S0-BYG-052

Cynthia Harrod-Eagles is the author of the hugely popular Morland Dynasty novels, which have captivated and enthralled readers for decades. She is also the author of the War at Home series, which is an epic family drama set against the backdrop of World War I. Cynthia's passions are music, wine, horses, architecture and the English countryside.

By Cynthia Harrod-Eagles

The Bill Slider series

Orchestrated Death
Death Watch
Necrochip
Dead End
Blood Lines
Killing Time
Shallow Grave
Blood Sinister
Gone Tomorrow
Dear Departed

The Morland Dynasty series

The Founding
The Dark Rose
The Princeling
The Oak Apple
The Black Pearl
The Long Shadow
The Chevalier
The Maiden
The Flood-Tide
The Tangled Thread
The Emperor
The Victory
The Regency
The Campaigners
The Reckoning
The Devil's Horse
The Poison Tree
The Abyss

The Hidden Shore
The Winter Journey
The Outcast
The Mirage
The Cause
The Homecoming
The Question
The Dream Kingdom
The Restless Sea
The White Road
The Burning Roses
The Measure of Days
The Foreign Field
The Fallen Kings
The Dancing Years
The Winding Road
The Phoenix

War at Home series

Goodbye Piccadilly:
War at Home, 1914

Keep the Home Fires
Burning: War at Home, 1915

The Land of My Dreams:
War at Home, 1916

The Long, Long Trail:
War at Home, 1917

Till the Boys Come Home:
War at Home, 1918

Pack Up Your Troubles:
War at Home, 1919

Cynthia Harrod-Eagles

Orchestrated Death

sphere

SPHERE

First published in Great Britain in 1991 by Macdonald and Co
Paperback published in 1992 by Warner Futura
This reissue published by Sphere in 2019

1 3 5 7 9 10 8 6 4 2

Copyright © Cynthia Harrod-Eagles 1991

The moral right of the author has been asserted.

A CIP catalogue record for this book
is available from the British Library.

ISBN 978-0-7515-7533-0

Typeset in Plantin by Palimpsest Book Production Limited,
Falkirk, Stirlingshire
Printed and bound in Great Britain by Clays Ltd, Elcograf S.p.A.

Papers used by Sphere are from well-managed forests
and other responsible sources.

Sphere
An imprint of
Little, Brown Book Group
Carmelite House
50 Victoria Embankment
London EC4Y 0DZ

An Hachette UK Company
www.hachette.co.uk

www.littlebrown.co.uk

1

Absence of Brown Boots

Slider woke with that particular sense of doom generated by Rogan Josh and Mixed Vegetable Bhaji eaten too late at night, followed by a row with Irene. She had been asleep when he crept in, but as he slid into bed beside her, she had woken and laid into him with that capacity of hers for passing straight from sleep into altercation which he could only admire.

He and Atherton, his sergeant, had been working late. They had been out on loan to the Notting Hill Drug Squad to help stake out a house where some kind of major deal was supposed to be going down. He had called Irene to say that he wouldn't be back in time to take her to the dinner party she had been looking forward to, and then spent the evening sitting in Atherton's powder-blue Sierra in Pembridge Road, watching a dark and silent house. Nothing happened, and when the Notting Hill CID man eventually strolled over to put his head through their window and tell them they might as well push off, they were both starving.

Atherton was a tall, bony, fair-skinned, high-shouldered

young man, who wore his toffee-coloured hair in the style made famous by David McCallum in *The Man From UNCLE* in the days when Atherton was still too young to stay up and watch it. He looked at his watch cheerfully and said there was just time for a pint at The Dog and Scrotum before Hilda put the towels up.

It wasn't really called The Dog and Scrotum, of course. It was The Dog and Sportsman in Wood Lane, one of those gigantic arterial road pubs built in the fifties, all dingy tiled corridors and ginger-varnished doors, short on comfort, echoing like a swimming pool, smelling of Jeyes and old smoke and piss and sour beer. The inn sign showed a man in tweeds and a trilby cradling a gun in his arm, while a black labrador jumped up at him – presumably in an excess of high spirits, but Atherton insisted it was depicted in the act of sinking its teeth into its master's hairy Harris crutch.

It was a sodawful pub really, Slider reflected, as he did every time they went there. He didn't like drinking on his patch, but since he lived in Ruislip and Atherton lived in the Hampstead-overspill bit of Kilburn, it was the only pub reasonably on both their ways. Atherton, whom nothing ever depressed, said that Hilda, the ancient barmaid, had hidden depths, and the beer was all right. There was at least a kind of reassuring anonymity about it. Anyone willing to be a regular of such a dismal place must be introspective to the point of coma.

So they had two pints while Atherton chatted up Hilda. Ever since he had bought the Sierra, Atherton had been weaving a fiction that he was a software rep, but Slider was sure that Hilda, who looked as though the inside of a magistrates' court would hold no surprises for her, knew perfectly well that they were coppers. Rozzers, she might even call them; or Busies? No, that was a bit too Dickensian: Hilda couldn't be more than about sixty-eight or seventy. She had the black, empty eyes of an old snake, and her hands trembled all the time except, miraculously, when she pulled a pint. It was hard to tell whether she knew everything that went on, or nothing. Certainly she looked as though she had never believed in Father Christmas or George Dixon.

After the beer, they decided to go for a curry; or rather, since the only place still open at that time of night would be an Indian restaurant, they decided which curry-house to patronise – the horrendously named Anglabangla, or The New Delhi, which smelled relentlessly of damp basements. And then home, to the row with Irene, and indigestion. Both were so much a part of any evening that began with working late, that nowadays when he ate in an Indian restaurant it was with an anticipatory sense of unease.

After a bit of preliminary squaring up. Irene pitched into the usual tirade, all too familiar to Slider for him to need to listen or reply. When she got to the bit about What Did He Think It Was Like To Sit By The Phone Hour After Hour Wondering Whether He Was Alive Or Dead? Slider unwisely muttered that he had often wondered the same thing himself, which didn't help at all. Irene had in any case little sense of humour, and none at all where the sorrows of being a policeman's wife were concerned.

Slider had ceased to argue, even to himself, that she had known what she was letting herself in for when she married him. People, he had discovered, married each other for reasons which ranged from the insufficient to the ludicrous, and no one ever paid any attention to warnings of that sort. He himself had married Irene knowing what she was like, and despite a very serious warning from his friend-and-mentor O'Flaherty, the desk sergeant at Shepherd's Bush.

'For God's sake, Billy darlin',' the outsize son of Erin had

3

said anxiously, thrusting forward his veined face to emphasise the point, 'you can't marry a woman with no sense-a-humour.'

But he had gone and done it all the same, though in retrospect he could see that even then there had been things about her that irritated him. Now he lay in bed beside her and listened to her breathing, and when he turned his head carefully to look at her, he felt the rise inside him of the vast pity which had replaced love and desire. *Tout comprendre c'est tout embêter*, Atherton said once, and translated it roughly as 'Once you know everything it's boring'. Slider pitied Irene because he understood her, and it was that fatal ability of his to see both sides of every question which most irritated her, and made even their quarrels inconclusive.

He could sense the puzzlement under her anger, because she wanted to be a good wife and love him, but how could she respect anyone so ineffectual? Other people's husbands Got On, got promoted and earned more money. Slider believed his work was important and that he did it well, but Irene could not value an achievement so static, and sometimes he had to struggle not to absorb her values. If once he began to judge himself by her criteria, it would be All Up With Slider.

His intestines seethed and groaned like an old steam clamp as the curry and beer resolved themselves into acid and wind. He longed to ease his position, but knew that any shift of weight on his part would disturb Irene. The Slumber-well Dreamland Deluxe was sprung like a young trampoline, and overreaction was as much in its nature as in a Cadillac's suspension.

He thought of the evening he had spent, apparently resultless as was so much of his police work. Then he thought of the one he might have spent, of disguised food and tinkly talk at the Harpers', who always had matching candles and napkins on their dinner-table, but served Le Piat d'Or with everything.

The Harpers had good taste, according to Irene. You could tell they had good taste, because everything in their house resembled the advertising pages of the Sundry Trends Colour Supplement. Well, it was comforting to know you were right, he supposed; to be sure of your friends' approval of your stripped pine, your Sanderson soft furnishings, your oatmeal Berber, your Pampas bathroom suite, your numbered limited-edition prints of bare trees on a skyline in Norfolk, the varnished cork tiles on your kitchen floor, and the excitingly chunky stonewear from Peter Jones. And when you lived on an estate in Ruislip where they still thought plastic onions hanging in the kitchen were a pretty cute idea, it must all seem a world of sophistication apart.

Slider had a sudden, familiar spasm of hating it all; and especially this horrible Ranch-style Executive Home, with its picture windows and no chimneys, its open-plan front garden in which all the dogs of the neighbourhood could crap at will, with its carefully designed rocky outcrop containing two poncey little dwarf conifers and three clumps of heather; this utterly undesirable residence on a new and sought-after estate, at the still centre of the fat and neutered universe of the lower middle classes. Here struggle and passion had been ousted by Terence Conran, and the old, dark and insanitary religions had been replaced by the single lustral rite of washing the car. A Homage to Catatonia. This was it, mate, authentic, guaranteed, nice-work-if-you-can-get-it style. This was Eden.

The spasm passed. It was silly really, because he was one of the self-appointed guardians of Catatonia; and because, in the end, he had to prefer vacuity to vice. He had seen enough of the other side, of the appalling waste and sheer stupidity of crime, to know that the most thoughtless and smug of his neighbours was still marginally better worth protecting than the greedy and self-pitying thugs who preyed on him. You're a bastion, bhoy, he told himself in O'Flaherty's voice. A right little bastion.

The phone rang.

Slider plunged and caught it before its second shriek, and Irene moaned and stirred but didn't wake. She had been hankering after a Trimphone, using as an excuse the theory that it would disturb her less when it rang at unseasonable hours. There were so many Trimphones down their street now that the starlings had started imitating them, and Slider had made one of his rare firm stands. He didn't mind being woken up in the middle of the night, but he was damned if he'd be warbled at in his own home.

'Hullo, Bill. Sorry to wake you up, mate.' It was Nicholls, the sergeant on night duty.

'You didn't actually. I was already awake. What's up?'

'I've got a corpus for you.' Nicholls' residual Scottish accent made his consonants so deliberate it always sounded like corpus. 'It's at Barry House, New Zealand Road, on the White City Estate.'

Slider glanced across at the clock. It was a quarter past five. 'Just been found?'

'It came in on a 999 call – anonymous tip-off, but it took a while to get on to it, because it was a kid who phoned, and naturally they thought it was a hoax. But Uniform's there now, and Atherton's on his way. Nice start to your day.'

'Could be worse,' Slider said automatically, and then seeing Irene beginning to wake, realised that if he didn't get on his way quickly before she woke properly, it most certainly would be.

The White City Estate was built on the site of the Commonwealth Exhibition, for whose sake not only a gigantic athletics stadium, but a whole new underground station had

6

been built. The vast area of low-rise flats was bordered on one side by the Western Avenue, the embryo motorway of the A40. On another side lay the stadium itself, and the BBC's Television Centre, which kept its back firmly turned on the flats and faced Wood Lane instead. On the other two sides were the teeming back streets of Shepherd's Bush and Acton. In the thirties, the estate had been a showpiece, but it had become rather dirty and depressing. Now they were even pulling down the stadium, where dogs had been racing every Thursday and Saturday night since Time began.

Slider had had business on the estate on many an occasion, usually just the daily grind of car theft and housebreaking; though sometimes an escaped inmate of the nearby Wormwood Scrubs prison would brighten up everyone's day by going to earth in the rabbit warren of flats. It was a good place to hide: Slider always got lost. The local council had once put up boards displaying maps with an alphabetical index of the blocks, but they had been eagerly defaced by the waiting local kids as soon as they were erected. Slider was of the opinion that either you were born there, or you never learnt your way about.

In memory of the original exhibition, the roads were named after outposts of the Empire – Australia Road, India Way and so on – and the blocks of flats after its heroes – Lawrence, Rhodes, Nightingale. They all looked the same to Slider, as he drove in a dazed way about the identical streets. Barry House, New Zealand Road. Who the hell was Barry anyway?

At last he caught sight of the familiar shapes of panda and jam sandwich, parked in a yard framed by two small blocks, five storeys high, three flats to a floor, each a mirror image of the other. Many of the flats were boarded up, and the yard was half blocked by building equipment, but the balconies were lined with leaning, chattering, thrilled onlookers, and

7

despite the early hour the yard was thronged with small black children.

A tall, heavy, bearded constable was holding the bottom of the stairway, chatting genially with the front members of the crowd as he kept them effortlessly at bay. It was Andy Cosgrove who, under the new regime of community policing, had this labyrinth as his beat, and apparently not only knew but also liked it.

'It's on the top floor I'm afraid, sir,' he told Slider as he parted the bodies for him, 'and no lift. This is one of the older blocks. As you can see, they're just starting to modernise it.'

Slider cocked an eye upwards. 'Know who it is?'

'No, sir. I don't think it's a local, though. Sergeant Atherton's up there already, and the surgeon's just arrived.'

Slider grimaced. 'I'm always last at the party.'

'Penalties of living in the country, sir,' Cosgrove said, and Slider couldn't tell if he were joking or not.

He started up the stairs. They were built to last, of solid granite, with cast-iron banisters and glazed tiles on the walls, all calculated to reject any trace of those passing up them. Ah, they don't make 'em like that any more. On the top-floor landing, almost breathless, he found Atherton, obscenely cheerful.

'One more flight,' he said encouragingly. Slider glared at him and tramped, grey building rubble gritting under his soles. The stairs divided the flats two to one side and one to the other. 'It's the middle flat. They're all empty on this floor.' A uniformed constable, Willans, stood guard at the door. 'It's been empty about six weeks, apparently. Cosgrove says there's been some trouble with tramps sleeping in there, and kids breaking in for a smoke, the usual things. Here's how they got in.'

The glass panel of the front door had been boarded over. Atherton demonstrated the loosened nails in one corner, wiggled his fingers under to show how the knob of the Yale lock could be reached.

'No broken glass?' Slider frowned.

'Someone's cleaned up the whole place,' Atherton admitted sadly. 'Swept it clean as a whistle.'

'Who found the body?'

'Some kid phoned emergency around three this morning. Nicholls thought it was a hoax – the kid was very young, and wouldn't give his name – but he passed it on to the night patrol anyway, only the panda took its time getting here. She was found about a quarter to five.'

'She?' Funny how you always expect it to be male.

'Female, middle-twenties. Naked,' Atherton said economically.

Slider felt a familiar sinking of heart. 'Oh no.'

'I don't think so,' Atherton said quickly, answering the thought behind the words. 'She doesn't seem to have been touched at all. But the doc's in there now.'

'Oh well, let's have a look,' Slider said wearily.

Apart from the foul taste in his mouth and the ferment in his bowels, he had a small but gripping pain in the socket behind his right eye, and he longed inexpressibly for untroubled sleep. Atherton on the other hand, who had shared his debauch and presumably been up before him, looked not only fresh and healthy, but happy, with the intent and eager expression of a sheepdog on its way up into the hills. Slider could only trust that age and marriage would catch up with him, too, one day.

He found the flat gloomy and depressing in the unnatural glare from the spotlight on the roof opposite – installed to deter vandals, he supposed. 'The electricity's off, of course,'

Atherton said, producing his torch. Boy scout, thought Slider savagely. In the room itself DC Hunt was holding another torch, illuminating the scene for the police surgeon, Freddie Cameron, who nodded a greeting and silently gave Slider place beside the victim.

She was lying on her left side with her back to the wall, her legs drawn up, her left arm folded with its hand under her head. Her dark hair, cut in a long pageboy bob, fell over her face and neck. Slider could see why Cosgrove thought she wasn't a resident. She was what pathologists describe as 'well-nourished': her flesh was sleek and unblemished, her hair and skin had the indefinable sheen of affluence that comes from a well-balanced protein-based diet. She also had an expensive tan, which left a white bikini-mark over her hips.

Slider picked up her right hand. It was icy cold, but still flexible: a strong, long-fingered, but curiously ugly hand, the fingernails cut so short that the flesh of the fingertips bulged a little round them. The cuticles were well-kept and there were no marks or scratches. He put the hand down and drew the hair back from the face. She looked about twenty-five – perhaps younger, for her cheek still had the full and blooming curve of extreme youth. Small straight nose, full mouth, with a short upper lip which showed the white edge of her teeth. Strongly marked dark brows, and below them a semicircle of black eyelashes brushing the curve of her cheekbone. Her eyes were closed reposefully. Death, though untimely, had come to her quietly, like sleep.

He lifted her shoulder carefully to raise her a little against the hideously papered wall. Her small, unripe breasts were no paler than her shoulders – wherever she had sunbathed last year, it had been topless. Her body had the slender tautness of unuse; below her flat golden belly, the stripe of white flesh looked like velvet. He had a sudden vision of her, strutting along a foreign beach under an expensive sun, carelessly self-conscious as a young foal, all her life before her, and pleasure still something that did not surprise her. An enormous, unwanted pity shook him; the dark raspberry nipples seemed to reproach him like eyes, and he let her subside into her former position, and abruptly walked away to let Cameron take his place.

He walked around the rest of the flat. There were three bedrooms, living-room, kitchen, bathroom and WC. The whole place was stripped bare, and had been swept clean. No litter of tramps and children, hardly even any dust. He remembered the grittiness of the stairs outside and sighed. There would be nothing here for them, no footprints, no fingerprints, no material evidence. What had become of her clothes and handbag? He felt already a sense of unpleasant anxiety about this business. It was too well organised, too professional. And the wallpaper in each room was more depressing than the last.

Atherton appeared at the door, startling him. 'Dr Cameron wants you, guv.'

Freddie Cameron looked up as Slider came in. 'No sign of a struggle. No visible wounds. No apparent marks or bruises.'

'A fine upstanding body of negatives,' Slider said. 'What does that leave? Heart? Drugs?'

'Give me a chance,' Cameron grumbled. 'I can't see anything in this bloody awful light. I can't find a puncture, but it's probably narcotics – look at the pupils.' He let the eyelids roll back, and picked up the arms one by one, peering at the soft crook of the elbow. 'No sign of usage or abusage. Of course you can see from the general condition that she wasn't an addict. Could have taken something by mouth, I suppose, but where's the container?'

'Where are her clothes, for the matter of that,' said Slider. 'Unless she walked up here in the nude, I think we can rule out suicide. *Someone* was obviously here.'

'Obviously,' Cameron said drily. 'I can't help you much, Bill, until I can examine her by a good light. My guess is an overdose, probably by mouth, though I may find a puncture wound. No marks on her anywhere at all, except for the cuts, and they were inflicted post mortem.'

'Cuts?'

'On the foot.' Cameron gestured. Slider hunkered down and stared. He had not noticed before, but the softly curled palm of her foot had been marked with two deep cuts, roughly in the shape of a T. They had not bled, only oozed a little, and the blood had set darkly. Left foot only – the right was unmarked. The pads of the small toes rimmed the foot like fat pink pearls. Slider began to feel very bad indeed.

'Time of death?' he managed to say.

'Eight hours, very roughly. Rigor's just starting. I'll have a better idea when it starts to pass off.'

'About ten last night, then?' Slider stared at the body with deep perplexity. Her glossy skin was so out of place against the background of that disgusting wallpaper. 'I don't like it,' he said aloud.

Cameron put his hand on Slider's shoulder comfortingly. 'There is no sign of forcible sexual penetration,' he said.

Slider managed to smile. 'Anyone else would simply have said rape.'

'Language, my dear Bill, is a tool – not a blunt instrument. Anyway, I'll be able to confirm it after the post. She'll be as stiff as a board by this afternoon. Let me see – I can do it Friday afternoon, about four-ish, if it's passed off by then. I'll let you know, in case you want to come. Nice-looking kid. I wonder who she is? Someone must be missing her. Ah, here's the photographer. Oh, it's you, Sid. No lights. I hope you've got yours with you, dear boy, because it's as dark as a mole's entry in here.'

Sid got to work, complaining uniformly about the conditions as a bee buzzes about its work. Cameron turned the body over so that he could get some mugshots, and as the brown hair slid away from the face, Slider leaned forward with sudden interest.

'Hullo, what's that mark on her neck?'

It was large and roughly round, about the size of a half-crown, an area of darkened and roughened skin about halfway down the left side of the neck; ugly against the otherwise flawless whiteness.

'It looks like a bloody great lovebite,' Sid said boisterously. 'I wouldn't mind giving her one meself.' He had captured for police posterity some gruesome objects in his time, including a suicide-by-hanging so long undiscovered that only its clothes were holding it together. Decomposing corpses held no horrors for him, but Slider was interested to note that something about this one's nude composure had unnerved the photographer too, making him overcompensate.

'Is it a bruise? Or a burn – a chloroform burn or something like that?'

'Oh no, it isn't a new mark,' Cameron said. 'It's more like a callus – see the pigmentation, where something's rubbed there – and some abnormal hair growth, too, look, here. Whatever it is, it's chronic'

'Chronic? I'd call it bloody ugly,' Sid said.

'I mean it's been there a long time,' Cameron explained kindly. 'Can you get a good shot of it? Good. All right, then, Bill – seen all you want? Let's get her out of here, then. I'm bloody cold.'

A short while later, having seen the body lifted onto a

stretcher, covered and removed, Cameron paused on his way out to say to Slider, 'I suppose you'll want to have the prints and dental records *toot sweet!* Not that her teeth'll tell you much – a near perfect set. Fluoride has a lot to answer for.'

'Thanks Freddie,' Slider said absently. *Someone must be missing her.* Parents, flatmates, boyfriend – certainly, surely, a boyfriend? He stared at the bare and dirty room: *Why here, for heaven's sake?*

'The fingerprint boys are here, guv,' Atherton said in his ear, jerking him back from the darkness.

'Right. Start Hunt and Hope on taking statements,' Slider said. 'Not that anyone will have seen anything, of course – not here.'

The long grind begins, he thought. Questions and statements, hundreds of statements, and nearly all of them would boil down to the Three Wise Monkeys, or another fine regiment of negatives.

In detective novels, he thought sadly, there was always someone who, having just checked his watch against the Greenwich Time Signal, glanced out of the window and saw the car with the memorable numberplate being driven off by a tall one-legged red-headed man with a black eyepatch and a zigzag scar down the left cheek. I *could tell 'e wasn't a gentleman, Hinspector, 'cause 'e was wearing brown boots.*

'Might be a good idea to get Cosgrove onto taking statements,' Atherton was saying. 'At least he speaks the lingo.'

14

2

All Quiet on the Western Avenue

A grey sky, which Slider had thought was simply pre-dawn greyness, settled in for the day, and resolved itself into a steady, cold and sordid rain.

'All life is at its lowest ebb in January,' Atherton said. 'Except, of course, in Tierra del Fuego, where they're miserable all year round. Cheese salad or ham salad?' He held up a roll in each hand and wiggled them a little, like a conjurer demonstrating his bona fides.

Slider looked at them doubtfully. 'Is that the ham I can see hanging out of the side?'

Atherton tilted the roll to inspect it, and the pink extrusion flapped dismally, like a ragged white vest which had accidentally been washed in company with a red T-shirt. 'Well, yes,' he admitted. 'All right, then,' he conceded, 'cheese salad or rubber salad?'

'Cheese salad.'

'I was afraid you'd say that. I never thought you were the sort to pull rank, guv,' Atherton grumbled, passing it across. 'Funny how the act of making sandwiches brings out the

15

Calvinist in us. If you enjoy it, it must be sinful.' He looked for a moment at the bent head and sad face of his superior. 'I could make you feel good about the rolls,' he offered gently. 'I could tell you about the pork pies.'

The corner of Slider's mouth twitched in response, but only briefly. Atherton let him be, and went on with his lunch and his newspaper. They had made a para in the lunchtime *Standard:*

> *The body of a naked woman has been discovered in an empty flat on the White City Estate in West London. The police are investigating.*

Short and nutty, he thought. He was going to pass it over to Slider, and then decided against disturbing his brown study. He knew Slider well, and knew Irene as well as he imagined anyone would ever want to, and guessed that she had been giving him a hard time last night. Irene, he thought, was an excellent deterrent to his getting married.

Atherton led a happy bachelor life in a dear little terraced artisan's cottage in what Yuppies nowadays called West Hampstead – the same kind of logic as referring to Battersea as South Chelsea. It had two rooms up and two down, with the kitchen extended into the tiny, high-walled garden, and the whole thing had been modernised and upmarketised to the point where its original owners entering it through a time warp would have apologised hastily and backed out tugging their forelocks.

Here he lived with a ruggedly handsome black ex-tomcat called, unimaginatively, Oedipus; and used the lack of space as an excuse not to get seriously involved with any of his succession of girlfriends. He fell in love frequently, but never for very long, which he realised was a reprehensible trait in him. But the conquest was all – once he had them, he lost interest.

Apart from Oedipus, the person in life he loved best was probably Slider. It was certainly the most important and permanent relationship he'd had in adult life, and in some ways it was like a marriage. They spent a lot of time in each other's company, were forced to get on together and work together for a common end. Atherton knew himself to be a bit of a misfit in the force – a whizz kid without the whizz. He thought of himself as a career man, a go-getter, keen on advancement, but he knew his intellectual curiosity was against him. He was too well read, too interested in the truth for its own sake, too little inclined to tailor his efforts to the results that were either possible or required. He would never be groomed for stardom – he left unlicked those things which he ought to have licked, and there was no grace in him.

In that respect he resembled Slider, but for different reasons. Slider was dogged, thorough, painstaking, because it was in his nature to be: he was no intellectual gazelle. But Atherton not only admired Slider as a good policeman and a good man, he also liked him, was even fond of him; and he felt that Slider, who was reserved and didn't make friends easily, depended on him, both on his judgement and his affection. It was a good relationship, and it worked well, and if it weren't for Irene, he thought they would have been even closer.

Irene disliked Atherton for taking up her husband's time which she felt ought to be spent with her. He thought she probably suspected him vaguely of leading Bill astray and keeping him out late deliberately on wild debauches. God knew he would have done given the chance! The fact that Slider could have married someone like Irene was a fundamental mark against him which Atherton sometimes had difficulty in dismissing. It also meant that their relationship

17

was restricted mainly to work, which might or might not have been a good thing.

Slider looked up, feeling Atherton's eyes on him. Slider was a smallish man, with a mild, fair face, blue eyes, and thick, soft, rather untidy brown hair. Jane Austen – of whom amongst others Atherton was a devotee – might have said Slider had a sweetness of expression. Atherton thought that was because his face was a clear window on his character, which was one of the things Atherton liked about him. In a dark and tangled world, it was good to know one person who was exactly what he seemed to be: a decent, kindly, honest, hard-working man, perhaps a little overconscientious. Slider's faint, worried frown was the outward sign of his inner desire to compensate personally for all the shortcomings of the world. Atherton felt sometimes protective towards him, sometimes irritable: he felt that a man who was so little surprised at the wickedness of others ought surely to be less puzzled by it.

'What's up, guv?' he asked. 'You look hounded.'

'I can't stop thinking about the girl. Seeing her in my mind's eye.'

'You've seen corpses before. At least this one wasn't mangled.'

'It's the incongruity,' Slider said reluctantly, knowing that he didn't really know what it was that was bothering him. 'A girl like her, in a place like that. Why would anyone want to murder her *there* of all places?'

'We don't know it was murder,' Atherton said.

'She could hardly have walked up there stark naked and let herself in without someone seeing her,' Slider pointed out. Atherton gestured with his head towards the pile of statements Slider had been sifting through.

'She walked up there at some point without being seen. Unless all those residents are lying. Which is entirely possible.

18

Most people seem to lie to us automatically. Like shouting at foreigners.'

Slider sighed and pushed the pile with his hands. 'I don't see how any of them could have had anything to do with it. Unless it was robbery from the person – and who takes all the clothes, right down to the underwear?'

'A second-hand clothes dealer?'

Slider ignored him. 'Anyway, the whole thing's too thorough. Everything that might have identified her removed. The whole place swept clean, the door knobs wiped. The only prints in the whole place are the kid's on the front-door knob. Someone went to a lot of trouble.'

Atherton grunted. 'There are no signs of a struggle, and no sounds of one according to the neighbours. Couldn't it have been an accident? Maybe she went there with a boyfriend for a bit of sex-and-drugs naughtiness, and something went wrong. Boom – she's dead! Boyfriend's left with a very difficult corpse to explain. So he strips her, cleans the place up, takes her clothes and handbag, and bunks.'

'And cuts her foot?'

'She might have done that any time – stepped on the broken glass from the front door for instance.'

'In the shape of the letter T? Anyway, they were postmortem cuts.'

'Oh – yeah, I'd forgotten. Well, she might have been killed somewhere else, and taken up there naked in a black plastic sack.'

'Well, she might,' Slider said, but only because he was essentially fair-minded.

Atherton grinned. 'Thanks. She's not very big, you know. A well-built man could have carried her. Everyone indoors watching telly – he could just pick his moment to walk up the stairs. Dump her, walk down again.'

19

'He'd have to arrive in a car of some sort.'

'Who looks at cars?' Atherton shrugged. 'In a place like that – ideal, really, for your average murderer. In an ordinary street, people know each other's cars, they look out of the window, they know what their neighbours look like at least. But with a common yard, people are coming and going all the time. It's a thoroughfare. And all the living-room windows are at the back, remember. It would be easy not to be noticed.'

Slider shook his head. 'I know all that. I just don't see why anyone would go to all that trouble. No, it's got a bad smell to it, this one. A setup. She was enticed there by the killer, murdered, and then all traces were removed to prevent her from being identified.'

'But why cut her foot?'

'That's the part I hate most of all,' Slider grimaced.

'"I don't know nothin' I hate so much as a cut toe,"' Atherton said absently.

'Uh?'

'Quotation. Steinbeck. *The Grapes of Wrath*.'

The duty officer stuck his head round the door, registered Slider, and said, 'Records just phoned, sir. I've been ringing your phone – didn't know you were in here. It's negative on those fingerprints, sir. No previous.'

'I didn't think there would be,' Slider said, his gloom intensifying a millimetre.

The disembodied face softened: everybody liked Slider.

'I'm just going to make some tea, sir. Would you like a cup?'

Nicholls came into Slider's room in the afternoon holding a large brown envelope. Slider looked up in surprise.

'You're early, aren't you? Or has my watch stopped?'

'Doing Fergus a favour. He's tortured with the toothache,' Nicholls said. He and O'Flaherty were old friends, having gone through police college together. He called O'Flaherty 'Flatulent Fergus', and O'Flaherty called him 'Nutty Nicholls'. They sometimes dropped into a well-polished routine about having been in the trenches together. Nicholls was a ripely handsome Highlander with a surprising range of musical talents. At a police concert in aid of charity he had once brought the house down by singing 'The Queen of the Night' aria from *The Magic Flute* in a true and powerful soprano, hitting the cruel F in alt fair and square on the button. Not so much the school of Bel Canto, he had claimed afterwards, as the school of Can Belto.

'So much tortured,' Nicholls went on, rolling his Rs impressively, 'that he forgot to give you these. I found them lying on his desk. I expect you've been waiting for them.'

He held out the envelope and Slider took and opened it.

'Yes, I was wondering where they'd got to,' he said, drawing out the sheaf of photographs and spreading them on his desk. Nicholls leaned on his fists and whistled soundlessly.

'Is that your corpus? A bit of a stunner, isn't she? You'd best not let the wife see any of these, or bang goes your overtime for the next ten years.' He pushed the top ones back with a forefinger. 'Poor wee lassie,' he said. 'No luck ID-ing her yet?'

'We've got nothing to go on,' Slider said. 'Not so much as a signet ring, or an appendix scar. Nothing but this mark on her neck, and I don't know that that's going to get us anywhere.'

Nicholls picked up one of the close-ups of the neck, and grinned at Slider. 'Oh, Mrs Stein – or may I call you Phyllis?'

'You know something?'

Nicholls tapped the photograph with a forefinger. 'You and Freddie Cameron I can understand, but I'm a wee bit surprised young Atherton hasn't picked up on this.'

'Perhaps he didn't see it at the flat. And we've been waiting for the photographs,' Slider said patiently.

'Tell me, Bill, did you notice anything about her fingers?'

'Nothing in particular. Except that she had very short finger-nails. I suppose she bit them.'

'Ah-huh. Nothing of the sort, man. She was a fiddle-player. A vi-o-linist. This is the mark they get from gripping the violin between the neck and the shoulder.'

'You're sure?'

'Well, I couldn't swear it wasnae a viola,' Nicholls said gravely. 'And the fingernails have to be short, you see, for pressing down on the strings.'

Slider thought. 'They were short on both hands.'

'I expect she'd want them symmetrical,' Nicholls said kindly. 'Well, this gives you a way of tracing her, anyway. Narrows the field. It's a closed kind of world – everyone knows everyone.'

'I suppose I'd start with the musicians' union,' Slider hazarded. Like most people, he had no idea how the musical world was arranged internally. He'd never been to a live symphony concert, though he had a few classical records, and could tell Beethoven from Bach. Just.

'I doubt that'd be much use to you,' Nicholls said. 'Not without the name. They don't have photographs in their central records. No, if I were you, I'd ask around the orchestras.'

'We don't know that she was a member of an orchestra.'

'No, but if she played the fiddle, it's likely she was on the classical side of the business rather than the pop. And if she wasn't a member of an orchestra, she'd still likely be known to someone. As I said, it's a closed world.'

'Well, it's a lead, anyway,' Slider said, getting up with renewed energy and shuffling the photographs together. 'Thanks, Nutty.'

Nicholls grinned. 'N't'all. Get yon Atherton onto it, I should. I heard a rumour he was havin' social intercourse with a flute-player at last year's Proms. That's why I was surprised he didn't recognise the mark.'

'If it was a mark on the navel, he'd have spotted it straight off,' Slider said.

It was a mistake to try to go home at half past five, as anyone more in the habit of doing so than Slider would have known. The A40 – the Western Avenue – was jammed solid with Rovers and BMWs heading out for Gerrard's Crawse. Slider was locked in his car for an hour with a disc jockey called Chas or Mike or Dave – they always seemed to have names like the bark of a dog – who burbled on about a major tailback on the A40 due to roadworks at Perivale. So he was further hindered in his desire to forget his work for a while by finding himself stationary for a long period on the section of the road which ran beside the White City Estate.

Sometime this afternoon Freddie Cameron would have done the post. Slider had been to one or two out of interest, in order to know what happened, and he had not wished to attend this one. It was a particularly human horror, this minute and dispassionate mutilation of a dead body. No other species practised it on its own kind. He felt inexplicably unnerved at the thought. For some reason this particular young woman refused to take on the status of a corpse but remained a person in his mind, her white body floating there like the memory of someone he had known. She was in the back of his head, like the horrors seen out of the corner of the eye in childhood: like the man with no face behind the bedroom door after Mum had put the light out. He knew he mustn't look at it, or it would get him; and yet the half-admitted shape called the eye irresistibly.

He tried to concentrate on the radio programme. A listener had just called in, apparently – to judge by the background

23

noise – from some place a long way off that was suffering from a hailstorm, or possibly an earthquake. A distorted voice said, 'Hullo Dive, this is Eric from Hendon. I am a first-time caller. I jussliketsay, I lissnayour programme every day, iss reelly grite.' Slider remembered being told that soundwaves never die, simply stream off into space for ever and ever. What would they make of that, out on Alpha Centauri Beta?

He was going home early in the hope of scoring some Brownie points after the storms of the last few days. It struck him as a dismal sort of reason for going home, and he thought enviously of Atherton heading back to his bijou little cottage, a few delectable things to eat, and a stimulating evening with a new young woman to be conquered. Not that Slider wanted stimulation or a new young woman – he was too tired these days for the thought of illicit sex to do other than appal him; but peace and comfort would have been nice to look forward to.

But the house, which he hated, was Irene's, decorated and furnished to her requirements, not his. Wasn't it the same for all married men? Probably. Probably. All the same, the three-piece suite seemed to have been designed for looking at, not sitting on. All the furniture was like that: it rejected human advances like a chilly woman. It was like living in one of those display houses at the Ideal Home Exhibition.

And Irene cooked like someone meting out punishment. No, that wasn't strictly fair. The food was probably perfectly wholesome and well-balanced nutritionally, but it never seemed to taste of anything. It was joyless food, imbued with the salt water of tears. The subconscious knowledge that she hated cooking would have made him feel guilty about evincing any pleasure in eating it, even if there had been any.

When they were first married, Slider had done a lot of the cooking in their little bedsit in Holland Park. He liked trying

24

out new dishes, and they had often laughed together over the results. He examined the memory doubtfully. It didn't seem possible that the Irene he was going home to was the same Irene who had sat cross-legged on the floor and eaten chilli con carne out of a pot with a tablespoon. She didn't like him to cook now – she thought it was unmanly. In fact, she didn't like him going into the kitchen at all. If he so much as made a cup of tea, she followed him round with a J cloth and a tight-lipped expression, wiping up imaginary Spillings.

When he got home at last, it was all effort wasted, because Irene was not there. She had gone out to play bridge with the Harpers and Ernie Newman, which, had he thought hard enough, he should have known, because she had told him last week about it. Slider had said sooner her than him, and she'd asked why in a dangerous sort of way, and he'd said because Newman was an intolerable, stuffed-shirted, patronising, constipated prick. Irene primmed her lips and said there was no need for him to bring bowels into it, he wasn't talking to one of his low Met friends now, and if he spent less time with them and more with decent people he'd be able to hold a civilised conversation once in a while.

Then they had had a row, which ended with Irene complaining that they never went anywhere together any more, and that was more or less true, not only because of his job, but because they no longer liked doing the same kind of things. He liked eating out, which she thought was just a waste of money. And she liked playing bridge, for God 's sake!

Actually, he was pretty sure she didn't like bridge, that she had only learned it as the entrée to the sort of society to which she thought they ought to belong. The Commissioner and his wife played bridge. He didn't say that to her of course, when she badgered him to learn. He just said he didn't like card games and she said he didn't like anything, and he had found that hard to refute just for the moment. His concerns seemed to have been whittled down to work, and slumping in front of the telly for ten minutes before passing out. It was years since he had stayed awake all the way through a film. He was becoming a boring old fart.

Of course, that wasn't congenital. He had lots of interests really: good food and wine and vintage cars and gardening and walking in the country and visiting old houses – architecture had always been a passion of his, and he used to sketch rather well in a painstaking way – but there just didn't seem to be room in his life any more. Not time, somehow, but room, as if his wife and his children and his mortgage and his job swelled like wet rice year by year – bland, damp and weighty – and squeezed everything else out of him.

No Brownie points tonight, then. No peace either – the living-room was occupied by the babysitter, who was watching a gameshow on television. A ten-second glance at the screen suggested that the rules of the game comprised the contestants having to guess which of the Christian names on the illuminated board was their own in order to win a microwave oven or a cut-glass decanter and glasses. The applause following a right answer was as impassioned as an ovation for a Nobel-prize winner.

The babysitter was fifteen and, for some reason Slider had never discovered, her name was Chantal. Slider regarded her as marginally less competent to deal with an emergency than a goldfish, and this was not only because, short of actual self-mutilation, she had done everything possible to make herself appear as ugly and degenerate as possible. Her clothes hung sadly on her in uneven layers of conflictingly ugly colours, her shoes looked like surgical boots, and her hair was dyed coke-black, while the roots were growing out blonde: a mind-

26

numbing reversal of the normal order of things which made Slider feel as if he were seeing in negative.

To add to this, her eyelids were painted red and her fingernails black, she chewed constantly like a ruminant, and she wore both earrings in the same ear, though Slider assumed that this was fashion and not absent-mindedness. She was actually quite harmless, apart from her villainous appearance, and her parents were decent, pleasant people with a comfortable income.

She looked up at him now with the intensely unreliable expression of an Old English sheepdog.

'Oh, hullo, Mr Slider. I wasn't expecting you,' she said, and a surprising hot blush ran up from under her collar. She fingered her Phurnacite hair nervously. She was in fact desperately in love with him, though Slider hadn't twigged it. He had replaced Dennis Waterman in her heart the instant she discovered that Dennis Waterman was married to Rula Lenska. 'Shall I turn this off?'

'No, it's all right. I won't disturb you. Where are the children?'

'Matthew's round his friend Simon's, and Kate's in her room reading.' They eyed each other for a moment, trapped by politeness. 'Shall I fix you a drink?' Chantal asked suddenly. It was like a scene from *Dynasty*. Slider glanced around nervously for the television cameras.

'Oh – er – no, thanks. You watch your programme. Don't mind me. I've got things to do.'

He backed out into the hall and closed the door. Fix him a drink, indeed! He looked round, wondering what to do next. No comfort, he thought. He really hadn't anything to do. He was so unused to having time on his hands that he felt hobbled by it. He decided to go upstairs and see Kate, who hadn't been awake when he left that morning, and whom he hardly ever saw at night because she usually went to bed before he got home. The door of her room was closed, and through it he heard the muted tones of what must surely be the same radio programme.

'Hullo, Mike. This is Sharon from Tooting. I jussliketersay, I lissnayour programme all the time, iss reely grite . . .'

Or perhaps there was only ever one, an endless loop of tape run by a computer from a basement somewhere behind Ludgate Circus.

He stopped on the dim landing, and suddenly the dead girl was there with him, ambushing him from the back of his mind: the childlike fall of her hair and the curve of her cheek, the innocence of her nakedness. He put his fingers to his temples and pressed and drew his breath long and hard. He felt on the brink of some unknown crisis; he felt suddenly out of control.

Kate must have heard something – she called out 'Is that you, Daddy?' from inside her room. Slider let out his breath shudderingly, drew another more normal. He reached for the door handle.

'Hullo, my sweetheart,' he said cheerfully, going in.

3

Drowsy Syrups

It was an old-fashioned morgue, cold and high-ceilinged, with marble floors that echoed hollowly when you walked across them, and a sink in the corner with a tap that dripped. There was a strong smell of disinfectant and formalin, which did not quite mask a different smell underneath – warmer, sweetish and dirty.

Cameron, fresh from the path unit at one of the newer hospitals, contrasted this chilly old tomb with the low-ceilinged, strip-lighted, air-conditioned, rubber-tile-floored place he had just left. He felt a vague fondness, all the same, for the old morgues like this which were fast disappearing. Not only had he done his training in such places, but the architecture reminded him cosily of his primary school in Edinburgh. All the same, he decided to leave his waistcoat on.

His dapper form enveloped in protective apron and gloves, he bent forward over the pale cadaver on the herringbone-gullied table, his breath just faintly visible on the cold air as, whistling, he made the first sweeping incision from the point of the chin to the top of the pubic bone.

'Right then, here we go,' he said, reaching under the table with his foot for the pedal which turned on the audio recorder. Out of sheer force of habit he reached up and tapped the microphone with a knuckle to see if it was working, and it clunked hollowly. The assistant watched him phlegmatically. He had tested the machinery himself as a matter of course, as he always did, as Cameron knew he always did; but Cameron had no faith in machines. He had done his training in the days of handwritten notes, and even then he had known fountain pens to go wrong.

Now, like a cheerful gardener pruning roses, Cameron snipped through the cartilages which joined the ribs, freed them from the breastbone, separated the breastbone from the collarbones, and then with the economical force of long practice, opened out the two sides of the chest like cabinet doors. Inside, neatly disposed in their ordained order, were the internal organs, displayed like an anatomical drawing in a medical textbook before his enquiring eyes.

Slider was not present. Cameron had phoned him earlier to say that he would not be posting the girl until six-thirty, in case he wanted to come, but Slider had refused. Cameron thought his old friend sounded distinctly odd. He hoped old Bill wasn't going to crack up. Many a good man had gone that way: Cameron had seen it in the army as well as in the force, time and time again, and it was always the quiet, conscientious ones you had to watch. When a man had worry at work and worry at home – well, pressure started to build up. And poor old Bill's Madam was not exactly the Pal of the Period.

The words *male menopause* floated through his mind and he dismissed them irritably. He disliked jargon, particularly inaccurate jargon. When a man of forty-odd started fancying young girls, it was either because things were not right at home, or he was trying to prove something to himself – in either case, it was nothing to do with hormones. Not that Bill was chasing skirts, of course – he simply wasn't that sort – but it came to the same thing. He was jumpy, distinctly jumpy.

'I'd like to come, Freddie, but I've got a heap of reports I've been putting off,' Slider had said. 'It's quiet now, and I daren't put them off again.' Now this was transparently an excuse. Cameron knew how much there was to do when a division handled a murder case – the Incident Room to be set up, thousands of statements to go over – no need to go dragging in reports. Then Slider had given a nervous laugh and added unnecessarily, 'You know what paperwork is.' When a close friend starts talking to you like an idiot, Cameron considered, you knew there was something seriously on his mind.

Still whistling, and wielding his large knife with a flourish, more the jolly family butcher now than the cheerful gardener, he removed the internal organs in turn, weighed, sliced and examined them, and took sections for analysis, which the assistant sealed in sterile jars and labelled while Cameron watched sternly. He had a natural horror of unlabelled specimens. When the body was completely eviscerated, he made a lateral cut across the scalp from ear to ear, freed the tissues from the bone, and drew the front half of the scalp down over the face like a mask, and the rear half down over the neck like a coalman's flap. Then with an electric bone-saw he cut through the cranium and lifted the top off the skull, much as he had taken the top off his boiled egg that morning, and with very little more effort. With a little more cutting and snipping, he was able to slide his hands in under the brain and lift it out whole. He laid it on the slab and sliced it like a rather pallid country loaf.

'All normal,' he said. As he worked, he had spoken his

commentary aloud for the machine, and between comments he whistled. Sometimes he forgot to touch the foot pedal, so the whistle got recorded too. This was particularly trying for the audio-typist who transcribed his reports, for the machinery played the whistle back at a pitch which was quite painful through an earpiece. She had spoken to him again and again about it, and he always apologised profusely, but it made no difference. He had always whistled. He had begun it as a student thirty years ago, an assumption of insouciance which was designed to deceive himself more than other people, and to stop him thinking of the cadavers as human beings; and the habit was so ingrained by now he wasn't even aware he was doing it.

'Right, I think that will do,' he said at last, switching off the machine and nodding to the assistant. 'I'll be off then. I've got two more to do at Charing Cross before I've finished, and I promised Martha I wouldn't be late tonight. She's got some ghastly people coming in for drinks.' He looked at his watch. 'Not much chance of making it before they leave, thank God, but I'll have missed the traffic, anyway.'

'Goodnight, then, sir,' said the assistant. When the doctor had gone, he had his own tasks to perform. The body would have to be stuffed and sewn up, the skull packed and the scalp drawn back into place and stitched, and the viscera disposed of in the incinerator. When this was done, he returned the body to the trolley and, because he was a bit of a perfectionist in his own way, he fetched a damp cloth and cleaned it up. Dead bodies don't bleed, but they leak a bit.

With a gentle hand he wiped the pink-tinged bone-dust from the face. Poor kid, he thought. It was tragic when they caught it as young as that. And pretty too. From her label he could see she was unidentified, which struck him as odd, because she didn't look like the kind of girl no one would miss. Still, sooner or later, someone would want her, so she ought to be made a bit decent. Kindly he smoothed the hair back to hide the stitches, and then wheeled her back to her waiting numbered drawer in the mortuary.

When you're born, and when you die, a stranger washes you, he thought, as he had thought a hundred times before. It was a funny old life.

It was silly weather for January, warm and sunny as April never was, and all down Kingsway there were window boxes crammed with yellow daffodils. Pedestrians were either looking sheepish in spring clothes, or self-righteous and hot in boots and overcoats, and the bus queues were suddenly chatty.

Only the paper-seller outside Holborn Station looked unchanged and unchangeable in his multifoliate sweaters, greasy cap, and overcoat tied in the middle with baling-string. His fingers were as black and shiny as anthracite from the newsprint, as was the end of his nose where he had wiped it with his hand. He scowled in disproportionate rage when Slider asked him where the Orchestra's office was.

'Why don't you buy yourself an *A ter Z?*' he enquired uncharitably. 'I'm not Leslie Fuckin' Welch, the fuckin' Memory Man, am I? I'm here to sell papers. Right? *Noos*-papers,' he added fiercely, as if Slider had queried the word. Slider meekly bought the noon edition of the *Standard*, asked again, and was given very precise directions.

'Next time ask a bleedin' policeman,' the paper-seller suggested helpfully. Am I that obvious? Slider thought uneasily as he walked away.

The office turned out to be on the third floor of a building that had known better days, one of those late-Victorian monsters of red brick and white-stone coping, a cross between a ship and a gigantic birthday cake. Inside were marble-chip

33

floors and dark-panelled walls, and a creaking, protesting lift caged like a sullen beast in the centre of the entrance hall, with the stairs winding round it.

There was a legend on the wall inside the door, and Slider looked up the Orchestra office's location, considered the lift, and took the stairs, flinching when the lift clanged and lurched into action a moment later, and loomed past him, summoned from above. He didn't like its being above him, and hurried upwards while coils of cable like entrails descended mysteriously inside the shaft.

On the third floor he found the half-frosted door, tapped on it, and entered an office empty of humanity, but otherwise breathtakingly untidy, crammed with desks, filing cabinets, hat stands, dying pot plants, and files and papers everywhere in tottering piles. On the windowsill amongst the plants was a tin tray on which reposed a teapot, a caddy, a jar of Gold Blend, an opened carton of milk, and a sticky teaspoon. The empty but unwashed mugs were disposed about the desks, evidence to the trained mind that coffee-break was over. A navy-blue cardigan hung inside-out over the back of a chair which stood askew from a desk on which the telephone rang monotonously and disregarded.

Soon there were brisk footsteps outside in the hallway, the door was flung open, and the cardigan's owner hurried in, bringing with her the evocative scent of Palmolive soap, and reached for the telephone just as it stopped ringing.

She laughed. 'Isn't it maddening how they always do that? I've been waiting for a call from New York all day, and just when I dash out to the loo for a second . . . Now I suppose I'll have to ring them. Can I do something for you?'

She was a small, slight, handsome woman in her forties; shiny black hair cut very short, large-nosed face carefully made-up, a string of very good pearls around her neck. Slider would have known even without looking that she was wearing a white blouse, a plain navy skirt with an inverse pleat at the front, navy stockings, and black patent-leather court shoes with a small gold bar round the heel. He felt he knew her well: he had met her a hundred times in the service flats round the back of Harrods or the Albert Hall; in Kensington High Street; in Chalfont and Datchet and Taplow. Her husband would be a publisher or an agent, something on the administrative side of The Arts, and their son would be at Cambridge.

Slider smiled and introduced himself and proffered his ID, which she declined gracefully with a wave of the hand, like someone refusing a cigarette.

'How can I help you, Inspector?'

Slider was impressed. Few people nowadays, he found, could call a policeman 'Inspector' or 'Officer' without sounding either self-conscious or rude. He produced the mugshot.

'I'm hoping you may be able to identify this young woman. We have reason to believe she may be a violinist.'

The woman took the picture and looked at it, and said at once, 'Yes, she's one of ours. Oh dear, how awful! She's dead, isn't she? How very dreadful. Poor child.'

That was quick of her, he thought. 'What's her name?'

'Anne-Marie Austen. Second fiddle. She hasn't long been with us. What was it, Inspector – a traffic accident?'

'We don't yet know how she died, Mrs—'

'Bernstein. Like the composer,' she said absently, looking at the photo again. 'It's so awful to think this was taken after she – I'm sorry. Silly of me. I suppose you must get used to this sort of thing.'

She looked up at Slider, demanding an answer to what ought to have been a rhetorical question, and he said, 'Yes and no,' and she looked suitably abashed. He took the photo back from her. 'As I said, Mrs Bernstein, we don't yet know

35

the cause of death. Do you know if she had any chronic condition, heart or anything, that might have been a factor?'

'None that I know of. She seemed healthy enough – not that I saw much of her. And she hadn't been with us long – she came from the Birmingham about six months ago.'

'I was wondering,' Slider said musingly, running his fingers along the edge of the desk, 'why she hadn't been missed? If one of your members doesn't turn up, don't you make any enquiries?'

'Well, yes, normally we would, but this is one of our quiet periods. We're often slack just after Christmas, and in fact we haven't any dates for the Orchestra until the middle of next week.'

'I see. And you wouldn't contact your members in the mean time?'

'Not unless some work came in. There'd be no need.'

'When did the Orchestra last work together?'

'On Monday, a recording session for the BBC, at the Television Centre, Wood Lane. Two sessions, actually – two-thirty to five-thirty, and six-thirty to nine-thirty.'

'Was Anne-Marie there?'

'She was booked. As far as I know she was there. I don't attend the sessions myself, you know, but at any rate, nobody has told me she was absent.'

'I see.' Another little piece had slipped into place in Slider's mind – well, quite a big piece really. It explained why the girl was in that area in the first place. She finished work at nine-thirty at the TVC, and half an hour or so later she was killed less than half a mile away. Probably she had met her murderer as soon as she came out of the Centre. Someone might have seen her walk off with him, or get into his car. 'Did she had any particular friends in the Orchestra?'

Mrs Bernstein shrugged charmingly. 'Really, I'm not the

36

person to answer that. I work mostly here in the office – I don't often get to see the Orchestra working. The personnel manager, John Brown, would be able to tell you more about her. He's with the players all the time. And she shared a desk with Joanna Marshall – she might be able to help you.'

'Shared a desk?'

'Oh – the string players sit in pairs, you know, with one music stand and one piece of music between them. We call each pair a desk – don't ask me why.' Slider gave her an obedient smile in response to hers. 'Desk partners, particularly at the back of the section, are quite often close friends.'

'I see. Well, perhaps you could put me in touch with Miss Marshall, and Mr Brown. And would you give me Miss Austen's address, too?'

'Of course, I'll write them down for you.' She went to a filing cabinet and brought out a thick file containing a computer print-out of names and addresses. Flicking through it she found the right place, and copied the information onto a piece of headed paper in a quick, neat hand.

'The phone number of the office is here at the top of the sheet, in case you want to ask me anything else. And I'll put my home number too. Don't hesitate to contact me if you think I can help.'

'Thank you. You're very kind,' Slider said, pocketing the paper. 'By the way, do you know who was her next of kin?'

'I'm afraid I don't. The members are all self-employed people, you see, and it's up to them to worry about that sort of thing.' The quick dark eyes searched his face. 'I suppose she was murdered?'

'Why do you suppose that?' Slider asked impassively.

'Well, if it was all above board, if she'd tumbled downstairs or been run over or something, you'd have said, wouldn't you?'

'We don't yet know how she met her death,' he said again, and she gave him a quick-knit smile.

'I suppose you have to be discreet. But really, I can't imagine anyone wanting to kill a child of her age, unless—' She looked suddenly distressed. 'She wasn't – it wasn't—?'

'No,' said Slider.

'Thank God!' She seemed genuinely relieved. 'Well, I should think Joanna Marshall would be your best bet. She's a nice, friendly creature. If anyone knows anything about Anne-Marie's private life, it'll be her.'

Out in the street again, Slider tried the name out on his tongue. Anne-Marie Austen. Anne-Marie. Yes, it suited her. Now he knew it, he felt as though he had always known it.

John Brown's telephone number produced an answering machine inviting him tersely to leave a message. He declined. Joanna Marshall's number produced an answering machine giving the number of a diary service, which Slider wasn't quick enough to catch the first time round. He had to dial again, pencil at the ready, and took down a Hertfordshire number. The Hertfordshire number rang a long time and then produced a breathless woman with a dog barking monotonously in the background.

'I'm so sorry, I was down the garden and the girl seems to have disappeared. Shut up, Kaiser! I'm sorry, who? Oh yes, Joanna Marshall, yes, just a minute, yes. Today? And what time? Oh, I see, you want to know where she is? Shut *up*, Kaiser! Well, I'm afraid I can't tell you, because she's not working this afternoon. Have you tried her home number? Oh, I see. She's not in trouble, is she? Well, all I can tell you is that she's on tonight at the Barbican. Yes, that's right. Seven-thirty. Kaiser get *down*, you foul dog! I'm sorry? Yes. No. Of course. Not at all. Goodbye.'

Slider left the telephone box and walked back into

Kingsway. The sunshine and warmth had persuaded the proprietor of an Italian café to put tables outside on the pavement, and two early lunchers were sitting there, remarkably unselfconscious, eating pizza and drinking bottled lager, blinking in the sunshine like cats. A mad impulse came over Slider. Well, why not? His morning cornflakes were a distant memory now, and a man must eat. He hadn't been in an Italian restaurant in years. He lingered, looking longingly at the tables on the pavement, and then went regretfully inside. He'd feel a fool. He hadn't their sureness of youth and beauty and each other.

He plunged into the dark interior, into the smell of hot oil and garlic, and felt suddenly ravenous and cheerful. He ordered spaghetti with pesto and *escalope alla rustica*, and half a carafe of red, and it came and was excellent. The frank, pungent tastes worked strangely on his palate, accustomed as it was to sandwich lunches and grilled chops and boiled vegetables at night: he began to feel almost drunk, and it was nothing to do with the wine. Anne-Marie, he thought. Anne-Marie. His mind turned and fondled the name. Was she French? Did she like Italian food? He imagined her sitting opposite him now: garlic bread and gutsy wine, talk and laughter, everything new and easy. She would tell him about music, and he would regale her with the stories of his trade which would all be new to her, and she would marvel and be amused and admire. Everything was interesting and wonderful when you were twenty-five. Until someone murdered you, of course.

'You only just caught me. I was just going out for something to eat,' said Atherton.

'I've had mine. And I've found out who the girl is.'

'I deduced both those facts – you smell of garlic and you're looking smug.'

'I also know why she was where she was: she was working at the TVC that evening.'

'Lunch can wait. Tell me all,' Atherton said. He sat down on the edge of a desk, raising a cloud of dust into the streams of sunlight that were fighting their way through the grime on the windows of the CID room, which no one had ever washed in the history of Time. Everyone else was out, the telephones dozed, and the room had that unnatural midday hush.

Slider told him what he had learned that morning. 'It's possible that whoever killed her knew that the Orchestra wouldn't be working again for ten days, and that therefore she wouldn't be missed. Stripping the body, too – they'd have expected it to delay us for weeks. After all, if it hadn't been for Nicholls identifying that mark on her neck—'

'Unlike Nicholls, I didn't have the benefit of seeing it. And unlike you, by the way.'

'All right, sonny – how would you like to go back to tracing stolen videos?'

It was a familiar joking exchange of sass and threat, but suddenly there was a harsher note in it that surprised both of them, and they eyed each other with some embarrassment. Atherton opened his mouth to say something placatory, but Slider forestalled him. 'You'd better go and get your lunch, hadn't you? Who's minding the shop, anyway?'

'Fletcher. He's in the bog.'

Slider shrugged and went away to his own room, angry with himself, and a little puzzled. Everyone needed help in this job – why was he suddenly so defensive?

Freddie Cameron phoned.

'I've got the forensic reports from Lambeth, Bill. I've just sent off a full copy of the post-mortem report to you, but I thought you'd like to know straight away, as it's your case.'

'Yes, thanks, Freddie. What was it?'

'As I thought – an overdose of barbiturate.'

'Self-administered?'

'I think it very unlikely. The puncture was in the back of the right hand, damned awkward place to do it to yourself. The veins slide about if you don't pull the skin taut. Anyway, I found the puncture as soon as I got her into a good light, and it was the only one, so there's no doubt about that. But there was some very slight subcutaneous bruising of the left upper arm and right wrist. I'd say she was handled by an expert – someone who knew how to subdue with the minimum force, and without damaging the goods. Professional.'

'Left upper arm and right wrist?'

'Yes. It seems to me that if she was sitting down, for instance, someone could pass their arm right round her body from behind and grip the wrist to hold it still while administering the injection with the other hand.'

'Or there might have been two of them. She'd probably struggle. No other marks? No ligatures?'

'Nothing. But they wouldn't have to hold her for long. She'd have been unconscious within seconds, and dead within minutes.'

'What was it, then?'

'Pentathol.'

'Pentathol?'

'Short-acting anaesthetic. It's what they give you in the anteroom of an operating theatre to put you under, before they give you the gas.'

'Yes, I know that. But it seems an odd choice.'

'It produces deep anaesthesia very quickly. Of course, it also wears off very quickly – except that this poor child was given enough to fell a horse. Wasteful chaps, murderers.'

'And you're sure that's what it was? No other drugs?'

'Of course I'm sure. As I said, this stuff normally wears off very quickly, but if you administer enough of it, it paralyses the victim's respiratory system. They stop breathing, and death follows without a struggle.'

'Presumably only a doctor would have access to it?'

'Yes, but even then, not every doctor. It would have to be an anaesthetist at a hospital, or someone with access to hospital theatre drugs. An ordinary GP who wrote out a prescription for it wouldn't get it. Not what I'd call the murderer's usual choice. It's eminently detectable, and so difficult to come by that I should have thought the source would be easily traceable. Now if it were me, I'd have—'

'I think they wanted it to be detected,' Slider said abruptly.

'What's that?'

'Well, look – there was no attempt to hide the body, or to make it look like suicide. They must have known she'd be found before long. And then there were the cuts on her foot.'

'Ah yes, the cuts. Inflicted after death, of course.'

'Yes.'

'With a very sharp blade. They were deep, but quite clean – no haggling. A strong hand and something like an old-fashioned cutthroat razor, but with a shorter blade.'

'A scalpel, perhaps,' Slider said quietly.

'Yes, I'm afraid so. Exactly like that.' There was a silence, filled only with the hollow, subaural thrumming of an open line. 'Bill, I'm not liking this. Are you thinking what I'm thinking?'

'It looks,' Slider said slowly, 'like an execution.'

'*Pour encourager les autres,*' Cameron said in his appalling Scottish French. 'The letter T – Traitor? Or Talker perhaps? But put pentathol, scalpel and a strong, steady hand together, and it comes out Surgeon. That's what I don't like.'

'I don't like any part of it,' Slider said. An execution? What could she have been into, that young girl with her unused body?

'Well, you should have your copy of the report this afternoon, with any luck. When's the inquest?'

'As soon as possible. At least we don't have any distraught parents clamouring for release of her body.'

'You've not ID'd her then?'

'Yes, but we've no next of kin yet, and no one's asked after her. No one at all.'

He must have sounded a little how he felt, for Cameron said kindly, 'She wouldn't have felt a thing, you know. It would have been very quick and easy, like a mercy killing. They just put her to sleep, like an old dog.'

4

Digging for Buttered Rolls

Anne-Marie Austen had lived in a shabby, three-storeyed Edwardian house off the Chiswick High Road. There were three bells on the front door, with paper labels: Gostyn, Barclay and Austen. A prolonged ringing at the lowest bell eventually produced Mrs Gostyn, the erstwhile owner of the house, who now lived as a protected tenant in the ground-floor accommodation with use of garden.

She was very old, and had presumably once been fat, for her thick, white, ginger-freckled skin was now much too big for her and hung around her sadly like borrowed clothes. She gripped Atherton's forearm with surprising strength to keep him still while she told him her tale of the glories from which she had fallen; passing on, when he showed signs of restlessness, to the iniquities of the Barclays on the first floor, who left their baby with a child minder so that they could both go out to work, and who hoovered at all hours of the evening which interfered with Mrs Gostyn's television, and who made the whole ceiling shake with their washing machine, she gave him her word, so it was a wonder the house didn't come down around her ears.

44

Miss Austen? Yes, Miss Austen lived on the top floor. She played the violin in an orchestra, which was very nice in its way, but there was the coming and going at all hours, and then practising, practising, up and down scales until you thought you'd go mad. It wasn't even as if it was a nice tune you could tap your feet to. You mightn't think it to look at her, but Mrs Gostyn had been a great dancer in her time, when Mr Gostyn was alive.

Atherton recoiled slightly from the arch look, and tried to withdraw his arm, but though the flesh of her hand slid about, the bones inside still gripped him fiercely. He murmured as little encouragingly as he could.

'Oh yes, a great dancer. Max Jaffa, Victor Sylvester – we used to roll the carpet back, you know, whenever there was anything like that on the wireless. Of course,' with a moist sigh, 'we had the whole house then. Lodgers were not thought of. But you can't get servants these days, dear, not even if you could afford them, and I can't climb those stairs any more.'

'Did Miss Austen have many visitors?' Slider asked quickly, before she could tack off again.

'Well, no, not so many. She was away a lot, of course, for her work – sometimes for days at a time, but even when she was home she didn't seem to be much of a one for entertaining. There's her friend – a young lady – the one she worked with, who came sometimes—'

'Boyfriends?' Atherton asked.

Mrs Gostyn sniffed. 'There have been men going up there, once or twice. It's not my business to ask questions. But when a young woman lives alone in a flat like that, she's bound to get into trouble sooner or later. Far be it from me to speak ill of the dead, but—'

Atherton felt Slider's surprise. There had been no official identification given out, no photograph in the press.

'How did you know she was dead, Mrs Gostyn?'

The old woman looked merely surprised. 'The other policeman told me, of course. The one who came before.'

'Before?'

'Tuesday afternoon. Or was it Wednesday? Inspector Petrie he said his name was. A very nice man. I offered him a cup of tea, but he couldn't stop.'

'He came in a police car?'

'Oh no, an ordinary car, like yours. Not a panda car or anything.'

'Did he show you his identification?' Slider tried.

Of course he did,' she said indignantly. 'Otherwise I wouldn't have given him the key.'

Atherton made a sound like a moan, and she glanced at him disapprovingly. Slider went on, 'Did he say why he wanted the key?'

'To collect Miss Austen's things. He took them away with him in a bag. I offered him a cup of tea but he said he hadn't time. Thank you very much for asking, though, he said. A very nice, polite man, he was.'

'Shit fire,' Atherton muttered, and Slider quelled him with a glance.

'I'm afraid I don't know this Inspector Petrie,' he said patiently. 'Did he happen to mention to you, Mrs Gostyn, where he came from? Which police station? Or did you see it on his identity card?'

'No, dear, I couldn't see it properly because of not having my reading glasses on, but he very kindly read it out to me, his name, I mean – Inspector Petrie, CID, it said. Such a nice voice – what I'd call a cultured voice, like Alvar Liddell. Unusual these days. Are you telling me there's something wrong with him?'

Atherton intercepted a glance from Slider and headed back to the car radio.

'I'm afraid there may have been some little confusion,' Slider said gently. 'I don't think I know Inspector Petrie. Could you describe him to me?'

'He was a tall man,' she said after some thought. 'Very nicely spoken.'

'Clean-shaven?'

She thought again. 'I think he was wearing a hat. Yes, of course, because he lifted it to me – a trilby. I remember thinking you don't see many men wearing hats these days. I always think a person looks unfinished without a hat on, out of doors.'

Slider changed direction. 'He arrived yesterday – at what time?'

'About two o'clock, I should think it was.'

'And you gave him the key to Miss Austen's flat? Did you go upstairs with him?'

'I did not. It's not my business to be doing that sort of thing, and so I've told Mrs Barclay many a time when she wanted delivery men letting in. I only keep the keys for the meter man and emergencies, that's what I've told her, besides going up and down those stairs, which is too much for me now, with my leg. Not that I'd give anyone the key, dear, but I've known the meter man for fifteen years, and if you can't trust the police, who can you trust?'

'Who indeed,' Slider agreed. 'And did you see him come down again?'

'I came out when I heard him on the stairs. He was very quick, only five or ten minutes. He had one of those black plastic sacks, which he said he'd got Miss Austen's things in. "To give to her next of kin, Mrs Gostyn," he said, and I asked him if he'd like a cup of tea, because it's not a nice job to have to do, is it, even for strangers, but he said no, he had to go. He said he had everything he needed and touched his hat to me. Such a nice man.'

47

'Has anyone else been up there since? Have you been up there?'

'I have not,' she said firmly. 'And besides, Inspector Petrie has the key, so I couldn't get in if I wanted to.'

Atherton came back, and spoke to Slider aside through wooden lips. 'Petrie my arse.'

'I'll go up,' Slider said quietly. 'See if you can get a description out of her. Don't bully her, or she'll clam up. And a description of the car.'

'You wouldn't like the registration number, I suppose?' Atherton enquired ironically, and turned without relish to his task while Slider went upstairs to lock the stable door.

Mrs Gostyn proved extremely helpful. From her Atherton learnt that the bogus inspector was a tall, short, fat, thin man; a fair, dark-haired red-headed bald man in a hat, clean-shaven with a beard and moustache, wore glasses, didn't wear glasses, and had a nice speaking voice – she was quite sure about that much. The car he drove was a car, had four wheels, and was painted a colour, but she didn't know which one.

Atherton sighed and turned a page. On the day of the murder, he learnt, Miss Austen had driven off in her little car at about nine-thirty in the morning and hadn't returned, unless it was while Mrs Gostyn was at the chiropodist between two and four in the afternoon. But her car wasn't there when Mrs Gostyn returned, and she hadn't heard her come in that night.

Atherton put his notebook away again. 'Thank you very much for your help. If you remember anything else, anything at all, you'll let us know, won't you?'

'Anything about what?' Mrs Gostyn asked with apparently genuine puzzlement.

'About Miss Austen or Inspector Petrie – anything that happened on that day. I'll give you this card, look – it has a telephone number where you can reach us, all right?'

He disentangled himself with diminishing patience and went upstairs after Slider, to find that his superior had already opened the flat door and gone in.

'Who needs keys,' he said aloud. 'What was it this time – Barclaycard or Our Flexible Friend?' He examined the lock. It was a very old Yale, and the door had shrunk in its frame, leaving it loose, so that the tongue of the lock was barely retained by the keeper. He shook his head. *Morceau de gateau,* opening that.

The door opened directly into a large attic room furnished both as living-room and bedroom. It was indecently tidy, the bed neatly made. Slider was sitting on it playing back the answering machine, which stood with the telephone on a bedside table.

He looked up as Atherton came in. 'Three clicks, and a female called Only Me saying she'd call back. Get anything from the old lady?'

'Nothing, again nothing. The girl went out in the morning and didn't come back. The rest is silence.'

Slider shook his head. 'She must have come back at some point – there's her violin in the corner.'

Atherton looked. 'Unless she had a spare.'

'Oh. Yes.'

The violin case was propped on its end in the corner of the room nearest the window. In front of it there was a music stand adjusted to standing height, on which stood open a book of practice studies. From a distance the music looked like an army of caterpillars crawling over the page. On the floor was other music scattered as if it had been dropped, and on a low table under the window was yet more, together with a metronome, a box containing a block of resin, two yellow dusters and a large silk handkerchief patterned in shades of brown and purple, three pencils of varying length, a glass ashtray containing an India rubber, six paper clips and a pencil-sharpener, and an octavo-sized manuscript book with nothing written in it at all It was the only untidy, living, lived-in corner of the flat.

Apart from the bedsitting room there was a kitchen and a bathroom. Together they went over every inch and found nothing. There were clothes in the wardrobe and in drawers, including three black, full-length evening dresses – her working clothes, Atherton explained. There were a few books and a lot of records, and even more audio-tapes, some commercial, some home-made. There were odds and ends and ornaments, a cheap quartz carriage clock, a plaster model of the leaning tower of Pisa, some interesting sea-shells, a nightdress case in the shape of a rabbit, a sugar bowl full of potpourri – but there were no papers. Diary, address book, letters, bills, personal documents, old cheque books – anything that might have given any clue to Anne-Marie's life had been taken.

'He got the lot,' Atherton said, slamming an empty drawer shut. 'Bastard.'

'He was very thorough,' Slider said, 'and yet Mrs Gostyn said he was only here five or ten minutes. I wonder if he knew his way around?'

The bathroom revealed soap, face cloth, towels, spare toilet rolls, bath essence – she seemed to have had a preference for The Body Shop – and no secrets. The medicine cabinet at first appeared cheeringly full, but it turned out to contain only aspirin, insect repellent, Diocalm, a very large bottle of kaolin and morphia, travel-sickness pills, half a packet of Coldrex, a packet of ten Tampax with one missing, a bottle of Optrex, four different sorts of suntan lotion, and three opened packets of Elastoplast. On the top of the cupboard stood a bottle of TCP, another of Listerine, a spare tube of Mentadent toothpaste, unopened, and right at the back and rather dusty, another packet of Elastoplast.

'No mysterious packages of white powder,' Slider said sadly. 'No syringe. Not even a tell-tale packet of cigarette papers.'

'But at least we have established some facts,' Atherton said, dusting off his hands. 'We know now that she was female, below menopausal age, travelled abroad, and cut herself a lot.'

'Don't be misled by appearances,' Slider said darkly.

The kitchen was long and narrow, with the usual sort of built-in units along one wall, sink under the window, fridge and gas stove. 'No washing machine,' Atherton said. 'I suppose she used the launderette.'

'Look in the cupboards.'

'I'm looking. Sometimes I dig for buttered rolls. Does it occur to you that we've nothing to go on in this case, nothing at all?'

'It occurs to me.'

There was a good stock of dry goods, herbs and spices, tea and coffee, rice and sugar, but little in the way of fresh food. A bottle of milk in the fridge was open and part-used but still fresh. There were five eggs, two packs of unsalted butter, a wrapped sliced loaf, and a piece of hard cheese wrapped in tin foil.

'She wasn't intending to eat at home that night, at any rate,' said Slider.

As he straightened up the word VIRGIN caught his eye, and he turned towards it. Behind the bread bin in the far corner of the work surface were two tins of olive oil, like diminutive petrol cans. They were brightly, not to say gaudily, decorated in primary colours depicting a rustic scene: goitrous peasants with manic grins were gathering improbable olives the size of avocados, from trees which, if trees could smile, would have been positively hilarious with good health and good will towards the gatherers.

Atherton, following his gaze, read the words on the face of the front tin. 'VIRGIN GREEN – Premium Olive Oil – First Pressing – Produce of Italy.' He pushed the bread bin out of the way. 'Two tins? She must have been fond of Italian food.'

The words set up echoes in Slider's mind of his lunchtime fantasy about her. Coincidence.

'She was,' he said. 'Packets of dried pasta and tubes of tomato purée in the cupboard.'

Atherton gave an admiring look. 'What a detective you'd have made, sir.'

Slider smiled kindly. 'And a lump of Parmesan cheese in the fridge.'

Atherton lifted the second tin and hefted it; unscrewed the lid and peered in, tilting it this way and that, and then applied a nostril to the opening and sniffed. 'Empty. Looks as though it's been washed out, too, or never used. I wonder why she kept it?'

'Perhaps she thought it was pretty.'

'You jest, of course.' He turned it round. 'Virgin Green, indeed. It sounds like a film title. Science fiction, maybe. Or pornography – but we know she wasn't interested in pornography.'

'Do we?' Slider said incautiously.

'Of course. She didn't have a pornograph.'

Slider wandered back into the living-room and stared about him, his usual anxious frown deepening between his brows. Atherton stood in the doorway and watched him. 'I don't think we're going to find anything. It all looks very professional.'

'Somebody went to a lot of trouble,' Slider said. 'There must have been something very important they didn't want us to know about. But what?'

'Drugs,' said Atherton, and when Slider looked at him, he shrugged. 'Well, it always is these days, isn't it?'

'Yes. But I don't think so. This doesn't smell that way to me.'

Atherton waited for enlightenment and didn't get it. 'Have you got a hunch, guv?' he asked. No answer. 'Or is it just the way you stand?'

But Slider merely grunted. He walked across to the music corner, the only place with any trace of Anne-Marie's personality about it, and picked up the violin case, sat down on the bed with it across his knees, opened it. The violin glowed darkly against the electric-blue plush of the lining with the unmistakable patina of age. It looked warm and somehow alive, inviting to the touch, like the rump of a well-groomed bay horse. In the rests of the lid were slung two violin bows, and behind them was tucked a snapshot. Slider pulled it out and turned it to the light to examine it.

It was taken on a beach in some place where the sun was hot enough to make the shadows very short and underfoot. A typical amateur holiday snapshot, featuring the shoulder and flank of a lean young man in bathing-trunks disappearing out of the edge of the picture, and Anne-Marie in the centre in a red bikini, one hand resting on the anonymous shoulder. She was laughing, her eyes screwed up with amusement and sea-dazzle, her head tilted back so that her dark bob of hair fell back from her throat. Her other hand was flung out – to balance her, perhaps – and was silhouetted sharply against the dark-blue sea in the background like a small, white starfish. She looked as though she hadn't a care in the world; her youthful innocence seemed the epitome of what being young ought to be like, and so seldom was.

Slider stared at it hungrily, trying to blot out the memory of her small abandoned body lying dead in that grim and dingy, empty flat. *Murdered.* But why? The white starfish hand, pinned for ever against time in that casual snapshot, had rested finally against the old and splintered wood of those dusty floorboards. She was so young and pretty. What could she possibly have known or done to warrant her death? Not fair, not fair. She laughed at him out of the photograph, and he had only ever known her dead.

One thing he was sure about – there was an organisation behind her death. That was bad news for him: if they were good, they'd have second-guessed him all the way along the line. But however good they were, they would have made one mistake. A benign God saw to that – one mistake, to give the good guys a chance, that was the rule. There was a good sensible reason for it, of course – that the criminals were working to a finite time-scale, and the investigators had for ever more to investigate – but Slider believed in a benign God anyway. He had to, to make sense of his world at all.

Atherton had evinced no interest in the photograph, but was staring intently at the violin. He took it from the case and turned it over carefully, and then said hesitantly, 'Guv?' Slider looked up. 'I think this violin might be something rather special.'

'What do you mean?'

'I'm no expert, but it's got A. Stradivarius written on it.'

Slider stared. 'You mean it's a Stradivarius?'

Atherton shrugged. 'I said I'm no expert.'

'It might be a fake.'

'It might. But if it were genuine—'

Slider noticed, as he had noticed before, how even under stress Atherton's grammar did not desert him. 'Yes, if it were,' he agreed.

One mistake. Could this be it?

'Take it. Find out,' he said. 'Find out what it's worth. But for God's sake be careful with it.'

'Tell your grandmother,' Atherton said, replacing it with awed hands. 'What now?'

'I'm going to see her best friend. You realise we still don't have a next of kin, thanks to Inspector Petrie? So it's the Barbican for me.'

'Wouldn't you like me to go for you? Concert halls are more my province than yours.'

'It'll be good for me to widen my experience,' Slider said. 'Rôle reversal.'

'That's dangerous,' said Atherton. 'The filling might fall out.'

5

Utterly Barbicanned

Slider left his car in the Barbican car park and immediately got lost. He had heard tales of how impossible it was to find your way around in there, and had assumed they were exaggerated: He found a security guard and asked directions, was sent through some swing doors and got lost again. He entered a lift which had been designed, disconcertingly, only to stop at alternate floors, and eventually, with a sense of profound relief, emerged into the car park where he had begun. At least now I know where I am, he thought, even if I don't know where I've just been.

He was contemplating his next move when the sound of footsteps made him turn, and he saw a woman coming towards him carrying a violin case. His heart lifted, and he went towards her like an American tourist in London who has just spotted the Savoy Hotel.

'Are you a member of the Orchestra? Can you tell me how to get to the backstage area from here?'

She stopped and looked at him – looked up at him in fact, for she was about six inches shorter than him, which made

Slider, who was not a tall man, feel agreeably large and powerful.

'I can't tell you, but I can take you,' she said pleasantly. 'It is a rabbit warren, isn't it? Did you know it's even given rise to a new verb – to be Barbicanned?'

'I'm not surprised,' Slider said, falling in beside her as she set off with brisk steps.

'They ought to issue us with balls of thread really. I only know one route, and I stick to it. One diversion, and I'd never be found again.' She glanced sideways at him. 'I'm not actually a member of the Orchestra, but I'm playing with them today. You're not a musician, are you.'

It was plainly a statement, not a question. Slider merely said no, without elaborating, and continued to examine her covertly. Though small she had a real figure, proper womanly curves which he knew were not fashionable but which, being married to a thin and uncommodious woman, he liked the look of. She was dressed in white trousers, pale blue plimsolls, a blue velvet bomber jacket, and a T-shirt horizontally striped in pale – and dark-blue. Her clothes were attractive on her, but seemed somehow eccentric, though he couldn't quite decide why. It made it difficult to deduce anything about her.

She led him through a steel door in the concrete wall and down a flight of stairs of streaked and dimly lit desolation. On the landing she suddenly stopped and looked up at him.

'I say, I've just realised – I bet you're looking for me anyway. Are you Inspector Slider?'

She regarded him with bright-eyed and unaffected friendliness, something he had rarely come across since becoming a policeman. Her face was framed with heavy, rough-cut gold hair which looked as though it might have been trimmed with hedge-cutters, and he suddenly realised what it was about her that made her seem eccentric. Her clothes were youthful, her face innocent of make-up, her whole appearance casual and easy and confident, and yet she was not young. He had never seen a woman of her age less disguised or protected against the critical eyes of the world. And framed by a background of as much squalor as modern building techniques could devise, she gazed at him without hostility or even reserve, with the calm candour of a child, as if she simply wanted to know what he was like.

'You're Joanna Marshall,' he heard himself say.

'Of course,' she said, as if it were very much of course, and held out her hand with such an air of being ready to give him all possible credit that he took it and held it as though this were a social meeting. Warmth came back to him along the line of contact, and pleasure; their eyes met with that particular meeting which is never arrived at by design, and which changes everything that comes afterwards.

As simple as that? he thought with a distant but profound sense of shock. The moment seemed scaffolded with the awareness of possibility – or, well, to be honest, of probability, which was infinitely more disturbing. Like the blind stirring of something under the earth at the first approach of the change of season, he felt all sorts of sensations in him turning towards her, and he let go of her hand hastily. At once the staircase seemed more dank and dreary than ever.

She resumed the downward trot and he hurried after her. 'How did you know who I was?' he asked.

'Sue Bernstein phoned me. She said you'd probably want to talk to me. I knew you weren't a musician, of course. Come to think of it, I suppose you do look like a detective.'

'What does a detective look like?' he asked, amused.

She flicked a glance at him over her shoulder, smiling. 'Oh, I hadn't any preconceived ideas about it. It's just that now I see you, I know.'

She shouldered through another pair of steel doors, and then another, and suddenly they were back in civilization: lights, sounds, and the smell of indoors.

She stopped and rounded on him again. 'It's so terrible about Anne-Marie. I suppose there's no doubt that it is her? I simply can't believe she's dead.'

'There's no doubt,' he said, and showed her one of the mugshots. She took it flinchingly, fearing God-knew-what sketch of carnage. Her first glance registered relief, her second a deeper distress. Few people in this modern, organised world ever see a corpse, or even the picture of a corpse. After a moment she drew a sigh.

'I see,' she said. 'Sue said it was murder. Is that true?'

'I'm afraid so.'

She frowned. 'Look, I want to help you, of course, but I've got to get changed and warm up, and I've only just got time. But I'm only on in the first piece – can you wait? Or come back a bit later? I should be finished by a quarter past eight – then I'll be free and I can talk to you for as long as you like.'

As long as you like. She looked up at him again, straight into the eyes. This directness of hers, he thought, was very disturbing. It was childlike, though there was nothing childish about her. It was something outside the range of his normal experience, and made him feel both exposed and off-balance – as if she were of a different species, or from a parallel universe where, despite appearance, the laws of physics were unnervingly different.

'I'll wait,' he said. 'Perhaps I could take you to supper afterwards,' he heard himself add. What in God's name was he doing?

'Oh, that would be lovely,' she said warmly. 'Look, I must dash. Why don't you go in and listen? The auditorium's through that door there.'

59

'Won't I need a ticket?'

'No, it won't be full, and no one ever checks. Just slip through and sit somewhere near the side, and then at the end of the first piece come back through here, and I'll meet you here when I've changed again.'

She was a quick changer; and at half past eight they were sitting down in an Italian restaurant nearby. The tablecloths and napkins were pale pink, and there were huge parlour palms everywhere, one of which shielded them nicely from the other diners as they sat opposite each other at a corner table. She moved the little lamp to one side to leave the space clear between them, put her elbows on the table, and waited for his questions.

Close to her, he wondered again about her age. Clearly she was quite a bit older than Anne-Marie: there were lines about her eyes, and the moulding of experience in her face. Yet because she wore no make-up and no disguise, she seemed younger; or, well, perhaps not really younger, but without age – ageless. It troubled him, and he took a moment to ask himself why, but he could only think it was because if she asked him a question about himself, he would feel obliged to tell her the truth – the real truth, as opposed to the social truth. And then, this immediacy of hers made him feel as though there were no barrier between them and that touching her, which he was beginning to want very much to do, was not only possible, but inevitable.

He had better not follow that train of thought. He got a grip on himself.

'I suppose we must make a start somewhere. Do you know of anyone who would have reason to want to kill your friend Anne-Marie?'

'I've been thinking about that, of course, and I honestly

60

don't. Actually, I can't imagine why anyone would ever want to kill anyone. Death is so surprising, isn't it? And murder doubly so.'

'Would you have found suicide less surprising?'

'Oh yes,' she said at once. 'Not because I had any reason to think she was contemplating it, but one can always find reasons to hate oneself. And one's own life is so much more accessible. Murder, though—' she paused. 'It's such an affront, isn't it?'

'I'd never really thought of it like that.'

'It must be awful for you,' she said suddenly, and he was surprised.

'Worse for you, surely?'

'I don't think so. I have no responsibility about it, as you have. And then, because I only knew her alive, I'll remember her that way. You only ever saw her dead – no comfort there.'

Why in the world did she think he needed comforting? he thought; and then, more honestly, amended it to how did she know he needed comforting?

'Who were her friends?' he asked.

'Well, I suppose I was her closest friend, though really, I can't say I knew her very intimately. We shared a desk, so we used to hang about together while we were working. I went to her flat once or twice, and we went to the pictures a couple of times. She hadn't been with the Orchestra long, and she was a private sort of person. She didn't make friends easily.'

'What about friends outside the Orchestra?'

'I don't know. She never mentioned any.'

'Boyfriends?'

She smiled. 'I can tell you don't know about orchestra life. Female players can't have boyfriends. The hours of work prevent us from mixing with ordinary mortals, and getting together with someone in the Orchestra is fatal.'

61

'Why?'

'Because of the talk. You can't get away from each other, and everyone bitches and gossips, and it's horribly incestuous. Men are much more spiteful than women, you know – and censorious. If a woman goes out with someone in the Orchestra, everyone knows all about it at once, and then she gets called filthy names, and all the other men think she's easy meat – just as if women never discriminate at all.'

'But Anne-Marie was very attractive. Surely some of the men must have made passes at her?'

'Yes, of course. They do that with any new woman joining.'

'And she rejected them?'

'She had a thing going with Simon Thompson on tour last year, but tours are a different matter: the normal rules are suspended, and what happens there doesn't count as real life. And I think she may have gone out with Martin Cutts once or twice, but that doesn't count either. He's just something everyone has to go through at some point, like chickenpox.'

Slider suppressed a smile and wrote the names down. 'I see.'

'Do you?'

He looked into her face, wondering how she had coped with the situation. She had said those things about being a female player without bitterness, merely matter-of-fact, as though it were something like the weather than could not be altered. But did she know those things from first-hand experience?

She smiled as though she had read his thoughts and said, 'I have my own way of dealing with things. I'll tell you one day.'

The waiter came with their first course, and they waited in silence until he had gone away. Then Slider said, 'So you were Anne-Marie's only friend?'

'Mmm.' She made an equivocal sound through her mouthful, chewed, swallowed, and said, 'She didn't confide in me particularly, but I suppose I was the person in the Orchestra who was closest to her.'

'Did you like her?'

She hesitated. 'I didn't dislike her. She was a hard person to get to know. She was quite good company, but of course we talked a lot about work, and that was mostly what we had in common. I felt rather sorry for her, really. She didn't strike me as a happy person.'

'What were her interests?'

'I don't know that she had any really, outside of music. Except that she liked to cook. She was a good cook—'

'Italian food?'

'How did you know?'

'I was at her flat today. There were packets of pasta, and two enormous tins of olive oil.'

'Oh yes, the dear old green virgins. That was one of her fads – she said you had to have exactly the right kind of olive oil for things to taste right, and she wouldn't use any other sort. The stuff was lethally expensive, too. I don't suppose anyone else could've told the difference, but she was very knowledgeable about Italian cooking. I think she was part Italian herself,' she added vaguely.

'Was she? Did you ever meet her parents?'

'Both dead,' she said succinctly. 'I think she said they died when she was a baby, and an aunt brought her up. I never met the aunt. I don't think they got on. Anne-Marie used to go and visit her once in a while, but I gathered it was a chore rather than a pleasure.'

'Brothers and sisters? Any other relatives?'

'She never mentioned any. I gather she had rather a lonely childhood. She went to boarding school, I think because the aunt didn't want her around the house. I remember she told me once that she hated school holidays because her aunt would never let her have friends home to play in case they made a mess. Wouldn't let her have a pet, either. One of those intensely houseproud women, I suppose – hell to live with, especially for a child. Have you spoken to her yet?'

'I didn't know until this moment that she existed. We asked your Mrs Bernstein, but she didn't know who the next of kin was.'

'No, I suppose she wouldn't,' she said thoughtfully. 'I suppose if it was me instead of Anne-Marie, it would be just the same. So the aunt won't know yet, even that Anne-Marie's dead?'

Slider shook his head. 'I suppose you don't know her name and address?'

'Oh dear! Did she ever tell me her aunt's name? I know she lived in a village called Stourton-on-Fosse, somewhere in the Cotswolds. The house was called something like The Grange or The Manor, I can't remember exactly. But Anne-Marie said it was a large house, and the village is tiny, so you ought to be able to find it easily enough. Wait a minute,' she frowned, 'I think I saw the name on an envelope once. Now what was it? I was going to the post box and she asked me to post it along with mine.' She thought for a moment, screwing up her eyes. 'Ringwood. Yes, that was it – Mrs Ringwood.'

She looked at him delightedly, as though waiting for praise or applause, but their main course arrived and distracted her.

'Mm,' she said, sniffing delightedly. 'Lovely garlic! You could give me matchboxes to eat as long as you fried them in garlic. I hope you like it?'

'I love it,' he said.

Long, long ago in his youth, before Real Life had happened to him, he had cooked for Irene on a grease-encrusted, ancient and popping gas stove in their little flat; and he had used garlic – and onions and herbs and wine and spices and ginger – and food had been an immediate and sensuous pleasure. So it still was, he could see, for Joanna. She seemed very close to him, and warm, and what he felt towards her was so basic it seemed earth-movingly profound. He wanted to take hold of her, to have her, to make good, wholesome, tiring love to her, and then to sleep with her all night with their bodies slotted down together like spoons. But did anything so simple and good happen in Real Life? To anyone?

Under the table he had a truly amazing erection, and it couldn't be entirely because of the garlic. He saw with an agony of disappointment what life could be like with the right person. He imagined waking up beside her, and having her again, warm and sleepy in the early morning quiet; eating with her and sleeping with her and filling her up night after night with himself. Just being together in that uncluttered way, like two animals, no questions to answer and none to ask. He wanted to walk with her hand in hand along some bloody beach in the sunset, with or without the soaring music.

The erection didn't go down, but the pressure seemed to even itself out, so that he could adjust to it, like adjusting to travelling at speed, all reactions sharpened. He watched her eating not only with desire, but also, surprisingly, with affection. He could see how the rough, heavy locks of her hair were like those sculpted on the bronze head of a Greek hero, soft and dense, pulling straight of their own weight. She ate with simple attention, and when she looked up at him she smiled, as if that were something obvious and easy, and then all her attention was on him.

She put out her hand for her wine glass, and almost before he knew what he had done, he intercepted it across the table. To his astonished relief, her warm fingers curled happily round his and returned his pressure, and the situation resolved itself simply and gracefully, like crystals forming at crystallising point. Nothing to worry about. He released her and they both went on eating, and Slider felt as though he were flying, and was utterly astonished at himself, that he could have done such a thing.

In the interval between the main course and dessert he went to the telephone to ring the station, and spoke to Hunt, who was Duty Officer.

'I've got a next of kin in the Austen case,' he said, and relayed the information about Mrs Ringwood. 'Can you put a trace on that, and get one of the local blokes to go round and inform her. She'll have to formally ID the body. And then we can have the inquest. Would you tell Atherton to get onto it first thing in the morning?'

'Righto, guv,' said Hunt.

'Also I want him to get Mrs Gostyn in to make a statement and see if she can help us put together a photofit of this Inspector Petrie.'

'Okay, sir. Anything else?'

There was, but not for his ears. 'Is Nicholls on the desk? Put me through to him will you?'

To Nicholls he said, 'Listen, Nutty – will you ring Irene for me, and tell her not to wait up. I've got a lot of interviews to do, and I won't be back until very late.'

'Sure I'll tell her,' he said, but with the end of the sentence clearly open for the unspoken words *but she'll not believe it.*

'Thanks, mate.'

'Okay Bill. Cheeroh. Be careful, won't you?'

That, thought Slider, was like telling a man about to go over Niagara Falls in a barrel not to get his feet wet.

★ ★ ★

'Tell me about that last evening,' he said over the profiteroles.

'We were on until nine-thirty at the Television Centre. We packed up—'

'Did you finish on time?'

She smiled. 'You bet. Otherwise they have to pay us overtime. We're fierce about that. We packed up – that would take five minutes or so – and then I'd arranged with a couple of the others – Phil Redcliffe and John Delaney and Anne-Marie – to go for a drink.'

'Which pub did you use?' he asked, having a sudden dread that it would be The Dog and Scrotum, which after all was the nearest pub to the TVC.

'We always go to The Crown and Sceptre – it's Fullers, you see,' she said simply, and he nodded. For a beer-drinker, it was that simple. 'As I was going out, Simon Thompson asked me if I was going for a drink, and I said yes but Anne-Marie was coming, and he said in that case he didn't want to come, and that delayed me a bit—'

'Why didn't he want to come if she was going?' Slider interrupted.

'They'd been having a bit of trouble.' She grimaced. 'Look, I don't want you to make too much of this, but I'll tell you about it, because *someone* will, so it had better be me. I told you Anne-Marie and Simon had been together on tour?'

'Yes, you did. Do you mean they were having an affair?'

'Oh, it didn't really amount to that. Being on tour is sort of like fainlights—' She demonstrated the crossed fingers of childhood games. 'It doesn't really count. People sleep together, go round together, and when they get back to England, it's all forgotten. Anne-Marie and Simon were like that, except that after the last tour in October, to Italy, Anne-Marie tried to carry it on. Simon didn't like that because he's got a permanent girlfriend, and Anne-Marie—' She paused.

67

'Well, she got a bit funny about it. She insisted that Simon had been serious about her, that they had decided to get married, and that now he was trying to get out of it.'

'Did you believe her?'

'I don't know. There must have been something in it, surely? Simon said she was just making it up, of course, but then he would, wouldn't he? He started saying all sorts of nasty things about her, that she was unbalanced and so on, but I don't know what the truth of it was. Anne-Marie just gave it up after a while and left him alone, but he made a great performance out of not having anything to do with her – changing tables in the coffee-bar if she sat down near him, not going for a drink with a group of us if she was included – that sort of thing.'

'I see,' Slider said encouragingly, hoping that he would. 'How did she seem to you that last day? Did she seem in her normal spirits?'

'I didn't notice really, one way or the other. She'd been a bit quiet since that trouble with Simon – a bit low, you know, withdrawn. As I said, I never thought she was a particularly happy person, and that could only make it worse.'

Slider nodded. 'So you spoke to Simon Thompson, and then what? You went out to your car?'

'Yes. We were all in separate cars, of course. Phil and John had already gone, and with Simon stopping me – oh, and I talked to John Brown as well about something, the fixer, so I was the last one out. Anne-Marie had rushed off when she saw Simon coming. She left her car outside, you know in that narrow bit to the side of the main gate where the Minis and small cars are parked.'

'Yes, I know. Did she drive a Mini?'

'No, she had a red MG – just about the one thing in her life she really loved, that car. Anyway, as I came out, she was just running back across the yard towards me. She said she was glad she'd caught me, and why didn't we go to The Dog and Sportsman instead. That's another pub, along the—'

'I know,' Slider said. I knew it, he thought flatly. I should never have drunk on my own manor.

Joanna eyed him curiously. 'Well, it's a horrible pub, and in any case Phil and John had already gone. I said so, and she seemed quite put out, and tried to persuade me to go to The Dog, just the two of us, but I didn't want to, and in the end she just left me and went back to her car. I went to The Crown and Sceptre, and of course she never showed up. I don't know if eventually she did go to the other pub, or if she – if they—' She stopped.

'Did she say why she wanted to go to the other pub?' Slider asked, not without sympathy.

'No. She didn't give any reason. I've wondered since whether, if we'd gone with her, she might not have been killed. Do you think she could have known something was going to happen to her?'

Slider was thinking. 'At what stage did she change her mind? She was going to The Crown with you? She knew that's where you planned to go?'

'Oh yes, we always went there. And when she left the first time, when she went out to her car, she knew that's where we were going. In fact I think when she went past me as I was talking to John Brown she said something like "See you in there".'

'So something happened to make her change her mind when she was outside, going to her car. Did she speak to someone in the car park?'

'I don't know. When I came out she was already running back towards me. The men in the gatehouse might have seen something. There are always two of them on duty, and they'd have been able to see her car from their windows.'

'Yes,' Slider said, and made a note: *Gatekeepers!* and *Ask Hilda*. He looked up. Joanna was staring at him unhappily. 'What is it?'

'Maybe she was afraid, and wanted us to come with her for protection. Maybe if we'd gone with her—'

Slider felt compelled to offer her some comfort. 'I don't think it would have made any difference. I think it would just have happened some other time.'

Her eyes widened as she considered the implications of this. 'I don't think that helps very much,' she said.

The eating and drinking were over. He paid, and they walked out into the street. 'It was a good meal,' he said. 'I like Italian food.' He remembered Anne-Marie like touching a mouth ulcer he'd forgotten.

'You mind, don't you,' Joanna said. 'About Anne-Marie. Why do you? I mean, all murder is dreadful, but you must have seen some horrible cases in your time, worse than this. Why is it different?'

He wanted to ask how she knew, but was afraid of the answer. Instead he said, 'I don't know,' which was unoriginal, but true, and she accepted it at face value.

'I can't feel it much – not continuously. She still doesn't feel dead to me. She was so young, and I always thought her rather silly – not a particularly capable person. Vulnerable. It seems almost like cheating to kill someone so easy to kill.'

They stood looking at each other on the pavement. Now the moment had come, he didn't know how he could possibly ask her. He had no right to. He had nothing to offer – he could only take. But how, otherwise, were they ever to move from this spot? He looked at her helplessly.

'Can you be struck off, like doctors, for fraternising with witnesses?' she asked lightly. She had seen his trouble, and

70

was doing the job for him, making it easy for him either to go on or to go away. He knew how generous that was of her, and yet still he blundered.

'I'm married,' he said – blurted – and he actually saw it hurt her.

'I know that,' she said quietly.

'How do you know?' Now he was simply delaying, evading.

She shrugged. 'You have the look – hungry. Like a man with worms, you eat but it doesn't satisfy you.' She looked at him consideringly, and he was aware painfully that he had put this distance between them, that it was all his fault. 'I even know what she looks like,' she went on. 'Pretty, very slim, smart. Keeps the house spotless, and hasn't much sense of humour.'

'How can you know that?' he said uneasily.

He saw her suddenly tire of it. She had placed everything at his service, and he had been too weak and cowardly to do the right thing, one way or the other. She hitched her bag onto her shoulder and said, 'I'd better be going. Thank you very much for supper.'

Leave it be, let it go. Don't ask for trouble. Life is complicated enough as it is.

'Where do you live?' he gasped. One last breath before going under, one last grasp at the straw. She would say north or south, anything, not west, and that would be that. Let God decide. Yet if she said west, what then? She turned back the little she had turned away, and it seemed an effort, and she looked at him doubtfully, as if she were not sure whether to answer him or not.

'Turnham Green,' she said at last, with no inflection at all.

He licked his lips. 'That's on my way,' he said in a voice like fishbones. 'I live in Ruislip.'

'You can follow me,' she said, 'if you promise not to book me for speeding.'

71

His stomach went away from him like an express lift and he nodded, and they walked towards their cars, parked nose-to-tail down the side street. Even in his extremity he told himself he was not committed yet, that it would be perfectly easy for him to lose her on the cross-town drive. But of course she knew that too, and it was too late, by several hours at least.

The drive back to Chiswick was long enough for Slider to think of everything and fear everything several times over. It was close to twenty years since he had made love to anyone but Irene, and it was a long time – he paused – good God, was it really over a year? – since he had made love even to her. Large-scale social and moral considerations jostled for space in his cringing mind with mute and ignoble worries about custom, expectation, performance, and even underwear, to the point where desire was suppressed and he could no longer think of any good and sufficient reason to be doing what he was doing at all.

And yet still he followed her, almost automatically, keeping the taillights of her Alfa GTV just two lengths ahead of him, copying her lefts and rights like a colt following its dam, because doing anything else would have involved him in a decision he was no longer capable of making.

They stopped at last, parked, got out of their cars. Hollow excuses formed themselves inside his head, and if she had spoken to him or even looked back at him, he would probably have babbled them and fled. But she had her door key ready in her hand, opened her front door and went in, leaving it open for him, without once looking round, and so he simply followed, as if the moment for making the absolutely definitely final decision had not yet arrived.

Afterwards he wondered how much of his state of mind

she had guessed and was making allowance for. Inside the hallway of her flat she was waiting for him. She had not put on the lights or taken off her coat. She had simply put down her bags on the floor, and as he entered the half dark of the passage she put her arms round him inside his coat and lifted her mouth to be kissed.

Slider went tremblingly to pieces. No questions to ask and none to answer. He pulled the female softness against him and was kissing her ravenously, and her mouth and tongue led him with the lightness of a familiar dancing-partner. She moved her pelvis, and he could feel his erection like a rock between them, and he felt distantly, ridiculously proud. She broke off from kissing him at last, but it was only to lead the way into her bedroom beyond, which was lit dimly by the glow from a streetlamp outside – just light enough, and not too much.

There was the bed, a big double, covered by a counterpane. She went round to the far side and sat on the edge with her back to him and began to take off her clothes with neat, economical movements. So they were really going to do it, part of his mind said in amazement. He was glad she was letting him undress himself. His state of mind was so far gone he was no longer sure what he'd got on, or whether he could get it off without fumbling stupidly. By the time he was down to his underpants she had finished, and slid gracefully in under the sheets and looked at him calmly from the pillows. He pulled in his stomach and took off his pants. The air felt cold on his skin, but his erection felt so huge and hot he half thought it would warm up the room, like an immersion heater. What a ridiculous thing to think, he rebuked himself; but he must have smiled, for she smiled in response and pulled back the covers for him.

After all his fears, it was all so beautifully simple. He lay down beside her, feeling the whole length of her against his body warm and delicious; and before he could start wondering what she would expect of him by way of preliminaries, she drew him onto and into her so easily that he sighed in enormous relief, as if he were coming home. Being in her was both exotic and familiar in such piercing, blissful combination that he knew it could not last long. But it didn't matter – there would be time for everything later. He turned his mouth, nuzzling for hers, and as they connected he felt her lift and close on him, and that was it. He let go gratefully and flooded her as though all of his life he had been saving up for this moment.

Close and far away he heard her sigh 'Ah!' And then they were drifting out together into dark water, clean and complete as if newborn. A long time later she kissed his cheek and lay her face against his neck, and he slid over onto his back and took her in his arms, with her head on his shoulder, and it felt very good. He wanted to tell her he loved her, but he couldn't speak: everything was too vivid, as though all his nerve endings were exposed, and the difference between pleasure and pain was slight. He needed to be silent for a while, to discover whether this new and perilous existence could be sustained.

6

Moth and Behemoth

He woke gently, with that Christmas-Day feeling of something delicious having happened that he had forgotten about while asleep. He moved slightly and felt a responding movement beside him, and knew he was not in his own bed and not alone, and everything came back to him all-of-a-piece. He opened his eyes. In the light from the window he looked at her, curled on her side, sleeping quietly. The covers had slipped off her, and she seemed all made of curves, strongly indented at the waist, richly rounded at breast and hip. Her hair looked soft and heavy as if it were moulded from bullion, too dense to curl, each lock lying separately like the petals of a bronze chrysanthemum.

He reached out a hand to push it from her face and she smiled and moved her face to his hand. He smoothed her eyebrows and the smiling dents at the corners of her mouth, and her face felt pliant and flowing under his fingers as if he could shape her. He felt powerful. The world outside was dark and damp like something newborn, and it was all his. She shivered suddenly, and he drew her to him and pulled the covers over her. She stretched gratefully in the restored warmth, and her hand contacted his penis, and it rose to meet her.

'Hmm?' she enquired gently, her eyes still closed.

'Hmm,' he replied, running his hands over her shoulders and sides. She uncurled like a flower, and he seemed to flow into her effortlessly. This time they took time over it, seeking out pleasure softly, kissing and touching a great deal, and it was unbelievably good, unlike anything he had ever experienced before. He was happy and amazed.

'I love you,' he said afterwards, and then got up on his elbows and looked at her to see her reaction.

'Don't you think it's a little early to be saying that?' she asked, amused.

'Is it? I don't know. I've nothing to compare it with. I've never done this before, you know.'

'In that case, I'm very flattered.'

'I wish I'd met you years ago,' he said, as people will at such a moment.

'You wouldn't have liked me,' she said consolingly.

'Of course I would. You must have—' The green, luminous read-out of her bedside clock-radio caught his eye. He turned his head slightly and went cold with shock. 'Christ, it's twenty to seven!'

'Is it?' She didn't seem perturbed by the news.

'It can't be! We can't have slept the whole night through!'

'Not so much of a whole night,' she murmured, and then, seeing he really was upset, 'What's the matter?' But he was off her, rolling to the side of the bed, swinging his legs out, groping on the floor for clothes. She knew what was wrong, and her mouth turned down sourly.

'Christ,' he was muttering, 'that's done it. What the hell do I do now? Jesus.'

She propped herself up to look at him. 'You can't go home now,' she said reasonably. 'You've been out all night, and that's that. Come back to bed for a bit. Seven o'clock is early enough to start making excuses.'

But it was no good: the world had rolled onto him like a stone. All the clean simplicity had been delusion, his omnipotence had fled. There was going to be a row at home, and he was going to have to think of lies to tell. Probably Irene would not believe him, and he was going to feel bad about it whether she did or she didn't.

'Christ,' he muttered. 'Jesus.'

'Take it easy,' she said protestingly.

He shook his head, hunching his shoulders away from her. 'I'll have to make some phone calls,' he said miserably. 'I'm sorry.'

She looked at him a moment longer, and then got quietly out of bed on the other side, and drew a cotton wrap over her glowing nakedness. 'Phone's beside you. I'll go and make some tea.'

She padded away, and he understood that she didn't want to hear him lying, and that was nearly the worst thing of all. He reached for the phone.

Atherton was a long time answering. 'I was in the shower. What's tip? You're up early.'

'Actually, I haven't been to bed yet.'

'What?'

'Not my own bed. I've been out all night.'

There was a short and horrible silence. Then, 'I'm not hearing straight. Please tell me you don't mean what I think you mean.'

Slider could tell from his tone of voice that he really didn't think that's what it was, and the knowledge depressed him even further.

'I've been with Joanna Marshall. I'm at her place now.'

Another, slightly worse silence. 'Christ, guv, you don't mean—'

'I took her out for supper last night, and then—' No possible way of ending that sentence. Slider grew irritable with guilt. 'Oh, for God's sake, I don't have to draw you pictures, do I? You can use your imagination. You've done it yourself often enough.'

'Yes, but I—'

'The thing is, I've got to tell Irene something. Can I tell her I was with you?'

'Oh great.' Atherton's voice hardened. 'She'll love me after that.'

'I don't think she likes you much anyway. It can't make any difference. Please. I'll ring her up and say we were working late at your house, and we had a few drinks, and it got too late to come home.'

'Why didn't you phone her from my place?'

'Oh God – it got too late, I thought she'd have gone to bed and I didn't want to wake her.'

'Jesus, is that the best you can do?'

'What the hell else can I say? Come on, for God's sake, back me up.'

'All right,' Atherton said shortly. 'But I don't like it. It's not like you, either. What's got into you?'

'Every dog has its day,' Slider said weakly.

'I mean, messing around with a witness—'

'She's not a material witness. For God's sake, what does it matter? It's going to be bad enough facing Irene – don't you give me a hard time as well.'

'All right, all right, don't bite me! I'll say whatever you want. I'm just worried for you, that's all.'

'Thanks. I'm sorry.'

'Take it easy.' The concern was naked in his voice. 'You going to phone Irene now? You going home?'

The idea made Slider shudder. 'I think it's best not to. I'll go down and talk to the next of kin – the aunt in the Cotswolds. Will you do the paperwork for me? You got my messages last night?'

'Yeah. Okay. I'll get old Mother Gostyn in this morning, and check out John Brown. And I thought I'd take the violin down to Sotheby's.'

'Good. And you might see if you can get hold of Anne-Marie's ex-boyfriend, this Simon Thompson type.'

'Okay. Will I see you later?'

'Depends what comes up. I'll phone you, anyway.'

'Right.' A pause. 'Are you taking her with you?'

The idea flooded Slider's brain with its bright originality. 'Well, I – yes, I thought I might.'

He heard Atherton sigh. 'Well – be careful, won't you, guv?'

'Of course,' he said stiffly, and put the phone down. Joanna came in with a mug of tea.

'Finished?'

'That was Atherton, my sergeant. He said he'll – back me up. You know.'

'Oh.' She turned her head away.

'But now I've got to—'

'I'll go and run my bath,' she said abruptly and left him again, her face expressionless. And that was the easy part, he thought, dialling his own number.

Irene picked it up at the second ring. 'Bill?'

'Hullo. Did I wake you up?'

'Where are you? What's happened? I've been worried sick!'

'I've been with Atherton, at his flat. Didn't Nicholls phone you?'

'He phoned yesterday evening to say you'd be late, that's

all. He didn't say you wouldn't be home at all. How late can you be, interviewing witnesses? What were they, night workers?'

Her anger was at least easier to deal with than hurt or worry. He felt guiltily grateful.

'They were musicians and they were giving a concert and we had to wait until they'd finished. Then Atherton and I went over some of the statements. We had a couple of drinks and – well, I didn't think I'd better drive.'

'Why the hell didn't you *phone*? I didn't know what had happened to you. You might have been dead.'

'Oh, darling – it got late, and we hadn't noticed the time. I thought you'd have gone to bed. I didn't want to wake you up—'

'I wasn't asleep. How do you think I could sleep, not knowing where you were? I don't care what time it was, you should have phoned!'

'I'm sorry. I just didn't want to disturb you. I'll know another time,' Slider said unhappily.

'You're a selfish bastard, you know that? Anything might have happened to you, with your job. I just sit at home wondering if I'm ever going to see you again, if some madman hasn't gone for you with a knife—'

'They'd have got in touch with you if anything had happened to me.'

'Don't joke about it, you bastard!' He said nothing. After a moment she went on in a lower voice, 'I know what it was – you and that bloody Atherton got drunk, didn't you?'

'We just had a couple of scotches—' He tried not to let the relief show in his voice as the danger disappeared up a side track. Let her go on thinking that was it!

'Don't tell me! I hate that man – he's always trying to set you against me. I know how you two go on when you're together – telling smutty stories and giggling like stupid little boys. You don't realise how he's holding you back. If it wasn't for him, you'd have been promoted long ago.'

'Oh come on, darling—'

'Don't darling me,' she said, but he could hear that the heat was going out of her voice. The new, sharp-edged grievance had been put aside for the old, dulled one. 'You should be a chief inspector by now – everyone knows that. Your precious bloody Atherton knows that. He's jealous of you – that's why he tries to hold you back.'

Slider ignored that. He made his voice as sensible and man-to-man as he could. 'Look, darling, I'm sorry you were worried, and I promise I'll phone if it ever happens again. But I'll have to go now – I've got a hell of a lot to do today.'

'Aren't you coming home to change?'

'I'll make do as I am. The shirt I've got on isn't too bad, and I'll get a shave at the station.'

The domestic details seemed to soothe her. 'I suppose it's no use asking you what time you'll be home tonight?'

'I'll try not to be late, but I can't promise. You know what it's like.'

'Yes, I know what it's like,' she said ironically, but she had accepted it. She had accepted it all. The boat had righted itself again. He rang off, and found himself sweating, despite the cold air of January.

He felt rather sick. So this was what it was like. He thought of the thousands of men there must be to whom such lying and dissembling were part of normal, everyday life, and wondered how they ever got used to it. And yet he had just coped, hadn't he? Coped well. Lied like an expert, and got away with it, and felt relief when she'd swallowed it. Self-disgust reached its peak. Perhaps all men were born with the ability, he thought. Well, he knew what they knew now.

The peak passed. He listened and heard water splashing

somewhere, and thought of Joanna, and at once the distress of the phone calls dropped off him cleanly, leaving no mark. He thought of making love to her, and heat ran under his skin. We can spend the whole day together, if she's not working. Oh pray she's not working! A whole day with her—!

That was the other half of it, wasn't it? And it was the fact that they could exist in complete isolation from each other that made the whole thing possible. What absolute shits we are, he thought, but it was without any real conviction. Oh pray she's not working today! And that she's got a razor in her bathroom with a half-way decent blade. He got up and padded in the direction of the splashing.

The man from Sotheby's, Andrew Watson, apart from being tall, slim, blond, and impeccably suited, was also possessed of that unmistakably upper-class beauty that stems from generations of protein diet and modern sanitation. It gave him the air of possessing youth and wisdom in equal, incompatible proportions. Actually, he couldn't possibly be as young as he looked, and be as senior as he was. Atherton's upbringing in Weybridge and his grammar-school education were weighing heavily on him. He felt, by comparison, as huge and ungainly as a behemoth. He saw himself looming dangerously over the other man as if he might crush him underfoot like a butterfly. And Andrew Watson's aftershave was so expensively subtle that for some time Atherton put it down to imagination.

All that apart, however, he was quite endearingly excited by the violin, the more endearingly because Atherton guessed he wanted to display only a calm, professional interest. After a long and careful examination, prolonged conference with a colleague, and reference to a book as thick as an eighteenth-century Bible, Watson seemed prepared to go over every inch of the fiddle again with a magnifying glass, and Atherton stirred restively. He had other things to do. And he wanted to be around when Mrs Gostyn was brought in. There had been no reply from her telephone that morning, so Atherton had arranged for one of the uniformed men to go round and fetch her.

At last Watson came back to him. 'May I ask where you obtained this instrument, sir?'

'You may ask, but I'm not at liberty to tell you,' Atherton replied. It was catching, that sort of thing. 'Is it, in fact, a Stradivarius?'

'It is indeed, and a valuable one – a very valuable one. My colleague agrees with me that this is a piece made by Antonio Stradivari in Cremona in 1707, which has always been known by the name of La Donna – The Lady,' he translated kindly. Atherton nodded gravely.

'There is, as you see, a particular grain to the wood forming the back of the instrument, which is very unusual and distinctive,' Watson went on, turning it over to demonstrate. Atherton looked, saw nothing very distinguishable, and nodded again. Watson resumed. 'The piece was very well known, and its history is well documented right up to the Second World War, when it disappeared, as so many treasures did, during the Nazi occupation of Italy. Since then there's been a great deal of speculation as to its fate, naturally. It would be of great interest –' his voice took on an urgency '– not just to me personally, but to the world, to know how it has come to light again.'

Atherton shook his head. 'If I could tell you, I would. You're quite sure this is the genuine thing?'

'Oh, quite! There are many features which make it unique. For instance, if you look at the scroll, here—'

'I'm happy to take your word for it,' Atherton said hastily.

Watson looked hurt. 'You can, of course, ask for a second opinion. I could recommend—'

'I'm sure that isn't necessary,' Atherton smiled politely, trying not to overshadow him with his colossal, Viking bulk. 'Can you give me an estimate of its value?'

'With a piece of this importance, it's always hard to say. It would depend entirely on who was at the auction, and there are often great surprises when rarities like this come to be sold. Prices can go far beyond expectations. But if you were to ask me to place it at auction for you, I should recommend that you put it in with a reserve price of at least seven or eight hundred thousand.'

'*Pounds?*'

'Oh yes. We don't deal in guineas any more.' Watson regained his composure as Atherton lost his. 'You must understand that this is a very rare and important instrument. And it's in beautiful condition, I'm glad to say.' He ran a hand over it with the affection of a true connoisseur, and then raised his speedwell eyes to Atherton's face. 'In fact it could easily fetch over a million. If you ever do come to sell it, I should feel privileged to handle the sale for you. And if you ever feel able to divulge its history, I should be extremely grateful.' Atherton said nothing, and Watson sighed and placed the violin gently in its case. 'It's a shock to see such a beautiful instrument lying in this horrible case – and with these horrible bows. I hope no one ever tried to play it with one of them.'

Atherton was interested. 'You think the bows – incongruous?' He chose the word with care.

'I can't believe any true musician would ever touch this violin with either of them,' Watson said with simple faith.

'I didn't know there were good bows and bad ones.'

'Oh yes. And good bows are becoming quite an investment these days. I'm not as well up on them as I ought to be, I'm afraid – they're a study in themselves. If you wanted to know

84

about bows, you should go and see Mr Saloman of Vincey's – Vincey's the antiquarian's, a few doors down in Bond Street. Mr Saloman is probably the leading authority in the country on bows. I'm sure he'd love to see this violin, too.'

'Thank you, Mr Watson,' Atherton said, restraining the urge to press his hand lovingly, and took his massive bulk and the Stradivarius out of Mr Watson's life.

First he went to find a phone and call the station. Mackay answered from the CID room to say that there was still no reply from Mrs Gostyn's telephone or door. Atherton felt a stirring of anxiety.

'Tell them to keep trying, will you? An old bird like her can't have gone far. She's bound to be back some time soon. I'll ring in from time to time and see if you've got her.'

He was then free to keep his appointment with John Brown, the Orchestra's personnel manager – a rosy, chubby man in his forties, with the flat and hostile eyes of the ageing homosexual. He received Atherton impassively, but with a faint air of affront, like a cat at the vet's, as of one on whom life heaps ever more undeserved burdens.

'She hadn't long been with us. She came from the Birmingham,' he said, as though thus dissociating himself from the business.

'Where in Birmingham?' Atherton asked ingenuously.

Brown looked scornful. 'It's an orchestra – the Birmingham Municipal Orchestra. She'd been there about three years. They could tell you more about her personal life than I could,' he added with a sniff.

'Had she any particular friends in the Orchestra?'

Brown shrugged. 'She hung around with Joanna Marshall and her lot, but then they shared a desk, so what would you expect? Most of them stay with their own sections in coffee-breaks and so on. I don't think she was particularly chummy

85

with anyone. Not the chummy sort. Out of hours, I couldn't tell you *what* she got up to.'

'Did she drink a lot? Take drugs – pot or anything like that? Was she ever in any kind of trouble?'

'How should I know?' Brown said, turning his head away.

'You didn't like her, did you?' Atherton asked, woman to woman.

'I neither liked her nor disliked her,' Brown said with dignity, refusing the overture. 'She was a good player, and no less reliable than the rest of them. That was the only way in which her personality could interest me in the slightest. I'm not paid to like them, you know.'

'What do you mean, no less reliable? Less reliable than whom?'

'Oh, they're always wanting releases to do outside work. With her it was wanting to go back and play for her old orchestra. They're all like that these days – greedy. No loyalty. Never think about how much work it makes for everyone else. She used to go up there at least once a month, and frankly I'm surprised they wanted her. I mean there must have been plenty of other extras they could have used, locally. She wasn't so wonderful no one else would do.'

Atherton let this sink in, unable yet to make anything of it. 'Did she have a boyfriend? Someone in the Orchestra, perhaps?' he asked next.

Brown shrugged again. 'I imagine so. They all have the morals of alley cats.'

'What, musicians?'

'Women,' he spat, his face darkening. 'I don't like females in the Orchestra, I'll tell you that for nothing. They're trouble-makers. They go round making factions and setting one against the other, whispering behind people's backs. And if you say anything to them, they start crying, and you have to lay off them. Discipline goes to pieces. We never had any of that kind of trouble before we started taking in females. But of course,' he sneered, 'it's the *law* now. We're not allowed to keep them out.'

Atherton's expression was schooled to impassivity. 'But wasn't there someone in particular?' he insisted. 'Some man in her section?'

The eyes slid away sideways. 'I suppose you mean Simon Thompson? They were together on tour, once. You should ask him about that, not me. It's not my business.'

'Thanks, I will.' Doesn't like women, Atherton thought. What else? 'When did you last see Miss Austen?'

'At the Centre on Monday, of course. You know that.'

'Yes, but exactly when? Did you see her leave, for instance?'

'I didn't see her leave the building, if that's what you mean. I was standing at the door of the studio handing out payslips. I gave her hers, and that's the last I saw of her. By the time I'd left the building they'd all gone.'

'How are they paid? Direct into the bank?'

'Yes – I just give out the notifications.'

'How much did she earn? I suppose you'd know that, wouldn't you?'

'I have the computer read-out, if you want to look at it. I wouldn't know offhand. They're all self-employed, and paid by the session, so it varies in any case from month to month, depending on how much work there is.'

'So if it was a quiet month, they'd all be a bit short?'

'Not necessarily. They all do work outside, for other orchestras. They might get other dates if we have no work.'

Brown brought forth the green striped paper, put it down on the table and flicked through it rapidly and efficiently.

'Here you are – Austen, A. Last month she grossed £812.33.'

'Was that about average?'

'I couldn't say. We were fairly busy last month, but it wasn't the best month of the year. There are always gaps around Christmas.'

Atherton calculated. So she was earning between ten and twelve thousand a year – not enough to have bought a Stradivarius, anyway, not even on the lay-away plan. It looked as though she must have been into some pretty big shit to have come by it. Over Brown's shoulder he took down the details of Anne-Marie's bank account and, watching his face from the corner of his eye, asked casually, 'Do you know what sort of violin she played?'

The reaction was one of simple, mild surprise. 'I've no idea. Joanna Marshall would probably know, if it's important to you.'

Well, if the Strad was the key to all this, Brown didn't know about it. 'Okay – so you gave Miss Austen her pay-slip, and that's the last time you ever saw her?'

The sulkiness returned. 'I've told you so.'

'And what did you do afterwards, as a matter of routine?'

'I went home and went to bed.'

'Is there anyone who can confirm that? Do you live here alone?'

The sulkiness was replaced by a dull anger – or was it apprehension? 'I share the flat, as it happens. My flatmate can tell you what time I got in.'

'Your flatmate?'

'Yes.' He spat the word. 'Trevor Byers is his name. You might have heard of him – he's the consultant orthopaedic surgeon at St Mary's. Is that respectable enough for you?'

Oho, thought Atherton, writing it down, is that how the milk got into the coconut? 'Eminently so,' he said, trying to goad him a little more. He decided to try the old by-the-way ploy. 'By the way, wasn't there some sort of trouble between you and Miss Austen? A quarrel, or something?'

Brown shoved his fists down onto the table and leaned on them, his red and angry face thrust forward.

'What are you trying to suggest? I didn't like her, I make no bones about it. She was a troublemaker. They're all troublemakers. There's no place for women in orchestras – I've said that. They're all trollops, and their minds are never on their jobs.'

'You disapproved of her relationship with Thompson.'

He controlled himself, straightening up and breathing hard. 'I've told you, that was none of my business. It was she who caused the trouble, talking about people behind their backs – telling lies—'

'About you?'

'No!' He took a breath. 'I couldn't care less about anything she said. And if you think I murdered her you're barking up the wrong tree – I wouldn't soil my hands. As far as her being a troublemaker's concerned, ask Simon Thompson about it. He'll tell you.'

'This is all purely routine, sir,' Atherton said soothingly. 'We have to ask about everything, however unlikely, and check up on everyone – all simply routine, you know.'

Back in his car he wondered about it. Brown a homosexual – Austen with too much money? Was she blackmailing him, perhaps? It's not illegal to be bent, but an eminent surgeon might perhaps not like it to come out. On the other hand— He sighed. Check everybody, he'd said, and there were a hell of a lot of them to check. Why couldn't the damned woman be a lighthouse keeper or something agreeably solitary, instead of a member of a hundred-piece orchestra of irregular habits?

And Bill's pure and perfect woman was beginning to sound a little tarnished. Making all possible allowance for Brown's prejudice, there must have been something unlikeable about Anne-Marie Austen. A faint frown drew down his fair brows. What was going on with old Bill? First he got a thing about the Austen girl, and now he had stepped right out of character and screwed a witness – a man who had never been unfaithful to his wife in however many years it was of marriage. It was all very worrying.

7

The Last Furnished Flat in the World

Slider drove at first as though he and the car were made of glass, breathing with enormous, drunken care, sometimes even holding his breath, as if to see whether anything would change, whether Joanna would disappear and he would find himself alone in his car in a traffic jam in Perivale again. His mind felt hugely, spuriously expanded, like candyfloss, blown out of its normal dimensions with the effort of encompassing the impossible along with the familiar. The new knowledge of Joanna was laid alongside his ingrained experience of Irene and the children, both occupying the space one had occupied before – an affront to physics, as he had learned at school.

He had never felt like this before. The trite words of every love song – but it was literally true. This was not just the intensification of a previously charted emotion, it was something entirely new, and he hardly knew what to do with it. In his life there had been one or two tentative teenage fumblings, and then there had been Irene, and he had never felt like this with Irene.

He didn't remember ever having felt anything intense about

Irene. He had proposed to her as the next, the correct thing to do: you left school, you got a job, then you got married. He had admired her for his mother's reasons, as the goal to attain, and had naturally assumed, since he was going to marry her, that he must love her.

Once married to her, he had behaved well by her because it was the right thing to do, and also, perhaps, because it was in his nature to sympathise. You've made your bed, his mother might have said if she'd ever known about his disappointment, and now you must lie on it. Well, so he had thought. But now he had to grapple with the possibility, wounding to the self-esteem, that he had dealt justly with Irene only because he had experienced no temptation to do otherwise.

But no, that was not the whole story. He had been married to Irene for fifteen years, and he had never known her, except in the sense that he recognised her and could predict pretty well what she would say or do in any situation. Joanna he had only just met, and he could not in the least predict her, and yet he felt as though he knew her absolutely, right to the bones. He felt that while anything she might do or say would probably astonish, it would never really surprise him.

The threatened crisis was here. He had deceived his wife. He had been unfaithful to her, slept with another woman, and told lies to cover up for it. Worse than that, he intended to go on doing it, as long and as often as possible. Broken things might be mended, but they could never be quite right again, he knew that: thus he had begun something that would change his whole life. There was peril implicit in it, and unhappiness for Irene and the children, and that peril was minutely perceived and understood. What he couldn't understand was why it entirely failed to alarm him; why, knowing that what he was doing was both wrong and dangerous to all concerned, he could feel only this huge and expanding joy, as though his life were at last unrolling before him.

Joanna, looking sideways at him, saw only a faint smile. 'What are you thinking about, dear Inspector?'

Happiness bubbled over into laughter. 'You really can't go on calling me Inspector!'

'Well, what then? Ridiculous though it seems, I don't know your first name.'

'It was on my identity card.'

'I didn't notice it at the time.'

'George William Slider. But I've always been called Bill, because my father's a George as well.' Saying his own name aloud made him feel ridiculously shy, as though he were sixteen and on his first date.

'Oh yes,' she said. 'Now I know, I can see it suits you. Do you like to be called Bill?'

'Well, hardly anyone does these days. There's still a lot of surname-calling in the force. The quasi-military setup, you see. I suppose it makes it seem a bit like public school. I always called Atherton by his surname, for instance. I simply can't think of him as Jim, though the younger ones do.'

'Did you go to public school?'

He laughed at the thought. 'Good Lord, no! Timberlog Lane Secondary Modern, that was me.'

'What a pretty name,' she teased. 'Where's Timberlog Lane?'

'In Essex, Upper Hawksey. It was a brand new school in those days, one of those Prides of the Fifties, knocked up to cope with the post-war bulge.'

'Where's Upper Hawksey?'

'Near Colchester. It used to be just a little village, and then they built a housing estate onto it – hence the school – and now it's practically an urban overspill. You know the sort of thing.'

'Yes, I know – there's the village green and the old black-smith's forge, carefully preserved, and backed up against it streets and streets of modern open-plan houses with a Volvo parked in front of each.'

'Sort of. And further back there's an older council estate – that was there when I was a child.'

'The rot had set in even then?'

'Mmm. It's funny – we lived in the old village, so we thought ourselves a cut above the estate people, the newcomers. But they thought themselves above us, because we had no bathrooms and only outside privies. But my father had nearly an acre of garden, and grew all our own vegetables. And he kept rabbits. And a donkey.'

'A donkey?'

'For the manure.'

'Ah. Messy, but practical. So you're a real country boy, then?'

'Original hayseed. Dad used to take me out into the woods and fields and sit me down somewhere and say, "Now, lad, keep your mouth shut and your eyes open, and you'll learn what there is to be learnt". I've always thought that was a very good training for a detective.'

'So you always meant to be a detective?'

'I suppose so. Once I'd got past the engine-driver stage. Reading all those Sherlock Holmes and Sexton Blake stories must have turned my brain.'

She smiled. 'I bet they're proud of you. Do they still live in Upper Whatsit, your parents?'

'Hawksey. Dad does – in the same cottage, still with the outside lavvy. Mum's – Mum died.' He still hated to say she was dead. The verb seemed somehow less destructive. 'What about your parents?'

'They're both alive. They live in Eastbourne.'

'Is that where you come from?'

'No, they retired there. I was brought up in London – Willesden, in fact. You see I've never strayed very far.'

'And are they proud of you?'

'I suppose so,' she shrugged, and then caught his eye and smiled. 'Oh, I don't mean they don't care about me or anything like that, but there were an awful lot of us – I was seventh of ten. I don't think you can care so intensely about each when you've got so many. And I left home so long ago I don't think of myself in relation to them any more. I expect they're glad I earn an honest crust and haven't ended up in Holloway or Shepherds' Market, but beyond that—' She let the sentence go. 'Are you an only child?'

'Yes.'

'Well, there you are then. Do you still visit your father?'

'Sometimes. Not so much now. There never seems to be time, and he never got on with—' He checked himself, and she glanced at him.

'With your wife? Well, I suppose you'll have to mention her sometime. What's her name?'

'Irene,' he said reluctantly. He didn't want to talk about her to Joanna. On the other hand, when he said no more the silence seemed to grow ominous and unnatural, and at last he said in a sort of desperation, 'Mum liked her very much. She was always glad we got married. But Dad couldn't get on with her, and after Mum died it got to be a bit of a strain going down there with Irene, and it looked rather pointed to go without her.'

'I suppose it is rather a long way,' Joanna said neutrally.

Another silence fell. Slider drove on, and the whole ugly, familiar, unnecessary edifice of in-law trouble crowded into his mind; cluttering the view, like those wartime prefabs that somehow never got taken down. Mum had been so proud when he'd married Irene. She saw it as a step-up – for her only son to marry a girl from the Estate, a girl who came from a house with a bathroom. Irene was 'superior'. She came from a 'superior' family, people who had a car and a television and went abroad for their holidays. Irene's mother didn't go to work, and had a washing-machine. Irene's father worked in an office, not with his hands.

Mum's perceptions and her ambitions were equally uncomplicated. Her Bill had got a good education and a good job, and now he was marrying a superior girl, and might one day own his own house. He thought with a familiar spasm of hatred of Catatonia, and how Mum would have loved it. Well, they said men always married women like their mothers.

Dad, on the other hand, had somehow managed to avoid the standardisation of state education. He could read and write and his general knowledge was extensive, but his approach to life had not been moulded. He lived close to the earth, and on his own terms, clear-sighted and sharp-witted as wild animals were. Stubborn, too, like his donkey. He had said Irene wouldn't do, and he had stuck by that. To be fair, he had never really given her a chance, or made allowances for her youth and inexperience. What had been nervousness on her side, Dad saw as 'being stuck up'. Slider, seeing both sides, as was his wont, had been unable to reconcile them.

But they had gone on putting up with each other as people will, rather than risk open breach. Slider remembered with muted horror those Sunday visits. Oh the High Tea, complete with tinned salmon and salad and a fruit cake and trifle with hundreds-and-thousands on the top! The polite, monotonous conversation; the photograph album and the walk round the garden and the glass of sweet sherry 'for the road'. It was a pattern which might have endured to this day, had Mum not died and ended the necessity for dissembling.

'What did he do, your father?' Joanna asked suddenly. 'Are you from a long line of policemen?'

'God, no, I'm the first. Dad was a farm-worker.' Even after all these years he still said it with a touch of defiant pride, legacy of the days when Irene, ashamed, would tell people her father-in-law was a farmer, or sometimes an estate-manager. 'The cottage we lived in was a tied cottage, but by the time Dad retired things had changed, and the new generation of estate workers wouldn't have wanted to live there, so they let him stay on. He'll die there, and then I suppose they'll gut it and modernise it and put in central heating, and let it to some account executive as a weekend cottage.'

He knew he sounded bitter, and tried to lighten his tone. 'You wouldn't recognise the farm Dad worked on now. When I was a kid, it used to have a bit of everything – a few dairy cows, some pigs, a bit of arable, chickens and ducks and geese wandering about everywhere. Now it's all down to fruit. Acres and acres of little stunted fruit trees, all in straight rows. They grubbed up all the hedges and filled in all the ditches and planted thousands of those dwarf trees, in regiments, right up to the road. It's like a desert.'

How could fruit trees be like a desert? his logic challenged him as he lapsed into silence. But they gave the impression of desolation, all the same. Joanna laid a hand on his knee for an instant and said as if to comfort him, 'Things are changing now. They're beginning to realise their mistake and replant the hedgerows—'

'But it's too late for the hedgerows I knew,' he said. He turned his head for an instant to look at her. Her eyes, which he had thought were plain brown, he now saw were richly tapestried in gold and tawny and russet, glowing in the sunlight. 'That's the terrible thing about my job,' he added. 'By its very nature, almost everything I do is done too late.'

'If it makes you so unhappy, why do you do it?' she asked, as people had asked before, as he had asked himself.

'Because it would be worse if I didn't,' he said.

Simon Thompson lived in a flat in the Newington Green Road, where people lived who couldn't yet quite afford Islington. It was above a butcher's shop and must, Atherton thought, be one of the last furnished flats in the world. He walked up the dark and dirty stairs to the first floor and stopped before the gimcrack, cardboard door with the sticky-paper label. The stairs went on upward, more sordidly than ever, and a smell of nappies and burnt fat slid down them towards him.

Thompson opened the door violently at the first knock as though he had been crouched behind it listening to the foot-falls. On the phone he had sounded nervous, protesting and consenting almost simultaneously. Presumably he was well aware that he was the person, after Joanna Marshall, who would be presumed to have been closest to Anne-Marie Austen.

'Sergeant Atherton,' he stated rather than asked. 'Come in. I don't know why you want to speak to me. I don't know anything about it.'

'Don't you, sir?' Atherton said peacefully, following Thompson into a flat so perilously untidy that it would have taken a properties-buyer a month at least to recreate it for a television serial.

'In here,' Thompson said, and they entered what was evidently the sitting-room. There was a massive and ancient sofa, around which the flat had probably been built in the first place, and a set of mutually intolerant chairs and tables. A hi-fi system occupied one wall, incongruously new and expensive, and at least answering the question as to what

98

Thompson spent his income on. It seemed to have everything, including a compact-disc player, and was ranked with a huge collection of records, tapes and discs, and a pair of speakers like black refrigerators.

Everything else in the room was swamped with a making tide of clothes, newspapers, sheet music, empty bottles, dirty crockery, books, correspondence, empty record sleeves, apple cores, crumpled towels, and overflowing ashtrays. The windows were swathed in net so dirty it was at first glance invisible. Curtains lay folded, and evidently laundered, on the window-sill waiting to be rehung, but even from where he stood Atherton could see the thick film of dust on them.

'I hardly knew her, you know,' Thompson said defensively as soon as they were inside. He turned to face Atherton. He was a small and slender young man of ripe and theatrical good looks. His hair was dark and glossy and a little too carefully styled, his skin expensively tanned, his eyes large and blue with long curly lashes. His features were delicately pretty, his mouth full and petulant, his teeth white as only capping or cosmetic toothpaste could make them. He wore a ring on each hand and a heavy gold bracelet on his right wrist. His left wrist was weighed down with the sort of watch usually called a chronometer, which was designed to do everything except make toast, and would operate under water to a depth of three nautical miles.

He was the sort of man who would infallibly appeal to a certain kind of woman, who would equally infallibly be exploited by him. 'Spoilt', Atherton's mother would have put it more simply. A mummy's boy: all his life women had made a pet of him, and would continue to do so. Probably had elder sisters who'd liked dressing him up when he was a toddler and taking him out to show off to friends. He was also, Atherton noted, extremely nervous. His hands, held before him defensively, were never still, and there was a film of moisture on his deeply indented upper lip. His eyes flickered to Atherton's and away again, like those of a man who knows that the corpse under the sofa is imperfectly concealed, and fears that a foot may be sticking out at one end.

'May I sit down?' Atherton said, digging himself out a space at the end of the sofa and sitting in it quickly before the tide of junk could flow back in. 'It's purely a matter of routine, sir, nothing to worry about. We have to talk to everyone who might be able to help us.'

'But I hardly knew her,' Thompson said again, perching himself on the arm of the chair opposite, with the air of being ready to run.

Atherton smiled. 'No one seems to have known her well, from what we're told, but you must have known her better than the rest. After all, you did have an affair with her, didn't you?'

He licked his lips. 'Someone told you that, did they?' He leaned forward confidentially. 'Look here, I've got nothing to hide. I went to bed with her a couple of times, that's all. It happens all the time on tour. It doesn't mean anything. Anyone will tell you that.'

'Will they, sir?' Atherton was writing notes, and Thompson took the bait like a lamb. Lamb-bait?

'Yes, of course. It wasn't serious. She and I had a bit of fun, just while we were on tour. So did lots of people. It ends when we get back on the plane to come home. That's the way it's played. But then when we got home she started to pretend it had been serious, and saying I'd promised to marry her.'

'And had you?'

'Of course not,' he cried in frustration. 'I never said anything like that. And she kept hanging around me and it was really embarrassing. Then when I told her to get lost, she said she'd make me sorry, and tried to make trouble with my girlfriend—'

'Oh, you have a girlfriend, then, have you sir?'

Thompson looked sulky. 'She knew about that from the beginning, Anne-Marie I mean. So she knew it wasn't serious. Helen and I have been together for six years now. We've been living together for two years. Anne-Marie knew that. She threatened to tell Helen about – well, about the tour.' His indignation had driven out his nervousness now. 'It would've really killed Helen, and she knew it, the bitch. And when she first joined, I thought she was such a nice girl. But underneath all that baby-face business, she was a nasty piece of work.'

Atherton listened sympathetically, while his mind whirled at Thompson's double standards. 'And did she in fact tell your girlfriend?'

'Well, no, fortunately she never did. She phoned a couple of times, and then put the phone down when Helen answered. And she kept hanging around me in the bar during concerts and saying things in front of Helen, suggestive things, you know. Well, Helen's very understanding, but there are some things a girl can't stand. But she gave it up in the end, thank God.'

Atherton turned a page. 'Can I have some dates from you, sir? You first met Anne-Marie when?'

'In July, when she joined.'

'You hadn't known her before? I believe she was at the Royal College?'

'I went to the Guildhall. No, I hadn't come across her before. I think she worked out of London.'

'And then you went on tour together – when?'

'In August, to Athens, and then to Italy in October.'

'Did you – sleep together on both tours?'

'Well, yes. I mean – yes, we did.' He looked embarrassed for once, perhaps realising that the return engagement might be construed as having aroused expectations.

'And it was when you came back from Italy that she started "making trouble" for you?'

Thompson frowned. 'Well, no, not immediately. At first it was all right, but after a week or so she suddenly started this business about marrying me.'

'What made her change, do you think?'

He began to sweat again. 'I don't know. She just – *changed.*'

'Is there anything you said or did that might have made her think you wanted to go on seeing her?'

'No! No, nothing I swear it! I'm happy with Helen. I didn't want anyone else. It was just meant to be while we were on tour, and I never said anything about marrying her.' He lifted anxious eyes to Atherton's face, passive victim looking at his torturer.

'After that session at the Television Centre on the fifteenth of January – what did you do?'

'I came home.'

'You didn't go for a drink with any of your friends?'

'No, I – I was going to go with Phil Redcliffe, but he was going with Joanna and Anne-Marie, and I wanted to avoid her. So I just went home.'

'Straight home?'

There was a faint hesitation. 'Well, I just went for a drink first at a local pub, round here.'

'Which one?'

'Steptoes. It's my regular.'

'They know you there, do they? They'd remember you coming in that night?'

He looked hunted. 'I don't know. It was pretty crowded. I don't know if they'd remember.'

'Did you speak to anyone?'

'No.'

'You're sure of that, are you? You went to a pub for a drink and didn't speak to anyone?'

'I – no, I didn't. I just had a drink and came home.'

'What time did you get home?'

Again the slight hesitation. 'I don't know exactly. About half past ten or eleven o'clock, I think.'

'Your girlfriend will be able to confirm that, I suppose.'

Thompson looked wretched. 'She wasn't here. She was at work. She's on nights.'

'She's a shift-worker?'

'She's a theatre nurse at St Thomas's.'

Atherton's heart sang, but he betrayed no emotion. He wrote it down and said without pausing, 'So no one saw you at the pub, and no one saw you come home?'

Thompson burst out, 'I didn't kill her! I wouldn't. I'm not that type. I wouldn't have the courage, for God's sake! Ask anyone. I had nothing to do with it. You must believe me.'

Atherton only smiled. 'It isn't my business to believe or not believe, sir.' He had found that calling young men 'sir' a lot unsettled them. 'I just have to ask these questions, as a matter of routine. What sort of car do you drive, sir?'

He looked startled. 'Car? It's a maroon Alfa Spyder. Why d'you want to know about my car?'

'Just routine. Downstairs, is it?'

'No, Helen's borrowed it – hers is being serviced.'

'And your young lady's full name, sir.'

'Helen Morris. Look, she won't have to know about – you won't tell her about – on tour and all that, will you?'

Atherton looked stern. 'Not if I don't have to, sir. But this is a murder enquiry.'

Thompson subsided unhappily, and did not think to ask

103

what that meant. A few moments later Atherton was in his own Sierra and driving away, mentally rubbing his hands. He's lying, he thought, and he's scared shitless – now we only have to find out what about. And best of all, the girlfriend is a theatre nurse. A much more promising lead, he thought, even than the Brown one.

The Lodge, Stourton-on-Fosse, had evidently never been anyone's lodge, and from the look of it Slider deduced that if Anne-Marie had been poor, it was not hereditary. It was an elegant, expensive, neo-classical villa, built in the Thirties of handsome red brick, with white pillars and porticoes and green shutters. Its grounds were extensive and immaculate, with a gravelled drive leading from the white five-barred gate which looked as though it had been raked with a fine-toothed comb and weeded with tweezers.

'Crikey,' said Joanna weakly as they drove slowly past the gate to have a look.

'Is that all you can say about it?'

'It's the smell of money making me feel faint. I never knew she came from this sort of background.'

'You said it was a large house in the village.'

'Yes, but I was thinking of a four-bed, double-fronted Edwardian villa, the sort of thing that goes for a hundred and fifty thousand in North Acton. You need practice to imagine anything as rich as this.'

'Did she never give any hint that there was money in the family?'

'Nary a one. She lived in a crummy sort of bedsit – oh, you've seen it, of course – and as far as I know, she lived off what she earned in the Orchestra. She never mentioned private income or rich relatives. Perhaps she was proud.'

'You said she didn't get on with her aunt.'

'I said I got that impression. She didn't say so in so many words.' Slider stopped the car and turned it in a farm gateway. 'Are you going to drive in?'

'On that gravel? I wouldn't dare. No, I'll park out in the lane.'

'Then I can wait for you in the car.'

'I thought of that too.'

'I bet you did.' She leaned over and kissed him, short and full, on the mouth. He felt dizzy.

'Don't,' he said unconvincingly. She kissed him again, more slowly, and when she stopped he said, 'Now I'm going to have to walk up the drive with my coat held closed.'

'I thought it would give you the courage to face people above your station,' she said gravely.

He pushed her hand away and wriggled out, leaning back in for one last kiss. 'Be good,' he said. 'Bark if anyone comes.'

An elderly maid or housekeeper opened the door to him and showed him into a drawing-room handsomely furnished with antiques, a thick, washed-Chinese carpet on the polished parquet, and heavy velvet curtains at the French windows. Just what he would have expected it to look like, judging from the outside. Left alone, he walked round the room a little, looking at the pictures. He didn't know much about paintings, but judging by the frames these were expensive and old, and some of them were of horses. Everything was spotless and well polished, and the air smelled of lavender wax.

He made a second circuit, examining the ornaments this time, and noting that there were no photographs, not even on the top of the piano, which he thought unusual for a house of this sort, and particularly for an aunt of her generation. It was a remarkably impersonal room, revealing nothing but that there had been, at some point in the family's history, a lot of money.

He perched on the edge of a slippery, brocade sofa, and

then the door opened and two Cairn terriers shot in yapping hysterically, closely followed by a white toy poodle, its coat stained disagreeably brown around eyes and anus. Slider drew back his feet as the terriers darted alternately at them, while the poodle stood and glared, its muzzle drawn back to show its yellow teeth in a continuous rattling snarl.

Mrs Ringwood followed them in. 'Boys, boys,' she admonished them, without conviction. 'They'll be quite all right if you just ignore them.'

Slider, doubting it, regarded Anne-Marie's aunt with astonishment. He had been expecting a stout and ample aunt, a tightly-coiffeured termagant; but Mrs Ringwood, though in her late fifties, was small and very slim, with bright golden hair cut in an Audrey Hepburn urchin. Her jewellery was expensively chunky, her clothes so fashionable that Slider had seen nothing remotely like them in the high street. She sat opposite him angularly, her thin legs crossed high up, her heavy bracelets rattling down her arms like shackles. The whole impression was so girlish that unless one saw her face, one would have thought her in her twenties.

Slider began by offering his condolences, though Mrs Ringwood showed no sign of needing or welcoming them.

'It must have been a terrible shock to you,' he persisted, 'and I'm sorry to have to intrude on you at such a moment.'

'You must do your job, of course,' she conceded reluctantly. 'Though I may as well tell you at once that Anne-Marie and I were not close. We had no great affection for one another.'

Didn't anyone like the poor creature? Slider thought, while saying aloud, 'It's very frank of you to tell me so, ma'am.'

'I would not like anything to hamper your investigation. I think it better to be open with you from the beginning. You believe she was murdered, I understand?'

'Yes, ma'am.'

'It seems very unlikely. How could a girl like that have enemies? However, you know best I suppose.'

'You brought Miss Austen up from childhood, I believe?'

'I was made responsible for her when my sister died,' Mrs Ringwood said, making it clear that there was a world of difference. 'I was the child's only close relative, so it was expected that I should become responsible for her, and I accepted that. But I did not think myself qualified – or obliged – to become a second mother to her. I sent her to a good boarding school, and in the holidays she lived here under the charge of a governess. I did my duty by her.'

'It must have been something of a financial burden to you,' Slider tried. 'School fees and so on.'

She looked at him shrewdly. 'Anne-Marie's school fees and living expenses were paid for out of the trust. Her grandfather – my father – was a very wealthy man. It was he who built this house. Rachel – Anne-Marie's mother – and I were brought up here, and of course we expected to share his estate when he died. But Rachel married without his approval, and he disowned her and left everything to me, except for the amount left in trust for Anne-Marie's upbringing. So you see I suffered no personal expense in the matter.'

'Anne-Marie was the only child of the marriage?'

Mrs Ringwood assented.

'And when she finished school, what happened then?'

'She went to the Royal College of Music in London to study the violin. It was the only thing she had ever shown any interest in, and for that reason I encouraged her. I insisted that she could not remain here doing nothing, which I'm afraid was what she wanted to do. She was always a lazy child, giving to mooning about and daydreaming. I told her she must earn her own living and not look to me to keep her. So she did three years at the College, and then went to the

Birmingham Municipal Orchestra, and took a flat in Birmingham. The rest I'm sure you know.'

'How much did you know about her life in London?'

'Nothing at all. I rarely go to London, and when I do I shop and take lunch with an old friend. I never visited her there.'

'But she came to see you here?'

'From time to time.'

'How often did she come?'

'Three or four times a year, perhaps.'

'And when was the last time?'

'Last year – October, I think, or November. Yes, early November. She had just been on a tour with her Orchestra.'

'Did she mention any particular reason for visiting you at that time?'

'No. But she never discussed her personal life. She came from time to time, on a formal basis, that's all.'

'Did you pay her an allowance?'

She looked slightly disconcerted at the question. 'While she was at the College, I was obliged to. Once she had her own establishment and was capable of earning her own living, I considered my obligations as having ceased.'

'Did you ever give or lend her money?'

She looked pinker. 'Certainly not. It would have been very bad for her to think that she could come to me for money whenever she wanted to.'

'She had no other income? Nothing except her salary from the Orchestra?'

'Not that I was aware of.'

'Did you know that she owned a very rare and valuable violin, a Stradivarius?'

Mrs Ringwood displayed neither surprise nor interest. 'I knew nothing about her private life, her London life. I am not interested in music, and I know nothing about violins.'

Slider did not press this, though surely everyone must know what a Stradivarius was, and anyone would be surprised if a penniless relative turned out to own one. He felt Mrs Ringwood was departing somewhat from her self-imposed duty of complete openness.

'On that last visit, in November, did she talk about any of her friends?'

'I really cannot remember at this distance what she talked about.'

'But you said she had just been on tour – presumably then she must have mentioned it to you?'

'She must have spoken about it, I suppose. The places she'd been to, and the concerts she'd done. But as to friends—' Mrs Ringwood looked irritable. 'As far as I knew she never had any. When I was her age I was always up and doing – parties, tennis, dances – scores of friends – and admirers. But Anne-Marie never seemed to have any interest in anything, except drooping about the house and reading. She seemed to have no *go* in her at all!'

Slider was beginning to form a much clearer picture of Anne-Marie's childhood, and the clash of personalities that was inevitable between this former Bright Young Thing and an introverted orphan who cared only for music. Mrs Ringwood's perceptions about her niece would not be likely to be helpful to him. Instead he tried a shot in the dark. 'Can you tell me who her solicitor was?'

Was there a very slight hesitation before she answered?

'The family solicitor, Mr Battershaw, attended to her business.'

'Mr Battershaw of—?'

'Riggs and Felper, in Woodstock,' she completed, faintly unwillingly. Slider appeared not to notice, and wrote the name down in his careful secondary-modern-taught hand. He looked up to ask the next question and his attention was drawn to the French windows behind Mrs Ringwood, just a fraction of a second before the dogs also noticed the man standing there, and rushed at him, barking shrilly.

'Boys, boys!' Mrs Ringwood turned with the automatic admonition, but the newcomer was in no danger. The yappings were welcoming, and the attenuated tails were wagging. 'Ah, Bernard,' Mrs Ringwood said.

He stepped forward into the room, a tall, thin man a year or two older than her, dressed in a suit of expensive and extremely disagreeable tweed, and a yellow waistcoat. His face was long, mobile and yellowish, much freckled. He had a ginger moustache, grey eyebrows sparked with red, and thin, despairing, gingery hair, combined into careful strands across the top of his freckled, balding skull.

As he stooped in, he put up a hand in what was obviously an automatic gesture to smooth the strands down, and Slider noticed that the hand, too, was yellow with freckles, and that the nails were rather too long. The man smiled ingratiatingly behind his moustache, but his eyes were everywhere, quick and penetrating under the undisciplined eyebrows.

Slider, freed of the dogs' vigilance, stood politely, and Mrs Ringwood performed the introduction. 'Inspector Slider – Captain Hildyard, our local vet, and a great personal friend of mine. He looks after my boys, of course, and he often pops in on his way past. I hope he didn't startle you.'

Slider shook the strong, bony yellow hand, and the vet bent over him charmingly and said, 'How do you do, Inspector? What brings you here? Nothing serious, I hope. Has Esther been parking on double yellow lines?'

Slider merely gave a tight smile and left it to Mrs Ringwood to elucidate if she wanted.

'I suppose you've come to look at Elgar's foot?' she said.

'It was kind of you to drop by, but I'm sure it's nothing serious. Tomorrow would have done just as well.'

'No trouble at all, my dear Esther,' Hildyard said promptly. Slider watched them, unimpressed. Something about them struck a false note with him. Had she warned him off, provided him with the excuse? Was there some kind of collusion between them, and if so, why?

'I'll look at it while I'm here,' Hildyard went on. 'Don't want the little chap suffering. By the way, Inspector, is that your car out in the lane?'

'Yes,' said Slider. He met the vet's eyes and discovered that they were grey with yellow flecks, and curiously shiny, as if they were made of glass, like the eyes of a stuffed animal. 'Is it in your way?'

'Oh no, not at all. I was merely wondering. As a matter of fact, that was partly why I called in. We keep an eye on each other in a neighbourly way in this village, and a strange car parked near a house like this is always cause for concern.'

He paused. With five pairs of eyes on him, watchful and waiting, Slider felt pressed to take his leave. He moved, and the dogs rushed upon him, yapping.

'I'd better be on my way,' he said. 'Thank you for your help, Mrs Ringwood. Nice to have met you, Captain Hildyard.'

Hildyard bowed slightly, and Mrs Ringwood smiled graciously, but they were waiting side by side for him to leave with a palpable air of having things to say as soon as he was out of earshot. There was more between them than vet and client. Old friend? Or something closer?

'Who was that utterly bogus character in the hairy tweeds?' Joanna asked as he got in and started the engine. 'He looked like a refugee from a Noël Coward play.'

'He purported to be one Captain Hildyard, the local vet.'

111

Slider drove off, feeling relief at the putting of some distance between him and the house.

'He gave me a fairly savage once-over as he passed. Why only purported to be?'

'Oh, I suppose he's a vet all right,' Slider said tautly.

'He seems to have ruffled you.'

'He had long fingernails. I absolutely abominate long fingernails on men. And I don't like people who use military rank when they're not in the army.'

'I said he looked bogus. What was he doing there, anyway?'

'It did seem rather opportune, the way he suddenly appeared. But on the other hand, the dogs of the house evidently knew him all right, and he said he'd called because he was worried by a strange car being parked near the house, which is not only reasonable, but even laudable.'

'You do like to be fair, don't you?' she said. 'I bet you're Libra.'

'Close,' he admitted. 'I'm told I'm on the cusp. But listen, he had long fingernails, which is not only disgusting, but I would have thought a distinct handicap for a vet.'

'Perhaps he's such an eminent vet he only does diagnoses from X-rays, and never has to shove his hands up things like Mr Herriot.'

'Maybe. Still, I found out a couple of things, despite the aunt's unwillingness.'

'Why was she unwilling?'

'That's what I hope to find out. She told me, you see, that Anne-Marie had nothing but her income from the Orchestra. But when I asked casually who her solicitor was, she gave me the name.'

'Anne-Marie's solicitor, you mean?'

'Of course.'

'I'm not with you. What's significant about that?'

'Well, look, ordinary people don't have a solicitor. Do you have one?'

'I've consulted one on a couple of occasions. I couldn't exactly say I "have" one.'

'Precisely. If you talk about "having" a solicitor, it suggests a continuing need for one. And the only continuing need I can think of is the management of property, real or otherwise.'

'Aha,' Joanna said.

'Exactly,' Slider agreed. 'So what we do now is have some lunch, and then go in search of the Man of Business. Shall we find a pub, or would you prefer a restaurant?'

'Silly question – pub of course. You forget I'm a musician.'

8

Where There's a Will There's a Relative

'Has it occurred to you,' said Joanna as they strolled into The Blacksmiths Arms a few villages further on, 'that the pub is the only modern example of the old rule of supply and demand?'

'No,' said Slider obligingly. They had chosen the pub because it had a Pub Grub sign and sold Wethereds, and when they got inside they found it smelled agreeably of chips and furniture polish.

'It's true,' she said. 'In every other field of commerce the rule has broken down. The customer bloody well has to take what the supplier feels like supplying. Complaining gets you nowhere. You can look dignified and say "I shall take my custom elsewhere" and the least offensive thing they'll say is "Suit yourself".'

'I suppose so. Well?'

'Remember what pubs used to be like in the sixties and seventies? Keg beer, lino on the floor, no ice except Sunday lunchtimes, never any food. Now look! They've actually changed in response to public demand, which is a total denial of the Keynes theory.'

'What, Maynard?' he hazarded.

'No, Milton.'

They reached the bar. 'What will you have?'

'A pint please.'

'Two pints, then,' Slider nodded. It was lovely to be in a pub with someone other than Irene, who never entered into the spirit of the thing. The most she would ever have was a vodka and tonic, which Slider always felt was a pointless drink. More often she would ask, with a pinching of her lips, for an orange juice, than which there was nothing more frustrating for a beer-drinker. It makes it quite clear that the asker really doesn't want a drink at all and would sooner be anywhere but here, thus at a stroke putting the askee firmly in the wrong and destroying any possibility of enjoyment for either.

They ordered ham, egg and chips as well, and went to sit down in the window seat, where the pale sunshine was puddling on a round, polished table. Joanna drank off a quarter of her pint with fluid ease and sighed happily.

'Oh, this is nice,' she said, smiling at him, and then an expression of remorse crossed her face so obviously that Slider wanted to laugh.

'You were thinking that if Anne-Marie hadn't died we wouldn't be sitting here at all.'

'How did you know?'

'Your face. It's like watching a cartoon character – everything larger than life.'

'Gee, thanks!'

'No, it's nice. Most people are so world-weary.'

'Even when they've nothing to be weary about. Poor things, I think it's a habit they get into. It must be terrible never being able to admit to enjoying anything.'

'So why are you different?' he asked, really wanting to know.

She gave the question her serious consideration. 'I think because I never have time to watch television.' He laughed protestingly, but she said, 'No, I mean it. Television's so depressing – the universal assumption of vice. I don't think it can be good for people to be told so continuously that mankind is low, evil, petty, vicious and disgusting.'

'Even if it is?'

She contemplated his face. 'But you don't think so. That's much more remarkable, considering the job you do. How do you manage to keep your illusions? Especially as—' She broke off, looking confused.

'Especially as what?'

'Oh dear, I was going to say something impertinent. I was going to say, especially as you aren't happily married, either. Sorry.'

Considering they had just spent the night making torrid love together, considering he was being unfaithful to his wife with her, 'impertinent' was a deliciously inappropriate word, besides being pretty well obsolete in this modern age, and he laughed.

He had never in his life before felt so at ease in someone's company. More even than making love with her, he wanted to spend the rest of his life talking to her, to put an end to the years – his whole life, really – of having conversations inside his head and never aloud, because there had never been anyone who would not be bored, or contemptuous, or simply not understand, not see the point, or pretend not to in order to manipulate the situation. He knew that he could talk to her about absolutely anything, and she would listen and respond, and a vast hunger filled him for conversation – not necessarily important or intellectual, but simply absorbing, unimportant, supremely comfortable chat.

'Talking of your job,' she said, following Humpty Dumpty's

principle of going back to the last remark but one, 'shouldn't you be asking me questions to justify bringing me along with you? I shouldn't like you to get into trouble. Come to think of it, you've been pretty indiscreet, haven't you, Inspector? I mean, suppose I did it?'

'Did you?'

'No, of course not.'

'Well, there you are, then,' Slider said comfortably.

'I'm worried about you,' she said. 'You seem to have no instinct for self-preservation.'

Where she was concerned, he thought, that was painfully true. The number of things he ought to be worried about was multiplying by the minute, but he was completely comfortable, and her left leg was pressed against his right from hip to knee. He roused himself with an effort. 'Tell me about your friend Simon Thompson, then.'

'No friend of mine, the slimy little snake,' she said promptly. 'However, I don't suppose he could have been the murderer. He's like a kipper – two-faced, and no guts.'

'Never mind supposing. You've been reading too many books.'

'True,' she admitted, and then tacked off again. 'On the other hand, and come to think of it, he might just have been capable of it. These self-regarding people can be surprisingly ruthless, and he had convinced himself that she was the Phantom Wife-Phoner.'

'Come again?'

'Oh – well – you know I told you that people often do things on tour that they wouldn't do at home? Of course everybody knows about it, but everybody keeps quiet about it. Except that once or twice people's wives have received anonymous phone calls spilling the beans, and of course that makes terrible trouble all round. Well, after Anne-Marie and

117

Simon had split up, he put it about that she was the Phantom, and that made things very nasty for her, because of course there will always be people who says things like "there's no smoke without fire".'

'Do you think she was the Phantom?'

'No, of course not. What possible reason could she have for wanting to do that?'

'What reason could anyone have?'

She thought, and sighed. 'Well, I don't think it was her. Poor Anne-Marie, she never made it to the top of the popularity stakes.'

Slider drank a little beer, thoughtfully. 'When she and Simon were having their affair – did they get on well? Were they friendly?'

'Oh yes. They were all over each other. Martin Cutts said it made him feel horny just to look at them.' She frowned as a thought crossed her mind. 'They did have a quarrel on the last day in Florence, come to think of it. But they must have made it up, because they sat together on the plane coming home.'

'What was the quarrel about?'

'I don't know.' She grinned. 'I had my own fish to fry, so I wasn't particularly interested.'

He felt a brief surge of jealousy. Other fish? 'Tell me about Martin Cutts,' he said evenly.

She leaned her elbows on the table and cupped her face. 'Oh, Martin's all right as long as you don't take him seriously, and hardly anyone does. He simply never grew up. He got fossilised at the randy adolescent stage, and feels he has to have a crack at every new female that crosses his path, but he doesn't mean anything by it. He's quite childlike, really – rather endearing.'

Slider thought he knew the type, and anything less endearing was hard to imagine. Dangerous, selfish, self-regarding – and what had been his relationship with Joanna? But he didn't want to wonder about that. Fortunately the food arrived at that moment and prevented his asking any really stupid questions. The food was good: the ham was thick and cut off the bone, moist and fragrant and as unlike as possible the slippery pink plastic of the sandwich bar; the chips were golden, crisp on the outside and fluffy on the inside; and the eggs were as spotlessly beautiful as daisies. They ate, and the simple pleasure of good food and good company was almost painful. O'Flaherty's voice came to him from somewhere in memory, saying 'A lonely man is dangerous, Billy-boy'.

'Thank heaven for pub grub,' Joanna sighed, echoing his pleasure.

'I suppose you must eat out a lot,' Slider said.

'It's the curry syndrome,' she said cheerfully. 'One of the hazards of the job. When you're on an out-of-town date, you have to get a meal between the rehearsal and the concert, which is usually between five-thirty and seven, and nothing is open that early except Indian restaurants. And when you're playing in town, you want to eat after the show, and you have a couple of pints first to wind down, and by that time the only thing *left* open is the curry-house.'

'It all sounds horribly familiar,' Slider said. 'You could be describing my life.' Then he told her about his late meals with Atherton and The Anglabangla and his lone indigestion, and that brought him back to Irene and he stopped abruptly and ate the last of his chips in silence. Joanna eyed him sympathetically as though she knew exactly what he was thinking, and he thought that she probably did. But married life is different he told himself fiercely. If he and Joanna were married, they wouldn't go on having cheerful, chatty, comfortable lunches together like this. Of course they wouldn't. It would all change. A lonely man is a dangerous man, Billy-boy. He gets to believing what it suits him to believe.

Atherton decided, as he was in the area, to check out Thompson's story as far as the pub, Steptoes, was concerned. He found it moderately busy, filled with suited young men in run-down shoes and smart women with tired faces under hard make-up – the office crowd, and how, he wondered, could they get away with it? He ordered a pint of Marston's and a toasted cheese sandwich and got chatting to the governor, a short and muscle-bound ex-boxer, who in turn introduced him to the Australian barmaid who had been on duty on Monday night.

To Atherton's surprise they both said they knew Simon Thompson and his girlfriend, the nurse. They came in a lot, usually with a crowd of other musicians and nurses. The two professions seemed to go together for some reason. But neither barmaid nor governor remembered seeing Simon on the Monday night.

'But we were busy,' the barmaid pointed out in fairness. 'The fact that I didn't see him doesn't mean to say that he wasn't here.'

Which was true, Atherton thought, and just about what you could expect with this job.

Slider left Joanna to wander about Woodstock while he went in to see the solicitor.

Mr Battershaw was at first reluctant to believe that Anne-Marie was dead at all. 'I shall have to see a death certificate,' he said more than once; and, 'Why wasn't I informed before this?'

Patiently Slider explained about the difficulty of identifying the body and tracing the next of kin. 'I've just been to see

Mrs Ringwood, and she gave me your name and address. I understand that you were Miss Austen's solicitor?'

Once properly convinced that Anne-Marie was no more, Battershaw became co-operative. He was a big, gaunt man in his late fifties, with surprised, pale eyes and a long jaw, which made him look like a bloodless horse. He offered Slider tea, which Slider refused, and under steady questioning settled down to tell the family story.

'Anne-Marie's grandfather, Mr Bindman, was the client of my predecessor here, the younger Mr Riggs. He's retired now, but he told me all about Mr Bindman. He was a self-made man, who started off as the son of a penniless refugee who came over during the First World War. Our Mr Bindman set himself up in business and made his fortune, built himself that lovely house, and was altogether a pillar of society.'

'What sort of business?'

'Boots and shoes. Nothing exciting, I'm afraid. Well now, he was married twice – his first wife died in 1929 or '30 – and he had a son, David, by his first marriage, and two daughters, Rachel and Esther, by his second wife. David was killed in 1942 – a great tragedy. He was only eighteen, poor boy – just joined up. He'd only served a few weeks. And the second Mrs Bindman was killed in the Blitz, so there were just the two little girls left.

'Mr Bindman doted on them both, but the younger girl, Rachel, was his pet. Esther married in 1957, and Gregory Ringwood was a very solid young man, steady and reliable, just the sort a careful father would approve of. But later the same year Rachel fell in love with a violin player called Austen, and that was a different matter altogether.'

'How old was she?'

'Oh, let me see – she'd be eighteen or nineteen. Very young. Well, Mr Bindman was very definite in his ideas. He loved

121

music, and it was he who encouraged Rachel to go to concerts, and even bought her gramophone records and her own radio-gram. But when it came to marrying a fiddle-player – that wasn't good enough for his pet. He told her there was no future in it, and that Austen would never be able to earn enough to keep her, and forbade her to marry him, or even see him again. Rachel, I'm afraid, was a very strong-willed young woman, very like her father, in fact, and they spent two years or so quarrelling fiercely about it. Then in the end, as soon as she was twenty-one and the old man could no longer prevent her, she married Austen, and broke her father's heart.' Battershaw sighed. 'Mr Bindman reacted in the only way he knew: he cut her out of his will, and vowed never to speak to her again.'

'Pretty drastic,' Slider said mildly.

'Oh, positively Victorian! Mind you, I'm sure he would have changed his mind in the end, given time, because he adored Rachel, and she'd have found a way to get round him. I think he probably just wanted to register his disapproval in the time-honoured way. But unfortunately time wasn't on his side. The following year, 1960, Anne-Marie was born, and Rachel attempted a reconciliation, and there were signs that the old fellow was softening; but then when Anne-Marie was a year old, Rachel and her husband were both killed in a car crash.'

'How dreadful.'

Battershaw nodded. 'That was the year I joined the firm, and in a short time I saw old Mr Bindman age ten years. He blamed himself, as people will after the event, and poured out all the love he should have given to Rachel onto the little girl. And he changed his will, leaving half the estate to his daughter Esther, and the other half in trust for Anne-Marie.'

The words fell into Slider's mind like pieces of a jigsaw

slotting into place. Mrs Ringwood's hesitations aside, there was so often money at the bottom of things. When there's a way, there's a will, he thought.

'What were the terms of the trust?' he asked.

Battershaw looked disapproving. 'I'm afraid they were very ill-advised, and I argued strenuously with Mr Bindman about them, but he was a stubborn old man, and wouldn't budge an inch. Money was to be released from the income to pay for Anne-Marie's upbringing and education, but the capital and any accrued interest were not to be handed over to her until she married.' He shook his head. 'He didn't trust women to handle money, you see – he thought they needed a man to guide them. Of course, I'm sure he didn't anticipate the way things fell out. He must have expected that Anne-Marie would marry straight from school, and that he would still be around to approve or even arrange the marriage.'

'And then, presumably, he would have changed the terms?'

'Indeed. Oh, I did my best to persuade him anyway. I begged him at least to put a date to the winding-up of the trust, so that she would inherit either when she married or when she reached the age of, say twenty-five, but he wouldn't have it. I dare say that given time I could have brought him round to it, but there again time was not on our side. Rachel's death had broken his health, and he died within a year of her, leaving Anne-Marie in a most invidious position, without a penny she could touch until and unless she married.'

Slider mused. 'Did Mrs Ringwood know the terms of the trust?'

'Indeed. She is the other trustee, you see, along with myself.'

'And Anne-Marie? Did she know?'

Battershaw looted a little disconcerted. 'Now, it's a strange thing, if you had asked me that question a year ago I would have had to say I didn't know. I had never discussed the matter with her, and I have strong doubts as to how much Mrs Ringwood would have thought wise to tell her. The terms of the trust, you see, are certainly an encouragement to improvident marriage, and—' He paused, embarrassed.

'She might have married just anyone, simply to get away from home?' Slider offered.

'Yes,' Battershaw said gratefully. He cleared his throat and continued. 'But then last autumn Anne-Marie made an appointment to see me.'

'Can you tell me the exact date?'

'Oh, certainly. I don't remember offhand – I think it was towards the end of October – but Mrs Kaplan, my secretary, will be able to tell you. It will be in my diary.'

'Thank you. So Anne-Marie came to see you – here? In this office?'

'Yes.'

'And how did she seem?'

'Seem? She was very well – quite sun-tanned, in fact. I remember I commented on the fact, and she said she had just come back from Italy. She had been on a tour with her Orchestra, I think, but she'd always been fond of Italy.'

'Was she happy?'

Battershaw seemed puzzled. 'Really, Inspector, I don't quite know. I had had very little personal contact with Anne-Marie, not enough to know how she was feeling. All I can say is I didn't notice that she seemed *un*happy.'

'Of course. Please go on.' Slider rescued him from these uncharted seas. 'What did she want to see you about?'

'She wanted to know the exact terms of her grandfather's bequest to her. I told her—'

'Just a moment, please – did she ask you what were the terms, or did she already know the terms, and ask you to confirm them?'

Battershaw looked intelligent. 'I understand you. As I remember, she said that she understood she had no money of her own until she married, and asked me if that were true. Of course, I told her that it was.'

'And what was her reaction?'

'She didn't say anything at once, although she looked rather thoughtful, and not entirely pleased, which was understandable. Then she asked if there were any way round it, any way of changing the provision of the will. I told her there was not. And then she said, "You are quite sure that the only way I can lay my hands on my money is to get married?" Or words to that effect. I said yes, and then she got up to go.'

'That was all?'

'That was all. I asked if there were anything else I could do for her, and she said no.' The anaemic horse smiled almost roguishly. 'I think she said "Not a thing", to be precise.' The smile disappeared like a rabbit down a hole. 'That was the last time I saw her. It's hard to believe the poor child is dead. Are you quite sure it was murder?'

'Quite sure.'

'Because I hate to think that she might have – laid hands on herself, for the want of money. That would not at all have been her grandfather's intention.'

'We're confident it wasn't suicide,' Slider said. His mind was elsewhere. 'Did Miss Austen have any relatives on her father's side?'

'None that I know of. Her father was an only child, I know, so there would not have been aunts and uncles, or cousins. There may have been second cousins, but I never heard of any.'

Slider tried a long shot. 'Did she have any relatives in Italy? Was Austen perhaps part-Italian?'

Battershaw looked merely bewildered. 'I never heard that

he was. But really, I had nothing to do with him at all. Mrs Ringwood would be the person to ask.'

'Of course. Thank you.' Slider got up to go. 'Your secretary will give me the date of that meeting?'

'Yes, indeed.' Battershaw accompanied him to the door, and Slider checked him before he could open it.

'By the way,' he said, 'the estate was a large one, was it?'

'Quite large. The capital was soundly invested.' He named a sum which made Slider's eyebrows rise.

'And who does it all go to, now that Miss Austen is dead?'

Battershaw looked unhappy now, a pale horse with colic. 'Mrs Ringwood is the residuary legatee,' he said.

'I see. Thank you,' said Slider.

Slider walked out into the smeary, intemperate sunshine and stood there for a moment, blinking. The tangle of the case, he felt, was beginning to resolve. He could see ends of string that he could begin to wind in. The favoured sister; the dead favoured sister's child – helpless, hapless infant; the dutiful daughter who had never been properly appreciated, forced to take care of the rival for her father's love; the money that should have been hers, and was now hers again. No wonder she hadn't wanted to talk about it, he thought. But motive doesn't make a case. All the same . . .

Suddenly he remembered Joanna. While he had been engrossed with Battershaw he had entirely forgotten her. It was one of the reasons he loved his job: it had the power to absorb him completely, so that it became his refuge, the one place where he could escape from wearying self-consciousness.

But coming back to the thought of Joanna was refreshment and renewal. She was sitting in the window of the tearoom they had appointed as meeting-place, and she didn't see him for a moment, so that he was able to look at her unobserved.

Her face was already familiar to him, but now he saw it in the unmerciful sunlight in all its planes and textures, its shapes and inconsistencies, its simple uniqueness. There was all the evidence of a lifetime of experience entirely separate from him. She had lived, and living had marked her. She had spent perhaps half her allotted span, without him – he more than half of his, without her. Of all the thousands of days and nights, they had spent only one together. But still, looking at her, he had the extraordinary feeling of belonging. This was how it was, then, he thought. His righteous place was on her side of the glass, ranged with her against the incoming tide of the rest of the world, and it didn't matter a damn that he knew nothing she knew: he knew *her*.

She saw him. The focus of her eyes changed and she smiled and he went in.

Sunshine or not, it was only January, and the gathering darkness as they drove back to London affected their mood, dampening their lightness with the realisation of their problems. Slider voiced it unwillingly as he drew up outside her house.

'I mustn't be too late back tonight.' She made a small turning-away movement of her head, and he recognised it as hurt, which hurt him. 'We could go out for a quick bite to eat, if you like,' he said tentatively.

She turned back to look at him clearly. 'No, that would waste time. Let's have a drink here, and a snack if you like. I'll light the fire.'

'I'll have to make some phone calls,' he said, and then added hastily, 'to Atherton, and the station. I haven't called in all day.'

'It's all right,' she said. 'You must do what you have to.'

But when they went in the phone began instantly to ring, and she sprinted for it and picked it up before the answering-

127

machine could intercept. Slider felt a chill of foreboding even before she made polite responses into the receiver and then turned to offer it to him.

'For you,' she said. It was too dark in the hall to see the expression of her face, but her voice said clearly enough that she knew the day was over for them.

It was O'Flaherty. 'Izzat you, Billy? Christ, we been trying to get yez all day. Atherton said y' might be there. Jaysus, are you at that owl caper, now?'

'What is it, Pat?' Slider forbore to rise to the bait.

'Ah, the world's a wheel o' fortune, so it is,' O'Flaherty remarked cryptically. 'Well, I'm sorry to spoil your shenanigans, but you'd better come in here straight away, me fine Billy, and thank God and Little Boy Blue that we never phoned your owl lady to ask where y' were.' Little Boy Blue was what O'Flaherty called Atherton. They had a robust but not unfriendly contempt for each other.

A complex blend of relief, disappointment and apprehension was having its effect on Slider's bowels, and he said impatiently, 'For Christ's sake, Pat, what's happened?'

'The owl woman, Mrs Gostyn. They been trying to raise her all day, and getting anxious as time went on and she never showed up. So Boy Blue goes in troo the winder and finds her dead on the floor.'

The receiver suddenly felt slippery and cold in his grasp. In the darkness of the unlit hall he sought Joanna's eyes, and her face seemed to swim unattached in the shadows. Then she reached out and switched on the light, and everything was ordinary again, and he only felt very tired.

'How did it happen?' he asked.

'Well, she might've slipped and banged her head on the fender,' O'Flaherty said with an emphasis on the word 'might' that told Slider all he needed to know.

'I'm on my way,' he said. Joanna turned away and went into the kitchen, which he recognised as her way of relieving him of responsibility for her. Their day was over; but under the surface of churning reactions there was still a peacefulness, because she was there, and they felt what they felt about each other, which meant that they couldn't *not* go on being together in some way or another, and so everything was all right really, wasn't it?

9

Other Fish?

Atherton had set his alarm to get him up with the birds, but what he was in fact up with was a disgusting crunching and slurping noise from under the bed, where Oedipus had retired to eat a mouse. Atherton got out of bed with a curse, and on his hands and knees cautiously lifted the corner of the counterpane. In the fluffy twilight the cat looked at him over its shoulder with yellow headlamp eyes and a tail hanging out of the corner of its mouth.

'Just be sure you eat it all,' Atherton said, remembering the time he had found four abandoned feet on his pillow, and headed for the bathroom. He had a hot shower, shaved under it, washed his hair, and then stood under the streaming, steaming water and thought about Slider.

It was really the most extraordinary thing to have happened. He hadn't met the Marshall woman, of course, but even if she combined all the feminine charms, it was hard to see how she could have got Slider off the rails of a lifetime in a matter of hours. To have slept with her – and really slept — the first evening of their acquaintance, and then to have taken her with him when he went out on police business, was so far out of character for his superior that Atherton, who believed in Love only as a theoretical possibility – as something that hadn't been definitely disproved – could only think that Slider was heading for some kind of a breakdown.

There was no fool like an unpractised fool, he thought, turning off the water and stepping into a very large, thick bath sheet – Atherton took washing very seriously – and to his knowledge Slider had never been unfaithful to Irene before, probably not even in thought. He was one of those rarities, a truly virtuous man, and Atherton, who was all for Slider's getting out from under Irene's thumb on principle, didn't know whether the poor sap could handle it. If he was going to go off the rails, he'd probably do it in a spectacular way, and to be heading for that kind of crisis in the middle of a murder investigation was catastrophic.

There were plenty of people in the department, he thought as he wielded the hairdryer, who would be happy to clamber a step higher up the ladder by treading on the head of anyone else, however much they liked them, who seemed not to have his entire mind on his job. And Slider, as Atherton was aware, had been passed over for promotion before because of department politics. All in all, it behoved Atherton to get his head down and produce something to show up at the next meeting, because so far they seemed to have got precisely nowhere.

He dressed, checked quickly under the bed – Oedipus had departed, leaving only a forlorn scrap of grey fur – and went off to St Thomas's to try to intercept Helen Morris as she came off duty.

Slider was woken by Kate spilling tea onto his chest as she climbed onto the bed balancing a mug.

'Time to get up, Daddy,' she said, her bubblegum-sweet

breath stertorous with the effort of retaining at least some of the tea within the mug. Slider elbowed himself sufficiently upright to field it before she scalded him again.

'Thank you, sweetheart,' he said dopily, and tried for the sake of her feelings to sip. It had been one hell of a session last night. He felt as though he had only just gone to sleep. He felt as though he had been beaten all over, and he had a smoke-headache and a dire feeling of oppression in his sinuses. He abandoned the attempt at creative parenthood, put the mug on the bedside table and flopped back onto the pillows with a groan.

'You mustn't go back to sleep, Daddy – you've got to get up,' Kate said severely. She eyed him curiously like a bird eyeing a wormhole. 'Were you drunk last night?'

'Of course not,' Slider mumbled. 'Why d'you say that?'

'Mummy thought you were.'

He opened one eye. 'She didn't say that,' he said with some assurance. Kate shrugged her birdlike shoulders.

'She didn't say so, but I bet that's what she thought anyway. She's cross about something, and she said you were very late coming home, and when Chantal's dad comes home late *he's* usually drunk.'

'You think too much,' Slider said. 'Anyway, I was working, not drinking. You know, don't you, that I have to work funny hours sometimes?' She shrugged, unconvinced, and opened her mouth to deliver more opinions. Desperate to deflect her, Slider said unguardedly, 'What are you going to do today?'

The already opened mouth dropped still further in amazement at his stupidity. 'But it's the school *fair* today,' she said with huge and patient emphasis, like a nurse in a home for the senile. 'I'm going to be on a *stall*. I'm going to be a *Mister Man*. Mummy's made me a costume and *everything]*'

'Oh, is that today?' Slider said feebly.

Kate sighed heavily, blowing a strand of sticky, light-brown hair across her face. 'Of course it's today. You *know* it is,' she said inexorably.

'I thought it was next week,' Slider said with a growing sense of doom.

'Well, it isn't.' She eyed him suspiciously. 'You are coming, aren't you?'

'Darling, I can't. I've got to go to work.'

Violent despair contorted her features. 'But Daddy, you promised!' she wailed.

'I'm sorry, sweetheart, but I can't help it. I've got an important case on at the moment, and I just have to go in to work. It's a murder case – you know what that is, don't you?'

'Of course I do. I'm not stupid,' she said crossly. 'But you don't really have to go, do you? Not all day?'

'I'm afraid so.'

'Is that why Mummy's cross?'

'I don't think she knows yet,' Slider said weakly. 'Get off the bed, darling, I have to go to the bathroom.'

'I *bet* she doesn't know,' Kate said with relish, bounced off the bed and hared off downstairs, a delighted harbinger of doom. Blast the child, Slider thought as he plodded what felt like uphill to the bathroom. He urinated, stood for a pleasurable moment or two scratching himself, and then started to run a bath. The running water made so much noise he didn't hear Irene behind him until she spoke.

'Is it true?'

'Is what true?' he temporised.

'Kate says you've got to work today.' Her voice was icy, and he turned to see how bad it was. It was bad. Her lips were thin and white, which made her look five years older than her true age. It was an unlovely expression, he thought, on any woman. He felt around in his mind for a moment for

133

guilt, and could find nothing new there, only the familiar old sorts with which he was almost comfortable. Joanna was there, but as a loosely woven, shining net of pleasure, and the glow coming off the thoughts of her seemed to be protecting him from feeling anything bad about it.

'I'm afraid so,' he said, and drew breath to add some extenuating detail, but she was in first.

'I'm surprised you bothered to come home at all,' she said bitterly. 'It hardly seems worth it. Why don't you move in with Atherton? At least you won't disturb him coming in all hours of the night – especially if it's him you're sitting up drinking with.'

Slider allowed himself a touch of impatience. 'Oh come on! I wasn't drinking last night, as you know perfectly well. I was working. I told you the old lady, the only witness in this blasted case, was found dead. You know how much work that means. And,' he added, managing to work up a bit of momentum. 'I think it's a bit much for you to go telling Kate I came in drunk.'

He thought the false accusation would sidetrack her, but she only said with deep irony, 'And now I suppose you've got to go in again?'

'Yes, I've got to,' he returned her words defiantly.

'And you couldn't possibly have told me earlier, of course?'

'No, of course I couldn't. I didn't know earlier, did I?'

'You realise that it's Kate's fair today. Of course, she's only been looking forward to it for weeks.'

'Well, I can't see that that—'

'And that Matthew's playing in the match today. His first chance in the school team. Which you said you were so proud of.'

'Oh God, is that today as well? I'd forgotten—'

'Yes, you're good at forgetting things like that, aren't you?

134

Things to do with your home and family. Unimportant things – like the fact that you were supposed to take Kate and me to the fair and then take Matthew on to the match. You forgot that you were supposed to be *here* for a change.'

'Well, I can't help it, can I?' he defended himself automatically. 'What do you want me to do, tell Division I'm busy?'

Irene never answered inconvenient questions. 'One day,' she said bitterly. 'Just one day. Is that so much to ask? Of course I wouldn't expect you to do anything for me, but I would have thought you could spare a few hours for your children, when they've been looking forward to it so much. But you're much too busy. I should have expected it.'

'It's my job, for God's sake!' he cried, goaded.

'Your job,' she said in tones of withering scorn.

'It's an important case—'

'So you say. But I'll bet you one thing – it won't get you anywhere. It won't get you promoted. And shall I tell you why? Because you run around like their little dog, working all the hours God sends, at their beck and call, and they don't respect you for it, oh no! They're going to keep you down because you're too useful for them to promote you!'

'Oh for God's sake, Irene, do you think I'd do it if it wasn't necessary? Do you think I like going to work on a Saturday?'

Suddenly things changed. Her face, taut with anger, seemed to loosen. She was no longer playing a part in her own personal soap opera: she looked at him for once as though she really saw him; she looked at him with a sadness of disillusion which hurt him unbearably.

'Yes,' she said. 'I think you do. I think you prefer working at any time to being with us.'

It was too close to the truth. He stared at her helplessly, wanting to reach out his hands to her, but it was too long since they had touched habitually for the gesture to be possible without intolerable exposure. If he reached out and she rejected him, it would hurt both of them too much. The distance they had established between them was the optimum for being able to continue living together, and this was not the moment to change the parameters.

'Oh, Irene,' was all he managed to say from the depths of his pity.

'Don't,' she said abruptly, and went away.

Slider sat down on the rim of the bath and stared at his hands, and longed suddenly and fiercely for Joanna, for someone not filled to the brim with obscure and irremediable hurt. He remembered Atherton once saying that the best thing you could give to someone you loved was the ability to please you. He didn't know where Atherton got it from, but it was true. He loved Joanna not least because he could so easily give her pleasure; but he was not so naive that he didn't know that might easily be true of the beginning of any affair.

Sighing, he rose and got on with his shaving and bathing and dressing, thinking about the Irene problem and the Joanna not-problem in uncoordinated bursts, while the back of his mind leafed endlessly through the documents of the case. His mind was like Snow White's apple, one half sweet, one half poisoned.

'Miss Morris?'

'You must be Sergeant Atherton. They rang me from downstairs to say you wanted to see me.'

Helen Morris was plump and pretty with friendly dark eyes and neat, short brown hair. She had the deliciously scrubbed-clean look of all nurses, and dark shadows under her eyes which could be the result of night-duty, Atherton supposed. On the other hand, he had already made enquiries downstairs before he came up to this floor, which put him at an advantage over the weary nurse.

'I'm sorry to make your working day longer, but I wanted to talk to you alone,' he said, giving her a disarming, non-alarming smile.

She didn't respond. 'I don't like doing things behind Simon's back,' she said.

Atherton smiled ever more genially. 'It's purely a matter of routine – independent confirmation, that's all.'

She put her head up a little. 'I've complete confidence in Simon. He had nothing whatever to do with – with what happened to Anne-Marie.'

'Well, that's all right then, isn't it?' Atherton said blandly, turning as if to walk with her along the corridor.

Finding she seemed to have agreed to it, she shrugged and went along. 'I must have a cup of coffee,' she stipulated.

'Fine. We can talk in the canteen.'

They walked along the wakening corridors and into the canteen, which was filled with the hollow, swimming-bath sounds of a half-empty public place early in the morning. There was a pleasant smell of frying bacon, and the bad-breath smell of instant coffee. A number of nurses were breakfasting, but there were plenty of empty tables to enable them to sit out of earshot of anyone else. Atherton bought two coffees, and sat down opposite her across the smeared melamine.

'I suppose you know why I'm here,' he began, working on the principle of letting people put their own feet in it first.

She shrugged, stirring her coffee with an appearance of calm indifference. He admired her nerve; though he supposed that after a night in the operating theatre, anything that happened out here might seem tame. On the other hand, she had a full and sexy mouth which just now was set in lines of discontent, and the attitude of her body as she leaned on

137

one elbow seemed expressive not only of tiredness but also unhappiness.

'How well did you know Anne-Marie Austen?' he began.

'Hardly at all. I saw her backstage a few times, and once or twice she was in a group of us that went for a drink after a concert – that sort of thing. I knew her to speak to, that's all.'

'She wasn't a particular friend of your boyfriend's?'

She had lifted her cup two-handed to her lips, and now made a small face of distaste and put the cup down without drinking. Now was that the coffee, or his question?

'I knew about her and Simon in Italy, if that's what you're getting at.'

'Someone told you?'

'These things have a way of getting about in an orchestra.'

'Did you mind about it?'

She looked at him with a flash of anger. 'Of course I *minded*. What do you think? But there was nothing I could do about it, was there?' He kept his silence, and after a moment she went on, 'You may as well know – she wasn't the first.' She smiled unconvincingly. 'Musicians are like that. It's the stress of the job. They do things on tour that they wouldn't do at home, and it would be stupid to make a big thing about it. As long as it ended at the airport, that's what I always said – and it did.'

'Always?'

'Simon and I have been together a long time, and I know him pretty well. With all his faults, he's always been fair to me. He would never have carried on with her after the tour. That was all on *her* side.'

She met Atherton's eyes as she said these noble lines, as people do who are bent on convincing you of something they don't really believe. She keeps up a good shop-front, he thought, but she's too intelligent not to know what he is.

'So Anne-Marie wasn't willing to let things go?'

Her lips hardened. 'Because they'd been to bed together, I suppose she – fell in love with him, or something. She started chasing him, and Simon felt sorry for her, and I suppose she took it for encouragement.'

'How do you mean, chasing him?'

She took it for a criticism, and looked at him defiantly. 'It wasn't just my imagination, you know – ask anyone. She was pretty blatant about it. She hung around him, kept asking him out for drinks, even phoned the flat a couple of times.'

'It upset you,' he suggested.

She shrugged. 'I just pretended nothing was happening. I wouldn't give her the satisfaction.'

'You didn't like her much, I gather?'

'I despise women like that. They've got to have a man – any man. They don't care who. It's pathetic.'

'But I would have thought a girl as pretty as her wouldn't have any trouble finding a boyfriend,' he said as though thoughtfully.

She looked a little disconcerted. 'People didn't like her. *Men* didn't like her. Look, I know you think I was jealous—'

'Not at all,' Atherton murmured.

'But it wasn't that. I had nothing to be jealous of. I just thought she was – weak.'

Atherton absorbed all this, and tried a new tack. 'Tell me about that day – the Monday.'

'The day she died?' She frowned in thought. 'Well, I'd been on duty Sunday night. I got home on Monday morning about half past eight. Simon was in bed. I got in with him and we went to sleep. He got up about half past twelve and made some lunch – scrambled eggs, if you want to be particular – and brought them in, and then he got dressed and went off to work.'

'At what time?'

139

'Well, he had a session at half past two, so it would be about half past one, I suppose. I didn't particularly notice, but he'd leave about an hour to get there.'

'And you were on duty again that night?'

'Yes.'

'When did you next see Mr Thompson?'

'Well, it would be the next morning, when I got home.'

'So you didn't see him between the time he left home on Monday – about half past one in the afternoon – and Tuesday morning at – what? – half past eight?'

'I've said so.' He said nothing, and she went on as if compelled. 'We were both working. I was here all night, and Simon was working until half past nine.'

'And then he went home?'

'He had a drink, and went home.'

'That's what he told you?' She was looking at him warily now. 'But you see, I happen to know that he came here to the hospital when he left the TVC that Monday evening. And why would he come here, if not to see you?'

She whitened so rapidly that he was afraid she might actually faint, and for a long moment she said nothing, though her dark eyes were intelligent, thinking through things at great speed, not focused on him. At last she said faintly, 'He wasn't here. He didn't—'

'You didn't see him? You didn't, by any chance, arrange to meet him and hand over a certain package?'

'No!' she protested, though it came out as hardly more than a whisper. She was evidently badly shaken, but Atherton knew that there would not have been time for Thompson to come here to the hospital, collect the drug, and still be back in time to murder Anne-Marie by the established time. If he were the murderer, his purpose in coming here must surely have been to establish his alibi, and Helen Morris ought therefore to be claiming to have seen him, not the reverse. It looked as though, if he did it, she was not in on it.

Her mind had been speeding along on a different track, however. She said, 'Look, I can guess what you're thinking, but there's no way in the world I could have got hold of any drugs. It's checked and double-checked every night. If anything was missing, it would be discovered at once. And Simon couldn't have got hold of anything, either. They're incredibly security-minded at this hospital.'

'Yes, I know. That's how I know he came here on that Monday night. And you're quite sure he didn't come here to see you?'

She hesitated, and Atherton watched with interest the struggle between her loyalty to Thompson, which wanted to bail him out of possible trouble, and her intelligence, which told her that if she changed her story now, it would look suspicious. In the end she said, 'I didn't see him. But he might have come to see me, and not been able to find me.'

Clever, thought Atherton.

'Look,' she went on with a touch of irritation. 'I'm very tired. Can I go home now? You know where to find me if you want to ask me any more questions. I'm not going to leave the country.'

Atherton rose and smiled graciously at the irony. He was not displeased with the interview. Someone intelligent and determined – and she was both – could overcome the problem of falsifying the drugs record; and he had established to his own satisfaction that she was not as sure of Thompson as she claimed to be. She knew he was a shit; she was also nervous and worried. She had by no means told Atherton everything. Perhaps she knew where Thompson had been that evening. Or perhaps she didn't know, and wondered.

* * *

141

Out in the clear air of the morning, Slider found himself ravenously hungry. He had declined breakfast at home in the company of his grieving son, his self-righteous daughter and his tight-lipped wife. Consequently he had a little time in hand; enough to drive to a coffee-stall he knew in Hammersmith Grove where they made bacon sandwiches with thick, white crusty bread of the sort he remembered from his childhood, before everyone went wholemeal. The other early workers made room for him in companionable silence, and they all sipped their dark-brown tea out of thick white mugs like shaving-pots and blinked at nothing through the comforting steam.

Restored, he drove to Joanna's house. She opened the door as he was parking the car and stood watching him until he came up the path. Discovering her again was a series of delightful shocks which registered all over his body. She had on a pair of soft and faded grey cord trousers, tucked into ankle-boots, and a buttercup yellow vyella shirt which seemed to glow in the colourlessness of a winter morning. She looked wonderful, but best of all, so approachable, so accessible. He put his arms round her and she turned her face up to him, smiling, and she seemed both familiar and dear. He caught the scent of her skin, and it seemed so surprising and exciting that he already knew the smell of her so well, that it gave him an erection.

'Hullo,' she said. 'How did you sleep?'

'Like the dead. And you?' It didn't matter what they said. He felt suddenly safe and optimistic.

They went into the house and she shut the door behind them with a practised flick of one foot. In his arms again, she pressed against him and felt his condition. 'Have we time?' she asked simply.

His stomach tightened. He was not yet used to such directness. 'What time is he coming?'

She cocked his watch towards her. 'Twenty minutes.'

'Then we've time,' he said, taking her face in his hands and kissing her. With one hand on the wall to guide her, she backed with him down the passage to the bedroom.

Martin Cutts turned out to be about forty-five, a small, almost delicate man with the very black hair and very white skin of the Far North, and the carefully upright gait of the back-sufferer. He had an alert face and an engaging smile, and was as jewel-bright as a bluetit – in a sapphire suede jacket over a canary-yellow roll-neck sweater. Slider was regarding with some suspicion and even contempt a man of that age who would dress so brightly, until it occurred to him depressingly that he was merely jealous of a man who he suspected might once have been Joanna's lover, and then he laid himself out to be affable.

Joanna had arranged the interview for Slider at her house, since there were things Cutts would not be able to say at home in front of his wife, as Slider, newly sensitive on that score, had appreciated. Joanna now left them tactfully alone and went and had her bath, and the thought of her naked and soapy in the steam beckoned distractingly from the corner of Slider's mind.

He cleared his throat determinedly and said, 'It was good of you to give me your time like this.'

'Not at all,' Cutts said, seating himself carefully on the arm of the chesterfield. 'It was good of you to let me answer your questions here rather than at home.' He crinkled his eyes in what Slider realised with a start was a conspiratorial grin. It brought home to him all over again his new status as a Man of the World, a Man with a Bit on the Side, and he wasn't sure he liked it.

'Perhaps you'd tell me how you got to know Miss Austen,'

he asked, poising his pen above his pad in the manner which laid obligation on the interviewee to give one something to write down.

Cutts was not unwilling. 'Well, of course I knew her in Birmingham,' he began, and Slider hid his surprise and nodded safely instead.

'You were in the same orchestra?'

'For a short time. She joined just before I left to come to London.'

'Did you have an affair with her while you were both in Birmingham?'

Martin Cutts did not seem at all put out by the question. He answered as if it were as natural a thing as having his hair cut. 'I went to bed with her, yes, but it wasn't really what you'd call an affair. I had to be more careful up there, of course, because I was between wives.'

Slider was puzzled. 'I don't follow.'

'I'd just divorced my first wife, and hadn't yet married my second,' he explained obligingly.

'Yes, but why did that mean you had to be more careful? Surely—'

'Well, obviously,' Cutts said as if it were, indeed, obvious, 'if you're not married and you go about with a single girl, she's bound to take you more seriously and try to pin you down. If you've got a current wife, you're safe. She knows she can't have you. That's the beauty of it.'

Slider nodded unemphatically at this remarkable philosophy. 'Do you think Miss Austen was on the look-out for a husband?'

'Well, they all are underneath, aren't they? Mind you, she didn't particularly show it in those days, not like later. She was pretty chipper, and it was all quite light-hearted. We had a lot of fun, and no hard feelings on either side when we parted.'

'She struck you as being happy – contented with life?'

'Oh yes. She'd got her own place, and she'd just bought a car, and I think she was enjoying being away from home and having her freedom. I don't think she'd been happy as a child.'

'Did she talk to you about her childhood?'

'Not in detail, but I gathered she was an orphan, and she'd been brought up by an aunt who hated her and wanted her out of the way. Am I telling you things you already know?'

'I'd like to have your impressions,' Slider said. 'It all helps to build up the picture. Did she tell you why the aunt hated her?'

'Personality clash, I think,' he said vaguely. 'She was always being shoved out of the way, sent to boarding school and so on. And apparently the aunt kept her short of money while she was at college, even though she was pretty well-off – the aunt, I mean.'

'Did Miss Austen ever intimate to you that she might have expectations? A legacy or something of that sort?'

He watched Cutts under his eyebrows for some reaction, but the other man only smiled to himself.

'Expectations. Nice old-fashioned expression. No, she never said anything of that sort. But she did live in a pretty swanky flat, so perhaps she had come into some money. Or it might have belonged to the aunt, I suppose. It wasn't like a young person's flat, now I come to think of it.'

'How do you mean?'

'It was one of those luxury service flats, you know, with a porter in the hall and everything laid on. More the kind of place you'd expect to find rich old ladies with Pekineses. And it struck me—'

He stopped, as if it had only just struck him. Slider made a helpfully interrogative sound.

'Well,' Martin Cutts went on, 'it never struck me as being very cosy or homelike. There was never anything lying around.

It didn't look as though anyone lived there – it was more like one of those company flats, where all the furniture and decorations have been done by a firm. Everything coordinated, like a luxury hotel. Awful, really.'

Slider thought of the shabby bedsitter and then, involuntarily, of the bare council flat, and the anomaly threatened to overload the circuits. He needed to move on, to let the subconscious get to work on it.

'After you left Birmingham, did you keep in touch with each other?'

'Oh no,' said Cutts, and the words 'of course not' hung on the air.

'As far as you were concerned, you never expected to see her again?'

He shrugged. 'I'd married my present wife, you see, and Anne-Marie and I were only ever a bit of fun. She understood that all right.'

But did she, Slider thought. He considered her childhood, the impersonal luxury flat, the desperate attempt to persuade Simon Thompson to marry her, the number of people who had said 'I didn't really know her'. No one, he thought, had ever wanted her. She had never been more than used and rejected, and Joanna, casual and incurious, was the nearest that poor child had ever had to a friend. The loneliness of her life and death appalled him. He wanted to shake this self-satisfied rat by the neck, and hoped for a whole new set of reasons that he had never been in Joanna's bed.

'But when she joined your present orchestra, you took up with her again?' he managed to say evenly.

'Oh, it wasn't really like that. We were friendly, of course, and I think we may have gone to bed a couple of times, but there was nothing between us. She was perfectly all right until she had this bust-up with Simon Thompson.'

'And what happened then?'

He looked away. 'She – approached me.'

'Why do you think she did that?'

'Shoulder to cry on, I suppose.' The eyes returned. 'She really was cut up about it, poor kid. She said Simon had proposed marriage to her, and then backed out. I didn't believe that – I mean Simon may be a prize prat, but he isn't stupid – but she evidently believed it, so it was all the same as far as she was concerned.'

'What form did this "approach" take?'

'She asked me to go for a drink with her after a concert one night, and when we'd had a couple, she asked me back to her flat.'

'And you went to bed with her?' Slider concealed his fury, he thought, very well.

'Yes. But I don't think it was me she really wanted. Her heart didn't really seem in it. I suppose she was still hankering after Simon.'

'Was it just the one occasion?'

'No, a few times. I can't remember – four or five perhaps.'

'And when was the last time?'

'Just before Christmas. After our last date – the Orchestra's last date, I mean – before the Christmas break.'

Slider nodded. 'Tell me what happened.'

Martin Cutts looked helpless, as if he didn't know what he was being asked. 'We had a few drinks, and went back to her flat. Like before.'

'And went to bed together?'

'Yes.'

'And how did she seem to you? Happy? Sad? Worried?'

'Depressed, I'd say. Well, she was worried, for a start, because she'd lost her diary. That may sound silly to you, but it's a major disaster for a musician. And she was worried that

Simon was going to make trouble for her in the Orchestra – that phone-call business. Do you know about that? Oh, right. But there was more than that.' He paused, evidently marshalling his thoughts. His eyes were a very bright blue, but small and rather round, which made him look more than ever like a bird with its head on one side. 'After we'd made love, she started to cry, and went on about how nobody cared about her, and that she hadn't got a boyfriend and so on. I was a bit pissed off about that – I mean, nobody likes being wept over – so I tried to jolly her up a bit, and then I thought I'd slope off. But when I tried to get up, she clung to me, and started really crying, and saying she was frightened.'

'Frightened? Of what?'

'She didn't say. She just kept saying "I'm so afraid. I'm so afraid" over and over, just like that. And sobbing fit to choke. Got herself really worked up.'

'And what did you do?'

'Well, what could I do? I held her and patted her a bit, and when she quietened down, I made love to her again, just to cheer her up.'

'I see,' Slider said remotely.

Martin Cutts eyed him unhappily. 'What could I do?' he said again. 'People on their own do get depressed around Christmas. It's not nice being on your own when everyone else is with their families, but I couldn't take her home with me, could I? And she wouldn't go back to her aunt. I felt rotten leaving her, but I had to get home.'

'How was she when you left her?'

'Quiet, she wasn't crying any more, but she seemed very depressed. She said something like "I can't go on any longer". I said of course you can, don't be silly, and she said, "No, it's all over for me".'

'Were those her actual words?'

'I think so. Yes. Well, you can imagine how I felt, leaving her like that. But then, when we met again in January, she seemed to be all right again – quiet, you know, as if she'd resigned herself. Then when I heard she was dead, I naturally thought she must have killed herself, and I felt terrible all over again. But she didn't, did she?'

'It wasn't suicide,' Slider acknowledged.

'So there was nothing I could have done, was there?' he appealed.

Slider had no wish to let him off the hook of responsibility, since what he had done must have added to Anne-Marie's overall misery, but he could hardly blame Cutts for her murder. *Quiet,* he thought, *as if she'd resigned herself.* But to what? Had she foreseen her death? What had she done to bring it upon herself? Perhaps, lonely and unwanted as she was, she had really ceased to care if she lived or died – until, of course, that last moment in the car park when the realisation had come upon her (how?) that it was going to happen, and she made the one last futile effort to escape, one last pathetic flutter of a bird in a trap.

Joanna came in cautiously, pink and scented, and looked from one to the other. 'The voices had stopped, so I thought you'd finished.'

Slider roused himself. 'Yes, we've finished. For the moment, anyway. Thank you, Mr Cutts.'

'Mr Cutts?' Joanna said in ribald derision. 'Mr *Cutts.*'

And Cutts reached out a hand and grabbed her by the neck, pulling her against his chest in an affectionate death-lock. It was not a lover's gesture, but it was the more disturbing for that, for Slider could easily imagine what depths of intimacy might have preceded such casual man-handling.

'Don't chance your arm, woman,' Cutts said, grinning, and

when he released her she slipped an arm round his waist and gave him a brief, hard hug.

Catching Slider's eye she said, almost apologetically, 'Martin and I are old friends, you know.'

Cutts smiled at Slider disarmingly. 'Yeah, Jo and I go back a long way. I hope you're taking good care of her – she's a remarkable woman.'

This, Slider knew, was where he was supposed to smirk and say something complacent along the lines of *she certainly is* or *I'm a lucky man,* thus accepting gracefully the implied compliment that Cutts knew that he was Joanna's lover and was assuring him that he had no rival here. But Slider's feelings were too new and unfamiliar to him, and above all too large and too overwhelmingly important for such social backgammon. He could do no more than mutter something stiff and graceless, and feel a fool, and angry. Joanna gave him a thoughtful look, and led Martin Cutts away to show him out, leaving Slider alone to regain his composure.

Accustomed to marital warfare, he expected her to reenter the room with a rebuke, and made sure he got his blow in first. 'You certainly know some really lovely people. Are they all like him in your business, or is he better than most?'

She stood before him, looking at him without hostility. In fact, there was even a smile lurking under the surface.

'Oh, Martin's not too bad a bloke, if you don't take him seriously. He's like a greedy child let loose in a sweetshop, except that his lollies are women's bodies. He has to prove himself all the time.' She put her arms round Slider's unyielding neck, and her breasts nudged him like two fat, friendly puppies. 'And you know, about fifty per cent of all men would behave exactly like him, given his opportunities. Why do so few men ever grow up? It's depressing.'

She laid her mouth against his, waiting for him to react,

but he struggled with his resentment and would not kiss her back. She drew her head back to look at him enquiringly. 'What are you so mad about?'

It was hovering on his lips to demand whether that man had been her lover, but he saw in time the amusement lurking in her dark eyes and knew that she was just waiting for him to ask. He thrust the thought away. It was of no interest to him, he told himself sternly.

She followed his struggles, recorded minutely in his expression, 'You're quite right,' she said. 'It's impossible to be jealous of someone like Martin. He isn't real. He's a sort of sexual Yogi Bear, always snitching picnic baskets, and being chased by Mister Ranger.'

Slider began to laugh, his resentment dissolving. 'I don't deserve you,' he said.

'Of course you don't,' she assured him. 'I'm a remarkable woman.'

10

Through the Dark Glassily

'Are you sure Atherton won't mind?' Joanna said as they sped
northwards through the blissfully empty streets. It was another
clear, sunny day, but there was a small and bitter wind much
more in keeping with the bare trees. Joanna was wearing an
overlarge and densely woolly white jacket, so that with her
dark eyes and pale face she looked like a small, stout polar
bear. Slider glanced sideways at her with affection, thinking
how natural it seemed already to have her beside him in the
car.

'Of course he won't. Why should he?'

'I can think of lots of reasons. For a start, he may not have
enough food for three if he was expecting to feed two. And
for another, he might want to have you to himself.'

'He's my sergeant, not my wife. Anyway, if we're going to
go over the case, we need you there. You were the person
closest to Anne-Marie.'

'That sounds perilously thin to me, and I'm not even a
detective. He's bound to see through it.'

'He's my friend as well as my partner. And I need you.'

152

'Ah well, there's no answer to that, is there? Do I call him Atherton as well? Or should I make an attempt at Jim?'

Atherton's face, when he opened the door, was carefully schooled to show nothing of his feelings either of annoyance or surprise, and he invited them in politely. Joanna eyed him, unconvinced.

'I hope you don't mind too much having me here? It was terribly short notice, I know, with no shops open. You don't have to feed me, if there isn't enough.'

'There's enough,' he said economically. 'Go on in, take your coats off.'

Slider glanced at him defensively, and followed Joanna in under Atherton's door-holding arm. The front door opened directly onto the living-room, a haven of deep armchairs, crammed bookshelves, and a real fire leaping energetically in the grate and reflecting cheerfully in the brass scuttle.

'Oh, what a gorgeous room!' Joanna said at once. She turned to Atherton an innocent face. 'I had an elderly aunt once who lived in an artesian cottage, and it wasn't a bit like this.'

Atherton walked into it. 'You mean artisan cottage,' he said, his eyebrows alone deploring her ignorance.

'Oh no,' she said gravely, 'it was very damp.'

There was a brief silence during which Slider watched Atherton anxiously, knowing he was proud, and more accustomed to using Slider as his straight man than being one himself. But an uncontrollable smirk began to tug at his lips, and after a moment he gave in to it and grinned along with Joanna.

'You should have told me she was silly,' he said to Slider. 'Have a drink and enjoy the fire. What will you have?'

Oedipus, who had been stretched out belly to the flames, got up politely and came across to wipe some of his loose hair onto Joana's pink velvet dungarees. She bent and offered him a hand, and he arched himself and walked under it lingeringly, by inches.

'Gin and tonic if there is, please. What's his name?'

'Oedipus. Bill?'

'Same please. Thanks.'

'Why Oedipus?'

'Because Oedipus that lives here, of course. Really, you are very dull.'

Slider was surprised at the rudeness, but Joanna grinned and said, 'There are two sorts of people in the world, those who quote from *Alice*—'

'And those who don't.'

'Alice?' Slider said blankly.

'*In Wonderland,*' Atherton elucidated, and smiled at Joanna on his way to the kitchen. Slider sat down, acknowledging, while not necessarily understanding, that the simple fact of sharing a quotation with Joanna had changed Atherton from not-very-well-concealed hostility to open partisanship. There was nowt queerer than intellectuals, he told himself resignedly; unless it was cows.

Joanna had taken the armchair by the fire, and Oedipus now jumped up onto her lap, sniffed it delicately, turned round once, and settled himself majestically with one massive, Landseer paw on each of her knees. Atherton brought all three glasses at once in his large, long hands, distributed them, and settled himself.

'Well, what first?' he said. 'You've seen the preliminary report on Mrs Gostyn?'

'Yes, and there's no doubt, except that there's every doubt,' Slider sighed. 'Beevers went round there, didn't he?'

'Yes. The carpet was rucked up, as if she'd put her foot on it and it slid away from her. He tested it, and it was slippery enough to have done that. She would have fallen backwards and struck her head on the corner of the fender. There was a smear of blood there, and the wound was consistent, according to Freddie Cameron, in shape, kind and force needed, with such a fall. Sufficient in a woman of her age and general condition to have proved fatal. No sign of a struggle, or of forcible entry—'

'But there wouldn't have been.' Slider interrupted, staring into his glass darkly. 'She knew him, didn't she? That nice Inspector Petrie – why shouldn't she let him in? I should have warned her—'

'Come on, Bill, it's not your fault. We don't even know it was him. Why should he come back? He'd got what he came for the first time.'

'Maybe he came back to silence her. She was the only one who could identify him.'

'We don't know that it wasn't an accident. She might have got nervous and stepped back from him, for instance, and just slipped.'

Slider smiled. 'I thought he wasn't even there?'

Atherton looked a little put out. 'Someone was there all right. Beevers interviewed the couple upstairs, the Barclays, and they think they heard someone moving about in Anne-Marie's flat, about the time we reckon it happened.'

'He went back for something. Something he'd forgotten the first time. What?'

'The violin?'

'Got to be. And then went downstairs to stop Mrs Gostyn's mouth. One out of two, better than nothing.'

'Well, it's possible,' Atherton conceded. He gave a grim sort of smile. 'The Barclays are moving out, going to stay with her mother in Milton Keynes. That's a sign of desperation if ever I heard one.'

'Scared?'

The grin widened. 'They wouldn't let Beevers in. Even after he put his ID through the letterbox. He persuaded them to phone the station and Nicholls gave them a description and the number of his car. Even then, when they let him in, Mrs B was standing well back with the baby clutched in her arms, while Mr B tried to look menacing with a large spanner.'

'It's all very well, but they must have been terrified,' Joanna said indignantly. 'Two of their neighbours murdered . . .'

'You haven't seen Beevers,' Atherton said. 'He's all of five-foot-five, completely spherical, with a chubby little phizog like a teddy bear. He looks about as dangerous as a scatter cushion.'

Joanna, unconvinced, turned to Slider. 'What was that about a violin? Surely it would have been in her car? She had it with her at the session.'

'That's what we would have assumed. We haven't found her car yet, of course, but we certainly found a violin in her flat, so either someone took it back there, or she had two.'

'Not that I know of,' Joanna said. 'I only ever saw the one. But in any case, why would anyone want to risk going back there to collect it?'

'Because it's extremely valuable, of course,' said Atherton.

'But it was nothing special,' she said, puzzled.

'You call a Stradivarius nothing special?'

Now Joanna laughed. 'She didn't have a Strad! She had a perfectly ordinary German fiddle, nineteenth-century, nice enough, but not spectacular.'

'Are you sure?' Slider asked.

'Of course I'm sure!' She looked from one to the other. 'I sat next to her, remember, I saw it hundreds of times. She bought it for nine thousand. She had to take out a bank loan to buy it.'

'Nevertheless,' Slider said, 'we found a Stradivarius in her flat, in an old, cheap case with two cheap bows.'

'I took it to Sotheby's to have it valued,' said Atherton. 'They think it might be worth as much as a million pounds.'

Joanna's lips rehearsed the price silently, as if she didn't understand what the figures meant. Then she shook her head. 'I don't understand. Where would she get a fiddle like that? How could she possibly afford it? And why didn't she use it? How could anyone who owned a Strad like that not play it?'

'Maybe she thought it was too valuable to use,' Slider hazarded.

Joanna shook her head again. 'It isn't like that. A fiddle's not like a diamond ring. You have to play them, use them. Even the insurance companies understand that.'

'Then the only other explanation is that she didn't want anyone to know she had it.'

'Stolen?' Joanna said, but Slider could see she didn't believe that, either. 'Look, fiddles like that are like – like famous paintings. You know, Sunflowers or the Mona Lisa. They don't just appear and disappear. People know them, and they know who has them. If one had been stolen, everyone would know about it. You'd have the details somewhere.'

'Are you quite sure she didn't play it? Would you really know what violin she was playing, if you had no particular reason to notice?'

'It's one of the first things you discuss when you get a new desk partner,' she said without emphasis. 'What sort of fiddle do you play? How much was it? Where did you get it? That sort of thing. And you get used to the sound of it. There are all sorts of little peculiarities you have to adapt to. Even if you never look at the thing, you'd know instantly if your partner played on a different instrument, especially if it was

157

one of Stradivarius quality. It just wouldn't sound the same.'

Atherton, at least, understood; Slider accepted without understanding because it was her. Their drinks were finished, and Atherton said, 'Let's eat, shall we? Feed the beast. Would you two like to lay the table while I do things in the kitchen? You'll find everything in that drawer, there.'

A little while later they were seated round the gate-leg table eating smoked mackerel pâté and hot toast, and drinking Chablis. Oedipus also had a chair drawn up to the table, where he sat very upright with his eyes half closed, as if he could hardly bear the sight of such unattainable delicacies.

'He's better if he sits where he can see,' Atherton said without apology. 'Otherwise his curiosity sometimes gets the better of his manners.'

'This is delicious,' Joanna said. 'Did you make the pâté yourself?'

Atherton looked gratified at the compliment. 'Marks and Sparks. Purveyors of comestibles to the rich and single. One of the truly great things about not being married and having children is that you never have to eat boring food. You can have what you like, when you like.'

'Oh, I agree,' Joanna said. 'I'd sooner not bother to eat if there's nothing interesting around. I like small amounts of really exotic things.'

Slider looked at them grimly. 'All right for you youngsters. You wait until you grow up. Bird's Eye Beefburgers and Findus Crispy Pancakes will catch up with you in the end.'

'I shall never be that old,' Atherton said with a delicate shudder. 'I'll go and get the next course.'

'Can I help?' Joanna said dutifully, but he was already gone. He returned very soon with a recipe-dish pheasant, reheated. 'Marks and Spencer?' Joanna said.

'Wainwright and Daughter,' Atherton corrected. 'I always

thought Daughter was the other bloke's name – you know, Mr Daughter.'

He added Egyptian new potatoes, Spanish broccoli, and Guatemalan petits pois.

'Harrods?' Joanna tried.

'Marks and Spencer,' he said triumphantly. 'Air travel and greenhouse forcing have effectively eliminated the seasons.'

'And freezing,' Joanna added.

'Nothing can eliminate freezing, unless you go and live on the equator. Have some more Chablis.'

While they ate, Slider told them about his interview with Martin Cutts, and Anne-Marie's fear. Atherton listened attentively, and then said, 'I know you think she was mixed up in something really heavy, and that this was a gang murder of some kind, but you know there's nothing to go on. The boys from Lambeth went over her flat with a fine-tooth comb and found absolutely zilch.'

'The boys from Lambeth?' Joanna asked.

'The Metropolitan Police Forensic Science Laboratories, at Lambeth.'

'But they wouldn't,' Slider said patiently. 'That's what really convinces me, that the whole thing was so carefully organised. They haven't made a single mistake, except for the violin.'

'It's circular thinking to say that because there's no evidence it means that they were too good to leave any. Why flog a dead horse? The Thompson lead is much better. It only wants working up a bit to look presentable.'

'All right, tell me the way you see it,' Slider sighed.

'Point one: Thompson had a good reason for wanting to get rid of her. She was being a bloody nuisance.'

'That's not much of a motive.'

'Better than no motive at all. Anyway, point two: his girlfriend is a theatre nurse and has access to the drug used to kill Anne-Marie.'

'Except that none was missing. You know we checked with all the hospitals first thing.'

Atherton shrugged. 'If she was smart enough to steal it she'd be smart enough to forge the records, or cover up the theft in some way. Whoever got the stuff would have to do that.'

'Well, go on.'

'Point three: Thompson lied about where he was that evening. He says he went for a drink at a certain pub – where no one remembers seeing him – and then went straight home. But the hall porter at the hospital saw him there that night – he's seen him often enough picking up his girlfriend to recognise him.'

'Well, maybe he was picking her up that night, too.'

'But she says she didn't see him. Why would he go there, unless to see his girlfriend? Or, if he did go there to see her, why is she lying?'

'It's not much,' Slider said, shaking his head.

'Oh come on,' Joanna interrupted, having restrained herself long enough, 'you can't believe that weed Simon Thompson murdered Anne-Marie? He's a complete rabbit.'

Atherton looked at her. 'Well, as it happens, I agree with you, but that isn't evidence, is it? And Bill will tell you that there are plenty of murderers – particularly domestic murderers – who don't look as if they could or would hurt a fly. Now, I've got a Polish cheesecake to finish off with, delicious enough to make a strong man weep, and the coffee's made. If you'd like to go and sit by the fire, I'll bring it all over on a tray and we can be comfortable.'

Slider settled in the armchair by the fire and Joanna sat on the floor by his feet. Atherton shut the remains of the pheasant in the fridge, and Oedipus pretty soon came mooching back in to enjoy the second-best pleasures of the fire and Slider's trousers, which being light grey showed up either black or white hair most satisfactorily. When everyone had plate, fork, cup and glass disposed about them, Atherton settled himself on the sofa and said, 'All right, Bill. Let's hear what you think.'

'There are several things about this case that bother me,' he began slowly. 'I haven't yet begun to put them together. But look – her body was stripped naked, surely to prevent her from being identified? But then her foot was marked after death in a way that looked like a signal or warning to someone. She lived in a modest way in a poky little bedsitter, but she had in her possession a violin worth almost a million pounds. Her aunt says she had no money but what she earned as a musician, but in Birmingham she lived in an expensive luxury flat. She had a large inheritance that she couldn't get her hands on until she married, and suddenly after the trip to Italy she made a desperate attempt to persuade Simon Thompson to marry her. When the attempt failed, she seemed depressed, and told Martin Cutts she was afraid. Just before Christmas her diary goes missing, and she's murdered at a time when it's most likely she won't be missed for a considerable time. On the night of her murder she goes out to her car, and then comes running back to try to persuade Joanna and the others to go with her to a different pub.'

He stopped, and there was silence, except for the crackling of the fire and the suddenly audible purring of Oedipus, now seated in Atherton's lap.

'So what does it all add up to,' Atherton said. It wasn't a question.

'One thing is obvious – the Birmingham connection's got to be followed up. John Brown said that she still went up

161

there on a regular basis, to play for her old orchestra.' He turned to Joanna. 'Is that likely?'

She frowned. 'We all do outside work when we can get it, and Ruth Chisholm – their fixer – is much nicer than our horrible old Queen John, who wouldn't put a woman on the call list to save his life. But she was very lucky they wanted her. There must have been plenty of other people – local people – after the work.'

'So it's quite possible that she wasn't really working for her old orchestra, but simply putting that forward as a reason for going up there.'

'But why did she want to go up there?'

'Why would anyone want to go to Birmingham?' Atherton agreed. 'But on the other hand, why put forward a reason at all? Why not just go and tell no one.'

'Presumably,' Slider said slowly, 'on instructions.'

Atherton looked at him sidelong. 'You still believe there's a big organisation behind all this?'

He shrugged. 'Otherwise, as you say, why give a reason at all?'

'You don't know yet that she didn't go there to work,' Joanna said.

'Easy enough to find out,' Atherton said. 'I suppose that means you'll be putting in another 728, Bill?'

'What's a 728?' Joanna asked obediently.

'Permission to leave the Metropolitan Area,' Slider supplied. 'We have to apply for it if we go out on police business.'

Atherton grinned. 'It also means overtime, expenses, petrol money, pub lunches – no wonder the uniformed branch think we have an easy life. And who will you take with you, he asked him innocently?'

'Norma,' Slider said promptly.

'The hell you will!'

162

'Who's Norma?' Joanna asked, still the obedient feed.

'WDC Swilley,' Atherton said with relish. 'We call her Norma for obvious reasons. She's good fun, drinks like a fish, swears like a matelot – typical CID, in fact. But I don't think it's on, Bill. Stopping off for a pub lunch with Beevers or me is one thing, but cock-au-van is going too far.'

The phone rang, and while Atherton was out of the room Joanna turned to lean on Slider's knees and say, 'Do you really think Anne-Marie was involved with some big criminal organisation? It seems so unlikely to me.'

'You prefer Atherton's theory?'

'There must be other explanations. But if it came to it, I'd prefer your theory to his.'

'Why?' he asked, genuinely interested.

'Because you're better looking than him.'

Atherton came back looking triumphant. 'They've found Anne-Marie's car. A forensic team's going over it right now. Also the report on Thompson's car has come in. Nothing of great interest except some long, dark hairs. Very long, dark hairs.'

'You said his girlfriend was dark,' Slider said.

'Short and curly,' Joanna supplied, muted.

'Where was the car found?'

Atherton's triumphant smile widened a millimetre. 'In a back street in Islington, about half a mile from where Thompson lives. Within walking distance, as you might say.'

'But surely,' Joanna protested, 'no one would be so stupid as to abandon the car of someone they've just murdered so close to their own home?'

'You'd be surprised just how stupid most people really are.'

'Who's on duty – Hunt, isn't it?' said Slider. 'Do you mind if I give him a ring?'

'Use the one in the kitchen,' Atherton said. Left alone, he

and Joanna eyed each other cautiously, and then Atherton cleared his throat. Joanna's eyes narrowed in amusement.

'I suppose you're going to warn me off. You're very protective of him, aren't you?'

'You know he's married, don't you?'

'Yes. Yes, I know.'

'Very married. He's never had an affair before – he's just not the type.'

'Is there a type?'

'He's got two kids and a mortgage and a career. He's not going to leave all that for you.'

'Did I expect him to?'

'I'm just warning you for your own good.'

'No you're not,' she said evenly.

He squared up to her. 'Look, any man can get carried away, and if he did leave home in the heat of the moment, it would be disastrous for him. It would ruin him, and I don't just mean materially. He's one of the few really honest men I know, he has a conscience, and the worry and guilt he'd feel about leaving his wife and family would ruin any happiness he might have with you.'

She suppressed a smile. 'You're going very far, very fast. Isn't that what's called jumping to conclusions?'

'The fact that he's done it at all means it's pretty serious. You don't know him like I do. He's not like us – he's from a different generation. He can't take things lightly. And he's very – innocent – about some things.'

'Well,' she said, and looked away, and then back again. 'I think he's old enough to make up his own mind, don't you?'

Atherton rubbed the back of one hand with the fingers of the other, a nervous gesture of which he was unaware. 'I don't want you to put him in a position where he *has* to decide.

Don't you see, once that happens he'll be unhappy whichever way he chooses.'

'I don't see that I can help that,' she said seriously.

Atherton felt anger rising, that she took it all so lightly. 'You could break if off, now, before it goes any further.'

'So could he.'

'But he won't. You know that. If you would just leave him alone—'

Now she smiled. 'Ah, but he'd have to leave me alone, too. Have you thought of that?'

Atherton jerked away from her and walked to the fireplace, beat his fist softly on the mantelpiece. 'You could discourage him,' he said at last, his back to her. He was afraid he would lose his temper if he looked at her. 'You could do that.'

'I could,' she conceded. She looked at his tense back thoughtfully. 'I still think, however, that it's his business to decide for himself, not yours or mine.'

He returned. 'It just shows how much you really care for him! You have no scruples about destroying his life, do you?'

She looked at him carefully, as if wondering whether it was worth trying to make him understand. Then she said, 'I don't believe that the status quo is the only workable configuration, or that maintaining it is necessarily the primary purpose of life. Life is rich in possibilities, and on the law of averages alone, some of them are bound to be an improvement.'

Atherton said sharply, 'You'll make a lot of people very unhappy.'

'I don't happen to believe that happiness is the primary purpose of life, either.'

'Crap!' Atherton said explosively. She shrugged and said no more.

In a moment Slider came back. 'I think I'd better take you

165

home,' he said. 'Things are about to hot up.' He glanced from her to Atherton. 'Were you two quarrelling?'

'Discussing,' Atherton said carefully. 'Our views on a number of things are very different.'

'Nonsense,' Joanna smiled. 'We were quarrelling over you – trying to see which of us loves you best.'

Slider grinned, not believing her. 'Who won?'

'I think it was a draw,' she said, and was rewarded by a brief and quirky smile from Atherton.

In the car he said, 'What were you talking about while I was on the phone?'

'He was trying to persuade me to give you up.'

'Oh!' He sounded dismayed. 'What did you say?'

'That you were old enough to make up your own mind.' It was not entirely what he wanted to hear, as she knew very well.

He sighed. 'Why do things have to be so complicated?' he said helplessly, like so many before him.

'That's how life is. Easy, but not simple.'

'All right for you to say it's easy,' he said resentfully.

'But it is. One always knows what the alternatives are.'

'Perhaps I haven't got your courage.'

'It's not a matter of courage.'

They stopped at the lights. 'Don't be so tough. What is it a matter of?'

'Approach, I suppose. Like pulling off a plaster. There's the inch-by-inch approach. Or you can give one good rip and have done. You always know at the beginning what the end will be, so I always think you might as well – just jump.'

He looked at her, feeling so much and so complicatedly that he couldn't articulate it. The lights went green, and he started off again automatically, without being aware of it.

'All the same,' she said after a moment, 'don't make the mistake of thinking that you can't cope and I can.'

He glanced at her, perplexed. 'But you can cope with anything,' he said.

'Oh yes, I know,' she said wryly. 'That's the trouble. That's what will finish me in the end.'

He wanted to protest that he was not Atherton, that he did not understand riddles; but he found that – and of course – he did. The love he felt for her, knowing its way better than he did, was fierce and tender in such mingled proportions – a cross between ravishing and cherishing – that he felt scoured, shaken, emptied out; and, with that, curiously strong, like a man who had been on a fast. Forty days and forty nights. Stronger than her – and how was that possible?

They arrived at the house. He wanted to make love to her, to sink into her and never surface again. She was the warm precinct of the cheerful day that he never wanted to leave.

'Will you come in?' she asked when he didn't move.

'No, I must go home.'

'And you said you didn't have courage.'

She sat quite still for a moment or two, and then as she began to move he said, 'You know it's Anne-Marie's funeral tomorrow.'

'No, I didn't know. Are you going to it?'

'Privately, not officially. Would you like to come with me?'

'Yes. I'd like to go. In all this it's so easy to forget about her.'

She looked at him seriously to see if he understood what she meant, and of course he did. He touched her face with the tips of his fingers, and then kissed her – on the mouth, but like a benediction.

'I'll pick you up,' he said.

★ ★ ★

167

But even forewarned, he hadn't expected the funeral to be so depressing. It turned warm during the night and began to rain, and it went on raining dismally all day, and was so dark that eleven in the morning seemed like four in the afternoon. Added to that there were hardly any mourners, which made everything seem somehow worse. Of course, she had had no relatives apart from the aunt, but Slider had expected there to be friends, people from her past life, though he could not have said who they might be. As it was, Anne-Marie Austen's home life was represented by Mrs Ringwood, attended by her housekeeper and Captain Hildyard, the solicitor, and an old man who seemed to be Mrs Ringwood's gardener; from her working life there was only Joanna, and Martin Cutts.

'I expect others would have come if it hadn't been short notice,' Joanna said without conviction.

'Sue Bernstein phoned Ruth Chisholm in case anyone from up there wanted to come, but it looks as though no one could make it,' Martin Cutts said.

'I suppose it's too far for them,' Joanna said.

'Nonsense. Birmingham is closer to here than London.'

'Oh. Well, probably they're working today,' Joanna said unconvincingly.

The service was distressingly bald and devoid of spiritual uplift to Slider, who liked his church High or not at all, and could never get over the feeling that the modern translation of the Prayer Book, by being so ugly, was sacrilegious. There was nothing, in fact, to take his mind off the fact that Joanna was seated on the further side of Martin Cutts, and that when she started crying Cutts put his arm round her and she rested her cheek on his shoulder. Slider hated him, with his ready, slippery ease of showing physical affection. Why couldn't I ever have been like that? he wondered resentfully. What Cutts gave and received so easily cost him so much pain and effort.

The committal at the graveside was brief, and as soon as was decently possible everyone hurried away to seek shelter. Slider found himself accosted by Mrs Ringwood, with Captain Hildyard looming supportively at her shoulder.

'I'm surprised to see you here, Inspector,' she said. 'Are you the official police presence?'

'No, ma'am. I'm here in my private capacity.'

She raised an eyebrow. 'Private capacity? What could that be? You weren't a friend of my niece, were you?'

'No, ma'am. But I do feel very much involved in the case – enough so to wish to pay my respects.'

'How refreshing to learn that you chaps have room for human feelings,' Hildyard put in, smiling yellowly behind his moustache to show that it was a joke, though his eyes were as boiled and glassy as ever. They swivelled round to stare at Joanna. 'And you, young lady – were you a friend of our poor, dear Anne-Marie?'

Joanna seemed upset, almost angered by the look and the words. She stared at his tie, avoiding his eyes, and said brusquely, 'I shared a desk with her in the Orchestra. What about you? I never heard her mention you as a friend of hers.'

It sounded rude, challenging, and Hildyard's eyes seemed hostile, though he spoke evenly enough. 'I've known the poor child since she was tiny. Being so much of another generation from her, I hardly like to claim I was a friend, but I know she looked on me with trust and affection. It's the privilege, perhaps, of my profession to win a place in the hearts of our young clients. Many's the time I've popped in to attend to her pony's colic or her puppy's worms, and believe me there's no surer way to win a child's love.'

'Perhaps you'd like to come back to the house for a glass of sherry,' Mrs Ringwood said abruptly to the air in general. Slider was reminded of his Latin lessons at school, when he had learned to construct a sentence that 'expects the answer *no.*' Mrs Ringwood's inflection had just the same effect.

'No thank you, ma'am. I have to be getting back to London,' Slider said, and by a turn of his body managed to place himself alongside Mrs Ringwood on the gravel path, which was only wide enough for two. Hildyard was forced to drop back beside Joanna. 'By the way, Mrs Ringwood,' he went on, lowering his voice and approaching her ear under the umbrella, 'did you ever visit Anne-Marie in Birmingham, after she joined the Orchestra there?'

'Certainly not. Why should I want to visit her?'

'You never went to her flat?'

'I had no reason to.'

'So you've no idea what sort of place it was? Whether she rented it? Whether she shared it with anyone?'

She evinced impatience. 'None at all. I've told you before, Inspector, I knew nothing about her personal life. I suggest you ask some of her musician friends.'

Slider thanked her, and collected Joanna and escaped by a side-path. So it hadn't been the aunt's flat – that disposed of that possibility. But something had been said today – something, sometime, by somebody – that was important, and he just couldn't bring to mind what it was. A bell had been rung in the back of his mind, but it was too far back to be of any help. He left it alone, knowing his subconscious would throw it back to him sooner or later, and returned his attention to Joanna.

Martin Cutts had just asked her if she would go with him to the nearest pub for a pint. She replied with a shake of the head and a single graphic glance towards Slider; at which he grinned, kissed her easily on the lips, said 'See you Wednesday, then,' and left.

'It's half past two closing out here,' she said. Her voice sounded so strange that Slider glanced at her, to find that she

170

was grey with cold and misery and within an inch of tears. He hurried her to the car, wanting to get them away from this place, wanting, absurdly, to take Anne-Marie with them too. She had been a musician as well, and even if no one had loved her, she had once known the companionship of pubs and the easy kisses of Martin Cutts. The contrast was too harsh – it seemed cruel to leave her behind.

In the car he put on the heater and the blower and drove as fast as the rain would allow back towards the sanity of London. As the car warmed up, Joanna revived.

'Well,' she said first, 'so that's that. Not my idea of a funeral. When I go, I want hundreds of people crying their eyes out, and then going off and getting good and drunk and saying what a great person I was.'

'Yes,' said Slider comprehensively.

'A proper service in the church, too, with candles and hymns and the real words out of the Prayer Book. Not that second-rate, poor man's substitute; that New Revised Non-Denominational Series Four People's Pray-in, or what-ever the bloody thing's called.' She glared at him, and suddenly cried out, 'It isn't fair!' and of course she wasn't talking about church services. But he was glad, in a way, that it hadn't been the old-fashioned service, because the familiar words would have reminded him of Mam's funeral. They always did, when he heard them on television or in a film, and still they made him cry. Funerals above all reminded you that there was no going back, that every day something was taken from you that you could never have back.

After a while she said in a small voice, 'When I die, will you promise to see that I'm buried properly, not like that? And I'll promise the same thing for you.'

'Oh, Joanna,' he said helplessly, and took her hand into his lap for comfort.

When they reached Turnham Green, however, she revived with the suddenness of youth. 'I'm starving. Do you know what I fancy – a hamburger! A proper one, not a McDonald's. Shall we go to Macarthurs?'

'I can't,' he said relunctantly. 'I've got to go to the station. There's a mass of things to be done, and the meeting to prepare for, I'm sorry.'

'Some love affair this is,' she said, but jokingly, making it easy for him.

'I'll try and call in later, on my way home. If I can't, I'll phone anyway.' She looked so forlorn that he offered his own particular foothold of comfort. 'Don't worry, we can't lose each other now. We can't stop knowing each other.'

She gave him an impish grin, 'Count your chickens! Don't forget once I start working again you'll have two impossible schedules to coordinate!'

'Look at this, guv,' Atherton said, bouncing his Viking length through the open door of Slider's room. 'Anne-Marie's bank statement – and very interesting reading it makes.'

'Midland Bank, Gloucester Road branch?'

'I expect she opened it when she was at the Royal College,' Atherton said wisely. 'Though with her swanky connections, you'd think it would have been Coutts from birth.'

'But she never had any money of her own before, did she?' Slider spread out the pages. 'Well, the totals are pretty modest. No money here for buying Stradivariuses.'

'No, but look here, last August – see? Sundries, three thousand pounds.'

'Is that her pay from the Orchestra?'

'No, that shows up as salary – look, here, and here. But sundries, bloody sundries, is what they call deposits, cash or cheques, made by post or over the counter. And it's gone in no time – four big cheques to cash. Spent it. She must have had expensive habits.'

'No sign of the repayments on the bank loan Joanna mentioned?'

'Oh, that was paid off a long time ago. Look, this is more interesting. Go back a bit further, and what do you find. A big sundry here, five K, one for four here, five again, six and a half here. Roughly every month she pays in a big lump sum and then whips it out in cash. Now what do you make of that?'

'Could she have spent it all? Maybe she had a savings account.'

'Nothing's turned up. Maybe she played the market, or put it on the ponies. But I'm not so interested in where it went as where it came from. Do you know what I think?'

'Tell me,' Slider said indulgently.

'I think she was blackmailing somebody. Or some bodies.'

'And whoever she was blackmailing got fed up and killed her? Have you gone off your Thompson theory, then?'

'Not necessarily. It could be him she was blackmailing.'

'My Uncle Arthur could stick his wooden leg up his arse and do toffee-apple impressions,' Slider said mildly.

Atherton grinned reluctantly. 'Oh well, you're not the only one who can have a hunch, you know. There was something very sinister and unloveable about that young woman. I'm going to keep my eyes open.'

'You do that. Here's something to rest them on – the report on her car.'

'Blimey, the lab really pulled its finger out on that one, didn't it? What did they find?'

'Nothing out of the ordinary, except that on the front passenger seat there were traces of a white powder—'

'*A white powder!*'

'Behave yourself. A white powder which on analysis proved to be pyrethrum and –' he consulted the report – 'piperonyl butoxide.'

'Come again?'

'It's an insecticide with pretty general application. Kills fleas, lice, bedbugs, earwigs, woodlice and so on. Freely available from any garden shop, or Woolworth's – you might find it in any household. Poisonous if you ate enough of it, and can irritate the eyes and nasal tissues if you throw it about or inhale it.'

'It irritates my brain tissues,' Atherton said crossly. 'What's the use of that? She could have bought a tin of it at any time, for any purpose, and spilt some on the seat. Where does that get us?'

'Nowhere. Except that we didn't find a tin of anything like that in her flat. But the other thing was more interesting – also found on the passenger seat, but down the crack between the seat and the back.' He handed over a small square of paper which had originally been folded into four, but had since been crushed and creased and dirtied by its sojourn down the seat cushion. Opening it out Atherton saw that it was a sheet from a note-block, the sort of small pad you keep by the telephone. On it, written at a steep angle, as it might be by someone gripping the telephone receiver between chin and shoulder to leave both hands free, was the word *Salomon*, and a telephone number.

There was an instant of painful blankness, and then Atherton exclaimed, 'Saloman! Saloman of Vincey's!'

'You know who he is?'

'Vincey's of Bond Street, the antiquarian's. Saloman's their expert on violin bows. Andrew Watson, the bloke at Sotheby's, mentioned him when he was looking at the Stradivarius. Is this Anne-Marie's writing, do we know? I suppose we can

174

find out. Did she consult him? It's a lead, anyway, and we've precious few of those.'

Slider smiled at his excitement. 'Leads have a habit of fizzling out on closer inspection. I'll leave this one to you – you're getting to be the violin expert around here. By the way, someone ought to drop in at The Dog and Scrotum and have a chat with Hilda and the regulars. I know they all said they didn't see Anne-Marie that night, but that was the official line. A comfy, private chat ought to get the truth out of them, one way or the other. I suppose,' he added unconvincingly, 'as it's more or less on my way home—'

'Bollards,' Atherton said sweetly. 'You know very well you don't go home that way any more. I'll do it, guv – you shove off to love's young dream.'

'That's awfully good of you, old chap,' Slider said gravely. 'I thought you didn't approve.'

'If you see enough of her, you might get bored. Anyway, you know Hilda fancies me. She's more likely to come across for me than for you. It's my fresh young face and youthful charm – she can't resist 'em.'

Slider shuddered. 'What about the gatekeepers at the TVC?'

'Beevers did 'em. One of them thinks he remembers that she didn't get into the car, just went up to it and then ran back as if she'd forgotten something.'

'A note under the windscreen wiper, perhaps, telling her to meet the murderer at the pub?'

'Not if the murderer was Thompson.'

'You know what I think about that,' Slider said.

'Maybe she just fancied somewhere different for a change. You can make too much of something, you know.'

Slider met his eyes, and a great number of warnings passed in both directions, which neither was likely to take heed of.

11

Miss World and Montezuma

'Hey,' said Joanna, sitting up and looking down at him in the leaping firelight.

'Hmm?' One side of his body was too hot, the other icy from the draught under the sitting-room door; the floor was hard under his shoulder blades, the rug itchy under his buttocks. All the same, he would have preferred not to have to move for several more hours. Sleep had been in short supply lately.

'You sleep on your own penny,' she said. 'You're supposed to be amusing me.'

'I just did,' he murmured without opening his eyes. He felt the roughness of her hair and a brief pressure on his penis as she bent to kiss it.

'Sex is all very well, but I want you to talk to me as well.'

He groaned and rolled onto his side, and propped his head minimally with hand and elbow. 'What?' he said.

'You look so sweet and ruffled,' she grinned at him. 'Innocent.'

'You look like a dangerous wild animal,' he said. 'Most

people look vulnerable when they take their clothes off, but you're just the opposite. You look as though you might eat me.'

'I will if you like,' she offered equably.

'A drink first. All very well for you women – it takes it out of us men.'

'You women! Spoken from the depths of your vast experience, I suppose!'

'You don't have to have a baby to be a gynaecologist,' he said with dignity.

She rose fluidly to her feet. 'Can you drink gin and tonic?'

'Does a monkey eat nuts?'

Left alone, he sat up and turned his other side to the fire. He looked around him and wondered at the sense of peace and comfort that this room gave him. He had never, to his memory, sat on the floor in his own house, though he used to in the early days of his marriage when he and Irene had had their little flat. But at home he couldn't in any case have sat on the floor by the fire, since there was neither fireplace nor chimney. This room was neither smart nor elegant, nor even particularly clean, but it was a place where you could do nothing in perfect peace, a room that demanded nothing of you, imposed nothing on you.

A clinking sound heralded Joanna with a large glass in each hand. Ice cubes floated and bumped like miniature icebergs, lemon moons hung suspended, beaded with silver bubbles, and the liquid gleamed with the delicate blue sheen of a bloody large gin. The aromatic scent of it wafted sweetly to his nostrils.

'Lovely,' he said inadequately. She folded down beside him, and held her glass at eye level.

'Aesthetically pleasing,' she acknowledged.

'You're such an animal. It's all pleasure with you – pleasure and comfort.'

'Any fool can be uncomfortable.'

'But what about duty and responsibility?'

She turned her head to rub an itch on her nose against her shoulder, something he couldn't imagine Irene ever doing.

'Those too. One fits them in, you know. But one's first duty is to oneself.'

'All right for you. You don't have a wife and children.'

'Oh, these wives and children!' He looked irritated, and she went on, 'Well, if you can't make yourself happy, you aren't likely to have much success with anyone else, are you? What use would I be to you if I were unhappy?'

'If everyone thought like you—' he began, but she gave convention short shrift.

'Everyone doesn't. The whole point is that the philosophy of irresponsibility is only safe in the hands of the morally trustworthy. So drink your nice drink and don't worry about it. It takes a great deal of practice to become a dedicated hedonist.'

'In other words, you don't want to discuss it.'

'Uh-huh,' she concurred, leaning forward, her glass held clear of their bodies, to kiss him. She slid her tongue into his mouth and he was amazed to feel his instant reaction. Blimey, lad, he addressed his organ inwardly, you're pretty lively for your age. Doing yourself proud, aren't you? He reached behind him blindly for somewhere safe to put his glass so as to free his hands, and the phone started to ring.

Joanna removed her tongue from his mouth. '"Time watches from the shadow. And coughs when you would kiss".'

'Shall I get it? It's probably for me.'

But she was already up. 'I should have put the answering machine on.'

It was O'Flaherty, starting his week of nights, and fresh from his day off with an assumed and expansive outrage. 'It's gettin' to be a bloody trial trackin' you down, Billy me darlin'. I even rang The Dog an' Bloody Scorpion, till Little Boy Blue said I'd find you in Flagrante Dilecto, and I said to him, I said, that's a pub I never even heard of—'

'I hate to interrupt your Ignorant Man from the Bogs routine, but did you want anything in particular? It's cold away from the fire.'

'I think I got something for you,' O'Flaherty said, dropping abruptly out of role. 'Listen, there's this young feller asking for you. He says he's got something important to tell you, and it's got to be you because he's shit-scared of Atherton. Says Atherton's got it in for him. Wants to see you alone.'

'How d'you rate him?'

'I think he's the goods. Name of Thompson.'

'Christ.'

'Are you deaf, I said Thompson,' O'Flaherty said witheringly.

'Is he there now?'

'No, he wouldn't come to the station in case we locked him up. All this was on the dog an' bone. I got him holdin' fire in The Crown and Sceptic, but only God knows how long he'll stay put. Apart from bein' in mortal terror, he'll be as pissed as a bloody fart unless you get out there soon. Where are you now?'

'Turnham Green. I can be there in ten minutes. Listen, Pat, will you do me a favour? Will you ring a certain person and say what's happened and that I don't know how long I'll be.'

'Ah, Jaysus, Billy—'

'Come on, Pat. Don't start that again.'

'Okay, okay, I'll do it. Now you'd better get for Chrissakes over to dat pub before yer man changes his mind.'

'All right, I'll speak to you later.'

He put the phone down and turned to find Joanna not looking at him. 'A certain person, forsooth,' she said, but quite mildly.

'Simon Thompson wants to see me, alone. Says he's got information for me. I've got to go and see him before he changes his mind.' She nodded acquiescence, turning her face away, sipping her drink and looking into the fire. All sorts of bits of him wanted badly to cleave unto her just then, but he reached for his clothes automatically, however unwillingly. 'I'm sorry.'

She shrugged.

'I'll ring you later, if it's not too late,' he said humbly.

She turned, contrite. 'Ring anyway, even if it is too late. I'll be awake.'

He dressed and kissed her goodbye before he left, but his mind had already left ahead of him.

The pub seemed full for a weekday. Slider stood just inside the door looking around so as to give Thompson a chance to accost him first. Neither, of course, knew what the other looked like, but he pretty soon picked out Thompson from Atherton's description – 'Miss World in trousers' – and from the way he was crouched over an untouched half pint with the preoccupied, inward-looking posture of an animal in pain. The eyes came round to the door, hesitated, went away, and returned to meet Slider's hopefully. Slider nodded slightly and went across and Thompson made room for him on the banquette. As soon as he was near enough, Slider could smell the other man's fear. This was no hoax.

'Mr Thomspon?'

Thompson nodded, still hunched wretchedly. 'You're Inspector Slider?'

'How did you know about me?'

'Sue Bernstein said you were in charge of the investigation. She said you seemed like a decent bloke. And she said you're going with Joanna Marshall, is that right?'

Slider coughed slightly, taken aback by the directness of the question.

'Well, I thought you were probably all right. Better than that Sergeant Atherton, anyway. He's got it in for me.' His voice rose a little in panic. 'He thinks I killed Anne-Marie. He's out to prove it, whatever it takes.' He seemed to flinch at the sound of his own words, and crouched lower, looking around him as if he expected Atherton to leap up triumphantly from under the table brandishing a tape recorder.

'I'm sure he doesn't think anything of the kind,' Slider said soothingly. 'We have to ask questions in order to get at the facts, that's all.'

Thompson looked at him hopefully, a film of sweat on his upper lip, his eyes fawning. 'You seem like a reasonable bloke. You don't think I killed her, do you?'

'Well, as a matter of fact I don't,' Slider said, 'but that's neither here nor there, is it?'

'Isn't it?'

'Well, if you really didn't do it, you've got nothing to worry about, have you?'

'It's all very well for you,' Thompson said bitterly, 'but if you were in my position you wouldn't be so cheerful. I had nothing to do with it. You must believe me. I was as horrified as anyone when I heard.'

'Perhaps a bit more horrified?' Slider suggested. 'Well, after all, you had had a relationship with her. You must have been closer to her than anyone else—'

'No one was close to that girl,' he interrupted with force. 'She was weird and – look, I'm sorry she's dead, but I can't help it. She was mixed up in something and it caught up

181

with her in the end. It was her own fault, that's how I see it.'

'What was she mixed up in?' Slider asked evenly, his heart jumping.

Thompson took the plunge. 'I don't know the details, but I'm pretty sure she was mixed up in some kind of smuggling racket. I got the idea she was beginning to want out, but she'd got in too deep. On the plane coming back from Italy she seemed pretty scared, but she wouldn't tell me what it was about.'

'Ah yes, Italy. Tell me about that. You and she were going around together, weren't you?'

He looked uncomfortable. 'It was just for the tour – that was understood. We'd done it before. We swapped rooms with some other people so that we could sleep together, and everything was all right until the last day, in Florence. We'd been out in the morning, poking around the junk shops in one of those alleys behind the main square – you know.' Slider, who had never been to Florence, nodded. 'Then I said how about getting some lunch and she suddenly said no, she had to go and see somebody. Just sprang it on me like that – never mentioned anything about it before. Well, when you're spending a tour together, you sort of expect to know what the other person's doing, don't you?'

Again Slider nodded.

'So naturally I asked her who she had to see all of a sudden, and she wouldn't tell me. Got quite nasty about it. Eventually she said if I really wanted to know she was going to see her cousin Mario, but it was none of my business, and I never gave her a moment's privacy and – things like that. Suddenly we were quarrelling and I didn't know how I got into it.'

'You think she deliberately engineered the quarrel – so as to get away from you?'

Thompson nodded eagerly. 'Yes, that's it. And she was different, too – jumpy and nervous, looking over her shoulder as if she thought someone might be watching her. Anyway, we argued a bit, and she stormed off, and I – well, I sort of followed her. I didn't really mean to. I was just walking in the same direction at first, because that was the way I wanted to go, and then because I was angry I sort of got the idea that I'd follow her and see where she went and then later I'd face her with this cousin Mario nonsense . . .' His voice trailed off.

'You were jealous, perhaps?' Slider suggested. Thompson shrugged. 'Did she see you following her?'

'I don't think so. I had a job to keep up with her, mind you, because she went a hell of a long way, right off the tourist track, and after a while I got scared of losing her, because I'd never have found my way back. I had no idea where I was.'

'Did she seem to know where she was going?'

'Oh yes. She never hesitated. And she took lots of little alleys and back streets and so on. I'd never have remembered the way – it was too complicated.'

Cautious, thought Slider. How the hell did she miss an incompetent bloodhound like Thompson? 'Where did you eventually end up?'

'In an ordinary street, with houses and a few shops on either side. Not a tourist street. Not smart. And then she turned into a doorway.'

'A shop?'

'I didn't see. I was a bit behind her, and when she went in I didn't like to go too close in case she came out again suddenly, and spotted me. So I stood in a doorway further down the street and waited. I kept thinking, suppose there's a back way? Suppose she goes out the back way, I'm really in trouble.'

'You didn't notice the name of the street, I suppose,' Slider said without hope.

Thompson looked eager and said, 'Yes, I did. The doorway I was standing in was right opposite the street sign, so I was sort of staring at it for ages. I remembered it because it was so inappropriate – Paradise Alley, only in Italian, you know.'

Blimey, Slider thought, a fact. Someone actually remembers something.

'Go on.'

'Well, she was in there I don't know how long, but it seemed a long time to me, maybe ten minutes, and when she came out she was carrying a bag.'

'What sort of bag? How big?'

'I think you call them carpet bags. You know, like a big sports bag, but soft – canvas I think – and with handles on the top. About this big.' He offered his hands about thirty inches apart.

'Was it heavy?' Thompson looked puzzled. 'How did she walk with it? Did she walk as if it was heavy?'

'Oh,' he said, enlightened. 'No, not really. She just walked normally. Well, I ducked back into the doorway until she'd gone past and then followed her again until we got near the main square and I recognised where I was, and I turned off to the side. But she must have turned off down the next street, because a minute later when I came into the square I bumped into her. She didn't look too pleased to see me, but I put it down to we'd just had a quarrel. So I asked her what was in the bag. Well, it was a natural question, wasn't it?'

'Perfectly. What did she say?'

'I thought for a minute she wasn't going to tell me. I thought she'd tell me to mind my own business. But then she sort of laughed and said olive oil.'

'Olive oil?' Slider was perplexed. Little wheels were whirring and clicking, but the patterns were making no sense.

'Olive oil, two tins, that's what she said. Well, she was nuts on cooking, I knew that. She said it was a special sort you couldn't get in England, and her cousin Mario got it for her to take back.' He shrugged, distancing himself from the whole mess.

'You say she laughed,' Slider said. 'Did she seem happy? Excited?'

'It wasn't that sort of laugh,' Thompson said doubtfully. 'More sort of – as if she was having a secret laugh at me. She wanted to get shot of me, anyway, that was for sure because I said I was going to get some lunch and asked her to come with me, and she said she was going back to the hotel and shot off like a scalded cat.'

'When did you see her next?'

'In the hotel room when I went back to get my fiddle for the seating rehearsal that evening. She was already there in the room when I arrived.'

'Did you see the bag again?'

'Yes, it was there on the end of her bed. I asked her, actually, if her cousin had given it to her, because it seemed rather a nice sort of thing just to be giving away. She didn't answer right off – looked a bit shifty, you know, as if she was wondering what to say – then she said he'd only lent it to her and that he'd be collecting it from the hall that evening. I'd have followed it up, but she jumped up and said she wasn't waiting for the Orchestra coach, that she wanted some fresh air so she was going to walk to the hall. And she just went. I think she wanted to get away from me, in case I asked her any more questions.'

'She took the bag with her?'

'Yes, and her fiddle case.'

'So you never got to see inside the bag?'

'No. She had it with her in the rehearsal, under her chair, but she must have passed it to this Mario when rehearsal finished, because she didn't have it later. But I've a fair idea what was in it, all the same, and it wasn't olive oil.' He looked at Slider expectantly.

'Not olive oil?' said Slider obediently.

'No. I'm pretty sure it was another fiddle, and a valuable one at that.'

Slider jumped, though he showed nothing more than interest on the outside. 'Why do you think that?'

'Because I was sitting behind her in the seating rehearsal and at the conceit, and the fiddle she was playing at the concert wasn't the same one that she was playing during rehearsal.'

'Are you sure?'

'Positive. I knew her usual fiddle, because the varnish was very dark and there was a tiny bit of beading broken off just by the chin-rest which showed up very pale against the dark varnish. But the one she had in the concert was much lighter and when she rested it on her knee I saw it had an unusual sort of grain on the back. But most of all, it sounded different – much, much better. I'd say it was a very valuable one. It might have been a Strad or an Amati or something, in which case it would be worth a fortune.'

'You weren't able to get a closer look at it, I suppose?'

'No, but I'll tell you what – she was very close with it during the interval. She never put it down for a moment – she put it back in the case, and then stood holding the case, even while she had a cup of coffee. Now I've never seen her do that before. I've never seen anyone do that.'

'So you think she collected a valuable violin from this cousin Mario in order to smuggle it to England, swapped it with her own violin, and passed that to him in the carpet bag sometime between the rehearsal and the concert?'

'That's what I think. That night back at the hotel, when she was in the bathroom, I tried to get a look at it, but her fiddle case was locked and obviously I couldn't break it open. That was another thing that convinced me, because she didn't usually lock her case.'

'But surely,' Slider said slowly, 'someone would have noticed that she wasn't playing her usual instrument.'

Thompson looked puzzled. 'Well they did – I did. I noticed.'

'What about her desk partner? Surely she would have noticed straight away?'

Thompson looked disconcerted, and then frowned, evidently upset at having his theory overturned. Then his brow cleared and he looked excited, for a moment almost boyish. 'I remember now – Joanna wasn't at the concert! That's right! She and Anne-Marie went for something to eat after the rehearsal, and Joanna came down with Montezuma's Revenge, and couldn't play the concert. Screaming diarrhoea. Normally we would all just have moved up one, but there was already an odd desk at the back because Pete Norris had broken his finger in Naples, so they just put Hilary Tonks up beside Anne-Marie, and of course she wouldn't know what Anne-Marie normally played.'

But Anne-Marie couldn't have relied on Joanna's being put out of action. Unless she slipped her something during their meal. But was that likely? Slider could hear Atherton's voice saying, *these are deep waters, Watson.*

'How easy would it be to smuggle a violin? What happens to them on the plane?'

'The other instruments go in the baskets, which are loaded in the hold, but usually fiddle players carry their violins with them on the plane, for safety. The instruments get listed on

187

a cartel for the customs, but no one ever checks them, except to see there's the right number. I mean, if you went out with one and came back with two, someone might notice, but not otherwise.'

'Did Anne-Marie carry hers onto the plane with her on the way home?'

'I can't remember. I think so. I'm not sure.'

'Not sure?'

He looked apologetic. 'It's like an extra arm, you see. You expect a fiddle player to be carrying a fiddle, so you don't really notice. I can't be sure, but I think she did.'

Slider nodded, thinking. 'Did you ever tell Anne-Marie what you suspected?'

'No. I thought it was none of my business. In any case, if she'd managed to smuggle a Strad in, good luck to her. We'd all like one.' He frowned again. 'But actually, I never saw her play it in England. If she did smuggle one in, I suppose she must have sold it.'

'So it wasn't over that that you quarrelled?'

'Quarrelled? Oh—' Surprisingly, he blushed. 'No – that was – but it wasn't my fault. There was never meant to be anything between us after the tour – she knew that. Lots of people did it. And at first it was all right. She behaved just as usual. And then suddenly she seemed to change, started hanging round me, trying to get me to go for drinks with her and that sort of thing. She even tried to get her position changed so she could sit next to me. I told her I was happy with my girlfriend and told her to stop pissing me off. And then she turned nasty, and threatened to tell my girlfriend, and said that I'd led her on and promised to marry her and stuff like that.'

'And had you?'

'No!' His indignation sounded genuine. 'I don't know why she said that. I think she must have been going off her trolley.

I never said anything about marrying her. You must believe me.' Slider's face was neutral. 'Helen does,' he added pathetically.

'You told people that she was the person making anonymous phone calls to players' wives, I believe?'

He turned a dull red. 'Well – yes – I suppose so. I was angry – I wanted to get back at her for trying to make trouble. I thought it might stop her.'

'And did it?'

'Well, something did. She left me alone, anyway.'

'Did it make trouble for her in the Orchestra?'

He shrugged. 'If you mean that business with John Brown, he didn't like her anyway. He doesn't like women in orchestras.'

'Tell me about the day she died. You must have seen her at the Television Centre?'

'Of course. But she hadn't given me any trouble since Christmas. I still tried to avoid her, though, just in case.'

'How did she seem to you?'

'Seem to me?'

'Was she happy, sad, frightened, worried?'

'Nothing really. She was quiet. Didn't speak much to anyone. That's how she usually was. I didn't notice anything different.'

'You'd arranged to go for a drink afterwards?'

'With Phil Redcliffe, yes, but during the second session he told me that Joanna and Anne-Marie were coming too. I think he felt sorry for Anne-Marie. I didn't argue with him, but when we finished I went to Joanna and told her that if Anne-Marie was coming, I wasn't going, and she sort of shrugged and said it was up to me – you know the way she is. She's never got any time for people's feelings. So I didn't go.'

'You went where instead?'

189

'I went home. Well, I went and had a drink first . . .' He slowed nervously. 'I had a drink at a pub near home—'

'You may as well tell me the truth,' Slider said kindly. 'We know you didn't go to Steptoes that evening. We know that you did go to St Thomas's. We know that you had someone in your car that night, and that someone wasn't Miss Morris.' Thompson paled sentence by sentence, and Slider added the last one almost tenderly. 'Someone with long, dark hair – hair about the same length and colour as Anne-Marie Austen's. We found some of her hairs on your car upholstery, you see.'

'Oh Christ,' Thompson whispered. For a moment Slider thought he was going to be sick, or faint. 'I know what you're thinking. I know what Sergeant Atherton thinks, but I swear—'

'Tell me what you did when you left the Television Centre.'

He swallowed a few times, and then said, 'I did go to the hospital.'

'Yes, I know. What for?'

'I went to meet someone. One of the nurses. Not Helen. She's – it's someone I've been seeing a bit recently. Helen doesn't know, you see. She wouldn't understand.'

I bet she wouldn't, Slider thought. 'All right, give me her name and address, and we'll check it out. I suppose she'll be able to confirm that she was with you – until when?'

'After midnight,' Thompson said quickly. Slider wondered why he picked on that hour. 'We went back to my flat and had a drink and – and, well, I drove her home in the early hours. I don't know exactly when, but it was certainly after midnight.'

'Her name and address.'

He licked his lips. 'I can't. I can't tell you. She's married, you see. Her husband – she said she was doing overtime because they were short-staffed. If he found out—'

'Mr Thompson, don't you realise that this young lady,

whoever she is, is your alibi? I promise you that we'll be as discreet as possible when we interview her, but you must give me her name.' Thompson shook his head unhappily. 'You realise that if you refuse, we're bound to wonder about your story? There are certain pieces of evidence which suggest—'

'Oh Christ, you still think I killed her! I swear I didn't! Why should I? She was nothing to me!' Slider said nothing, and Thompson dropped his gaze, concentrating on pushing his beer mug round and round by the handle. 'Look,' he said at last. 'I'll speak to her. Ask her what she thinks. If she says it's all right, I'll ring you. Or get her to ring you.' He looked up desperately. 'It's the best I can do. I can't give her away, just to save myself.'

Well, there's a turn up, Slider thought. Chivalry from this little shit. Of course, it was possible that he wanted time to speak to the nurse in order to coordinate stories, but Slider didn't think so. Whatever Atherton thought, Slider didn't believe that Thompson was the murderer.

They left the pub together. Outside Slider said, 'Have you got transport, or can I give you a lift somewhere?'

'My car's over there.' He gestured towards the Alfa Spyder parked on the corner. 'How did you find the hairs in it? Or was that a trick?' he asked suddenly.

Slider shook his head. 'That day when you came in to the station to make a statement, we took it round the back and went over it.'

'Are you allowed to do that?' Thompson demanded with a little return of vitality.

'Oh yes,' Slider said gently. Thompson sagged again, and turned away to trail miserably over to his car. Slider watched him go, but his attention was not all for Thompson. Some sixth sense was nagging at him, pulling him towards the alley on the other side of the pub. Something had moved there in the shadows. He walked slowly back, making a bit of business with straightening his raincoat belt, so that he could glance down the alley under his raised arm.

There was nothing. And yet something had disturbed him. It was an animal sense of danger that policemen develop, an instinct about being watched: a sort of subliminal awareness of more incoming stimuli than can be accounted for. He walked back to his car, more certain than ever that the tree up which Atherton was barking contained only a mare's nest full of red herrings.

O'Flaherty looked up. 'Did you get him?'

'Yes. Did you ring Irene?'

'I did. I told her you'd not be home till late.'

'What did she say?'

'She said nothing.' He regarded his friend massively, mournfully. 'I'm askin' you to be careful, darlin'. Now that's all. I'm asking you that, for this isn't a bit like you.'

Slider tried to smile, and found it a surprising effort. 'What a lot of interest you and Atherton are taking in my welfare these days. I can't meet either of you without getting spoonfuls of advice.'

'It's because we love you,' O'Flaherty said with a con man's sincerity.

'It's because you've nothing better to think about.'

'Well, sure, you could be right. And how was your Thompson type?'

'Scared stiff. And look, Pat, there was something else. When I came out of the pub, I had that old, old feeling. Someone was watching us.'

O'Flaherty's face pricked up as visibly as a dog's ears. 'Ah, Jaysus, I knew there was something else! Did you get sight of him?'

'I saw nothing. Why?'

'There was a feller hanging round the station when I came in tonight, and there was something about him that rang a bell, but I just couldn't place him in me memory.'

'What sort of man?'

'Professional lounger. Little runt of a man like a bookie's tout. A real little shit, you know, and Billy, I may be bad at names, but I never forget faeces. I seen him before on the watch, but for the life of me I can't pin him down.'

'I see. Well, I'll be careful. Keep trying to think where you've seen him before, and if you see him again, grab him.'

'I will. Sure and he may be nothin' to do with it at all, but—'

'Yes, but,' Slider agreed, and went to his room to write his report. When he had finished he sat for a while with his face in his hands, rubbing and rubbing at his eyes with the heels of his hands in a way which would make an oculist feel faint. His neck ached and he felt tired and depressed, and he wondered if he were sickening for a cold, and knew he wasn't really. It was just his mind trying to escape from things it didn't want to face up to.

Like going home. He tried to think seriously about going home, and found himself instead remembering Joanna sitting up on her knees, naked in the firelight. He wished he could have drawn her as she was just then. He imagined himself a great artist, and Joanna his famous model/mistress. He saw an attic room in Paris, plain white walls bathed in sunshine, Joanna lounging naked on a crimson velvet divan. Then he changed the studio into a self-catering studio flat in a holiday apartment block in Crete. A fortnight's holiday with Joanna after this case was cleared up – to recuperate because he'd had a breakdown through working too hard. And what would Freddie Cameron say about a man who ran away from reality as hard as that?

He smiled at himself and reached for the phone. A man must face reality, deal with his responsibilities, perform his duties, without sparing himself.

He dialled the number, and Joanna answered at the first ring.

'Were you crouched over it?'

'It was beside me. Are you all right? Do you want to come over?'

'It's late. It isn't really fair to put upon you like that.'

'Oh nuts. Who do you think you're talking to?'

'I need you,' he said with difficulty.

'I need you too.' As easy as that. 'Will you stop wasting time?'

He drove by a roundabout route, checking frequently in his rear-view mirror, and when he got to Turnham Green he parked around the corner from Joanna's and walked the rest, eyes and ears stretched, passing her door and pausing beyond the streetlamp to test the air. Nothing. He returned to her house and knocked softly on the door and she let him in at once and said nothing until she had closed the door behind him.

'What was all that about? What were you doing?'

'Making sure I wasn't being followed.'

'That's what I thought. Are you in danger? Or is Irene on to you already?'

He didn't answer. He took her in his arms and buried his face in her hair and then her beck, revelling in the feeling and the smell and the accessible warmth of her. 'That last evening in Florence,' he said, muffled. 'You didn't tell me you went for a meal with Anne-Marie.'

'There was nothing unusual in that. We often ate together.'

'Tell me about it. Where did you go?'

She pulled her face back from him, considering. 'Actually,

I'd already eaten before the rehearsal, but she said she was hungry and wanted me to come with her, for the company. I didn't mind – you have to do something. We went to a restaurant nearby—'

'Who chose it? You or her?'

'She did. I wasn't eating – I just watched while she ate.'

'You didn't have anything at all? Nothing to eat or drink?'

'Well, she tried to persuade me to have a glass of wine to keep her company, but I don't like to drink before a concert. So I had a cup of coffee.'

'Was it brought in a cup? Or a pot?'

She looked puzzled. 'Just a cup of espresso, that's all. Why?'

'And when did you start feeling ill?'

'Ill? Oh, it was just a touch of the Montezumas – rather a bad one, though. I couldn't do the concert – just couldn't get off the pan.'

'That was back at the concert hall?'

'I felt a bit queasy as we were walking back. Then just as I was changing it struck. It must have been what I had for supper, I suppose. I had been a bit stupid and eaten some figs.' He didn't reply, and, watching his face she said, 'What are you saying? You don't mean—? Oh no! Come on, that's ridiculous.'

'Is it? I think you were deliberately put out of action for the concert.'

'But she couldn't have put anything in my coffee without my knowing it.'

'She chose the restaurant. That was all she needed to do.'

'Dear God!' She broke away from him and walked a few steps as though trying to distance herself from the unpleasant idea. 'But what was it all in aid of? Why should she want me out of the way?'

'It may be that was the night she swapped violins. She

played the Strad in the concert, and you were the one person who would notice.' She only looked at him, still disbelieving. 'Did you notice at any time that she had a large carpet bag with her?'

'Only the one she brought her dress clothes in. It was under her chair during the rehearsal.'

'And what did she do with it after the rehearsal?'

'I don't remember. I suppose she took it back to the dressing-room.'

'Try to remember. It's important.'

'Let me think. Let me think. What did we do? Wait, I remember now! We had to put our fiddles in a lock-up, because the dressing-rooms didn't lock. She asked me to take her fiddle for her while she took her bag to the dressing-room, and then we met again outside at the stage door.'

'So you didn't actually see what she did with the bag? Did she have it with her later?'

Joanna shrugged. 'I didn't notice. Once the Montezumas struck, I wasn't noticing anything.'

'So she might have given it to someone, or left it somewhere for someone to collect, while you were putting her fiddle away.'

She looked carefully at his thoughtful face. 'You really think she was mixed up with some smuggling racket? Some big organisation?'

'I don't know. It's possible.'

'I just can't believe it. Not Anne-Marie.'

'Well, it's only one possible theory. We've really nothing to go on yet.' She still looked unhappy and a little anxious, and so he took her into his arms, and said simply, 'Can I make love to you?'

In the bedroom, she undressed and lay on the bed waiting while he struggled with his own more complicated clothes, and she looked flat and white in the unfiltered streetlight, and when he was ready and she lifted her arms to him, they seemed to rise almost disembodied from a great depth, white arms lifting from a dark sea in supplication, like Helle drowning.

His flesh was cold against hers, starting into warmth where it touched her. He took her face in his hands and kissed her, for once the protector, not the supplicant. Just now she needed him for comfort and reassurance as much as he needed her. It was done between them quickly, not hurriedly but in silence, a thing of great need and great kindness, and no great moment. Afterwards she pulled the covers over him and eased him over onto his side, his head on her shoulder. She kissed him once and folded her arms round him, and feeling at once the blissful heat of her flesh start up all around him, he passed without knowledge into a deep, quiet sleep.

12

Guilt Edged

The shriek of the phone woke him so violently that he could feel his heartbeat pounding all over his body, and a sour, tight ball of panic in his throat. For a moment he didn't know where he was, and then almost immediately the panic resolved into the fear that he had slept the whole night through again, and had been missed at home, and was in trouble.

Cold air trickled down his body as Joanna sat up and reached for the receiver.

'Hullo? Yes. Yes he is. Just a minute.'

Slider sat up too, and sought out the green devil-eyes of the digital clock, and found it was half past two. The air in the bedroom was evilly cold. The weather must be changing. Joanna gave him the receiver and he took it back under the covers with him.

It was O'Flaherty, of course. 'Are you never goin' to go home at all?'

'What's up, Pat?'

'Trouble. You'd better get back here quick – I'll fill you in on the details when you get here. Your little pal Thompson has bought it.'

'Dead?' So soon? Slider felt an undersea confusion working about in his brain. How could it be so soon?

'As mutton. So would you please, sir, very kindly get your for Chrissakes arse over here?'

The Alfa Spyder was parked outside a derelict house in a disagreeably neglected side street about a quarter of a mile from where Thompson lived. A late-night reveller, reeling home, had noticed something odd about the car and taken a closer look. Then, public-spirited despite his terror, he had telephoned the local police before declining to have anything more to do with it and heading rapidly and anonymously into oblivion.

Slider stared down at what had quite recently been Simon Thompson. He was lying across the front seats of his car, his legs doubled up, one arm hanging, and his throat was so deeply and thoroughly cut that only the spinal column was keeping his head on at all. There was blood everywhere. The seat and carpet were soaked with it, as were his left sleeve and the upper part of his clothing. With the tilting of his head, it had even run back into his hair and ears. His eyes were open and staring, his lips were parted, and his cosmetically white teeth had a brown crust around them.

On the floor of the car, under his trailing hand, there was a short-bladed surgical scalpel, presumably the murder weapon, though this was obviously meant to look like a suicide. Slider looked once more at those dark love-locks, dense and sticky with blood, and turned away, sick with anger and remorse.

They hadn't wasted any time. They had got to Thompson before Slider had even begun to be properly worried. He should have been more cautious. He *should* have worried, knowing what he thought they were. He might have prevented this.

The detective constable from 'N' District who had accompanied him, now handed him a small piece of paper. He was very young, and he looked very sick. Slider was interested to note with the professional part of his mind that a West Indian could be visibly pale, on the verge of greenness.

'We found this, sir, in his right hand. It was what put us on to you.'

Slider opened it out. It had been crushed rather than folded. In horribly uneven writing, speaking eloquently of great fear, it said, *Tell Inspector Slider. I did it. I can't stand it any more.*

The green young detective constable watched him, curiosity restoring some of the blood to his head. 'Do you know what it means, sir? Did you know him?'

'Oh yes,' said Slider. 'I know all about him.'

Slider didn't get home at all. At seven o'clock he had an enormous breakfast in the Highbury station canteen – fried egg, bacon, two sausages, tomatoes, fried bread, and several cups of tea – surprising himself with his own appetite until he remembered he had not eaten the night before. The food warmed him and started his blood running and his brain working, and the period before began to take on a comforting flavour of unreality. He almost stopped remembering that Simon Thompson had blood in his open eyes, that his eyelashes were stiff with it, like some weird punk mascara. At least he stopped minding about it.

Freddie Cameron, grumbling routinely, did the examination.

'What can I tell you?' he said to Slider on the phone. 'Cause of death asphyxiation, of course. The windpipe was completely

200

severed. I've sent the internal organs for analysis, but there's no indication of poisoning. Still, you never know. Suicides are notorious for liking a belt as well as braces.'

'Was it suicide?'

Cameron whistled a little phrase. 'You tell me. You're the detective. The wound was equally consistent with suicidal throat-cutting by a left-handed man, or homicidal throat-cutting by ditto standing behind the victim. Was your man left-handed?'

'I don't know.'

'He would also have had to be extremely determined. One never knows how difficult it is to cut a human throat until one tries, and there are usually a number of superficial, preliminary cuts in a case of suicide. It's quite unusual for a suicide to cut so deeply at the first attempt. The edges aren't haggled at all.'

'I suppose the weapon *was* the weapon?'

'No reason to suppose it wasn't.'

'I was surprised at the amount of blood.'

'Who would have thought the old man had so much blood in him? Well, it was a mighty cut, let's say. The heart would have gone on pumping for a moment or two. And alcohol expands the blood vessels.'

'Alcohol?'

'As in Dutch courage. Or Scotch courage in this case. I was nearly gassed when I opened the stomach. There must have been better than a quarter bottle of whisky, only just consumed. You want it not to be suicide, I gather.'

'Do you gather? No, really, I'd sooner it was, but I don't think it was.'

'Nor do I.'

'Opinions, Freddie? That's not like my cautious old medico,' Slider said with a faint smile.

'Firstly, I don't believe in that first-time cut. And secondly

201

there was a fresh chip out of one of his front teeth. The sort of thing that might happen if someone forced you to drink whisky straight out of a bottle, and you struggled.'

Slider was silent, feeling cold at this new image to add to the scenario. 'To render him passive, I suppose,' he muttered.

'Or to add colour to the suicide motif, I don't know. So you'll be looking for your left-handed murderer again, like any Agatha Christie gumshoe?'

'Mixed metaphor,' Slider warned. 'Or at least, mixed media. Anyway, by the evidence of the scalpel, we're looking for a left-handed surgeon.'

'Surgeons can cut with either hand, you ignoramus.'

'Can they?'

'Of course. I can myself. Surely you knew that? Was the note any help, by the way?'

'None at all. Very Agatha Christie, in fact.' Slider was glad to change the subject. 'Though I suppose anyone theatrical enough to commit suicide might easily have the bad taste to leave a melodramatic note. But would a left-handed murderer be clever enough to try a double bluff like that? There wasn't any bruising. I suppose?' he asked wistfully. 'After all, he must have been forced to write that note. You couldn't get up a bruised wrist for me?'

'Unless he was very courageous, the threat of a sharp blade at his throat would probably have been enough to make him write anything he was told to,' Cameron pointed out.

'He wasn't very courageous,' Slider said, thinking of Thompson bunched over his drink with the pain of his fear. The brave die once, he thought, but the frightened die many times over.

Atherton went with WDC Swilley to interview Helen Morris, and returned a sadder and wiser man.

'She was a little upset,' he told Slider, not meeting his eyes.

'Sit down,' Slider said. 'You look whacked.'

'So do you,' Atherton countered, and opened his mouth to offer his superior comfort, before wisely closing it again. He folded himself down into a chair and laid his long-boned hands on the edge of Slider's desk. 'Well, she identified the writing as Thompson's all right. His left-handed writing, she said.'

Slider's brows went up.

Atherton grimaced. 'Simon Thompson was ambidextrous. Apparently he was left-handed as a child, but playing the violin forced him to become right-handed. You can't play the fiddle back to front because the strings come out in the wrong order and you'd be bowing up when everyone else was bowing down.'

'Is that wrong?'

'Untidy. Anyway, Morris said he could write with either hand, but more usually wrote with his right hand, though for most other purposes he was completely ambidextrous.'

'Is nothing in this damned case ever going to be straightforward?'

'It seems straightforward enough to me, guv. In the emotional stress of his contemplated suicide, he reverted to his ingrained childhood habits, his natural left-handedness.'

'And the chipped tooth?'

'Suppose his hands were shaking? He could easily have done that himself.'

Slider shook his head. 'I wish I could go along with you. But I have an image of that human rabbit threatened by a very inhuman stoat with a sharp blade; so terrified, he writes the note, but in a last desperate attempt to tell the world all is not as it seems, he writes with his left hand, which Helen Morris at least will know is not usual.'

'But he cut his throat left-handed.'

'The murderer, who is very clever, as we know, notices that his victim is left-handed and proceeds to cut his throat for him in a consistent manner.'

Atherton lifted his hands and dropped them. 'That's pure Hans Andersen. The whole cloth. If the murderer was so very clever, why didn't he make the cut look more like suicide?'

'Perhaps he didn't know his own strength. More likely Thompson wouldn't sit still for a nice artistic haggling. One quick, hard slash, and it was all over.'

'Well, I dunno,' Atherton said, sighing. He rubbed the back of his left hand with the fingers of his right. 'It all seems a bit tenuous. If Thompson murdered Anne-Marie Austen, and then committed suicide, it would all make sense, and be so much simpler.

'And we could all go home to tea,' Slider finished for him. He could see that even Atherton had his moments of wanting to run away from reality. 'All the same, life is never that symmetrical.'

'And all the same again, there's actually no evidence that it wasn't suicide,' Atherton pointed out. 'Only your artistic sensibilities.'

There was a silence.

'Any luck at The Dog and Scrotum?'

'Nothing yet. But I'm not finished there, and I'm pretty sure Hilda knows something. I'm going to have another crack at her tonight.'

'Hilda always looks as if she's hiding something,' Slider said. 'Don't fall into that old trap.'

'We've got to have something to show up at the meeting, though. The Super's going to be asking questions about what we do all day.'

'Work our balls off.'

'Yes, but an oeuvre's not an oeuf.'

'Come again?'

'Skip it. Pearls before swine,' Atherton said loftily.

'Eggsactly,' Slider said with a quiet smile.

The young man was quietly spoken, neatly dressed, sensible – every policeman's dream of a witness.

'I noticed the car because it was an MGB roadster. I love MGs. I used to have one myself, but now we've got a kid it isn't practical.'

Married, with child, Atherton noted. Better and better.

'You didn't notice the registration number, I suppose?'

' 'Fraid not. Only that it was a Y registration.'

'Colour?'

'Bright red. I think they call it vermilion.'

He told his story. He had been waiting in the car park of The Dog and Sportsman for his wife, who was working the back shift at United Dairies in Scrubs Lane. They were both working every hour they could, to get together the deposit for a house. Now they had the baby, they wanted to get settled in a place of their own.

Who looked after the baby? – Denise's mum, who lived in the council flats in North Pole Road. That's why they met at The Dog and Sportsman. A bloke from the Dairies dropped Denise off there, Paul picked her up, and they drove round to collect the baby and then home to Latimer Road.

That particular evening he had got there a bit early, so he was just sitting in his car watching the traffic for Denise to turn up, when the roadster had come along. The girl was driving it very fast and flashily, screaming her tyres as she whipped into the car park, breaking hard, and backing into the space opposite him in one movement. When she got out of the car, he'd thought to himself that she was a pretty girl playing tough. She was dressed in a donkey jacket and jeans and short boots, which with a girl as pretty as that made you look twice all right.

What time was that? – About twenty to ten, more or less. He hadn't looked at his watch, but Denise usually got there about a quarter to, and it wasn't more than five minutes before she arrived. Maybe less.

Well, so this girl got out of the car and went towards the pub, and then this man appeared in front of her. No, he didn't see where he came from – he'd been looking at the car. He just sort of stepped out of the shadows between the parked cars. She stopped at once and they spoke a few words, and then they went back to her car and got in and drove away. That was all.

What did the man look like? – Well, he didn't get a close look at him. He was tall, and wearing an overcoat, a scarf, and one of those brown hats like Lord Oaksey wears on the television. What do you call them, trilbies? Not a young man. How did he know? Well, it was just a sort of impression. Besides, young men didn't wear hats, did they? He didn't see his face, because the hat and scarf sort of overshadowed it. He didn't think he'd recognise him again. Just a well-to-do, middle-aged man in a dark coat and hat.

Did she seem to know the man? What was her reaction to him?

The young man frowned in thought.

Yes, she knew him. She didn't seem to be surprised to see him there. Wait a minute, though – when she first saw him, she turned her head and looked quickly round the car park as if to check if anyone were watching. No, he was sure neither of them saw him. His lights were off and they didn't even glance his way. Just for the first minute he'd thought the man had stepped out to rob her, snatch her handbag or something, and that she'd looked around for help. But that wasn't it. And it was all over in a second. The man said something; she answered; he said something else; and they went back to her car and got in and drove back the way she had come, down Wood Lane towards Shepherd's Bush.

Atherton closed his notebook. 'Thank you very much, Mr Ringham. You've been very helpful. Now if you should remember anything else, anything at all, no matter how trivial it seems to you, you will be sure to let me know, won't you. You can reach me on this number.'

'Yes, okay – but look here, I won't be involved in anything, will I? I mean, I can't identify this man or anything, and I've got Denise and the kid to think about.'

Well, all witnesses have their limitations, Atherton thought, and reassured him with some vaguenesses and long words. In his own powder-blue Sierra, driving home to the sanctuary of his civilised little house, cat, real fire and elegant supper, he wondered how far this had got them. Enter Mr X in sinister trilby. He never trusted men who wore hats like that. So they now knew that she met the murderer at The Dog and Scrotum, and though the description was not promising, it might just as well have been Thompson. He was just the kind of jerk who would attempt to disguise himself by wearing a very obvious hat and muffler.

Anyway, at least they knew that she went to the White City in her own car. It would be worth interviewing the residents of Barry House again and asking about a red MGB. Surely someone must have noticed such a speciality car?

The atmosphere in the house was as icy as Slider had expected it to be.

Irene gave him a boiled stare and said, 'There's nothing for supper, except what's in the fridge. I wasn't to know you'd be home, and I'm not endlessly cooking meals to throw them away.'

'It's all right,' said Slider patient under insult. 'I can get myself something.' Even as he said it, he wondered what. Irene was not the sort of person to tolerate leftovers. The fridge would most likely be as innocent of food as an operating-table of germs – and for much the same reason. Atherton had long ago pointed out to him – in a different context of course – the correlation between lack of sexual outlet and an obsession with hygiene.

Both the children were home and had friends in, and Slider was able to use them, as so often before, as a screen. He asked Matthew about his football match, and sat through an interminable verbal action-replay. Matthew's friend, a pinch-nosed, adenoidal boy called Sibod, with such flamingly red hair that it looked like a deliberate insult, repeated everything half a beat behind, so that Slider got it all, or rather failed to get it at all, in an unsynchronised, faulty stereophony.

'So you won, then, did you?' Slider asked at last, groping for comprehension.

'Well, yes, we did win,' Matthew said with an anxious frown, 'and if we win again next Saturday against Beverley's, we win the Shield. Only they're very good, and if we only draw, it goes on goals, and we didn't do very well on goals.' From his worried expression, it was plain that the whole responsibility for their goal-less state rested on his shoulders. Like father, like son.

'Well, even if you don't win, it doesn't matter, as long as you do your best,' Slider said, as parents have said throughout the ages. Simon and Matthew both looked uncomprehending of his stupidity.

'But it's the Shield!' Matthew began, desperate to get this point across to unfeeling parenthood.

Slider forestalled him hastily. 'Matthew, is that bubble gum you're eating? I've told you again and again, I won't have you eating that disgusting stuff. Take it out and throw it away.'

'But you let me eat chewing gum,' Matthew protested. 'Only you can't make decent bubbles with chewing gum.'

'Chewing gum's different,' Slider said. The next question would be why. And since he didn't know, other than that it was personal prejudice, because the smell of bubble gum reminded him of the smell of the rubber mask they used to put over your face to give you gas in the dental hospital back in the dark ages of his childhood, he took refuge in authority.

'Please don't argue with me. Just do as I say. Take it out and throw it away, please – and wrap it in something first,' he added as Matthew, sighing heavily, stumped off towards the kitchen. Simon followed him, and he felt Irene's eye on him, saying as clearly as words, My how you love to play the heavy father, don't you? It's all Action Man, as long as it's only a couple of kids you have to stand up to.

He postponed being alone with her and her eye by going upstairs to see Kate, who was locked into one of her intensely private and uncomfortably ritualised games with Slider's least favourite of her best friends – a fat child called Emma who was so relentlessly sentimental and feminine that it made him squirm with embarrassment. When he pushed open the bedroom door, they were engaged in being schoolteachers to a class of six dolls, including a bald and one-legged Barbie of hideous aspect, a toy monkey and a bear. Emma's part at the point of his entry was confined to watching admiringly and breathing heavily through her mouth, but Kate was haranguing her victims in such tones of hectoring sarcasm that Slider wondered afresh if that was the way adults really appeared to children.

'I think I've told you before never, never to do that, haven't

I?' Kate was saying to the teddy bear. Slider had long ago named it Gladly, because its eyes were sewn on asymmetrically, and there had been a hymn he had sung in Sunday school when he was a child called 'Gladly my Cross I'd Bear'. Kate had accepted the name unquestioningly as she accepted all the incomprehensibilities of the grown-up world, as if they were nothing to do with her. Slider remembered being as young as that, with a mind gloriously untrammelled by a knowledge of the probabilities. When he was very small, he'd thought God's name was Harold, because of the second line of the Lord's Prayer, and it had not seemed at all surprising. Similarly he had believed for a very long time that there was a senior government official called The Lord Priwy, whose rod of office was an eel.

The thing, he thought, that marked him apart from his own children was that when he learned the truth of these matters it struck him as interesting and memorable. Nothing, he felt, would ever interest Kate beyond her own immediate sensations. She had already created herself in what she considered an acceptable image, and while that image would undergo subtle alterations year by year, the primary purpose of her life would always be the maintenance of whatever was the current version.

He regarded her sadly as she broke off her diatribe and looked at him with disfavour, minute fists on hips, lips narrowed in an uncomfortably familiar way. How was it, he thought, that without ever in the least intending to, we recreate our idiosyncrasies in our children? Already Matthew was exhibiting signs of Slider's overdeveloped sense of responsibility, his indecisiveness and tendency to worry about what he could not change. And Kate was turning day by day into a grotesque caricature of her mother. How could it have happened? For in sad truth, he had spent horribly little time with either of them since they were babies. Once they had settled into regular bedtimes, they had been lost to him. It must be Original Sin, he thought sadly.

He had intended asking his daughter about her fête, but she said, 'Go away, Daddy. We don't want you now,' and self-respect and a sense of duty obliged him instead to deliver a lecture on good manners. Kate listened to it with indifferent eyes and the patience of one who knows that resistance will only prolong the interruption. She was so different in that respect from Matthew, who would have flung himself into the situation with the burning conviction of a martyr, and ended in tears. Kate, Slider thought, had been born aged well over forty. Having finished with his bit of role-play, he left the room, and before he had shut the door behind him he heard Kate's instant resumption of hers: 'Now I'm sure you don't want me to have to smack you again, do you?' Even from his limited knowledge of Kate's games, he didn't think Gladly had much chance of talking himself out of that one.

And now there was no alternative but to descend to the realm of snow and ice, and face up to his other responsibility; his other, he supposed, creation – for Irene had not always been like this, and what could have shaped her apart from the interaction of his influence on her basic matter? She was sitting on the sofa staring at the television, though he knew she wasn't watching it. It was, however, The News, and one of the rules Irene had made for herself was that The News was important and mustn't be disturbed or talked during.

As far as he could see the news was itself and always the same: on the screen now was a battered street in some hot part of the world where houses are made of concrete filled with steel rods, like motorway bridges. An intermittent brattle of machine-gun fire was punctuating the urgent, segmented commentary, and interchangeable men in identical drab battledress were running and ducking and, presumably, dying. It struck him as odd how news of war, though it was repetitive and completely unsurprising, should be regarded as 'real' news, whereas anything which exemplified the kindness or inventiveness or compassion of human beings was included, if at all, only at the end of the bulletin as a sop to old ladies and housewives – the 'And finally' item.

All the same he was glad for the moment of the flickering images of death and suffering as a way to avoid talking to his wife. How many marriages were kept intact that way, he wondered wearily. His mind felt numb and exhausted with the effort of guilt and anxiety, and the frustration of being in the middle of a maze with no idea which was the way out, or even if there was one. Irene; the children; Anne-Marie; Thompson; Atherton; the Super: all revolved like Macbeth's witches, indistinct, dangerous, clamouring for his attention – all expecting answers from him, who had no idea even of the questions. O'Flaherty's voice waxed and waned like the sea, warning him of some danger in a booming, portentous voice; and far, far away, small and clear like something seen through crystal, was Joanna – almost out of reach, too far, and fading, fading . . .

'If you're going to fall asleep, you might as well go to bed,' Irene said, jerking him back out of a doze. The news had finished, to be replaced by that witless sitcom about a couple who had reversed their traditional roles, she going out to work while he stayed home and minded the house. The laughs were presumably generated by the sight of a man wearing an apron and not knowing how to operate the dishwasher. It was depressingly 1950s.

'Eh?' he said, trying to look interested in the programme. The man was holding a nappy and looking at the baby with a puzzled expression. Any minute now he would say 'Now which end does this go on?'

'It's useless sitting there pretending you're watching when you were snoring a minute ago,' Irene went on, and then, with an excess of vicious irritation, 'I hate it when your head slips over, and you keep jerking it up every three seconds!'

'I'm sorry,' he said humbly, meaning it, and she just looked at him with a resentment so chronic, so weary, that he was filled with a sense of helplessness. It was so vast that for a moment it seemed to blot out his personality entirely. He ought to take her hand, ask her what was wrong, try to reach her and comfort her, this woman whom he daily hurt and saddened; and yet how could he help her, when it was the simple fact of his existence which made her unhappy? He couldn't ask what was wrong, when there was nothing he could do to put it right, and the pity he felt was as useless, as unuseable, as that which he felt for the crumpled bodies on the television news film. That was the intractable, daily dilemma of married life, and it blocked the flow of tenderness, and finally even killed the desire for it.

'I'm sorry,' he said again. It would have been better not to have spoken, to have got up in silence and gone up to bed, leaving the unsayable unsaid. She knew it too. She turned her head away from him, a gesture of adult hurt he had seen her make almost all their lives together.

'For what?' she said.

For what indeed? For the fact that the only way he could live with his crippling sense of responsibility was to be a policeman and do the one thing he could do well to make the world a better place. Fat comfort.

'It isn't nice for me either,' he said at last. 'Never being home. Never seeing my children. Do you know, Kate looked at me just now like a stranger. She just stood there waiting for me to go away again.'

There were many things Irene might have said or done in

213

response to that appeal, but instead, after a short silence, she said in a neutral voice, 'Marilyn Cripps rang earlier on.'

The Cripps were a couple they had met some time ago at a garden party: he was a magistrate, and she was on the PC of Dorney Church and was a voluntary steward for the National Trust at Cliveden. They had a large detached house and a son at Eton, and Irene had been almost humble when after the first meeting Mrs Cripps had proved willing to continue the acquaintance. That was the kind of society she had always longed for; the sort she would have had as of right if Slider had only been promoted as he ought to have been. The wife of a police commissioner might mix on equal terms with the highest in the land.

'She asked us to a dinner party,' she went on unemphatically, 'but I couldn't accept without consulting you. With most husbands, of course, that would be just a formality, but with you I suppose it's hardly even worth asking.'

'Well, when is it, exactly,' Slider began dishonestly, for he knew her indifferent tone of voice was assumed.

'What's the point? Even if you say yes, when the time comes you'll call it off at the last minute, which is so *rude* to the hostess. Or you'll turn up late, which is worse. And even if you do go, you'll complain about having to wear a dinner jacket, and sulk, and sit there staring at the wall and saying nothing, and start like an imbecile if anyone talks to you.'

'Why don't you go without me?' Slider said cautiously.

'Don't be stupid!' She showed a flash of anger. 'We were invited as a couple. You don't go to dinner parties like that on your own. I wouldn't be so inconsiderate as to suggest it.'

There was nothing he could say to that, so he kept silent. After a moment she went on, in a low, grumbling tone, like a volcano building up to its eruption.

'I hate going out without you. Everyone looks at me so

pityingly, as if I were a leper. How can I have any kind of decent social life with you? How am I ever going to meet anyone. It's bad enough living on this estate—'

'I thought you liked this estate.'

'You know nothing about what I like!' she flared. 'I liked it all right as a start, but I never thought we'd be staying here permanently. I thought you'd get on, and then we'd move to somewhere better; somewhere like Datchet or Chalfont, where nice people live. Somewhere the children can make the right sort of friends. Somewhere where they give dinner parties!'

Slider managed not to smile at that, for she was deadly serious. 'Well, if you're not happy here, we'll move,' he said. 'Why don't you start looking round—'

'How can we move?' she cried, goaded. 'We can't afford anywhere decent on what you earn! God knows you're never here, you work long enough hours – or so you tell me – but where does it get you? Other people are always being promoted ahead of you. And you know why – because they *know* you've got no ambition. You don't care. You won't speak up for yourself. You won't make the effort to be nice to the right people . . .'

'There's such a thing as pride—'

'Oh! Pride! Are you proud of being everyone's dogsbody? Are you proud of being left all the rotten jobs? Being left behind by men half your age? They don't respect you for it, you know. I've seen you at those department parties, standing on your own, refusing to talk to anyone in case they think you're sucking up to them. And I've seen the way they look at you. You embarrass them. You're a white elephant.'

She stopped abruptly, hearing the echo of her own words, unforgivable, on the air. He was silent. Policemen should never marry, he thought dully, because they couldn't honour all their obligations and still do their job properly. And yet if

215

they didn't marry, like priests they wouldn't be whole people; and how could they do their job properly if they were in ignorance of the way ninety per cent of people lived?

For a fleeting, guilty moment he thought of Joanna, and how if he were married to someone like her it would be all right. No, not someone like her, but *her*. With her he could be a good policeman, and happy. Happy and good, and understood. His tired mind reeled. He mustn't think about Joanna in the middle of a row with Irene. That was bad.

'I'm sorry,' he said, 'but this is a very bad case I'm in the middle of, and—'

She didn't wait for him to finish. 'You can't even pay me the compliment of being angry, can you. Oh God!' She stared at him, furious and helpless, frozen like an illustration in the *Strand Magazine*. 'Baffled' was the word they would have used.

'Look, I'm sorry,' he began again, 'but this is a particularly horrible case. An old woman and a young man have been killed since the original murder, and I feel partly to blame for that. It's going to take up all my time and energy until I can get further forward, and that simply can't be helped. But I promise you, when it's over, we'll really get down to it and have a long talk, and try to sort things out. Will you try and be patient, please?'

She shrugged.

'And now I think I will go up to bed. I haven't had any sleep for ages, and I'm dead beat.'

Typically, once he had gone upstairs and undressed and cleaned his teeth and got into bed, he found himself wide awake, his mind ready and eager to tramp endlessly over the beaten ground of the case. In self-defence he took up his bedside book, a long-neglected and suitably soporific Jeffrey Archer, and thus was still sitting up reading when Irene came in.

'I thought you were dead beat,' she said neutrally. The heaviness of her tread spoke of her unhappiness: she had always been a brisk, light mover.

'Getting ready for bed woke me up, so I thought I'd read for a bit,' he said. She turned away to make her own preparations, and he watched her covertly while pretending to be engrossed in the book. In complete contrast to Joanna, she was a woman who looked better dressed than undressed: she had the kind of figure that clothes were designed to look good on, but which was of little interest viewed solely as a body. She was slender without being either rounded or supple; she had straight arms and legs, flat hips, and small, dim breasts which, he thought now, had only ever made him feel sad.

Once, in the few weeks at the very beginning of their marriage, they had both slept naked, but the idea was now so remote that it surprised him to remember it. After those first weeks, Irene had begun to wear her trousseau nightdresses because 'it was a shame to waste them', and he had begun to wear pyjamas because to continue naked while she slept clothed seemed too pointed, like a criticism.

She came back from the bathroom bringing the smell of toothpaste and Imperial Leather with her, neat and almost pretty in her flowered cotton nightgown and with her dark hair composed and shiningly brushed. She was so complete, he thought, but it was not a completeness which satisfied. It was a completeness which suggested that the last word had been said about her, and that nothing about her could be any different: this was Irene, and that was that.

Again, he thought, that was in complete contrast to Joanna, who in his thoughts of her seemed always to be flowing about like an amoeba, constantly in a state of change. Away from her he found it hard accurately to remember her face. Thinking about her at all had to be done cautiously, as if it might push the malleable material of her out of shape.

Irene stopped at the foot of the bed, and was looking at him, her head a little lowered, chewing her bottom lip in a way that made her appear uncharacteristically vulnerable. She had a barrel-at-the-edge-of-Niagara look about her which warned him that she was about to broach a dangerous subject, and he wished he could forestall her; but to do so was to admit that there was no longer any point in caring enough to quarrel, and he couldn't quite do that to her.

'What's the matter?' he asked when it was plain she needed a shove.

For another long moment she hesitated, teetering, and then, all in a rush, she said, 'I know all about her – your girlfriend.'

Strange how the body acknowledged guilt even when the mind felt none. For a moment the hot, peppery fluid of it completely replaced his blood and rushed around his body, making his heart thump unexpectedly in his stomach; yet even while that was happening he had replied calmly and without measurable hesitation, 'I haven't got a girlfriend.'

Irene made a restless, negating movement and went on as if he hadn't spoken. Of course, I've known for some time that something was going on, but I didn't know what. I mean, the fact that we haven't made love for fifteen months—'

He was stricken that she knew exactly how long it was. He could only have guessed. But female lives were marked out in periods and pills, and sex for them, he supposed, would always be tied to dates.

'And then, all those times that you're not here – well, some of them are work, I suppose, but not all of them. But I wasn't sure until quite recently what it was.'

'There's nothing going on. You're just imagining things,' he said, but she looked at him, and he saw in the depths of her expression not anger but a terrible hurt; and he saw in one unwelcome moment of insight how for a woman this was a wound which would not heal. A man whose wife was unfaithful would be consumed with anger, outrage, jealousy perhaps; but to a wife, unfaithfulness was a deep sickness that ate away at the bones of self.

'You don't have to lie to me,' she said. 'I could tell from their voices that they knew all about it, Nicholls and O'Flaherty, when they phoned me up with your excuses. And Atherton – I've seen the way he looks at me, pityingly. I suppose they all know – everyone except me. And laugh about it. What a gay dog you are! I bet they slap your back and congratulate you, don't they?'

'You're wrong, completely wrong—'

'I've put up with it so far. But now you've started sleeping the night with her, and using this case as your excuse, and I'm damned if I'll put up with that! It's disgusting! And with a girl young enough to be your daughter! How could you do a thing like that?'

So many things ran through Slider's mind at that moment that he was, mercifully, prevented from speaking. For one thing he was surprised that Irene, even in the grip of oratory, should describe Joanna as being young enough to be his daughter; and another considerable number of brain cells was preoccupied with the problem of how she could possibly have found out. No one at 'F' District would give him away, he would have staked his life on that, and the notion that she had put a private detective onto him was ludicrous. And underneath these preoccupations was the thought that these were shameful things to be thinking at such a moment, and that he should be feeling bad and guilty and remorseful at having hurt Irene.

And what he did say in the end came out sounding quite

calm and natural. 'You're completely mistaken. I haven't got a girlfriend, and I certainly wouldn't be interested in anyone young enough to be my daughter.'

'Oh, you liar!' she cried softly, and with a superbly unstudied movement flung a photograph down on the bed beside him. 'Who's this, then? A perfect stranger? Don't tell me you carry a perfect stranger's picture around in your wallet. You *bastard!* You've never carried a picture of me around with you, never, not even—'

She stopped and turned away abruptly, so that he shouldn't see her crying. Slider picked up the photograph, bemused and amused and relieved and sorry, and most of all just terribly, horribly sad. From the palm of his hand Anne-Marie looked up at him, all sun-dazzle and whipped hair and eternal, unshakeable youth, the little white starfish hand against the dark blue sea frozen for ever in that moment of joyful exuberance.

Loving Joanna had stopped him being haunted by Anne-Marie, but now it all came back to him in a rush; the pointless, pitiful waste of her sordid little death. They had put her down like an old dog, stripped her with the callousness of abattoir workers, and dumped her on the grimy floor of that grim and empty flat. He remembered the childlike tumble of her hair and the pathos of her small, unripe breasts, and a pang of nameless grief settled in his stomach. It was his old grief for a world in which people did such pointlessly horrible things to each other; sorrow for the loss of the world in which he had grown up, where the good people outnumbered the bad, and there was always something to look forward to. It was the reason he had taken this job in the first place, and the thing he had to fight against, because it unmanned him and made him useless to perform it. Oh, but he and his colleagues struggled day after day and could make no jot of

220

difference to the way things were, or the way things would be, and the urge to stop struggling was so strong, so strong, because it was hopeless, wasn't it?

Irene had turned again, and now flinched from the despair in his face. She had always known there was a streak of melancholy in him, which he had tried to hide from her as from himself; but until this moment she had not known how strong it was, or how deep it went. She remembered all at once those stories of policemen who drank themselves insensible the moment they came off duty, who took drugs, or rutted their way to oblivion through countless women's bodies; and of the policemen who committed suicide, unemphatically, like tired children lying down just anywhere to sleep. She wondered what it was that had held Slider together in the face of his own despair, and had little hope that it was her, except in so far as she and the children provided a kind of counter-irritant. She wondered how much longer it would work, and what would happen then; and whether, when the end came, she would have any right to resent her fate as victim of it.

She looked at him with the resignation of a woman who sees that she will never be as important to her husband as his work, and for whom to stop minding is the worst of the possible alternatives. Slider saw the resistance go out of her and was grateful, though he didn't know why it had happened.

He said, 'This is a photograph of the girl who was murdered, Anne-Marie Austen. The case I'm investigating. You can easily check that, if you don't believe me.'

She turned away. 'No,' she said. 'I believe you.' She pretended to be looking in a drawer, to keep her back to him, and her next words sounded curiously muffled. 'I shouldn't have looked in your wallet. I'm sorry.'

'It doesn't matter.'

'It does. I shouldn't have done it.'

He thought she was crying. 'Don't,' he said. 'Come to bed.'

But when she turned she was dry-eyed, only looked very tired. She got into bed beside him and lay down, not touching him, and then turned on her side, facing away from him, her sleep position. Slider put his book down and hesitated, looking down at her. So it was all right again. The danger was over. He had gone up the side turning and the posse had thundered past. It would be all right for a long time now because she would feel guilty about having wrongly accused him.

He wished that he could have made love to her then: it might have comforted them both, and given at least a semblance of resolution to what was otherwise unfinished business between them. But it had been too long since they last did it for habit to achieve the gesture, and he could not do it from the heart of any feelings for her. He switched out the light and lay down. Since there was Joanna, he thought in the dark, he could not do that.

13

A Woman of No Substance

The department meeting was held in the CID room, the other offices being too small to hold everyone simultaneously. The others were all there when Slider went in. WDC Swilley, who hated her real name of Kathleen so much that she actually preferred being called Norma, was sitting on one of the battered desks swinging her long, beautiful legs for the benefit of her colleagues. She was a tall, strong, athletic girl, with the golden skin, large white teeth, streaky-blonde hair, and curiously unmemorable features of a California Beach Beauty. Slider often had the feeling that he was the only member of the department she hadn't seduced, which he felt lent him a certain superiority over the others. Obviously she regarded him as a real person, while the others were only sex objects to her.

She smiled at him now and said, 'Here he comes, crumpled and in a hurry, the perfect example of the Married Middle-Management Man.'

'You missed out some. What about Menopausal?' said Beevers, sitting where he could get the best view of the famous

Legs, which often haunted his dreams. He was an almost circular young man, with thick, densely curly light-brown hair, and a rampant and disarming moustache. He was married to a tiny, round brown mouse of a woman called Mary. He adored her, but her serviceable legs only twinkled, never swung.

'How about Manic?' Atherton added.

'Not today,' Slider said, loosening his tie with an automatic gesture. 'Today I am a monument of calm. A man who has done his homework can't be shaken. Time you youngsters learned that – flair is no substitute for hard work.'

He looked around them as they groaned automatically. There was DC Anderson, just back from holiday and probably bulging with photographs he wanted to show around. He was keen on what he called 'artistic shots', which nearly all turned out to be various stages of a sunset reflected on sea and wet sand. The other DCs, wooden-headed, obsessive Hunt and quiet, introverted Mackay, were sitting solemnly side by side on hard chairs, bracketed by the sprawling charm of Swilley and Atherton, and counterpoised by stumpy Beevers, who had a bit missing from his brain and so could never be made to feel shame or embarrassment.

These, he thought, far more than the three in Ruislip, were his family; only if it were a family, he was probably the mother, while the Superintendent was the authoritarian father. They were one short at the moment, for the DCI, Colin Raisbrook, had suffered a mild heart attack and was on extended sick-leave. It was not yet clear whether he would be returning to the department. If they gave him early retirement, as Slider had long realised with an inward sigh, Irene would be expecting him to be promoted to DCI in Raisbrook's place; and if he was not, his life would be made extremely unpleasant.

'It's a filthy day,' Norma said unemphatically, staring out

of the window at the cold and steady rain, 'and due to get worse. Any moment now Dickson will come breezing through that door like an advertisement for cosmetic toothpaste, and I shall want to murder him all over again.'

'Hullo, Super!' Anderson chirruped, and Hunt obediently chanted the ritual reply.

'Hullo, Gorgeous!'

'If he calls me WDC Snockers once more, I shall murder him,' Swilley went on undeterred. 'I hate a man in authority who tries to be funny and then expects you to laugh.'

'I don't think he does,' Atherton said. 'I think he exists purely for his own gratification.'

This was too far above the head of Hunt, who brought the tone down to his own level by saying, 'But if you murdered him, Norm, what would you do with the body?'

'Sell it to the canteen,' Mackay suggested. 'Always roast pork on Wednesdays.'

'I thought they got that from Hammersmith Hospital,' Anderson joined in. 'Wasn't it Wednesday we had that pileup at Speake's Corner, the Cortina and the artic? Brought the Cortina driver out in pieces?'

'You lot don't get any better. All this fourth-form humour makes me tired,' Atherton said witheringly.

'You're always tired,' Swilley remarked with a sad shake of the head, and Anderson hooted.

'How would you know that, Norma? Let us in on your secret.'

They were interrupted, not before time in Slider's opinion, by the entry of Detective Superintendent Dickson. Dickson was large and broad and weighty, a prize bull of a man – no one would ever have thought of calling him fat – whose brisk movements, added to the sheer size of him, gave him an unstoppable impetus, like a runaway lorry. He had a wide,

225

ruddy, genial Yorkshire face, held in place by a spreading and bottled nose that spoke of a terrifying blood pressure. He had scanty, sandy hair, and a smile whose front uppers looked too numerous and regular to be his own.

He had survived years of being called Dickson of Shepherd's Bush Green by pretending that he had thought of it first, and had developed, like a compensatory limp, a passion for nicknames of his own. In a service fairly evenly divided between hard men pretending to be soft and soft men pretending to be hard, Dickson was in a category of one: a hard man pretending to be a soft man pretending to be hard. He drank whisky almost as continuously as he breathed, was never seen the worse for it, and one day would be found dead at his desk. Slider could never decide whether he would be glad or sorry at that moment.

'Good morning, lads. Good morning, Norma,' he breezed, favouring her with the full Royal Doulton. She glowered back. 'Sit down everybody. We've got a lot to get through this morning.'

It was some time before they had cleared away all the other matters and got to the murder of Anne-Marie Austen. Slider brought them up to date on what they had got so far, and then Dickson gathered their attention.

'I don't mind telling you that the powers that be are not too happy about this case – two more deaths, and nothing concrete to go on. Now either they're very good, or we're very bad, and either way we're going to lose it if we don't get something on the go. As far as the Thompson death goes, "N" District want to know if we think it's part of the same transaction and I take it that we do? All right. They'll do the legwork their end, and liaise with Atherton. Now, what have we got to follow up?'

'The Birmingham end ought to be looked into,' Atherton

said with an eye to the main chance. 'We know she was making regular trips there, and there's the question of the flat she rented which she oughtn't to have been able to afford. I could—'

'Right,' Dickson interrupted. 'Bill, you cover that. Take someone with you. Atherton, you're the musical genius around here – follow up this bloody violin. I don't believe no one's seen the thing since 1940. And get onto this Saloman bloke and find out all about him.'

'Yes, sir,' Atherton said, rolling his eyes at Slider.

'Beevers, I want you to check out the girl's aunt – your face isn't known down there. There's our money motive, strong and nice. Find out who she knows, where she goes, where she was that night. Find out about her trips to London. It's a small village, so you shouldn't have any trouble getting people to talk. Now, what else?'

'I'm convinced it's a large organisation behind it, sir,' Slider said.

'I know you are, and I have to admit it has that smell to me, but there's nothing to prove it isn't just a very ruthless individual.'

'The cuts on her foot, sir – did anything turn up about those?' Dickson didn't immediately answer, and Slider went on, watching him carefully, 'With the Italian connection, I couldn't help wondering if there wasn't some connection with the Family? Those cuts did make it look like a ritual killing.'

There was a short and palpable silence. Dickson's face went blank, his eyes uncommunicative. There's nothing I can tell you about that,' he said evenly. 'Nobody's got anything to say about the letter T.'

'Why shouldn't it be the murderer's initial?' Atherton said smoothly.

'Why indeed,' Dickson agreed, with an air of humouring him.

'Suggestion, sir,' Slider said quickly. Dickson's face became a wary blank again. 'Whether it's an organisation behind it or an individual, my guess would be that the Thompson death was meant to tie up the loose ends: murder, followed by remorse and suicide. I wonder if there might be some mileage in letting them think we bought it? If the villain or villains thought the heat was off—'

'What about Mrs Gostyn?' Atherton interposed.

'Accident. It might even have been one,' Slider said.

'We'd have to get the press to cooperate,' Dickson said, 'but it might just turn something up. I'm in favour. All right, I'll see to it.'

Slider nodded his thanks, but felt curiously unsatisfied. There was something about the way Dickson agreed that made him feel it had been decided beforehand by someone else. Something was going on. Cautiously, he slid a toe into the water. 'What about the Italian end, sir? This Cousin Mario? Can we get any cooperation on him or the house in Paradise Alley?'

Dickson's face grew redder with anger. 'I think you've got quite enough to be going on with already, finding out where she was killed, where the drug came from, what they did with her clothes, just for starters. And who's this bloke O'Flaherty says has been hanging around the station? Has he got anything to do with it?'

'I don't know—' Slider began, and Dickson roared like a bull.

'You don't know bloody much, and that's a fact. I'm telling you, all of you, that there are certain people who are not at all happy about the way this case is going, so let's get to it, and get something concrete down.' He rose to his feet like the Andes, glowered around them for an instant, and then transformed his features grotesquely into a fatherly grin. 'And

228

be careful, all right? You're not in this job to get your bloody heads blown off.'

He power-surged out of the room, leaving Slider feeling more than ever convinced that something was going on that they were not allowed to know about. Dickson had manufactured his rage to prevent the questions being asked that he was not prepared to answer. The others, however, were just shifting in their seats and muttering as if the headmaster had been in a nasty bate and given the whole school a detention.

'The mushroom syndrome,' Beevers said as if he had just thought of it. 'Keep us in the dark and shovel shit over us.'

'Very original, Alec,' Norma said kindly.

He turned his hairy lips upward and smiled graciously at her. 'There's one theory that no one's thought of, though.'

'Except you, I suppose?'

'Right! Thompson was murdered by a left-handed surgeon, wasn't he? And John Brown, the Orchestra personnel manager, is a raving bender and living with this bloke Trevor Byers, who just happens to be a surgeon at St Mary's. Suppose Austen was blackmailing them, and they got fed up with it and killed her. And Thompson somehow found out about it, and so they did him as well?'

He gazed around his audience triumphantly. Norma clasped her hands to her breast and whispered, 'Brilliant!'

Beevers accepted the tribute. 'This Mafia bullshit!' he went on kindly. 'Now the girl may or may not have smuggled a Stradivarius into the country, but there's no evidence she didn't just do it for herself, or that she ever did it more than once. And, with all due respect to you, guv, it's too clumsy to have been the work of a professional. This is a typical amateur setup, to me.'

'Brains and originality,' Norma remarked. 'You can't do without 'em.'

'Beevers can,' Atherton said.

'We had better leave no stone unturned, I suppose,' Slider said. 'But for God's sake be careful. Don't go blundering about and getting complaints laid against us.'

'Leave it to me, guv,' Beevers said, pleased. 'Softly softly.' He rose and headed for the door. 'Well, I'll love you and leave you. I'm going to—'

'Grin like a dog and run about the city,' Atherton suggested.

Beevers paused. 'Come again?'

'That's a quotation from Psalm 59,' Atherton told him.

Beevers gave him a superior smile. 'We're Chapel,' he said unassailably.

Slider was surprised to have Norma assigned to him for the trip to Birmingham, until she revealed that she knew Birmingham quite well, having lived there for many years. Since he could not take Joanna, both for professional reasons and because she was working, Slider was glad to have Swilley with him. He found her company restful, and he also considered her to be the best policeman in 'F' district, and nicer to look at than an *A to* Z.

'Do you know where this is?' he asked, proffering the address of the flat where Anne-Marie had lived while a member of the Birmingham Orchestra. Martin Cutts had wrenched it out of his memory, and Slider now proposed having a look at it, and if possible a chat with some of the other residents.

'Oh yes. That's part of the new development in the centre. Quite swanky, a bit like the Barbican when it was fashionable. Expensive, but very convenient for the city types.'

It turned out to be a steel-and-glass pillar which reflected the cloudy sky impassively. Slider squinted up at it. 'I should think the views from the top would be magnificent. I wonder where the entrance is?'

'Well hidden,' Norma said as they turned a second corner. 'I wonder if they ever get any mail delivered?'

They found it at last round the third side, a tinted glass door with a security button. When the buzzer sounded they pushed in to find themselves in a foyer which would not have disgraced the headquarters of a multinational consortium. It was four storeys high, fitted out with acres of quiet grey carpet, and the walls which were not sheer glass were panelled in wood. There were glassy displays of rubber plants in chromium tubs, and in the centre of the hall the largest tub of all contained a real, growing, and embarrassed-looking tree.

'Blimey,' Norma breathed in heartfelt tribute. 'Cop this lot!'

They waded their way through the deep pile towards the uniformed security guard who was standing behind an enormous mahogany-veneered desk which was a very irregular trapezoid in shape to prove it was not just functional. The opulence of it all made them feel faintly depressed, as perhaps it was meant to.

'Think of the rents!' Norma whispered.

'And the rates. And the maintenance charges.'

'You'd need a fair amount of naughtiness to pay for that lot,' Norma agreed.

The security guard was looking at them alertly as they completed the long haul to his desk, and before Slider could present his ID, he straightened himself perceptibly and said, 'Police, sir? Thought so. Which one is it you're interested in?'

Slider was amused. 'You have a lot of trouble here?'

'No sir, not a bit. No trouble. A lot of enquiries, though,' His left eyelid flickered.

'We're enquiring about a young lady who lived here about eighteen months ago, a Miss Austen.'

'Miss Austen? Oh yes, sir, she's in 15D, one of the penthouses. Very nice.'

Miss Austen or the flat? Slider thought. So the news of her death hadn't penetrated this far; and also she didn't seem to have given up the flat when she left Birmingham. 'Penthouse, eh?' he said. 'That must cost a bit. Any idea what the rent is?'

With a curious access of discretion, the guard wrote a figure down on his desk-pad and pushed it across with an arms-length gesture. Slider looked, and his eyes watered. Norma, looking over his shoulder, murmured 'Ouch!'

'How long has she lived here?' Slider asked.

'About, oh, four years I suppose. I could look it up for you.'

'Ever any trouble about the rent?'

'Not my department, sir, but I doubt it. The developers would be down on anything like that like a shot. What's she done, then?'

'I'm afraid she's dead.'

'Oh. I thought I hadn't seen her around for a while,' said the guard, and it wasn't even a joke. Such, Slider thought, was her epitaph, this enigmatic girl.

'Do you remember when you last saw her?'

The guard shook his head. 'Must have been a few weeks ago. I never saw much of her anyway, but it's like that in these flats. People don't draw attention to themselves. Besides, there's nothing to notice in a resident coming in or out. Strangers I'd notice – you know how it is.'

'What happens about visitors?'

'Anyone who comes in comes to the desk, and we make a note of it before we ring up to the flat, for security reasons. You can have a look at the books if you like. But of course if a resident brings in a guest themselves, there's no note kept.'

'I see. Well, I'd like to have a look at those books afterwards, but for the moment I'd like to see the flat. You have a key, I suppose?'

232

'Yes, sir. I'll get the pass key. I'll have to come up with you, though, and let you in. Regulations.'

'Are you allowed to leave your desk?'

'For five minutes, yes, sir. I lock the outer door, then anyone who comes has to ring and I hear them on this.' He patted the portable phone on his hip.

'Very security-conscious, aren't they?'

'Well, sir, there's a lot of influential people in these apartments.'

'Was Miss Austen an influential person?'

'I don't know exactly, sir. She didn't look it. I thought at first she was someone's mistress, but then she didn't seem the type. I suppose she must have been somebody's daughter.'

The sleek, silent lift smelled of wealth, and the door to the penthouse flat was solid wood with brass fittings and an impressive array of locks and bolts and chains.

'We needn't keep you,' Slider said kindly as the guard hesitated. 'You can trust us to leave everything as we find it.'

'Yes, sir. When you're ready to leave, if you wouldn't mind ringing down to me, and I'll come up and lock the door again. That's the house phone over there, the white one. And if you need anything else, of course.'

When he had gone, Norma padded further in and let out a soundless whistle. 'Boy oh boy, it's like a set off *Dallas*. Where did she get the money for a setup like this?'

'Thompson thought smuggling. Beevers thinks blackmail.'

'Impossible. It must have been something bigger – and more secure – than that. Dope distribution or something?' Slider shrugged. 'And why did she keep it on once she'd left the Orchestra?'

'Perhaps,' Slider said absently, 'it was her home.'

Home. Something Anne-Marie had never known much about; a word you would find it hard to apply to this place.

Norma had got it right when she said *Dallas* – it was like a film set, not like real life at all. It was furnished with the great expense, but with no individuality, and it was cold, impersonal. He wandered about, looking, touching, feeling faintly sick with distress. Thick pale carpets – skyscraper views over Birmingham through the huge, plate-glass windows – white leather sofas. A giant bed with a slippery quilted satin bedspread – teak and brass furniture – a huge, heavy, smoked glass coffee-table. A cocktail cabinet, for God's sake, and expensive, amorphous modern pictures on the walls.

It was like nothing in real life. It was utterly bogus. It was, he realised in a flash, the sort of thing a person with no experience might imagine they would like if they were very rich – a child's dream of a Hollywood Home. His mouth began to turn down bitterly.

'Sir?' Norma was standing by a bookcase in the corner of the living-room. He went over, and she handed him *A Woman of Substance by* Barbara Taylor Bradford. 'It was on television a while back, d'you remember?'

'Yes,' Slider said. 'Irene used to watch it.'

'It's about a kitchenmaid who rises to be head of a business empire. They used the real Harrods in the film as the department store she ended up owning.'

'Yes, I heard about it.'

'Rags to riches,' Normal went on. 'And look at these others – all the same kind of thing – sagas about wealthy, powerful women. It's the modern escapist fiction for women: luxurious settings, jetsetting heroines who are as ruthless and ambitious as men, and make fortunes and manipulate the lives of their minions.'

'Yes,' Slider said, looking around the room again. 'It fits.'

He saw it now. He stared at the row of crudely coloured, mental boiled sweets on the bookshelf before him and saw

234

Anne-Marie, orphaned as a young child, brought up by an aunt who resented her, sent off to boarding school to get her out of the way, foisted off on a governess during school holidays. He saw her as a child with no friends, horribly lonely, perhaps dogged by a sense of failure because she could not make people love her, turning to books as a refuge, entering a world where things could go the way she wanted them to: a world where the unpopular girl scored the vital goal at hockey and became the school's heroine; where the poor girl saved someone's life and was given a pony of her own. Then in adolescence, perhaps she turned to the stronger meat of romances, where the hero took off the plain girl's glasses and murmured, 'God, but you're lovely!'; and in young womanhood to the candyfloss of the eighties, the power-woman sagas.

Somehow temptation had come her way, a chance to enter a life of excitement and intrigue and make large sums of money; to be, as she probably saw it, rich, successful and powerful. Why should she refuse? It was illegal, but then who cared about her? Who would be hurt by her failure to be honest? Perhaps she even relished the idea of getting back at the law-abiding people of her childhood who had failed to love her.

He turned from the bookshelves, and imagined her alone here in this shiny, sterile apartment, feeding her vanity of riches and her illusions on pulp fiction, and fighting back the growing conviction that it was all a lie, that her new 'friends' were only using her and cared nothing for her. Was that why she had suddenly tried to marry Thompson, to get hold of her inheritance so that she could escape from the trap she had stepped into so willingly?

Pathetic attempt. The people she was involved with would be ruthless as no fictional characters were. They would not allow her to defect; and at the last moment, he thought, she had realised that. He remembered Martin Cutts's description of the last time he had seen her alone, and of her 'resignation' afterwards. Perhaps, until the very last moment, she had not minded the thought of dying, since life held so little for her.

He had been standing with the book in his hand staring ahead of him at nothing, but now he became aware that something was calling his attention, nagging at the periphery of his mind. He stood still and let it seep in. He was facing the open door into the kitchen, a showroom affair of antiqued pine cupboards and white marble surfaces and overhead units with leaded-light doors, and through the glass of the end cupboard, the one in his line of vision, he could see a vague shape and colour that were naggingly familiar.

'Yes,' he said abruptly, thrust the book into Norma's hand, crossed to the cupboard and snatched open the door. There it was in the corner: the familiar shape of the tin and haunting depiction of the goitrous peasants and the caring, sharing olive trees, and the large and gaudy letters VIRGIN GREEN. He picked up the tin triumphantly and turned with it in his hands.

'That's it,' he said. 'Virgin Green.'

'What is it, sir?' Norma asked, but without much hope of reply. She knew these moods of his, when a lot was going in and nothing much coming out.

'Virgin Green. There's got to be a connection.' And then he saw what he had not noticed before, or at least had not taken in, which was the name and address of the manufacturer, in truly tiny letters at the bottom of the back of the tin: *Olio d'Italia, 9 Calle le Paradiso, Firenze.*

Slider began to laugh.

Atherton paused outside Vincey's of Bond Street and allowed himself to be impressed. It was either very old, or very well faked, all mahogany and curly gold lettering, and the window display was austere. A heavy, blue velvet curtain hung from a wooden rail half way up at the back of the window, preventing anyone from seeing inside the shop, and its lower end was folded forward in elegant swathes to make a bed for the single article on display – a sixteenth-century lute on a mahogany stand.

Inside the shop was dark, and smelled dusty but expensive. An old Turkish carpet in dim shades of wine-red and brown covered the floor between the door and the old-fashioned high counter which ran the width of the shop. Around the walls were a few heavy, old-fashioned display cases containing a few curiously uninteresting ancient instruments. The atmosphere was arcane, fusty, and eminently respectable. Atherton supposed that ancient instruments must be of interest to somebody, or how could Vincey's continue to function? But the setup seemed precarious in the extreme, considering what rents and rates must be like in Bond Street.

The door had chimed musically when he opened and closed it, and by the time he reached the counter a man had come through the curtained door that led to the nether regions and was regarding him politely. He was small and shrunken and looked about sixty-five, though his face was sharpened by the brightness of his dark eyes behind gold-rimmed half-glasses, and distinguished by an impressive beak of a nose. He had a little straggly grey hair and a great deal of bare pink pate, on the extremity of which he wore an embroidered Jewish skullcap. The rest of his clothes were shabby and shapeless and no-coloured so that, given his surroundings, one might suppose he wore them as a sort of protective colouring. If he kept still, Atherton thought, only his eyes would give away his whereabouts.

'Mr Saloman?' Atherton was not really in any doubt. If ever a man looked like a Mr Saloman, it was he.

'Saloman of Vincey's,' said the man, as if it were a title, like Nelson of Burnham Thorpe. His hands, which had been down at his sides, came up and rested side by side on the edge of the counter on their fingertips. He had the ridged and chalky fingernails of an old man, and his fingers were pointed and the skin shiny and brown, as if they had been rubbed to a patina by years of handling old wood. As they rested there, Atherton had the curious feeling that they had climbed up of their own accord to have a look at him. It unnerved him, and made him draw an extra breath before beginning.

'Good afternoon,' he said as cheerfully as his normally cheerful face could contrive. 'I wonder if you could tell me if you have ever had any dealings with this young lady.'

Saloman did not at once take the proffered photograph. First he subjected Atherton's face to a prolonged examination; and when at last one of his hands relinquished its fingertip grip of the counter and came towards him, Atherton found his own hand shrinking back in reluctance to come into contact with those pointed, brown, animal fingers. Saloman took the photograph and studied it in silence for some moments, while Atherton watched him and formed the opinion that behind the old, hooknosed, impassive façade a very sharp mind was rapidly turning over the possibilities and wondering whether it would be better to know or not to know. Yes, I'm on to something, Atherton thought, with that rapid process of association and deduction which he thought was instinct.

'I have done business with her,' Saloman said at last, returning the picture with an air of finality as if the last word had been said on that subject. It put Atherton on the wrong foot, as it was meant to, and he had to think out the next question.

'Would you mind telling me what the business was and when it took place?'

It was not meant as a question. Saloman smiled the smile of a reasonable man. He almost shrugged. 'Would I mind? Why should I not mind? Who asks me? Young man, you have not told me who *you* are.'

It was a game as they both knew, for Atherton was perfectly well aware that he looked like a policeman. He brought out his ID, and Saloman took it and subjected it to such lengthy scrutiny that he might have been mentally setting it to music. At last he returned it and said, 'So. The young lady.'

'Yes. You did business with her, you said.'

'So, she brought me a violin one day, another day two bows. I valued them for her, and she asked if I would buy them. I bought them, and later I sold them at a profit. That is how my business supports itself – I hope it is not yet a crime? And now will you tell me why you want to know. Has the young lady got herself into trouble at last?'

'Why should you think so?'

Saloman smiled gently. 'Because she was very pretty and very young. In the end, life must catch up with the pretty and young, otherwise how could the old and ugly bear the injustice? What has she done, this one?'

'Nothing illegal, I assure you,' Atherton said, smiling in spite of himself. 'Can you remember when these transactions took place?'

Saloman shrugged. 'Remember? No.'

'But perhaps you keep records of purchases and sales?'

'Of course I do. I am a businessman. I pay tax, VAT. What do you think?'

Atherton, driven, said very precisely, 'Will you please look up in your records, and tell me when these transactions took place?'

Saloman smiled the smile of the tiger and brought out a large ledger and began to go through it from the back towards the front, slowly. Atherton could only abide in his breeches. His training, he told himself, must be at least as good as Saloman's.

It was a long wait. When he had been all through that ledger Saloman closed it and brought out another, and began again. Atherton gritted his teeth. At the end of something near half an hour, Saloman finally shut the book with a slam that raised an interesting cloud of dust, and said, 'In October 1987 she sold me a Guarnerius. In March 1988 violin bows, a Peccatte and a gold-mounted Tourte. So, this is what you want to know?'

'Did she give you her name?'

'It is here in the daybook, Miss A. Austen.'

'When she came in with the fiddle, in October 1987, did she know what it was, how much it was worth?'

'If she knew these things, why should she ask me to value it?'

Atherton ground his teeth. 'How did she react when you told her the value?'

He shrugged. 'Who can remember? Some are glad, some are not. I don't remember.'

'But you remember her?'

'She was a pretty young woman with a valuable violin.'

'How valuable? What did you give her for it?'

Saloman bent his head to the book again, though he must have known the figure already. 'Three hundred thousand pounds.'

'And the bows?'

'One hundred thousand for the two.'

'And you later sold these items at a profit?'

'Of course. That is my business.'

'Did she ever bring you a Stradivarius?' Atherton looked directly into Saloman's eyes. Was there a flicker? He couldn't be sure.

'No.'

'Are you sure?'

'I am sure.'

'Did you ask her where she got the Guarnerius and the bows?'

'No.'

'You didn't ask? You didn't require any proof of ownership from her?'

Now he sighed with faint reproach. 'People own things. Why should they have proof of ownership? They are family heirlooms, perhaps. A violin is not like a Rolex watch, my dear young man. I have from the police a list of stolen instruments, and these I look out for, always. What is not on the list I am free to buy and sell. Is it so?'

Saloman inclined his head at a helpful angle, but Atherton could hear the laughter in the air. The eight brown fingers, hooked over the rim of the counter, were grinning triumphantly at him. You have nothing on us, they said. You can't touch us.

'You've been most helpful,' Atherton said at last.

'I am always happy to help the police.'

'There is one more thing – can you lend me those daybooks for a while?'

'I need them for my daily business,' Saloman protested, but without emphasis.

'I can return them to you tomorrow. I'm sure you can manage for one day.'

Saloman inclined his head in consent and passed the books across the counter, but the brown fingers gripped them until the last moment before relinquishing them.

'Thank you very much,' Atherton said. He turned away with reluctance, feeling strangely unwilling to have Saloman unseen behind him on the short walk to the door. Outside,

Bond Street had never seemed so light and airy and lovely. He had the rest of the day to go through these damned ledgers to find something, but whatever he found, he knew it would at best only suggest, not prove. Saloman was a downy bird, if ever there was one. He had not even made the mistake of denying all knowledge of Anne-Marie, which was what convinced Atherton more than anything that he had been dealing with a very professional criminal.

14

Whom the Gods Wish to Destroy They First Make Rich

The personnel manager of the Birmingham Orchestra – what Slider had come to know was called 'the fixer' – was one Ruth Chisholm, a strong, handsome girl with foxy hair, bright cheeks, and pale, piercing eyes. She gave Slider the answer he was growing to expect about Anne-Marie Austen.

'I didn't know her very well. I don't think anyone did. She kept herself very much to herself. In fact –' she hesitated '– I don't think she was much liked in the Orchestra.'

'Why was that?' Norma asked.

'Well, to begin with, it was said she'd got the job in the first place through influence – someone had had a word with the powers that be and got her in. I don't know if that was true or not, but it's certainly true that she never auditioned for the part, which is unusual for a string player, and that got up people's noses a bit.' She smiled suddenly. 'Musicians are a funny lot. They'd jump at the chance to get their friends in, but if anyone else does it, they snap at them like piranha fish. In theory they like people to get on by ability alone, but it never works that way, and they know it.'

'Was she not good enough for the job?' Norma asked.

'Oh, she was a good player all right – and a good section player, what's more, which is rare. Nowadays they all want to be soloists, and that's no good when there are sixteen of you supposed to sound like one. Anne-Marie fitted in – musically, that is.'

'But not socially?'

'Well – I'll give you an example. She had a flat near the centre of town, which should have made her very popular. People need somewhere close to go, sometimes, between rehearsal and concert. But she never invited anyone back there. That's one of the things people said about her, that she was tight. And standoffish.'

'Was she well off?' Slider asked.

'A musician? You're kidding!'

'I thought she came from a wealthy family?'

She shook her head to signify that she knew nothing about that.

'Do you know who Anne-Marie's special friends were?' Norma asked next. 'Who she went around with?'

Before Ruth Chisholm could answer they were interrupted by an old man in porter's uniform, who sidled up to them and gave a conspiratorial cough into his fist.

''Scuse me sir, but would you be Inspector Slider, sir? Telephone call for you. If you'd like to come this way, sir, I'll put it through to you in the box.' He lowered his voice still further and gave a ghastly wink. 'That way it'd be more private, see.'

Slider gave Norma a glance and a nod, to tell her to get on with it, and followed the old man. A moment later he was easing himself distastefully into the booth in which someone had recently smoked a cigar – one of the things for which he often though the death penalty ought to be brought back.

244

The bell rang, and he picked up the receiver and found Nicholls on the line.

'Hullo, Bill? Ah, I've got a nurrgent message for you from your burrd.' He put so much roll into the last word that Slider couldn't identify it for a moment.

'Oh, you mean Miss Marshall?' he said superbly, and Nicholls chuckled.

'Well, if her face is as gorgeous as her voice, you're a lucky man. Anyway, this is it: apparently she's been working today with a guy called Martin Cutts – mean anything to you?' Slider felt the familiar spasm of jealousy and grunted ungraciously. One day, just one day! 'They were talking about the Austen girl, and it seems that he knows where she used to go to in Birmingham. Is this making sense to you?'

'Yes, yes, go on.'

'Okay. Well, it seems Austen bummed a lift offa this Cutts guy once, when he was coming up to Birmingham and her car had broken down, and she asked him to drop her off at the end of Tutman Street.'

'Tutman,' Slider said, writing.

'Aye. And Cutts says that he was at the kerb a while trying to get out into the traffic, and he saw her in his rear-view mirror as she walked away, going down Tutman Street briskly as if she knew where she was going.'

'Is that all?'

'Aye, that's it. Any use?'

'Could be. It's better than what I've got so far, which is nothing. Sweet eff ay.'

'You dear old-fashioned thing,' Nicholls chuckled. 'Nobody says that any more. Any message to send back to your woman?'

'Is she there?' Slider asked eagerly, feeling his heart leap about in his stomach in a disconcertingly adolescent way.

'No, she's at work. She phoned during the tea-break, as

245

soon as she could, so that we could relay this to you while you were still on the scene. Smart woman, eh?'

'She's wonderful. Okay Nutty, thanks. I'll phone her later myself and thank her properly.'

'I bet you will. I'll tell her that if she rings again.'

'Don't scare her off. How's your mum, by the way?'

'Much better, thanks. She's coming out of hospital tomorrow, thank God. I'm sick of looking after Onan – he smells.'

'Onan?' Slider asked, but with the feeling he was letting himself in for it.

'Her budgie. Cheeroh, then, Bill. Happy hunting. Love to Norma.'

Slider stepped gratefully out into the fresh air of the musty backstage corridor, and returned to where Norma was chatting animatedly with Ruth Chisholm. Her technique was terrific, as he had had occasion to notice before. She raised an eyebrow as he rejoined them, and relinquished the thread to him.

'Wasn't Anne-Marie friendly with Martin Cutts for a while?' he asked Ruth Chisholm.

'Friendly?' She grimaced. 'Well, I wouldn't call it that, exactly. They went around together for a while, until Martin left to go to London, but it wasn't anything serious. It never is with Martin. He has a different woman every few weeks.'

From which Slider gathered that she had been taken in herself at some point, and resented it.

'Do you know where Tutman Street is?'

'It's about five minutes' walk from here. One of the old back streets in the centre that hasn't been developed yet.'

'Is there a music shop there, or anything a musician might visit?'

'Not that I know of. There are lots of shops there, groceries and that sort of thing. Anyone might go there, really.'

'I see. Thank you.' He wound up the interview, and a few minutes later he was out in the street with Norma, and telling her about Joanna's message.

'She might not have stopped in Tutman Street,' Norma said. 'She might have gone through it to somewhere else.'

'Yes, I know. It's a slender thread, but it's all we've got.'

Norma looked a little smug. 'Especially since Ruth told me that Anne-Marie hasn't played for that Orchestra since last July.'

'What?'

'Yes – she lied about that. Ruth said why on earth would they book her when they had plenty of good players locally. So whatever she came back to Birmingham for, it wasn't to play in the Orchestra.'

'We'd better hope that it was Tutman Street she was visiting. Oh, by the way,' he remembered suddenly, 'why would anyone call a budgie Onan?'

Norma's face broke into a slow, spreading grin.

'Presumably because he keeps spilling his seed.'

Slider's benevolent deity had seen to it on his behalf that Tutman Street was only a short one. Even so, there would be a period of long and tedious labour involved in making their door-to-door investigation.

'You do that side, and I'll do this,' he said. It was a narrow street of early Victorian shops and houses, very run down and shabby, and the sort of thing that was being renovated and preserved like mad in King's Cross and east of Islington. Here it was simply suffering from the proximity of the new Centre development, and general urban deprivation.

At two he caught Norma between doors and took her round the corner to a greasy spoon for lunch.

'Because we must keep your strength up.'

'Tell me honestly, sir,' she said over hamburger, chips and beans, 'do you think there's any hope?'

'You sound like a Revivalist.'

'No, but really.'

'But really, no, I don't think there's any hope. These people make very few mistakes. But that isn't the point, is it? We just do what we can, and it has to do.'

'Slow and steady wins the race?'

'Only if the hare lies down for a kip, and frankly I've always thought that was a very unlikely story.'

She dabbled a chip in a puddle of tomato sauce. 'I think she was probably just passing through Tutman Street. It's quite close to Marlborough Towers, you know, where she lived. She was probably taking a short cut home.'

'Yes, I know. But we have to go through the motions.'

Late in the afternoon, Norma got a bite. She met with Slider out of sight round the corner, and said breathlessly. 'The owner of that paper shop recognised the mugshot. He said she often used to go to the grocer's shop further down on the other side, and his wife says they sell a special kind of olive oil that's imported in barrels, and you bring your own tin and they fill it up from the tap. They used to see Anne-Marie go past quite often with a tin.'

Slider was silent, his brow drawn with thought.

'I thought you'd be turning cartwheels.' Norma said reproachfully.

'I never know whether to cheer or sob whenever that damned olive oil comes into the picture,' he sighed. 'Come on then, let's go and see.'

The grocery shop was one of those tiny food stores turned into a supermarket by dint of adding a double-sided display down the centre and a cash register by the door. There was nothing unusual about it at first sight: there was the stack of battered wire baskets; the moth-eaten vegetables and brown-spotted apples in cardboard boxes; the freezer cabinet long overdue for defrosting piled high with Lean Cuisine, French-bread pizza and frozen chilli con carne; the cold cabinet sporting sticky, dribbling yoghurt tubs and packets of rubber ham; the chipped lino tiles on the floor and the film of dust over the less popular lines of tins and bottles.

Slider went in alone and wandered along the aisles, pretending to search for something. When he turned the end of the row and looked back towards the cash desk he saw something that alerted his instincts, something that was unusual about this shop. The owner had appeared from some-where and was standing by the till watching him, and he was not an Asian. He was white and middle-aged, and among the enduring stereotypes of Slider's childhood he would have been put down unerringly as good old Mr Baldergammon who runs the village shop. He was stoutish, pinkish, baldish, and respectable-looking, in a neat brown overall-coat. Had this been a television sitcom he would have been wearing a spot-less white grocer's apron, and his eyes would have twinkled benevolently from behind gold-rimmed half-glasses.

Slider moved towards him, his senses alert, and the man said, 'Can I help you, sir?'

He fell a long way short of his stereotype. Unaided by props, his eyes did not twinkle, but glared with muted hostility. He did not smile benevolently, and despite his words, he did not seem at all to want to help Slider, unless it was to help him out of the shop, and pronto.

'I'm looking for olive oil,' Slider said, meeting the eyes at the last moment. The grocer's remained stony.

'You passed it. Top shelf, right-hand side, down the end,' he said curtly.

Slider smiled an amiable smile and cocked an eyebrow at

a quizzical angle, expressions he did well and convincingly. 'Oh, well, actually, I'm looking for a special sort. A friend of mine cooked me an Italian meal and she says the olive oil you use makes all the difference. So naturally I asked her what sort she uses and she said it was called Virgin Green. Silly name, isn't it?'

'All we've got is what's on the shelf,' the grocer said coldly.

Slider smiled a little more ingratiatingly. 'But she told me you sell it here, only not in tins, in a barrel, like draught beer, so I thought as I was passing I'd call in and see if I could get some.'

'We don't sell it any more,' he said curtly.

'Oh, but I'm sure it wasn't very long ago she last got some from you. Are you sure you haven't got any, out the back, perhaps?'

The man made an involuntary movement with his eyes towards the door – presumably the door to the storeroom. It was no more than a flicker, quickly controlled, but Slider's scalp was prickling with the briny tension which filled the air. He could almost hear the clicking and whirring.

'I told you, we don't do it any more. Not enough call for it. It was too expensive.'

'Well, could you tell me where you got it from?'

'Italy,' he said impatiently. 'Is there anything else you want?' The question verged on the belligerent, and was obviously meant to be interpreted as *Why don't you piss off?*

'Oh, no, thanks, that was all,' Slider said, almost Uriah Heeping now, and departed. The grocer slammed the door behind him, and there was a distinctive little click which was the plastic sign hanging from the back of the door being turned to show 'Closed'. Slider went in search of Norma with a sweet singing of success in his ears.

He met her at the appointed rendezvous round the corner,

where she was engaged in cat-licking her face clean with the corner of a handkerchief and a pocket mirror. Her hair was ruffled, and her collar slightly askew.

'Anything?' he asked her, eyeing her condition. 'I hope you didn't take any risks.'

'There's an alleyway that runs right along the back to service the back yards. They all had high walls, but to an ex-PT teacher like me—' She shrugged. 'Piece of piss.'

'You were never a PT teacher,' Slider reminded her severely. 'Did you see anything?'

'The door was locked and the window was barred – pretty filthy too – but I hitched myself up and managed to have a look through it. It's just an ordinary storeroom, full of boxes and so on. But on one shelf there are about twenty tins like the one in Anne-Marie's flat.'

Slider sighed with pure pleasure. 'They've made a mistake. At last they've made a mistake – only a small one, but my God!'

'How did you get on?'

'He practically threw me out. Told me they didn't sell olive oil any more – no demand for it. My God, we must really have rattled him!' He stopped and sniffed. 'What have you been treading in?'

'I hate to think.' Norma said, making use of the kerb's edge. 'That yard was the resort of uncleanly creatures. Do you really think we're onto something?'

'I'm sure of it. A shop like that would never deny selling something they had in stock. Come on, my lovely girl, I'm going to buy you a drink. There must be a pub somewhere near here.'

'Anywhere, so long as there's a Ladies where I can clean myself up.'

* * *

251

'Thompson was right,' Atherton said triumphantly as Slider came in. 'She was smuggling!'

Slider simpered. 'Whatever happened to "Good morning, darling, did you sleep well?"'

'I've spent all night going through these daybooks and Anne-Marie's bank statements, and there are some remarkable correlations,' Atherton went on.

'You're not as much fun as you used to be,' Slider complained. 'What daybooks?'

'Saloman of Vincey's. It's an interesting exercise. The turn-over of that little shop is astonishing when you've been there and seen how empty it is.'

'In Bond Street you need an astonishing turnover,' Slider pointed out.

'All right, but look at these figures. Saloman admits to buying one fiddle from Anne-Marie, correct name and address, in October 1987. Now look at the bank statement.' Slider leaned over his shoulder and followed the line of the long forefinger. 'He pays her three hundred thousand pounds – which, by the way, my friend at Sotheby's thinks was on the high side for those days – and she makes a deposit of four thousand five hundred. In March '88 he admits to paying her a hundred thousand for two bows, and she makes a deposit in her account of fifteen hundred.' He looked up at Slider. 'I don't have to tell you, do I, that each of those deposits represents exactly one and a half per cent of the purchase price?'

'No, dear. But what happened to the rest of the money?'

'Yes, that's the question. The way I see it, Cousin Mario gives her the goods, she smuggles them in, sells them to Saloman, banks her cut, and sends the rest of the money to – someone.'

'Someone?' Slider said sternly.

Atherton ruffled his hair out of order. 'I haven't worked that bit out yet,' he admitted.

Slider ruffled the hair back again. 'Only teasing.'

'But look, we can take this further. There are only two occasions when Anne-Marie's name appears in the daybook, but every time she made a large deposit in her account, there's a corresponding sale around the same date at Vincey's. Sometimes the amounts don't match exactly, but she may have kept some cash back for immediate expenses – that's no problem. The other names used on those occasions are never the same twice. I don't know whether it would be worth checking them out.'

'I suppose they used her real name twice to make sure she was implicated and therefore couldn't rat on them,' Slider mused. 'That's quite feasible. There's no reason why she shouldn't have had a good fiddle and a couple of bows to sell, but more than that would look suspicious. But we know she didn't go on tour as often as once a month.'

Atherton shrugged. 'She needn't necessarily go with an orchestra. As long as she only took out one fiddle and came back with one, she was safe enough. And we do know that she was always taking time off from her Orchestra, ostensibly to play for outside concerns.'

'True – and we also know that she didn't play for the Birmingham Orchestra as she said she did.'

'What puzzles me is how they got her own fiddle back to her each time.'

Slider shrugged. They may simply have imported it legally, through the normal channels. All they'd have to do would be to pay the duty and VAT, which would be peanuts compared with the value of the fiddle she brought in.'

'But what was the scam, guv? I mean, the fiddles were sold openly at Saloman of Vincey's, and you'd have thought that if there was anything wrong with that setup, it would have been discovered long ago. I mean they knew all about it at Sothebys.'

'We'll have to check up on them, and the olive-oil company, and the shop in Tutman Street. But my hunch is that they'll all come out squeaky clean. They'd have to be, to be any use as a laundry service.'

Atherton's eyebrows went up. 'The Italian Connection. So you really think it was The Family after all?'

'I'd bet on it. An elaborate scheme to launder dirty money and pass it back to Italy where it could be used openly and legitimately. Of course, Anne-Marie's part must only have been a tiny one, one little wheel in a huge machine. And when she started to go wrong, she was simply eliminated.'

'Yes, but by whom? We don't seem to be any closer to knowing who actually killed her.'

'When we know how, we'll know who,' Slider said, but without conviction. 'But I'm afraid that aspect may turn out to be the least important of the whole business. I think I'd better go and talk to Dickson. Let me have a copy of those notes about the money, will you?'

When he came back in with the copy, Atherton lounged gracefully against the wall beside Slider's desk in the only patch of sunshine in the room. 'It looks as if you were right all along, guv,' he said. 'I was barking up the wrong tree with that Thompson business. But I wonder if we'll ever be able to prove it wasn't all legit.'

'I doubt it,' Slider said without looking up. 'That's the whole point of laundering.'

'But if a thing is a lie, it ought to be possible to nail it.'

'In an ideal world.'

'We might manage to squeeze them a bit on probability. Look, I did some more working out. We can tell from Anne-

Marie's bank statement that she must have been passing around two million pounds to that shop in Tutman Street, and how did they account for that? If olive oil costs, say, thirty pounds a tin—'

'What?'

'Oh yes.' Atherton was pleased at having surprised him. 'Extra virgin oil is very expensive. In Sainsbury's it's about two quid for a little tiny bottle. Now at thirty pounds a tin, they'd have had to record sales of around sixty-seven thousand tins a year to account for the money. And that would be about a hundred and eighty tins of it per day. Can you believe a little shop like that would sell all that much olive oil?'

'Probability isn't proof. And you can bet they've worked out their accounting problems. They needn't have passed all the sales through one shop or one class of goods. And we don't even know that that's where she took the money.'

'No, but she must have gone there for something.'

'And even if you did manage to nail that little shop, you'd only be snipping one tiny blood vessel in the system. You don't imagine that two million pounds was the summit of their ambitions, do you?'

'To quote you on that one, we do what we can, and it has to do. Your trouble is you take everything too seriously. If you can scoop up one little turd, the world is a sweeter place.'

'Thank you, Old Moore,' Slider said, not without bitterness.

She had drawn the heavy, port-coloured curtains against the dreary evening, and lit the fire, and it glinted off things half-hidden in corners and increased the Aladdin's Cave effect of the red Turkish carpet and the cushion-stuffed chairs and sofa.

'You're very late. Was it trouble?'

'I came by a roundabout route, and spent some time driving about watching my rear-view mirror.'

'I hope that's just paranoia.'

'Reasonable precautions, now they've seen my face.' He took her in his arms and kissed her. It seemed to have been a very long time since he had last done that.

After a while she rubbed a fond hand along his groin and remarked, 'At least you always carry a blunt instrument around with you.'

'Not always. Only when I'm with you.'

'You say such lovely things to a girl.' She tilted her head up at him, smiling a long, curved smile. 'Do you want to eat now, or afterwards? Speak now, because things will start to burn soon.'

He laughed. 'You're so basic. It's lovely.'

'It's healthy. Well?'

'Turn the gas off,' he said.

Much later they sat by the fire and ate steak with avocado salad followed by Gorgonzola with a bottle of Rully. Joanna was splendidly, unconcernedly naked – 'Saves on napkins,' she said – while Slider wore only his underpants, because her carpet was so prickly.

'You've changed so much,' she marvelled, 'in such a short time. That first night I met you, you were so reserved. You'd never have done something like this.'

'You've changed me,' he said, stroking her shoulder. 'And you aren't white at all. More butter-coloured.'

'Salted or unsalted?'

'Pure Jersey.'

'It's only the fire light,' she said, turning her head to kiss his hand, and he smiled and shook his head. All his senses seemed sharpened, all sensations heightened. The taste of the food and wine, the blissful heat from the fire on his skin, the shapes of light made by the flames, the small bright sounds of the fire and the ticking clock and the tap of cutlery on plate – everything seemed intensified, more itself, as if he had been transported into a world of paradigms. As perhaps he had, being in love.

They talked of nothing in particular, and gradually Slider fell silent, leaving the chatter to Joanna. She touched on a few subjects, and when they got to the cheese stage she asked him how the case was coming along.

'We're waiting for reports to come in on the shop and Vincey's. But I don't suppose they'll tell us much. If Anne-Marie was mixed up with a big, powerful organisation, it isn't likely we'll be able to pin her murder on them. They'll have covered their tracks.'

'Is that what bothers you?'

'What bothers me most is that if I'm right, my superiors will regard her as an unimportant side issue. People seem to have come to mean a great deal less than money nowadays.'

'Oh Bill!' She smiled, leaning forward to touch his knee. 'That's nothing new. Really, it's just the opposite – that only nowadays have people begun to feel that it's wrong for money to mean more than people. Think of the Victorian times. Think of Roman times. Think of any time in the past.'

He did not look convinced, so she changed the subject and told him about her day and the terrible conductor they were suffering from. She related a few musical anecdotes to him, and saw him trying to be amused and failing, and fell silent. Then, seeing he had allowed her to fail him, he felt guilty, and tried to make it up to both of them by making love to her again.

For the first time in his life he couldn't do it. Long after she had accepted the inevitable he went on trying, until at last she said gently, 'It's no use bullying yourself. If it won't, it won't.'

He rolled over onto one elbow and stared at her. This,

then, was the other side of that heightening of awareness – that everything hurt too much.

'I'm sorry,' he said helplessly.

'You shouldn't have tried. It's only made you sad.'

'I didn't want – I wanted us not to be separate.'

'Your feeling like that separates us. For heaven's sake, if you want to be sad in my company, go ahead and feel sad. You don't have to amuse me. You don't have to be on your best behaviour.'

He put out a hand and pulled a lock of her muddled hair. 'I know.'

'No. I don't think you do. Coming here to me is like – oh, I don't know – like going out to tea when you were a child. Best suit, party manners, a break from real life and bread-and-jam. I'm not real to you at all.'

He was surprised. 'You are! You're the most real thing in my life.'

'Then you should feel that you can be natural with me. Be gloomy, if that's how you feel.'

'But that wouldn't be fair on you.'

She jerked away from him and sat up. 'Oh, fair on me! What's fair on me? What do you think you're doing? When you happen to be here, and you're in a good mood, is that what you think is fair?'

'I don't understand,' he said helplessly.

'I can see that. It's because you don't put yourself to the trouble of thinking. Where will you be sleeping tonight, just answer me that?'

'At home, of course,' he said unhappily.

'Of course!'

'But you know that. What else can I do?'

'Nothing. Nothing. Forget it. Just don't talk about fairness.'

She stood up with an abrupt movement of exasperation or

hurt, he wasn't sure which, and stood with her back to him leaning on her folded arms on the mantelpiece.

'Joanna, I don't understand. I though you wanted me to be here. I don't want to hurt you. If it hurts you, me being here, I won't come,' he tried.

'Oh, for God's sake! Thank you for the extensive choice.'

He didn't know what else to say, and after a moment she said, 'I think you'd better go. We're only picking at each other.'

But not like this, he thought. He couldn't bear to leave her like this. He hesitated for a long time, and then went and put his hands on her shoulders and turned her. Her eyes were dry and bright and she looked at him searchingly, perhaps to see how much he understood, which was very little.

'When I was a child,' she said suddenly, 'My mother always wound the clock in the sitting-room on a Sunday afternoon, about five o'clock. It was a very evocative sound. And there was a drain in the kitchen under the sink that smelled of very old green soap. And the bricks the house was made of, when the sun warmed them, they smelled like caramel. But no one will ever say that sort of thing about any house of mine. I build my nest, you see, but nothing grows in it.'

Still he didn't understand, but wisely avoiding words, he kissed her on the forehead and the eyes and the lips, and after a while she responded, and they lay down on the hearth rug again and made love, this time without any trouble.

'You think this will make everything all right again,' she muttered at one point, and he did understand, dimly.

'I love you,' he responded. 'I love you.' He said it again and again, and never used her name because she was not separate from him then, she was part of his substance. Afterwards he lay heavy, like something waterlogged, in her arms, unable to make the terrible effort of moving.

'I'd better go,' he said at last.

'Hardly worth it. You might as well stay here. Move in, and save yourself the journey.'

'I can't,' he said automatically. Did she mean it or was she joking? He dreaded a revival of the argument.

But she only said, 'I know.'

'You don't sound convinced.'

'What do you want, a written guarantee?' she said, but without rancour. 'Go on, you dope. Get thee to thy clonery.'

'Here's the report on that company, Olio d'Italia.' Dickson said, gesturing Slider to a seat. The fragrance of whisky hung on the air all around him like aftershave. 'There was a certain amount of reluctance on the part of our Italian friends to press the enquiry, which in itself tended to confirm what you thought, Bill. There's mud at the bottom of every pool, and some of it's best left unstirred. Still, for what it's worth, they've sent us this profile, and it's pretty much what you'd expect.'

'Oh,' said Slider. Sometimes it wasn't nice to be proved right.

'Olio d'Italia, head office in Calle le Paradiso, however you pronounce that. Run by one Gino Manetti—'

'Cousin Mario,' Slider said. Dickson looked a question and didn't wait for the answer.

'The company itself is a subsidiary of Prodiutto Italiano imaginative names these people choose – which is a massive international concern dealing with all sorts of Italian produce – oil, pasta, tomatoes, olives, cheeses, grapes, dried fruit – you name it. The big boy at the head of the parent company is also, surprise surprise, called Manetti – Arturo Manetti. He lives in an enormous villa up in the hills above Florence. Fantastic place, so I'm told, servants, guard dogs, electric fence, armed bodyguards, the lot. Arturo is Gino's uncle, and others of his relations run other subsidiaries. Of course, the reason the Italian security didn't want to run the enquiries too hard is that Arturo is the local Capo.'

'I see.' This business of being proved right got worse and worse.

'Anyway, they've gone into the business, and it's all legit – except that it isn't, of course. They don't sell the oil in Italy at all, as we would have expected. The output of that particular subsidiary is all export, and the two biggest international customers are – want to guess?'

'England and America.'

'Britain and the States – got it in two. Their turnover is pretty big. In this country alone they do two hundred million. That's an awful lot of oil.'

'An awful lot of people like Italian food.'

Dickson looked at him sharply. 'Are you trying to be funny?'

'No, sir.'

'I've got a list of their outlets. Some of them are wholesalers, so I doubt if the list is complete as far as retailers go. Obviously they must all sell oil in some form, but I doubt whether more than one or two are actually bent – it wouldn't pay them to run the outfit that way. Your place in Tutman Street is on the list, and everything is backed up by the right paperwork. On paper everything is rose-scented, and that's the way it has to be, of course. No funny business. Nobody with a previous. They'll have people out all the time, agents, looking for likely recruits.

'Who recruited Anne-Marie, I wonder?' Slider said.

Dickson cocked his head. 'From what I gather, she was a cold-blooded unemotional, ambitious little cow. So she was ideal material, wasn't she? I mean, it was either that or the Foreign Office.' He leaned back and the chair creaked protest-ingly. 'The other end, the Vincey end, is even more difficult to finger.' He swivelled the chair and knocked a file off the desk with his elbow. Confining him in an office was like keeping a buffalo in the bathroom. 'Vincey's has been in existence as a business for over a hundred years on that same premises in Bond Street. Irreproachable address, first-class clientele and all that. The shop and the goodwill were purchased eleven years ago by an agent acting for an international antiques trading consortium, who had some very big American money behind them. The money traces back to a New York holding company with a Park Avenue address.'

'Swanky.'

'As you say. It's called AM Holdings, and the President of the company is called Walter Fontodi.'

'All impeccably above board?'

Dickson gave a savage smile. 'Squeaky bloody clean. If they could nail this AM Holdings they'd be happy folk over there. But they haven't yet found a way of touching it.'

'So the Vincey end is not a new exercise?'

'That's the way they work. That's the beauty of a family business, isn't it? You can take your time over things. If you don't benefit yourself, your son will, or your grandson. It's all in the bloody Family. That's a joke.'

Slider quirked his lips obediently.

Dickson rocked the chair back and let it fall forward with a thump that shook the floorboards. 'They buy up a place with a first-class record, and run it straight.' And I mean really straight – rates, taxes, VAT, the lot. They do that for a number of years before they ever start using it for their purposes. They want respectable, and they can afford to pay for it. Buying Vincey's and running it at a loss for a couple of years must have cost them a couple of million, but what's that to them? They're handling telephone numbers every year. Probably set it off as a tax loss.'

'And Vincey's really is respectable.'

'Yes, of course. They're simply buying and selling antiques, and if some of their customers are marked cards, so what? They never touch stolen goods. In fact, they're probably more honest than your average dealer. I'm told Saloman has an excellent relationship with the local police.'

'And who is Saloman?'

'Ah, that's an interesting detail. When they bought the business, it was on the market because the previous owner had died – that was the real, original Saloman. He was in his sixties, and he'd been running Vincey's since 1935. Apparently he was a fantastic old boy, a real expert, knew everything about stringed instruments, and a whale on bows. He'd been a concert violinist in his youth – apparently quite a good one – but for some reason gave it up and went into dealing, and specialised in antiquities.'

Slider raised his brows. 'You mean they took over his name and his reputation? The young man at Sotheby's sent Atherton to Saloman because he was an expert on violin bows.'

'Nice, isn't it? I suppose anyone who was around when the changeover took place would know the old boy had died, but the general public wouldn't, and by now I don't suppose anyone remembers.'

'So who is our Saloman?'

'His name isn't Saloman, of course. He isn't even Jewish, though he wears the hat. He's an Italian, name of Joe Novanto. Came over during the war as a refugee, after the Nazi occupation of Italy. He changed his name to Joseph Neves and got himself a job with Hill's of Hanwell, making violin bows, which apparently was his trade back home. When the war ended he stayed on in this country, and got a job at Vincey's.'

'So he really could do it?'

'Oh yes – that part was genuine all right. He was taken on

to repair and renovate bows and instruments they were handling, and he studied the ancient instrument trade under the real Saloman, so he was learning from an expert. And when Saloman died and the business was sold, he took over the name, the reputation, even the character. Of course, the fact that he'd been working there so long would help to confuse the issue – people would recognise him, and in time his identity got fudged over. I don't suppose many people go to a shop like that more than once in their lives.'

'And of course he really did know Saloman's stuff.'

'He's been doing it for twenty-five years.'

'But then, at what stage was he recruited? If it was the organisation that bought Vincey's when the old man died, was Neves already one of them?'

'God knows. I don't suppose we ever shall. But if you want my personal opinion I'd say yes. It's carrying the business of sleepers a hell of a long way, but these people work on a grand scale. You can afford to make plans that take fifty years to mature if it's your own flesh-and-blood that'll benefit. I'd say that Neves, or Novanto, was their man from the beginning, before he ever left Italy, and he was just slipped in when the opportunity came in case he was ever needed. But of course, there's nothing we can pin on him. He not only looks legit, he is, except for using Saloman's name, and that's not a crime.'

'So where do we go from here?'

Dickson looked at him carefully, and placed both his meaty fists on the desk top, making himself larger and squarer than ever. Body language? Slider thought. Dickson wrote the book on it! 'That's the part you're not going to like, Bill. I'm afraid you don't go anywhere: they're taking the case out of our hands.'

'Special Branch?'

'They've got their own operation going on the Family. They

know what they're doing. Come on, there's no use looking like that. You must have expected it. I'm only surprised they left it with us as long as they did.'

'And Anne-Marie?' Slider's lips felt numb.

'Well, she's a bit of a side issue really, isn't she? Besides, she was one of their own operators. Obviously they knocked her off when she started being a nuisance, and since they've cleaned up their own mess, you can't expect our boys to get too excited about it. There are bigger fish to fry, and Special don't want us mucking about and treading mud all over their carpet.'

'And Mrs Gostyn? And Thompson?'

Dickson shrugged. 'Look, I know how you feel, but it's more important to nail the blokes at the top than some two-by-four local operator. If we go poking sticks up the network looking for the murderer, we'll scare them into closing it down and a lot of hard work'll have been wasted. In any case, even if you could discover who murdered the Austen girl, it's seven to four on that he's dead by now. They don't tolerate failures, as you know, and anyone who draws attention to himself is a failure. Ipso bloody facto. They'll have topped him, no sweat.'

Slider merely looked at him, and Dickson replaced his fists with his elbows on the desk top and looked beguiling.

'It's not as bad as all that, come on. Instructions are to close the file officially. Thompson killed Austen and then committed suicide, and the old lady was just an accident. That's going on record, and it makes our figures very nice, I can tell you.'

'Our figures?' Slider repeated disbelievingly.

'They're letting us have the credit, officially, and since you did most of the slog, I'm putting it down to you, Bill. It goes on your record. Earns you quite a few more Brownie points. You'll be a Girl Guide in no time.'

265

Dickson sat back with an expansive smile, inviting Slider to look surprised, grateful, modest and hopeful in that order. The implied promise was in the air: the promise Irene had longed for, for so many years, was dangled, a golden vision, just within reach.

Slider stood up. 'Will that be all, sir?'

Dickson's smile disappeared like the sun going in. The granite showed through the red meat of his face, and his voice was hard and impatient.

'You're off the case. That's official, d'you understand? Forget it.'

As Slider passed the door of the CID room on his way back to his office, Atherton called to him, and he paused and looked in blankly. Beevers was there too, sitting on Atherton's desk reading a newspaper.

'Was it the report on Saloman?' Atherton asked 'Did Dickson have anything?'

'I never thought the old man would go for that schmucky Mafioso angle,' Beevers complained. 'He's always so keen on a good, solid money motive. Now I really think I'm onto something there. I've been breaking my balls over John Brown and his boyfriend, and I think there's something fishy about them.'

'Well, we know that,' Atherton said wearily.

'No, something else, I mean. Did you know that Trevor Byers was up before the disciplinary committee of the BMA about eighteen months ago? I can't find out what for, yet – they're as tight as a crab's arse about stuff like that – but it would account for why old Brown's so fidgety. And if Austen had found out about it somehow—'

'The case is closed,' Slider said, stemming the flood. 'Official, from the very top. We're all back on traffic violations.'

'Closed?' they chorused, like Gilbert and Sullivan.

'There are bigger fish to fry. Anything to do with The Family is for Special Branch alone. Hands off, do not touch. And Anne-Marie has become an unimportant side issue.'

In the momentary silence that followed, Atherton noted how Slider always talked about Anne-Marie and never about Thompson, as though the one were an intolerable outrage, and the other no more than he deserved. But he forbore to mention it. Instead he filched the paper out of Beevers' hand and opened it at the entertainments page.

'Oh well, that's that, then,' he said. 'At least we'll have our weekends to ourselves again. I wonder if there are any good shows on.'

'And you can find out if your children still recognise you,' Beevers said to Slider. 'Anyone fancy a cup of tea?'

Slider shook his head without even having understood what he had been asked, and walked away. When he had gone, Beevers turned to Atherton.

'What's up with him, then? Is he cracking up? I hear he took Norma to Birmingham for the day and never even laid a hand on her knee. I mean, that's not normal.'

'Oh shut up, Alec,' Atherton said wearily, turning a page.

Beevers looked complacent. 'Detecting's a young man's job. I've always said so and I always will.'

'Not when you reach forty, you won't.'

'These old guys can't take the pressure, you see. They let things get on top of them. The next thing you know, old Bill will start weeping over suicides and writing poetry. I always say—'

'Oh, stuff it!' Atherton said, getting up. He flung the newspaper in the bin and walked away, but Beevers simply raised his voice a little to carry.

'You're not so young any more either, are you, Jim? Time's running out for you too, old lad.'

Left alone, Beevers picked the newspaper out of the bin, smoothed it out, opened it at the sports page, and began to read. He whistled cheerfully and swung his rather short legs, which didn't reach the floor when he was perched on a desk. If they couldn't stand the heat, he thought with his usual originality, they should stay out of the kitchen.

15

A Runt is as Good as a Feast

Slider went back to his office and did a bit of desultory tidying up, which soon degenerated into sitting at his desk and staring moodily at the photograph of Anne-Marie. At the end of any case he usually felt a lassitude, a disinclination to work, once the momentary excitement of the result wore off, leaving only deflation and paperwork. But this was much worse, because he had no answers to the many questions, nothing to detract from the sense of injustice towards the victims.

The phone rang and he picked it up reluctantly. It was O'Flaherty. Even on the phone he sounded massive.

'I've got it, I've got it,' he chortled. 'I've remembered who the little runt was. It was Ronnie Brenner.'

'Half-inch Brenner? The bloke who used to sell hookey watches down the Goldhawk Road?'

'No, no, not him. He emigrated – oh, it must be two years ago.'

'Emigrated?'

'To Norfolk. He's gone straight, got a half-share in a chicken farm. Plays the trombone in the Sally Army band in Norwich.

He sent me a postcard, the cheeky sod. No, I'm talking about Ronnie Brenner: little feller, racecourse tout, bookies' runner, one-time unsuccessful jockey, tipster. You name it, he's done it, so long as it's to do with harses. He's always hanging about racecourses – Banbury and Kempton Park mostly, they all have their favourites. We've had him in on sus a few times for hangin' about stables with a pair of binoculars an' a little book, but we've never managed to nail him for anything. No previous, d'you see – that's why I had such a job trackin' him down in me memory. Sure, don't you remember we had a look at him for that doping business at Wembley in '88, but there was nothing on him.'

'Wembley? I don't remember. I think that was when I was away on holiday,' Slider said with an effort. 'I remember you all talking about it when I came back. A bit of excitement in the silly season.' His brain made a determined effort to catch up with him. 'But they don't have horses at Wembley, do they? I thought it was football.'

'The Harse of the Year Show, ya stewpot. Are you awake, son? The local lads pulled him in at Banbury for the same thing, and he laid his hand on his heart and swore he'd never do a thing like that to man's best friend. Touching, it was. There wasn't a dry seat in the house. Anyway, that's who it is. He lives in Cathnor Road. Didn't I tell you I never forget a shit?'

Slider's tired brain was whirling with fragments of conversations, free-associating and making no sense. Atherton's voice said *if you scoop up one little turd the world's a sweeter place*, and he tried to grab the words as they floated past. 'No previous . . . that doping business at Wembley. . . so long as it's to do with horses . . . Banbury . . . Cathnor Road . . . never forget a shit. . . if you scoop—'

'Billy, are you there, for Chrissakes? Would you ever speak

to me? It's a lonely thing to be a desk sergeant and unloved.'

'A lonely thing . . .' Slider took his head in his hands and shook his brain. 'Sorry Pat. I'm a bit tired. Thanks for the information, but it's come too late. The Austen case is closed – official, from the top. It's gone up to Special Branch, so there's nothing more I can do about it. I'm off the case.'

'So long as the case is off you,' O'Flaherty said warningly. 'Ah, don't take it so hard, darlin'. In a long life you'll see worse injustice than that.' Slider didn't answer. 'Brenner may have had nothing to do with it, but if I see him hangin' around I'll pull him in anyway. It doesn't do to let the flies settle.'

'Yeah, okay, thanks Pat,' Slider said vaguely.

'Listen, why don't you go home, insteada roostin' up there. Have an evening off for a change, while you can?'

'Yes, I think I will.'

'And if your wife calls, I'll tell her you're out on a case,' O'Flaherty added drily.

Slider's mind was not with him, and it took a moment before he said, 'Oh, yes, I – yes, thanks. Thanks, Pat.'

'And remind me to tell you some time,' O'Flaherty said very gently, 'what a stupid bastard you are.'

Slider collected his coat, and went out into the grey January afternoon.

The tall, shabby house on Cathnor Road had an air of long neglect and temporary desertion. Slider had been driving about, he hardly knew where, for so long that it was now dark. He had often found before that driving had the effect of releasing his subconscious mind to worry out problems in a way the conscious mind, being too cluttered, could not do; but this time the only conclusion he had come to was that, off the case or not, he wanted to find out what Ronnie Brenner had been up to.

271

The house was divided into flats, and since it was dark there ought to have been lights in at least some of the windows, but the building gave no sign of life as Slider passed it and parked a little beyond. He walked up the steps to the front door where there was a variety of bells, none of them labelled. He pressed a few at random, and then stood looking about him.

Almost opposite him was the turning that led to the cul-de-sac where The Crown and Sceptre stood. Ah, yes, he thought, that's why Cathnor Road had been ringing bells in his mind. And talking of ringing bells, he pressed a few more, and stepped back to look up at the windows. Almost at once he heard someone hiss from somewhere below him. A small and anxious face was craning up at him from the area door to the basement flat, which was hidden under the steps on which he stood.

'Mr Slider! Down here, quick! Come on, guv, quick as you like!'

The voice was hoarse with urgency, and he obeyed, running down the steps and then down the precipitous, dish-shaped flight into the area. Ronnie Brenner stood half concealed by his door, which he held just enough ajar for Slider to get through.

''Urry up, guv, please. It ain't safe,' he whispered, and Slider went past him into the flat, his senses alert. Brenner took a frightened and comprehensive look around outside, and then closed the door and chained it clumsily.

'Frough here,' he said, inching past Slider in the narrow, dark, malodorous passage and leading the way to the back of the house. 'We can't be seen in here – nothink don't overlook it.'

The room was a surprise to Slider. It was a living-cum-kitchen-cum-dining room, square, and well-lit from a window with a Venetian blind over it. One corner was equipped as a kitchen, and the rest was furnished with a square dining-table with barley-sugar legs, a shabby and almost shapeless sofa, two sagging armchairs covered in scratched and scarred leather, and bookshelves along one wall. Though shabby, it was spotlessly clean, and smelled, unlike the passage, not of damp and rotting plaster, but pleasantly of leather and neat's-foot oil.

There were photographs of horses everywhere, framed and hanging on the wall, pinned along the edges of the bookshelves, propped up on the table and the kitchen cabinet, cut out of newspapers and magazines and sellotaped to the fridge door and above the draining-board. At a quick glance Slider could see that all the books on the shelves were to do with horses and racing, ranging from serious turf and stud books to a row of Dick Francis novels in well-thumbed paperback. There was nothing surprising about the room except its existence here, in the basement of a slum house in Shepherd's Bush. Had it been transported, as it stood, to the flat above the stables of a respected stud-groom, Slider would have found it entirely in character.

Turning to face his host, Slider remembered him now, and remembered him as harmless. He was small, undersized, weakly-looking except for the whippy strength of his arms and hands, and the hard lines in his face which told of a lifetime's bitter and losing struggle with weight. He might once have been a handsome man, before the effects of deliberate starvation, exposure to the weather, and a diet of gin and cigarettes designed to stunt him, had browned and wrinkled and monkeyfied him. Under the brown he was at this moment very white, his features drawn and pinched with fear. Ronnie Brenner was plainly a very frightened man.

Slider addressed him kindly. 'Now then, Ronnie – who's been putting the frighteners on you?'

'Christ, Mr Slider, nobody don't need to say nothink. I seen what they do, haven't I? Was you followed, guv?'

'I don't think so. I came a very roundabout way. Is it as bad as that?'

'I wanted to tell you, guv, honest,' he said, fidgeting anxiously with the things on the table. 'I hung about the station for a bit hoping I'd see you, till I see that big Mick sergeant clocking me, then I come away a bit hasty. Him and me have had a brush now and then, see. I fought about phoning you, but I never done it. I never fought you'd come here.'

'Well I did, and here I am. What did you want to tell me?'

'I ain't done nothing, and that's the truth, guv, so help me. You got to believe me. This bloke phoned me up, see, out of the blue—'

'Which bloke?'

'I don't know. He never give me no name. He says, I know you, Ronnie, and I've got a little job for you, what'd pay you nicely.'

'He used your name like that?'

'Yessir. Straight out, Ronnie, he calls me.'

'Did you recognise his voice?'

'No, sir. Not to say who he was, but it's a kind of voice I've heard before. What I mean is, it was posh. Posher than yours. Not a Silver-Ring voice, see, but real posh, like the county nobs in the owners' enclosure.'

'Old? Young?'

'Not young. Middle-aged. An' he was ringing me from a coin box, and it must have been long distance because I kept hearing him put money in, every two bleeding seconds nearly. So anyway, he asks me to do this job for him. He says he wants me to find him an empty flat on the White City estate, make it so's he can get in, clean it out, and watch it for a couple of days to see who goes in and out of the block, what times an' that.'

'Did he say why he wanted you to do those things?'

'He says he wants to have a private meeting, and he wants him and his colleagues to be able to get there and go away again without no one seeing them. Well, it don't sound too bad, so I done it. Well, there's nothink against the law, is there?'

'Breaking and entering is against the law.'

'Yeah, but it was an empty flat, kids break in all the time. He couldn't steal nothink, could he? Just have a meeting there – well, I didn't know what the meeting was about and he never told me, but I said to him, I said, I ain't got no previous, I said, and that's the way I want it to stay. I don't want to get mixed up in nothink heavy, I said, and he said that's why I picked you, Ronnie, he said. I wouldn't want to have to do with no one what had a record.'

'He said that?'

'Yessir. And he said he'd pay me well and he did, no funny business. Two hundred and fifty a day, he paid me, in five and tens in a jiffy bag frough the letter box.'

'I don't suppose you kept any of the bags?'

'No, I frew 'em away.'

'You didn't notice the postmark?'

Brenner's face took on a gleam of hope. 'It was Birmingham. I spose that was where he was phoning from, long-distance.'

'And how was he to get the information from you?'

'He phoned me up every day at a certain time and I told him and he paid me. I done it five days, and I can tell you I was glad to get the money. I had a lot of bad luck recently, Mr Slider, and I had some heavy debts.'

'I believe you. Go on.'

'Well, I done it five days, like I said, and then he says all right, that's enough, and I never heard from him again. But then the next week I saw in the papers about the body being found in the flat, and, Christ, I can tell you, I nearly shat myself. I mean, I ain't never 'ad nothink to do with nothink like that! You know me, guv, I'm not in that class – wouldn't hurt a flea, and that's the truth. I didn't know what to do. I just stopped at home and kept the door locked. And then the bloke phoned me up again.'

'The same man?'

'Yessir. He didn't sound so smoove this time though. He sounded as if he was shitting himself an' all.'

'And what day was this?'

'The same day. It was in the papers the noon edition about the body being found, and he bells me the afternoon. I said to him straight off I didn't want nothink to do with him and his bloody money, and he said it wasn't no good me talking like that because I was right in it up to the nostrils.'

'Implicated.'

'That's it, guv, *implicated*. He said I'd got to do what he said or it'd be the worse for me, and he said I hadn't got to get in a panic because what I had to do was easy.'

'What did you have to do?'

'He says I've got to go back to the flats to look for the young lady's handbag.' Slider started, and Brenner nodded. 'That's right. He said it might be in all that building stuff lying about, 'cause he fought she might of thrown it out of the car or over the balcony, and if anyone found it we was all for the 'igh jump. Well, I didn't want to go back there, I can tell you, wiv the place crawling wiv plod – no offence, guv – but he says to me, talk bloody sense, he says, I could go round there like I was just sightseeing, but he'd stick out like a sore bloody fumb. Anyway, the long and the short of it is I went round there and I never found nothing. I told him

276

when he belled me, and he said to go back and look again, but I'd had enough, so I hooked it.'

'Where?'

Brenner looked apologetic. 'Isle of Wight. I fought I'd better get where he couldn't find me, and spend the money. But when it came to it, I couldn't spend it. I ain't never 'ad nothink to do with stuff like that, and it scared the shit out of me, guv, I can tell you. So Monday I come back and tried to get in touch with you, waited at the station to see you come out—'

'Why me, Ronnie? I'm flattered and all that, but . . .'

'Well, I knew Mr Raisbrook was in the cot, and I couldn't talk to none of them kids, all mouf and trousers. They ain't real. They don't know nothink what doesn't come out of a book. But I knew you was straight.' It was a simple and heartfelt tribute.

'Anyway, that night I see you going into The Crown, so I hung about outside in the alley, but you come out with another bloke, so I nipped off.'

'There was someone else there that night, too,' Slider said. 'You know that the man I was with was murdered the next day?'

'Was that 'im? Bloody 'ell, Mr Slider, what's going on? Is it drugs, or what?'

'Worse than that.'

'Something big?'

'Very big, I'm afraid.'

'I wish I'd never touched the bleedin' job,' Ronnie said bitterly, 'but it looked all right at the time. My bloke – is he going to be after me now?'

Slider paused a moment. 'I don't know. It depends on how quickly news travels. You see, we've officially dropped the case, and once they know that, they'll probably pull him out.

That means we'll never get the chance to get at him, unless there's anything else you can tell me about him.'

Brenner was a shade whiter even than before. 'Honest, guv, if I knew anything I'd tell you. I ain't holding back.'

'You said he seemed to know you—?'

'A lot of people know me, racing people. That don't mean nothing. His voice did sound a bit familiar, but all the racecourse toffs talk like that.'

'Well if you think of anything, anything at all—'

'I know. You don't need to tell me.'

'By the way, Ronnie, apart from that time outside The Crown, have you been following me, or watching me?'

'No,' he said promptly; and then his jaw sagged as he gathered the implication. 'Gawd 'elp us, he's been following you! He'll know you come here!'

'I don't think so,' Slider said as reassuringly as he could. 'I've been very careful. And as I said, once they know we've dropped it, they won't take any more risks. As long as you keep out of sight for the next few hours, you should be all right. Is there another way out of here?'

'If you climb out the winder, you can get across the garden, frough the fence, across the next garden and over the wall into the alley. I come in that way sometimes. There's a packing case this sider the wall, to give you a leg-up.'

'All right, I'll go out that way, just in case anyone's watching the front. But I don't think they'll bother you after tonight.'

'I hope they know that,' Brenner said woefully.

All the same, Slider parked a distance from Joanna's house and walked the rest, listening with his scalp. He had plenty to think about as he walked, and not much of it added up. Who the hell was the murderer? If he was someone who knew Ronnie Brenner, it was a natural assumption that he must be one of the racing fraternity, but then what was his connection with Anne-Marie? Or was he merely a hired hitman? But there were aspects of the case that made Slider feel restless with that as a conclusion; and he had also the infuriating feeling that there was something on the tip of his brain that he could not quite get to grips with – something he had seen out of the corner of his eye, or something someone had said in passing. If only he could remember what it was, he felt, all the unrelated threads would suddenly weave themselves together into a web strong enough to net the rabbit.

Joanna let him in. 'I haven't got long, you know. I'll have to leave in about an hour.'

He replied only with a preoccupied grunt. She took a close look at his face, and then ushered him without further comment in to the living-room, shoved him into an armchair and brought him a drink. Then she knelt at his feet and rested her arms on his knees and waited for him. Finally he drank a little, stroked her hair absently, and finally looked at her.

'What's happened?' she asked.

'They're closing the case.'

'Why?'

'Apparently they're convinced of the Family connection, and that makes it too big to handle locally. It's going up to the Yard, and they're making it official that Thompson killed Anne-Marie and then committed suicide.'

'To make the villains relax?'

'Partly. And partly because nobody really wants to know who murdered Anne-Marie. She was one of theirs, and they "tidied her up", and who cares?'

'Doesn't Atherton care?'

'Not really. He always said I took this case too personally, and I suppose I did. Atherton's a cool well-balanced personality, and the job is just the job to him.' He knew that wasn't entirely the truth, but it was near enough for the moment. 'But apart from my personal feelings, I hate to leave a job unfinished. There are so many loose threads—'

He lapsed into thought, and she sat quietly drinking her drink and watching him. Even through his preoccupation he felt her presence, just the being near and warming him. After a while he came back and said, 'I'm sorry, this isn't much fun for you.'

'Fun,' she said thoughtfully, 'We only met in the first place, you know, because Anne-Marie was murdered. Sometimes I can't take it in, and when I do, I feel terribly guilty about being so happy with you. She had such an awful life, when you think about it, and for so much loneliness to end like that is dreadful. There wasn't even anyone at her funeral. It's almost—'

Slider sat bolt upright, stopping Joanna in mid-sentence. His expression was so strange that for a moment she thought he was choking or having a heart attack. He grabbed her hand and gripped it so tightly that it hurt her, but he was unaware of it. Suddenly things were slotting into place so fast that he could hardly keep up with them.

'The funeral! At the funeral! I knew at the time someone had said something important, but I couldn't work out what it was, and it's been at the back of my mind ever since. Listen, you told me once that Anne-Marie had said to you that she wasn't allowed to have a pet when she was a child.'

'That's right – her aunt was too houseproud, and didn't want the mess, though I think Anne-Marie thought she forbade it simply out of spite, because of course she has dogs of her own.'

His eyes were very bright, but they were not focused on her. 'There were two things. I have it now. Somebody said – I think you said – that Stourton was nearer to Birmingham than to London. And the bogus vet said that he had known Anne-Marie all her life, and had often taken care of her pony and her puppy.'

'Yes he did. I remember it now. Why would he say that?'

'He made a mistake,' Slider said in a small, deadly voice. 'But what did—'

He gripped her hand even tighter. 'Don't speak!' He was frantic to take hold of the thread of his thoughts as the words tumbled through his brain. They put her down like an old dog. Someone who knew Ronnie Brenner. Piperonyl butoxide. Real posh, like the county nobs. A tall man with a nice voice. Known her since she was a child. A hat like Lord Oaksey wears—

Joanna eased her hand out of his grip and flexed it painfully. 'What is it?' she said very softly.

'We made a mistake at the very beginning. Freddie Cameron made a mistake. He said that only a hospital anaesthetist would have access to Pentathol. But it was he who said they put her down like an old dog. Said it to me as a joke, and I forgot it.'

She was listening, following.

'Vets have to be their own anaesthetists, don't you see? They don't just diagnose, like GPs, they do surgery as well. Pentathol and a surgeon's scalpel. And piperonyl butoxide kills fleas and lice as well as bedbugs and woodlice.'

'Flea powder!' she exclaimed. 'If a vet had traces of it on his clothes, and then sat down in the passenger seat of Anne-Marie's car—'

'He knew her from her childhood – that part was true, at least. He must have known how lonely and alienated she was. He may even have had long talks with her for all we know, got to know the way her mind worked, what her dreams were. It was he who recruited her.' Dickson's voice said in his head,

281

'It was that or the Foreign Office', and he shook it away as an irrelevance. 'Then she became dangerous and had to be put out of the way.'

'Why?'

'I think, because of the Stradivarius. I have a kind of feeling that playing it at that concert in Florence wasn't part of her orders. I think she took the opportunity of your being taken ill to play it for her own pleasure, and then, having played it, found she couldn't bear to part with it. She kept it instead of passing it on through the system. Then of course she was in trouble. She had to try to get hold of money, went to her solicitor to find out if there was anything coming to her, and discovered she was worth a fortune if only she could get married.'

'That's why she suddenly started pursuing poor old Simon!'

'He was her only hope. She had to move fast, she hadn't time to start from scratch, and the only other man she knew well was already married.'

'Martin Cutts.'

'He was probably more of a friend to her, for all his faults,' Slider said with distaste. 'When she found it was no use, she turned to him for comfort. She was beginning to get very frightened. She said to him, "I'm so afraid".'

'Yes, you told me,' Joanna said quietly.

'She was right to be. Already the order had gone out. The vet – Hildyard – knew Ronnie Brenner. Ronnie hangs out at Banbury racecourse, and that isn't far from Stourton. If we check, I think we'll find Hildyard was a regular there. We may even find he's the official racecourse vet. Ronnie has no previous – they'd never use anyone with a criminal record – but he looks shady enough, the type who'd do a job for cash without asking questions. Ronnie said his contact had a posh voice. And Mrs Gostyn mentioned his voice, too.'

'Who's Ronnie Brenner?'

He hadn't told her that part yet, but he shook the question away – no time now. 'Hildyard must have met Anne-Marie before Christmas – in London, I suppose. That was when he stole her diary, so he knew her movements, and knew she had a free period in January when no one would miss her. Ronnie found the empty flat for him and watched it to see when there was no one going in or out on a regular basis. Then Hildyard arranged to meet Anne-Marie at the pub that evening. I don't know how, but I imagine it was a prearranged signal. Something to do with her car – a note under the windscreen or something. She'd been resigned to her fate, but now suddenly she took fright. I suppose she guessed something was up, and now it was upon her she realised she didn't want to die.'

'Yes,' Joanna whispered. She was very pale.

'She ran back to try to get her friends to come with her, thinking that if she turned up at the pub with a group, he'd have to call it off. It would look like something she couldn't have helped, to have a bunch of friends tagging along. But of course, when it came to it, she found she hadn't any friends. She had to go alone.'

Joanna could see that he had forgotten that she was one of the 'friends' in question. She felt a little sick now, and kept her lips tightly closed. He was looking stretched and exhausted, but he went on.

'He met her in the car park, well muffled up, wearing a racing man's brown trilby – a hat like Lord Oaksey wears on the television. They didn't see Paul Ringham sitting in his car with his lights off, waiting for his wife. They left together in her car, with Anne-Marie driving. Perhaps she hoped then that she'd been mistaken. She'd known him all her life – maybe she persuaded herself that he really just wanted to talk.'

He finished his drink at a gulp and leaned back in the chair, rubbing his eyes. 'It all fits. But I could never prove it. No proof at all. And anyway, the case is closed – that's official.'

'Wouldn't they reopen it, if you told them what you've just told me?'

'No. I've no evidence. Besides, they aren't interested in Hildyard. They want the men at the top, and they don't want anything to disturb the setup until they're ready. Going after Hildyard would probably lead to them closing down the whole network and starting up again somewhere else. Anne-Marie simply isn't important enough. Oh God, what a world it is. What a bloody awful world.'

He rubbed and rubbed at his face, as if he might rub away his thoughts. There was more here, she could see, than Anne-Marie. This was the culmination of a long, long story of disappointment and disillusion, frustration and personal conflict. She put up her hands carefully to stop him rubbing, afraid he might hurt himself, and his hands closed like steel traps around hers, making her gasp with fear and pain.

'Hold on to me,' he said, staring at her fiercely. She could feel the unendurable tension through the contact of their hands. 'Hold on to me. I need you. Oh God.'

'You've got me,' she said. But she was afraid. She had never been this close to someone so near the breaking point, and she didn't know what to do. He was so overwound he might snap at any moment.

Instinct took over. He slid forward out of the chair, still holding her hands, and pushed her down onto the carpet. Then he made love to her, not even waiting to take off his clothes, merely undoing and parting them sufficiently for the act. He was not rough with her – he was even kind, but in an impersonal way which came from his character, a kindness which was ingrained in him and nothing to do with her. But she took him, accepted his need, and forgave him for being – as she knew he was – unaware of her as a person just then. She loved him, and knew that it was a kind of love which had made him turn to her to exercise the healing frenzy. All the same it was the beginning of sadness. When it was over he fell against her exhausted, and began to cry, and she held him while he said over and over, 'I'm sorry, I'm sorry.'

'It's all right,' she said. 'I love you.' But she knew it was not to her that he was apologising.

When she had gone to work, leaving him reluctantly, he got into his car and drove slowly around the streets. He couldn't rest. The idea of going home to Ruislip, of talking to ordinary people who didn't know what had happened, nauseated him. He couldn't have endured to explain anything to anyone. His mind threshed at the problem; and somehow the other problem, of Irene and Joanna, had become tangled up in it, so that it was both emotional and intellectual, and he felt he couldn't resolve the one without the other.

Perhaps if he could get Ronnie Brenner definitely to identify Hildyard as the man who had paid him to find the flat, they would let him take up the vet quietly and nail the murder to him without mentioning the organisation at all. It would be easy to impute some other motive to him, without mentioning the Family. If only he could do that, perhaps he would be able to go and live with Joanna, and then everything would be all right.

He must get a statement out of Ronnie straight away. He'd take him in to the station now, and then discuss some way of getting a tape recording of Hildyard's voice. He drove back to Cathnor Road and left the car parked outside The Crown and Sceptre where it was hidden amongst the customers' cars. He walked back to the house, and it was still dark and quiet;

the street seemed deserted, too. He went quickly and quietly down the area steps and stood in the shadow under the railings a moment, listening, but everything was still.

And then he saw that the door to Brenner's flat was not completely closed. He stepped closer and saw the dented and splintered wood of the frame where the jemmy had been inserted next to the Yale lock. His scalp began to crawl with a cold dread which worked its way down his body and settled in his feet and legs, weighting them. He pushed the door with a knuckle and it swung inwards into the dark hall, and the abused lock fell off with a thump and clatter that made him jump as though he had touched a live wire. The opening looked like a gaping mouth, and he shivered as he stepped into it. His hair had risen on his scalp so far that he could feel the cold air against the skin. Without realising it, he rose involuntarily on tiptoe as he started down the narrow, black passage.

Half way along his foot struck something that was blocking his way – something large, heavy and soft, a bundle on the passage floor. He drew out his pencil-torch and squatted down and shone it. Brenner's face leapt out of the darkness at him, contused and bulging, the eyes gleaming dully white like hard-boiled eggs stuffed into the sockets. The tip of a tongue, dark blue like a chow's, protruded from between clenched teeth, and there was a smear of blood at the corner of the mouth where he had bitten it. Around Brenner's neck was a length of plastic-coated wire, the sort you might use in a garden to support climbers. It was drawn so tight that it had disappeared into the concentric rings of swollen flesh to either side of it.

Slider heard himself whimper. He stood up, and his legs were trembling so much that he had to rest his hand against the wall to support himself until he regained control.

After a moment he made himself squat down again and

touch Brenner's skin. He felt cold. The murderer must have entered as soon as Slider left, he thought. He must have been watching. Was it Hildyard, or one of the organisation clearing up after him? Well, it hardly mattered now, to him or to Brenner. The only chance of linking Hildyard to the case was now gone. Slider stood up again, felt the blood leaving his head, and had to bend over for a moment until the ringing stopped. Then he walked away quickly, out of the flat, up the area steps, and across the road to his car.

16

Bogus is as Bogus Does

Outside the magic heat-ring of London a cold rain was falling, and in the wet darkness there was nothing to detract from his sense of nightmare. He got lost twice, and another time had to stop and find a phone box with a directory to look up the address. In between whiles, he drove fast. His reasoning mind had shut down, the circuits blown, leaving him in peace. The simple act of driving gave him a spurious sense of achievement, as if he really were getting somewhere at last.

In the village there were only streetlights outside the pub and the post-office stores, and beyond that all was in darkness. Country addresses in any case were always pretty esoteric – you had to be born there to know which was Church Lane, Back Lane, London Road. He drove around, wandering down dark, narrow lanes where unbroken hedges reared at him from the oblivion beyond the headlights, having to backtrack when he snubbed his nose against a dead end, and he found the place in the end completely by chance.

Neats Cottage. Was that a joke? he wondered. It was a pleasant, long, low cottage in the local grey stone with a lichen-gilded roof, typically Cotswold; but it had been horribly quaintified with lattice-paned windows, a front door with a bottle-glass peephole, and olde-worlde ironwork. And one end of the cottage had been bastardised with a hideous redbrick, flat-roofed extension with aluminium-framed windows. Slider presumed this must be the surgery.

The white garden gate gleamed preternaturally, and on it was a notice painted in black letters on white with the name of the cottage and then simply B. HILDYARD, MRCVS. Surprisingly restrained, he thought, for a man who had given himself away by unnecessary embroidery. The cottage appeared to be completely dark, but as Slider walked down the garden path he saw that in fact one window in the residential end was lit, but glowing only faintly behind thick red curtains. The man was still up. Well, no reason why not. There had been people in the pub, still. It couldn't be so very late.

Slider had no idea what he meant to do. He had come here simply on instinct, a very physical, unthinking instinct; and now, faced with the overwhelming normality of the place, he could think of nothing to do but to go up to the door and knock on it. The elaborate iron knocker did not seem to make much of a noise, and now he was closer he could hear music from within, too muted to identify. Good thick doors and walls, he thought. Then a light went on, a shadow fell across the square glass porthole, and it was flung abruptly wide. And there was the bogus vet, as Slider continued to think of him, towering over him like the Demon King in a pantomime, backed by the light and hard to see.

There was a moment of silence during which Slider had time to appreciate the folly of his being here at all, as well as the remarkable fact that he felt no fear. Indeed, he was aware of an insane desire to say something completely frivolous.

Then Hildyard said, 'You'd better come in.'

He looked past Slider's shoulder into the darkness, and then stepped back and to the side, blocking the way to the left, so that as he stepped over the threshold Slider had no choice but to turn right. Light and music were ahead of him. He obeyed the silent urging and entered a large and comfortable room. It was decorated in the chintz, brass and polished parquet tradition – Irene would have loved it, he thought. Even so, it was warm, pleasantly lit by shaded lamps, and made welcoming by a good log fire in the grate. Music issued from a stereo stack, turned low as for background. It was a classical symphony, Slider recognised, but he didn't know which one.

'Brahms – Symphony Number One,' Hildyard said, following the direction of his eyes. 'Do you like music? Or shall I turn it off?'

'Please don't,' Slider said. His voice seemed to come out with an effort, as though he hadn't used it for years.

'Won't you sit down?' There was nothing in Hildyard's voice or manner to suggest that this was anything but an ordinary social visit. Slider sat in the chintz-covered wing-back by the fire. The dented cushions of its opposite number suggested the vet had been sitting there. Doing what? Slider's roving gaze saw no paper, book, nor even drink to hand. He had just been sitting there, then, listening to the music. Waiting. For what?

Hildyard surveyed his visitor's face for a long moment and then said, as if he had just come to a conclusion, 'What will you have to drink? Whisky? Gin? A beer? I was just going to have one myself.'

'Thank you,' Slider said absently. The warmth, the easy chair, the music were all acting on his aching exhaustion, lulling him, soothing him. He didn't notice that he had made no choice, and his eyes followed Hildyard almost drowsily as he crossed to the table under the window and poured two stiff whiskies from an extremely cut-glass decanter into massive, heavy-bottomed tumblers. There was something about the cut glass that went with the chintz and brass, Slider thought vaguely. It was what Irene though of as Good Taste, and it struck him that it was as bogus as the ideal homes illustrated in the colour supplements – instant decor, everything coordinated, the taste that money could buy. Image without substance, slick, ready-made. Like Anne-Marie's flat in Birmingham. That's what's wrong with me, he thought: I've swallowed the Modern World, and it's made me sick.

He received the glass from the vet in a bemused way, his sense of unreality reaching a peak. He had no idea what he was doing here, what he could possibly achieve, even what he expected to happen. He felt that if he waited long enough he would hear his own voice, but that until he heard it he would not know what he was going to say. Hildyard sat down opposite him with his drink, watching him impassively, and probably assessing pretty accurately the state of his visitor's mind, Slider thought.

'This isn't an official visit,' was what Slider did eventually say.

'So I imagined. You've been taken off the case – grounded, as we used to say.'

'What?' Slider said stupidly.

'During the war. Air force,' Hildyard told him kindly. 'What a picnic that was! Never a dull moment. A lot of us never got over the peace, you know.' He glanced at Slider's hand. 'Drink your drink,' he urged pleasantly. Slider looked at the glass, suddenly wondering, and reading his thoughts, Hildyard said, 'It's just whisky. I've nothing to fear from you. I knew you'd been grounded before you did. Your Commissioner plays golf, you see.'

So he did. Slider remembered. 'And bridge,' he said vaguely. He sipped cautiously. The hot, wheaten taste flooded his mouth, burned pleasantly all the way down and settled in a warm glow in his stomach. The vapours rose instantly inside him, reminding him that he hadn't eaten all day.

'All the same,' Hildyard went on conversationally, 'I was half expecting you. Your presence at the funeral, for one thing. You've been behaving very oddly, you know. There's been talk – there may even be an investigation into your behaviour before very long. "Cracking up", isn't that what you chaps say? Too much pressure, too much work, not enough time off. Trouble at home, too. What are you doing here, at this very moment, for instance? I doubt whether you even really know yourself.'

Slider took a grip on his mind and dragged it away from the fire and the music and the irrelevancies of warmth and comfort.

'I wanted to talk to you. There are some questions I want to ask you, just for my own satisfaction.'

'And what makes you think I will answer any of your questions?' Hildyard leaned back comfortably in his chair and moved one long, bony finger gently to the music. It was the slow movement. 'Lovely piece this, don't you think? Did you know it was through my representatives that Anne-Marie was able to develop her musical talents? Her aunt wanted her to devote herself to something more reliable, especially given the trouble her parents' marriage had caused. But I persuaded her to let Anne-Marie study, and when she came out of the college, I dropped the right words in the right ears to get her into the Orchestra. She never knew that part, of course – but even talent needs a helping hand. Don't you think that was kind of me? But we all wanted Anne-Marie to stay close to home. It was a great blow when she moved to London. That, I think, showed ingratitude.' His smile was unpleasant.

'I should think her aunt would have been pleased,' Slider said with an effort.

'Well, perhaps. She didn't like Anne-Marie. Also she is a musical cretin. I hate to have to say such a harsh thing of my fiancée, but it's the truth. Oh, you didn't know I was going to marry Mrs Ringwood? A lady of mature charms, but none the worse for that; and if she is no friend to the muse, she will at least be very, very rich, especially as you people have had the kindness to wind up the investigation of her late niece. And I can always listen to my music in the privacy of my surgery. One can't have everything.'

'I suppose Mrs Ringwood will live only just long enough to make a new will,' Slider heard himself say. He was appalled, but Hildyard didn't seem to mind. Indeed, he chuckled.

'Come, come, am I so unsubtle? Rest assured, Inspector, that when Mrs Ringwood dies, be it soon or late, there will be nothing suspicious about her death. The doctor will have no hesitation in giving the certificate.'

'Then why did you kill Anne-Marie in that particular way? You could have made it look like a natural death, or even a convincing suicide.'

The vet's face darkened briefly, but he said in a normal-sounding voice, 'One has to award you points for frankness, at all events. Why on earth should you think I killed Anne-Marie?'

It was persuasively natural, and Slider made himself remember Anne-Marie's nakedness, Ronnie Brenner's blue tongue, the fact that Thompson had blood under his eyelids. He felt very tired. He wondered for a moment whether the whisky had been laced with something after all, and then dismissed the idea. Perhaps he really was just cracking up. If so, he had nothing to lose.

'Let's pretend,' he said thickly. 'Just a sort of parlour game.

Just for my own satisfaction. I think I've worked it all out, almost everything, but there are one or two points—'

'Do I owe you satisfaction?'

'Not particularly. But all the same, just for argument's sake, I suppose the Pentathol came from your surgery? Your records are all carefully kept, and all drugs fully accounted for, I imagine?'

'Naturally.'

'You arranged to meet her at the pub after her session at the Television Centre. You'd stolen her diary, so you knew she wouldn't be missed for several days. You went in her car. I suppose you'd left yours somewhere so it wouldn't be recognised?'

Hildyard gave a curious little seated bow. 'The trains from Oxford are very good, and frequent,' he said casually, not as if it were an answer to any question.

Slider nodded, accepting the point. 'Yes, Oxford. You had her drive you to the flat Ronnie Brenner had prepared for you. You took her in. You—' He stopped and swallowed. He couldn't say the next bit. 'Afterwards you took her clothes away and drove in her car to Oxford, transferred to your own car and drove home, and disposed of the clothes. I wonder how?' He though for a moment. 'I wonder, do you have a furnace of some kind? What about the bodies of animals you have to put down? I don't suppose everyone wants to bury their own pet.'

'There is a furnace at the back of the surgery,' Hildyard assented. There was an odd gleam in his eye. 'Very similar to the sort used in crematoria. Vaporises everything most efficiently.'

Slider nodded. 'Then you had to go back and clear out her flat, remove all her personal papers so that there could be no possibility she had left anything incriminating. But you forgot the violin – the Stradivarius. So you had to go back a second time. You must have thought, the way things were, that you had plenty of time. It must have been a shock to see in the paper that she'd been identified so soon. You panicked and killed the old lady—'

Suddenly Hildyard looked annoyed. 'My dear sir, do I look like the sort of man who panics? It was not I who killed the old lady, as you put it. That was a piece of bungled work. There was no necessity for it at all.'

'It may even have been an accident,' Slider said in fairness. 'Even we weren't sure about that. But it was you who dealt with Thompson, wasn't it? He was becoming a threat, getting too close to the truth; and in any case, it was a way to tie up all the loose ends. So you dumped Anne-Marie's car near his house, hijacked him somehow, forced him to write the suicide note, and cut his throat with one of your scalpels. It was clever of you to notice that he wrote left-handed and make the cut left-handed too. A friend of mine says that surgeons have to be able to cut with either hand. Is that true?'

'Oh yes. There are times when the angle of an operation is not accessible to a right-handed cut. Some of the best men operate with both hands simultaneously, holding several instruments in their fingers for quickness' sake.'

Slider was silent, thinking, and after a while Hildyard interrupted with a question of his own.

'I've been wondering how you did manage to identify Anne-Marie's body so quickly. I read in the newspaper report that she was stripped entirely naked and that there were no belongings with her to identify her; nor had she been missed by anyone.'

'The mark on her neck,' Slider said. He was very tired indeed, and closed his eyes for a moment. 'One of my men recognised it as a violinist's mark, so we went round all the orchestras with a photograph.'

'Ah, I see.' He looked thoughtful. 'But there would have been no way to disguise that in any case.'

Slider opened his eyes. 'No. But why the cuts on the foot? Why didn't you make the death look natural, like suicide?'

Something of Hildyard's self-possession left him. His expression wavered, his eyes narrowed with some emotion – anger perhaps? He pressed his lips together as though to prevent himself from speaking unwisely, but after a moment the words escaped him. 'I loved Anne-Marie. You can have no idea! She was my creation. She was my neophyte. I nursed and nurtured what there was in her—' He broke off just as abruptly, and the light in his eyes went cold. He turned his head away and said indifferently, 'Orders from the top must always be obeyed, whatever the individual thinks of them. Unquestioningly. Chaos otherwise. In business as in the services.'

'*Business,*' Slider said, struggling with the warm grip of the armchair, trying to get more upright to express his outrage. 'How can you call it business? If you really did know her all her life, how could you just murder her in cold blood, and feel nothing, and call it business?'

Hildyard rose abruptly and towered over him, but Slider was too far gone to feel any menace. His glass was taken from him by strong fingers and he heard the vet say, 'Damn it, I shouldn't have given you such a big one. I suppose you'd already been drinking before you came here. Come on, pull yourself together, you drunken fool! Can't have you passing out here. You shouldn't have come here anyway. Damn it, I shouldn't have let you in.'

And he still hadn't admitted anything, Slider thought. Not denied, but not admitted. He had no doubt that Hildyard was guilty; but even if the case hadn't been closed, none of this was admissible anyway. No witnesses. No witnesses? The strong hands were on his shoulders now, gripping like steel, and Slider tried to flinch away from them, belatedly alarmed. He loathed the touch which had so recently tightened the wire round Ronnie Brenner's neck.

'You aren't even worried, are you?' he said in bleared outrage. 'You're not human at all, you're a monster. You say you loved Anne-Marie, but you murdered her just because they told you to. And you killed Ronnie Brenner and then just came back here and lit the fire, as if it was all in a day's work.'

The hands were suddenly gone. Hildyard straightened upright and looked at Slider with sudden alertness. 'Killed Ronnie Brenner? What are you talking about?'

'You followed me to his house this afternoon, and when I came out you went in and killed him.'

The vet looked strange. 'No,' he said. 'I haven't been anywhere. I've been here all day.'

Slider struggled. 'Then what—'

'Listen!' Hildyard was suddenly tense, his whole body rigid, his head cocked in a listening attitude. 'Did you hear that?' he whispered. Slider shook his head, meeting the vet's eyes at last, and witnessed a curious phenomenon: the vet's yellowish face seemed to drain completely of blood, turning first white, and then almost greenish, waxy. His eyes seemed to bulge slightly in their sockets, his lips drew back involuntarily off his long teeth. Slider had never seen such terror in a man's face. It was not a pleasant sight.

'They followed you here,' Hildyard whispered. 'Oh, Jesus Christ.'

'Who? How?' Slider said, but the vet waved him to silence.

'Wait here. Keep quiet,' he whispered. He put down the glass he was holding and went to the door, opened it a crack and listened a moment, and then slipped out, moving on the balls of his feet, as soundlessly as a cat.

Slider waited. The fire crackled unimportantly. After a while he heaved himself out of the chair and went to the door which Hildyard had left open a crack. The air in the hallway was colder than in the room, and whistled unpleasantly into his ear as he applied it to the gap. He heard the slow, heavy tick of the longcase clock in the hall, and behind that the soft black silence of an empty house.

And then, distantly, a muted thud. It was a tumbling sort of thud, such as might be made by a stack of heavy, soft objects falling over. Slider opened the door wider, and then heard quite clearly from the other end of the house, the surgery end, the loud crash of breaking glass.

His mind was instantly stripped clean of lethargy and fumes. Adrenaline pumped through him as he shot across the hall, flinging open doors, understanding without words what that thud and crash meant. Dickson's voice, *They don't tolerate failures*, was with him as he raced across a dining-room, crashing his shins against a chair that got in his way, through the further door, and into the new part of the house, the extension, which still smelled of plaster. He crossed another small hallway, through a door into the waiting room, which smelled of that disinfectant that vets use, and through the final door into the surgery itself.

Stink of petrol, broken glass, a fierce blaze, dense smoke already building up. On the floor the fallen stack of Hildyard, sprawled face down, the back of his skull smashed by an expert blow to a pink pulp, shards of bone and strands of hair all mashed together. All this Slider gathered in a split second, and already the heat and smoke were too much. His eyes were streaming, he could hear himself coughing and feel the pain in his chest as he dropped to his knees. Must get out.

He took hold of the collar and shoulder of the vet's jacket

and tried to drag him backwards towards the door; but the man was an immense weight, and the door seemed an impossible distance away. Slider's mind stepped away from it all, away from the fire and the fear and all the multitude of agonies it had been suffering, and looked down on the scene from a great height, from a cool, dark, impenetrable distance. He was vaguely aware that this was a bad thing to do, but he couldn't now remember why, and he was so tired, and the darkness was too inviting for him to want to try.

17

The Stray Dog Syndrome

'Hullo?'

'Hullo, Joanna.'

'Bill! I didn't think I'd be hearing from you again.'

'Didn't you?' He sounded genuinely surprised.

'It's been a long time,' she said.

'I did phone once or twice before, but I got your answering machine, and I didn't want to talk to that.'

'I wish you had. At least I'd have known—'

'Known what?'

'That you – that you were still around.'

'I'm not really. Around, I mean. I'm away.'

'Oh.' She was determined not to ask questions. For three weeks she had waited with diminishing hope, feeling only that she must not be the one to ask.

After a silence he said, 'You aren't angry with me, are you?'

'No, not angry. Why should I be?'

'Did Atherton phone you?'

'He told me that you were in hospital but that it wasn't serious.'

'Is that all? Nothing else?'

'No. Was he supposed to?'

'I asked him to let you know what was going on. I suppose he forgot. There must have been a hell of a lot to do, especially with me away and Raisbrook not coming back.'

Forgot my arse! Joanna thought. She said, 'Where are you, then?'

'I'm staying with my father in Essex. They gave me long leave.'

'Upper Hawksey,' she remembered.

That's where I'm calling from now. The thing is – I wondered if you were going to have any time off in the next couple of days? I wondered if you'd like to come out here for the day? It's quite nice – country and all that.'

'Wouldn't your father mind?' She meant, *what about your wife*, and he understood that and answered all parts of the question.

'Irene's not here. She's at home with the children. I didn't want them to miss school. In any case, I'm supposed to be having peace and quiet. I've told Dad about you.'

Joanna's heart gave an unruly, unreasonable leap. 'Oh?'

'He's a good bloke.' He said it like a justification. 'I value his advice. I told him I wanted to ask you to come out, and he said he didn't mind. I think he wants to meet you, though he didn't say so out loud. Well, it's his generation, you know.'

'Yes.'

'Joanna, you're not saying much.'

'I don't know what to say.'

'Are you all right?'

'I'm not sure. I feel as if I've been going through a nightmare.'

'Yes, me too.' Understatement of the decade, she thought. 'Will you come, then? I'd like to have a chance to talk to you. But if you don't feel like coming out I shall quite understand.'

No you won't understand, you diffident bastard, she thought. 'Yes, I'll come, if you want me to. I could come tomorrow.'

'That would be perfect.'

'You'd better give me instructions, then.'

He was waiting for her at the end of the lane, and signalled for her to pull over onto the mud-strip lay-by. She obeyed and got out and stood looking at him, her heart in her mouth. His eyebrows had gone, and his front hair was stubbly, and across the top of his forehead the skin had a shiny, plastic look. His hands were still bandaged. Otherwise, there was no sign of what he had gone through.

But he had a skinned look, as though he had had too close a haircut. His face seemed to have lost flesh, so that his nose and ears were too prominent, and it made him look curiously young. He was wearing a shabby sweater, a pair of baggy cords, and Wellingtons too big for him, and she saw how these suited him much better than town clothes. He was a country boy by birth and blood, and he looked at home here against the bare hedges and the wide, flat, soggy brown fields.

The lack of eyebrows made him look surprised, and his smile was hesitant and shy. She loved him consumingly, and didn't know what to say, how to approach him, even if it were permitted to cross the gap between them.

He said, 'I think it would be best if you were to leave it here. It'll be quite safe, but with mine and Dad's down there already, the lane's getting a bit churned up. Dad's out at the moment. He's usually out all day. We've got the place to ourselves until teatime. Shall we go and have a drink and some lunch? I wasn't sure if you'd be hungry or not.'

He was talking too much, he knew, but he couldn't stop himself, and her silence was unnerving him. He had been

302

thinking about her for so long, and it had made her unreal in his mind. Now seeing her again he didn't know what he was feeling, what he was going to do, whether asking her here had been brave or stupid or right or selfish. They stared at each other awkwardly, out of reach.

'Are you all right?' she asked at last, and nodded towards his bandages. 'Those look a bit fearsome.'

He waved them. 'Oh, they're not as bad as they look. They're nearly healed now, but I wear the bandages to keep them clean. Practically everything I do here seems to involve getting filthy. It's very enjoyable.' He smiled tentatively, but she was still studying him.

'You look thinner. Or is it just the haircut?'

'Both. I had to have the haircut because I'd got singed in a couple of places. You see the old eyebrows are gone. They'll grow back, of course, probably thicker than before. I'll end up looking like Dennis Healey.' She didn't smile at his attempted joke, and he grew serious in his turn. 'Atherton got me out just in time. If it hadn't been for him – and you, raising the alarm . . . You saved my life between you.'

She turned her head away. 'Don't,' she said. 'For God's sake, no gratitude. I couldn't stand that.' She was suddenly nervous. 'That isn't what you asked me here for?'

'No. I – No. I wanted to see you. I had to talk to you.' He bit his lip. 'Let's get comfortable first. Come on, there's no sense standing about here.'

She fell in beside him and they walked up the muddy, rutted lane to the house. He led her into the kitchen where they shed their muddied footwear and he sat her at the table – wooden, and scrubbed, like a children's story, she thought – and gave her a gin and tonic.

'I had to send out for supplies for this,' he said, bringing her glass to her between bandaged palms. 'Dad only drinks beer, and homemade wine, and I wouldn't inflict that on you.'

'You didn't have to go to all that trouble. I could have drunk beer,' she said.

'I wanted you to have what you like.' He put the glass down in front of her, and their eyes met. He wanted to touch her, but he didn't know how to cross the space between them. He didn't know what she was thinking. She might not welcome the gesture. But she had come here, hadn't she? Or was that just curiosity?

The silence had gone on too long now. He turned away and fetched his own drink.

'Dad likes to have his tea when he gets in,' he said, 'so I thought we'd just have a light lunch, if that's all right?'

'Anything you like. Yes, that's fine.'

'Can you eat mushrooms on toast? I do them rather nicely.'

'That would be lovely. Can you manage, with your hands?'

'Oh yes. They don't hurt. Don't you do anything – just sit there. I've never had the chance to cook for you yet.'

The words pleased and pained her with their innocence. It was tender, and rather gauche, and she loved him all over again, and was afraid she was going to be asked to pay a second time. She watched him as he moved with assurance around the kitchen where he had grown up. He looked so much younger here, and it wasn't just the effect of the haircut. It was something to do with being back in the parental home. She had noticed before that people shed years when they were once more in the situation of being child to a father or mother.

As the gin eased the tension, he began to talk more naturally, about neutral subjects, and she listened, her eyes following him, her body relaxed. It was when they were sitting opposite each other with food to occupy their hands that he finally turned to the case.

304

'It seems incredible that I haven't spoken to you since the night Ronnie Brenner was killed. I don't really know how much you know. What made you ring the station, anyway?'

'I don't know,' she said, looking inward, her eyes dark. 'I just had a bad feeling about it: you seemed so strange. So I stopped at the first phone box and rang the station and asked to speak to your friend O'Flaherty, and when he said you weren't there, I told him everything. Of course, you might have gone home, but I couldn't check up on that. I expected him to tell me there was nothing to worry about, but he took it seriously, thank God. He told me he'd find out where you were and ring me straight back.'

She looked to see if he knew all this, but he nodded and said, 'Go on.'

'Well, apparently he sent a radio car round to whatsis-name's house, Brenner, and then of course it was red alert. O'Flaherty and Atherton put their heads together and decided the most likely thing was that you'd gone off to see the bogus vet, and Atherton just got in his car and drove like a mad thing.' She looked at him. 'He does care about you, you know.'

'Yes,' Slider said, looking at his plate. 'And did O'Flaherty phone you back? It must have been hell for you.'

'Not that time, but later. He called back in about ten minutes to tell me what they were doing to find you. But then I had to go on to work, and that was the longest evening of my life. God knows what I played like. It wasn't until I got home that I was able to find out what had happened. That was when Atherton phoned to tell me you were in hospital with shock and minor burns.'

That had been the beginning of the long wait and the slow decline of hope. She could not go and visit, in case Irene was there. She had tried ringing, but the hospital wouldn't give out information except to relatives. And then she had decided that if he wanted her, he would get in contact with her, and that if he didn't, she mustn't make it hard for him. So she had done nothing, and the silence had extended itself, and she had thought that that was her answer.

Now he said, 'They weren't pleased with me, you know. With Hildyard dead, they had to have some sort of investigation into him, and he turned out to be a pretty unsatisfactory customer. He was German by birth – his real name was Hildebrand. He studied veterinary surgery at Nuremburg until the outbreak of the war, and then he joined the Luftwaffe – Intelligence Corps.'

'So that's where he got the "Captain", was it?'

'I suppose so. Anyway, when the German army occupied Italy, he was seconded and given a sort of undercover job liaising with the pro-Nazi Italians, trying to crack the Italian Resistance. And apparently it was at that time that he made contact with the Mafia, and did himself quite a lot of good with under-the-counter deals. At all events, he got very rich, and when the Allies took over he was rich and powerful enough to disappear completely, even though he was a very wanted man.'

'Yes, I should think he was. Everybody would have been after his blood.'

'His only friends were the Mafia, and it looks as though they helped him to escape to England and establish himself. At all events, he disappeared for a while and when he resurfaced, there he was in Stourton-on-Fosse as respectable as you like, following his old trade of veterinary surgeon and digging himself into the local community.'

'And all that time being a sleeper? Or active? Or what?'

'I don't suppose we'll ever know. There's so much we don't know – like who killed Brenner, or Mrs Gostyn. Hildyard more or less admitted killing Thompson, or at least he didn't deny it. And Anne-Marie.' He was silent a moment, and then said, 'Anyway, they aren't going to follow it up. The shop in Tutman Street's closed, and the man I saw there has disappeared. We've evidently disturbed them enough to close down that particular network, and that means I'm not exactly flavour of the month up at the Yard. We'll be watching Saloman from now on, but I don't suppose they'll ever use him again.'

'One thing I've been wondering is how Anne-Marie actually passed the money on.'

'I've been thinking about that, too, and I think it must have been something idiotically simple. I think it was the olive oil tins. I can't account for 'em otherwise. She had two in each of her flats, and Atherton noticed they were quite clean and dry inside, as if they'd never been used. I think maybe she just shoved rolls of bank notes into them and carried them along to the shop, and was given another empty tin in exchange.'

'Surely it can't have been as simple as that?'

'Sometimes the simplest ideas work the best,' he said, and lapsed into silence.

'Well, at least Anne-Marie's murderer got his just deserts,' she said at last, trying to comfort him.

'You sound like Dickson. But it isn't a matter of that. That's just revenge.' He looked at her carefully. 'I want you to understand.' Then he changed his emphasis. 'I want *you* to understand.'

'Go on then. I'm listening.'

It took him a while to begin. 'It's not the way it is in books, you see, where the detective solves the problem and then goes home to tea. In real life, even if you solve the problem, that's only the beginning. You have to assemble all the evidence, construct the case, take it to court, and even then the villain might not go down. He might get off entirely, or he might get a suspended sentence and be straight back out on the street. It's a gamble. And all the time you're constructing the case against him, there's all the other crime going on, and you can't be in two places at once. You never win. You can't win. You never even finish anything. It's like grandmother's steps, only the villains keep just a nose ahead of you, always. And if you get one sent down, there's all the others still in business, you can't stop them all, and in a couple of years the one you got sent down comes out again and picks up where he left off. You never seem to get anywhere, and in the end it drives you crazy. If you let it.'

He looked to see if she was following, and she nodded.

'People have different ways of coping with the frustration. Of course there are some lucky enough or stupid enough not to feel it – like Hunt. And Beevers, too, in a way. Atherton copes by just switching off as soon as he leaves his desk, and concentrating on his social life, food and books and music and so on.'

'Playing the dilettante bachelor.'

'Yes. And it is an act, to an extent. He watches himself doing it, you know, polishes up his performance. Norma's a bit like that, too, only her act is being a tough guy. And there are some who drink, or take drugs, and some who just get brutalised.'

'And then there's you,' she suggested.

'I don't know really how I coped with it. I think, by believing that it was all worthwhile. But somehow from the beginning of this case it didn't work. I minded too much, and I don't know why, unless maybe it was just the last straw. But then I met you.'

She became very still, watching his face.

'You said once that I didn't see you as part of real life, and I think in a way you were right.'

She heard the words with a sense of foreknowledge and despair. He had asked her here to tell her it was over, too much a gentleman to do it other than face to face.

'You were my place to hide,' he went on. 'I see it now. I think I half knew it at the time, and it was very wrong of me to use you like that, but I can only say in my defence that my need was very great. I was right on the edge of a precipice and you were all I was holding on to.'

She nodded again, unable to speak. She couldn't believe that he was going to let her go, now that they had found each other against all the odds; but she knew, and she had always known, that nothing was more likely.

'I've had time to think while I've been here. It's a thing people hardly ever have, isn't it? Time on their own to think things out properly. Maybe that's why people so often get really basic things wrong. I've never really been on my own since I got married.'

He was coming to it now, she thought. She started to smile, and then realised that was inappropriate. He looked at her very seriously, and it made him look absurdly young, like an earnest sixth-former about to express his conclusion that what was really wanted was world peace and harmony.

'But down here I've had complete peace and quiet, with just Dad. He's very restful, you know – not a great talker. I've thought about everything – most of all about you. And I think that in spite of the way things have happened, you're the only real thing that's happened to me in – well, in the whole of my adult life, really.'

He smiled at her, and reached across for her hand, lifting it to his lips and kissing it – the tenderest gesture a lover can make. She thought it probably wasn't the time to say much more than that yet, so she got up and went around the table to him so that they could get their arms round each other, which was what they both needed most just at that moment.

Mr Slider came into the kitchen just when dusk was beginning to make it worthwhile to pull the curtains and switch on the light, and found Joanna peacefully making tea and boiling eggs while Bill watched the toast. The table was laid and the kitchen was warm and welcoming.

'Hullo, Dad. Get anything?' Bill said over his shoulder.

Mr Slider, who was occupied with pulling off his boots on the mat, only grunted. Joanna looked round and met his unsmiling gaze from under his eyebrows, but he nodded to her gravely and courteously.

'Went up to Hampton Wood in the end,' he said, padding over to the table in stockinged feet and sitting down. 'Got a couple of wood pigeons. Make nice eating by the weekend.' Joanna brought over the teapot, and he offered her the correct, modern courtesy. 'Have a good drive down?'

'Yes, thank you.'

'Ah. That you burning the toast, Bill?'

'Sorry, Dad.'

Father and son sat opposite each other, and Joanna sat between them, and looked from one to the other. They were so alike it made her feel oddly tearful. Mr Slider's grey, close-cropped hair grew in exactly the same way as Bill's honey-brown; his softly aged face and secret mouth must once have looked exactly like those of the man she loved. Most of all, there was in the lines of the older man's face, in the way his mouth curved and in the bright regard of his eyes, the look of a man who has loved another human being completely and success-fully, a sweetness that no subsequent loss can eradicate. She liked him, and felt she would have done even if he had not been Bill's father.

Bill and Joanna carried the conversation while Mr Slider made his meal with the economical movements of a man who has earned it. Eventually when they had all finished, Mr Slider pushed back his chair and said, 'Why don't you go and lay the fire, Bill? Joanna and me'll do the washing up.'

Bill gave a comical grimace and went off obediently, and Joanna began to clear the table with a sinking heart. I'm going to be warned off again, she thought; and I shall mind what this lovely old man says to me.

'I'll wash and you dry,' Mr Slider said. 'Don't want you getting dishpan hands.'

He was a slow and methodical washer, and managed to make the little there was go a long way. After the first few plates he looked up and saw her expression and gave her an amused and quirky smile.

'No need to look like that, girl. I'm only his father. I got nothing to do with it.'

'I don't think that's entirely true. Bill values your opinion.'

'Told you that, did he? Ah, well, we're a lot alike, Bill and me, except that I'm handsomer. And I'll tell you something – I like you.'

'I like you too.'

'Well, that's a start.' He went on washing. The next time he looked up it was gravely. 'It's a bad business, this. Bad for everyone. There are no winners when a man's torn between two women, and one of them's his wife. I was lucky. I loved Bill's mother, and I married her, and I never wanted no other. People talk a lot about why marriages break down, but there's only one reason – people stop loving each other, or they never did in the first place. Do you love Bill?'

'Yes. But I would never—' She stopped, embarrassed.

'No, I don't suppose you would.' He fished out an egg spoon and rubbed it minutely. 'Terrible stuff for sticking,

311

egg yolk. No, you'd never try to make up his mind for him. I never would either. I don't think you can make other people's decisions for them, or you shouldn't. The trouble with Bill is he's too sensitive.' He smiled suddenly, and his eyes seemed very blue. 'I know all parents say that. But Bill always was a worrier. Conscientious. He always tried to see both sides of everything, and be fair to everyone, and it gets in his way, see? His conscience runs ahead of his feelings and muddles him up. There, I think that's clean. Haven't got my close-up glasses on, so you'll have to keep an eye on me.'

She took the spoon and dried it without looking at it. 'What do you think he'll do?' It was foolish to ask, but everyone wants reassurance from time to time.

'I don't know. I wish I could tell you, because, to be honest about it, I like you, and I never liked Irene. She was never right for him – too sharp and go-ahead and looking at the prices of things. His mother though she'd sharpen him up, but I said to her, he's sharp enough in his own way. He sees more than most people, that's all. I'll tell you this much – whatever he does decide, it won't be easy for him. He'll take a long time deciding, and it'll hurt him. It'll hurt you, too,' he said, looking at her appraisingly, 'but I reckon you can take it. And you wouldn't want him, would you, if he was the kind of man that could decide a thing like that easily?'

'No. I suppose I wouldn't.' It wasn't much comfort.

They worked in silence for a while until Mr Slider said, 'There, last spoon, and that's the lot. You're a good little worker. And I tell you what.' She met his eyes and he smiled. 'I reckon Bill's got his head screwed on the right way. It may take a while, but I reckon he'll get it right in the end. And now I'm going to take my bath. Will you still be here when I get back?'

'I don't know,' she said, uncertain how long her visit was meant to last.

'Ah, go on, you don't want to be rushing off to London when you've just got here. Why don't you stay the night? We'll have a bit of supper later, and play a hand of cards. Do you play cribbage?'

'Yes, but—'

'That's all right. I'm past the age of being shocked. You stay and welcome. Fair enough?'

'Fair enough,' said Joanna.

She had to leave the next morning, early. She and Slider walked back down the lane together in silence.

'What's going to happen to us?' she asked at last. 'Have we got a future?'

'I hope so. I want us to have. Is that what you want?'

'I thought you knew that by now.'

He frowned. 'I want to be honest with you. It's going to be hard for me. I've been married a long time – I can hardly imagine not being married, now. And then there's the children – most of all, there's the children. They don't deserve to be made unhappy. Well, Irene doesn't either. It's not her fault.'

She listened to the hackneyed, deadly words, and all the arguments she might have raised passed unuttered through her mind. If he could not see them for himself, there was no point in her saying them.

'But on the other hand, I just don't think I could bear to go on without you now. You're too important to me. And if I want you, I shall have to do something about it, shan't I?'

She nodded, grateful for a man too honest to suggest he might have it both ways.

'What I want to ask you, and I know it will be hard for you, is to give me time. It will take me a while to work my way through this. Can you be patient? I've no right to ask you really, but—'

'I'll be patient. I'm thirty-six years old, and I've never been in love with anyone before. Just be as quick as you can,' she said.

He stopped and faced her and took her hands between his bandaged ones and could find nothing to say.

Looking down at their joined hands she said, 'Tell me something?'

'Anything.'

'What on earth were you doing, trying to rescue a dead bogus vet from the flames?'

He began very slowly to smile. 'I never even thought about it. It was a purely instinctive reaction.'

'You idiot! I love you.'

'I love you too,' he said. They resumed their walk towards her car. 'Did you know they're promoting me?' he said a little further on. 'Now that Raisbrook isn't coming back, they're making me Detective Chief Inspector.'

She looked at him quizzically. 'Why didn't you tell me before? You must be pleased. But I thought you said they weren't very happy with you?'

'They aren't promoting me because they're happy with me. It's a kind of consolation prize, because they aren't going to follow up the Austen case. No, not even that, less than that – it's a kind of booby prize. I've been a bloody nuisance, so they hand me a month's leave and a promotion to keep me quiet.'

She didn't know what to say. 'At least Irene must be glad,' she said at last.

'Irene always said they didn't value me. She was right about that, at least. Even when I get promoted, it's a kind of failure.'

'Don't,' she said, but he stopped her and gripped her hands.

314

'Oh, Joanna, I'm so afraid I'm going to fail you.'

She tried to smile. 'That isn't your fault. It's me. I've been a stray so long, it's hard for anyone to see me as anything else. A stray is no one's responsibility, you see. You might play with it when it comes up to you in the park, but you don't take it home.'

He looked distressed. 'Don't talk like that. Listen, it's going to be all right. It'll take time, that's all. Be patient with me.'

He took her to the car and watched her get in and fasten the seatbelt, and then he kissed her goodbye through the window, and she drove away. She waved to him before she turned the corner: jaunty and afraid, essentially no one's dog.

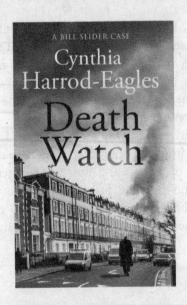

A BILL SLIDER CASE
Cynthia Harrod-Eagles
Death Watch

The lot of the working copper is getting harder: new
regulations, regular rousting by the top brass, a budget
tighter than a Victoria corset and a DC who thinks he's
in a John Le Carré novel makes it a trying time for
Detective Inspector Bill Slider.

Then when a noted womaniser dies in mysterious
fire in a sleazy motel and the whole of his murky past
comes to light, Slider begins to question whether this
was suicide . . . or murder.

And that's not the only thing Slider is questioning.
As soon as he's solved the motel mystery, Bill is going
to have to put his own house in order . . .

*

'Sharp, witty and well-plotted'
Times